DANGEROUS Obsessions

by J. M. Reines

PUBLISHED BY: J.M. Reines

This book is a work of fiction. Names, characters, businesses, organizations, places, events, and incidents are either the product of the author's imagination or are used fictitiously. Any resemblance to actual persons, living or dead, events, or locales is entirely coincidental.

Hardcover - ISBN: 979-8-9963814-0-1
Paperback - ISBN: 979-8-9963814-1-8
E-Book - ISBN: 979-8-9963814-2-5
Audiobook - ISBN: 979-8-9963814-3-2

Library of Congress Control Number: 2026914077
www.jmreines.com

Table of Contents

1
The Game

It wasn't time for the game. Her compulsions ached, and she needed the thrill. But it was too early. So, she waited.

Jessi sat at the edge of the weathered dock, watching as the last streaks of daylight sank behind the western mountains. The sky burned with color, amber fading into violet, then melting into the soft indigo of approaching night. A waxing moon was already lifting over the trees to the east, silvering the ripples on the water's surface. She drew in a slow, deliberate breath, letting the beauty settle over her like a fragile calm.

Leaning back, she stretched out along the dock, her oversized white cotton T-shirt whispering against the rough, sun-bleached boards. A few stars had begun to pierce the twilight, faint but steady. Her toes drifted lazily in the warm river, the gentle current brushing her feet as she swayed them back and forth. Only a month ago, the air had been sharp and cold, but an early heatwave made the water feel tepid, almost like silk.

Her gaze turned inward. The quiet, soft lapping of the water gave her space to think, dangerous space.

She didn't understand herself, not really. The impulses came like tides, unpredictable, overwhelming. Desire, punishment, escape, she could never tell which it was. All she knew was that once an idea took hold, it completely consumed her. The rush came in waves, the pounding in her chest, that reckless, breathless sense of being alive. But afterward, when the thrill ebbed, fear and shame took their place, leaving her hollowed out, depleted, dissatisfied, and questioning everything she thought she wanted.

She'd come to the dock to get away. After a long, numbing day, endless typing, shrill phones, and the relentless river of numbers on screen, Jessi felt scraped thin, every nerve dulled. Emptiness gnawed at her. All day, urgent restlessness burned beneath her skin. She ached for a jolt, something wild or reckless, any spark that could wrench her fully awake and alive.

Her car was parked in the small riverside lot at the head of the walking trail. From there, Jessi had followed the worn dirt path through the trees barefoot. The trail wound along the riverbank for nearly a mile before opening onto a quiet clearing, a handful of picnic tables, a patch of grass, and the old wooden dock stretching into the water. During the day, families and fishermen filled the space, but now it was deserted. The last light had faded, leaving her alone beneath a dim wash of moonlight and the rhythmic hum of crickets.

For nearly an hour, Jessi lay there. She watched the stars flicker awake. The glow of lightning bugs drifted lazily across the warm night air. The world felt suspended in a perfect, fragile calm. Then she stirred and glanced around to make sure she was alone.

Slowly, she sat up and peeled off her T-shirt, her only garment.

The cotton glided against her skin, revealing her pale, naked body beneath. The air was soft against her bare breasts and shoulders. She lay back again; her long, curly auburn hair spread out along the boards. Jessi felt the heat of the day still trapped in the wood beneath her. She let the evening breeze glide over her body like a quiet, forbidden comfort.

She closed her eyes and drew in a long breath, letting her thoughts settle in the fading warmth of the night. It was time to go. She opened her eyes, pulled herself upright, and gathered her things. She balled up her T-shirt and stuffed it into the small black nylon bag she'd brought. The soft jingle of her car keys echoed faintly inside as she zipped the bag shut.

Rising to her feet, she took one last look around the quiet park. In the distance, the city flickered like a mirage; neon lights and movement, life carrying on without her. Out here, the world felt hushed and forgotten. No one was around. She inhaled deeply, tasting the faint sweetness of honeysuckle in the river air, then turned toward the narrow dirt trail that led back through the woods.

As soon as she stepped beneath the canopy, the darkness seemed to fold over her. The earthy scent of pine and damp soil filled her lungs, while crickets and tree frogs pulsed in the night. The ground was soft beneath her feet, and the faint silver glow of moonlight filtered through the trees, guiding her just enough to see the path. The night air pressed close, its breath sliding across her exposed skin. It was both soothing and unsettling.

Her pulse quickened as she walked. Every rustle made her glance over her shoulder, though she kept moving, eyes searching the dim trail ahead until the trees finally began to thin. The faint hum of the highway returned, and then she saw it, her green Mustang sitting beneath the single parking lot light, the bulb tinted a dull purple, throwing hard-edged shadows across the pavement.

But she wasn't alone. Toward the center of the lot, a pickup truck was parked, two men perched on its tailgate with bottles in hand. Their laughter cut through the quiet, low and careless. Jessi froze. Slowly, she crouched down behind a patch of overgrown brush at the tree line, her heartbeat loud in her ears as she watched them, hoping they hadn't seen her.

Eventually, Jessi sank into a soft bed of pine needles, their faint scent rising with every movement. The forest floor was cool beneath her. She drew her knees close and peered through the branches toward the parking lot. The two men were still there, laughing, drinking, oblivious to her presence.

Will they never leave? She thought, irritation and anxiety winding together in her chest. Her eyes flicked to the black nylon bag beside her. Inside, her T-shirt waited, her escape, her safety net. All she had to do was pull it on, walk calmly to her car, and this whole thing would be over.

But that wasn't how it worked, not for her. To give in now would be cheating, a crashing failure. The "game," as she called it, demanded desperate risk.

Without it, there was no electrifying thrill. No frantic heartbeat hammering in her chest. No raw reminder that she was alive. So, she waited, muscles coiled and aching, breath brittle and shallow. The temptation gnawed at her with every savage minute. She loathed its presence, seductive and menacing, threatening to unravel the game.

Finally, movement. The men laughed one last time, tossing their empty bottles into the truck bed with dull clinks. The tailgate slammed shut, and they climbed into the cab. Jessi held her breath until the truck's red taillights disappeared beyond the curve of the road.

She exhaled sharply, adrenaline coursing through her. She reached into her bag for her keys. The metal felt cold against her palm. Rising quickly, she brushed pine needles from her legs and broke into a quiet trot toward the parking lot. Her thumb pressed the fob—chirp—and the Mustang flashed its lights in response.

In an instant, she was inside, slamming the door behind her, heart still racing. She started the engine, the familiar rumble grounding her as she took one last glance around the empty lot.

She pulled out, the night swallowing her taillights as she sped away.

It had been a sharp, fleeting thrill, and she'd survived it. But inside, Jessi could feel disappointment coiling tight. The rush drained away, leaving her restless. Soon, her mind would circle again, desperate for something riskier, darker, something to shatter this hunger with true exhilaration. There had to be more than this.

2
Kindred Spirits

Every Saturday evening, Amy and Traci would sweep into Jessi's apartment like a whirlwind, with chaos and laughter. They dropped their purses on the couch, claimed the bathroom mirror, and started their favorite playlist on a cell phone while they readied for the evening. It was a ritual that Jessi was used to and found amusing.

"Come on, Jess," Traci said, smoothing the hem of her dress. "Just this once. One song, one dance. Come with us."

Jessi rolled her eyes and laughed nervously as she sat at the edge of her couch, knees pulled up. "I'm fine. The club scene is just not my thing."

Amy shook her head as she added another layer of lip gloss. "You'd be amazing out there. The guys would be all over you."

Jessi just shook her head as she tugged at a small loop of string, twirling the twine around her fingers. The fact was that Jessi found the nightclub scene boring and a waste of time. She couldn't imagine seeing any meaningful relationship on a crowded and drunken dance floor.

And yet, every weekend, Amy and Traci kept asking. They never stopped believing that one night, Jessi might surprise them and say yes. The three had been friends since high school, and while Jessi rented her apartment independently, Amy and Traci shared an apartment in the same complex, just one unit over.

For some reason, Jessi's living room had become the unofficial weekend dressing room; makeup bags spread across the coffee table, shoes kicked off in the corner, mirrors angled just right for last-minute hair fixes.

"Come on, Jess," Traci would say, already shimmering in a revealing club dress. "It's not about being perfect. It's about having fun!"

Amy would lean in closer, applying a final coat of lipstick in Jessi's mirror. "Seriously, half the guys wouldn't even notice us if you were around."

But Jessi always shook her head with a soft smile, fingers curled around the string as she gazed at the TV screen. "You two go on and have fun. But, not too much fun."

Laughter bounced off the walls as the girls continued to prep for their night out. Then, a knock on the door. Jessi answered and found Rebecca standing in the hallway. "Hi Jessi. Was just seeing if Traci and Amy were here."

"They're in here making a mess as usual," Jessi said with a grin. "Come in."

Moving to the living room, Rebecca sat on the edge of a brown leather armchair; her hands folded in her lap. Jessi had only met Rebecca a couple of months before when she tagged along with Amy and Traci on one of their wild club-hopping evenings. She also lived in the complex and wasn't as loud as the other two, or at least didn't know how to join in their playful chatter. Jessi found Rebecca a little awkward but sweet. She seemed like someone who wanted to fit in with the crowd, but didn't quite know how to act.

Rebecca glanced around the room, taking in Jessi's unique decor. The one-bedroom unit had the same layout as her own apartment, with an open design: the living room and kitchen separated only by a counter with a couple of stools. The apartment had only two interior doors: one led to the bathroom, and the other to the bedroom, which had a folding closet door. Jessi's had character. In the living room, over her big puffy sofa, hung an old TWA Airlines poster, while an old movie poster for *The Lost Boys* was prominently displayed over the TV. On the bathroom door hung a life-sized poster of Jon Bon Jovi.

"Rebecca," Traci whined, slipping into a pair of tall boots, "you've got to come with us tonight. It's Saturday. No excuses."

"Seriously," Amy chimed in, leaning toward the mirror to fix her eyeliner. "Jessi is a homebody. If you don't come with us, we're kidnapping you."

Rebecca smiled nervously. "I'm not exactly dressed for clubbing." She stood and twirled around, like a model on a runway, showcasing her black AC/DC t-shirt, khaki shorts, and gray Converse high-tops.

"Oh, come on. I'm sure we can find something to wear between the three of us," Amy pleaded.

"Yeah. Come on, Becks," Traci added as she opened a cloth bag and began rifling through several garments inside.

Rebecca turned to Jessi and asked, "You're not going?"

Jessi leaned back on the couch and folded her arms, shrugging her shoulders with a smile. "I've got a date with the TV tonight."

Rebecca fidgeted as she turned back to Amy and Traci. "I don't think so, guys. Just not in the mood tonight."

Amy rolled her eyes. "You guys are wasting your talent on these four walls," she said as she and Traci ducked back into the bathroom to argue over eyeliner.

As the room grew quiet, Jessi shifted, hugging her knees. "You don't really want to go either, do you?" she asked softly, surprising Rebecca.

Rebecca blinked. Her throat tightened, but she nodded, just barely. "Not really."

Jessi let out a quiet laugh, almost relieved. "I thought I was the only one. Want to stay here with me and watch TV? I think there's a movie coming on."

Rebecca's heart skipped. The fact was that ever since she had met Jessi, she found herself with a huge infatuation. She had noticed Jessi's long curly auburn hair and her striking hazel eyes. But there was something about her smile that struck Rebecca; the way her lips curled and little dimples formed in her cheeks. She didn't even know if Jessi liked girls, and she was too timid to ask. She wanted to say *I'd love to stay here with you*, but the words trembled at the edge of her tongue, too bold to cross. She settled for a more subtle response. "Sure. If you'd like some company."

Just then, Amy and Traci came charging out of the bathroom, twirling and primping. "How do we look?" Traci asked with a grin.

"Oh my God," Jessi said mockingly. "You two are so gorgeous. I think I want to fuck you myself."

The two blondes burst into laughter as they poked each other and whirled in a circle. "Don't make promises," Traci giggled as she grabbed her purse.

Rebecca giggled at the banter and wanted to chime in with something witty, but she couldn't find the words. Her eyes flicked sideways to Jessi, who was laughing along with the teasing.

"Alright," Amy said as she adjusted her boobs in the dress. "We're off. You two have fun with your exciting TV watching... or whatever." With that, both girls kissed the tips of their own fingers, then firmly placed them on the lips of Bon Jovi's poster. Rebecca perceived the act as a sort of Saturday-night ritual. "We'll see ya," Traci said as they swept out the front door.

Suddenly, the apartment fell silent, all for the low volume on the television. A late-night comedy show was playing more for background noise than to draw attention. Jessi curled into her spot on the couch; a throw blanket draped across her lap. "You can see better over here on the couch if you want to sit over here."

"Oh, sure. Thank you," Rebecca responded nervously. She made her way over and sat a cushion away from Jessi, perched a little too upright, as if she wasn't sure how much space she was allowed to take.

"So…" Rebecca said, her voice just above the hum of the TV, "do you always let Amy and Traci raid your apartment like this?"

Jessi smiled faintly. "Pretty much every weekend. My place is, apparently, the official dressing room."

Rebecca gave a small laugh. "I can see why. It's… cozy. Feels easy to be here."

"Thanks," Jessi said, shifting to glance at her. The way Rebecca's eyes darted away didn't escape her. She could sense that Rebecca was nervous, maybe a little anxious.

Another stretch of quiet. Then…

"Do you, um… watch much TV?" Rebecca asked.

Jessi raised an eyebrow, amused at the randomness. "Sometimes. Mostly movies. Old ones, especially."

Rebecca perked up a little. "Really? Like what?"

Jessi looked up as she thought. "I like romances mostly. Old ones, with Cary Grant, or maybe Jimmy Stewart. Sometimes I like sci-fi."

"Who's Cary Grant?" Rebecca asked, her face a puzzled look.

Jessi cocked her head in perplexity. "You've never heard of Cary Grant?"

"Should I have? Maybe I have. If I see him, maybe I'll know who he is."

"Oh my gosh. We've got to educate you on the pleasures of classic movies," Jessi teased with a smirk. "What movies do you like?"

Rebecca felt a little flushed. She hoped she wasn't saying something wrong. "Uh… well… I like Marvel, some Star Wars."

Jessi nodded. "Okay. We can work with that." She raised the remote and began searching through channels. Her eyes were fixed on the screen. "So, tell me about yourself. Are you from here?"

"Atlanta," Rebecca answered. "I moved up here four years ago after graduating high school. Went to work at a Mike's Home Improvement, and now I'm living the dream," she said with a giggle.

"Let's see. If you graduated four years ago, that makes you…" Jessi looked up at the ceiling as she added in her head. "Twenty-two? Twenty-three?"

"Twenty-two," Rebecca said with a smile.

"You're just a puppy," Jessi teased. She tried to hold back a grin as she noticed Rebecca's face flush.

"How about you?" Rebecca responded. "How old are you? Or, am I supposed to ask?"

"Do I look that old?" Jessi said with a raised eyebrow.

"Oh, no. Not at all. I mean… I don't know if it's polite to ask."

Jessi laughed. "I'm just teasing you. I'm 26… an old lady." She looked around the room. "My walker is around here somewhere."

Rebecca let out a giggle, then covered her mouth.

"So, do you have a boyfriend?" Jessi asked.

"Well, I dated this guy all through high school. Josh. But, it didn't last after we graduated."

"Oh? What happened?"

"He was... how do I say... too possessive. Too clingy."

"I know how that is," Jessi said as she rolled her eyes.

"Then you have a boyfriend?" Rebecca's voice broke slightly.

"Not right now. Dated a few guys, one girl. Nothing ever worked out. Like you, they were too domineering. I'm too young to be tied down like that. You know?"

Rebecca's heart skipped. She did like girls, at least she had. "I dated this girl from work for a while, but we really didn't have much in common." She glanced over to scan Jessi's eyes, wanting to see her reaction.

Jessi caught Rebecca's glance, and Rebecca quickly looked away, cheeks warming. Jessi tried to hide a smile as she sensed Rebecca's infatuation with her. "So, you work at a home improvement store?"

Rebecca felt a tinge of disappointment that Jessi hadn't picked up on the 'dating a girl' remark. "Yeah, Mike's over on Waggoner Avenue. I'm in the flooring department."

"Well, your parents must be proud of you," Jessi responded with a grin. "You can get them a deal on flooring."

Rebecca looked down at the floor. "I wouldn't know. I don't really speak with them anymore. They don't approve of some of my life choices, you know."

Jessi's heart sank. "I'm so sorry, sweetie. I know how that is, too," she said as she reached over and placed her hand on Rebecca's.

"You don't speak with your parents either?"

Jessi's smile faded, and she leaned back to her end of the couch. "Well… my father left when I was just five… and my mother passed away two weeks after I graduated high school."

"Oh Jessi, I'm so sorry. I can't imagine."

"It's okay," Jessi said with a reassuring smile. "I've learned to deal with it. It's life… I guess."

Jessi leaned back, studying Rebecca with new eyes. Rebecca wasn't bold like Amy or Traci, and that was precisely what made her stand out. She was… careful. Tentative. And under that awkwardness, Jessi sensed something sincere.

“Let's talk about something else," Rebecca chimed in, attempting to change the subject. “So---what's with the kisses to Bon Jovi?”

Jessi turned to look over her shoulder at the poster hanging on the bathroom door. “Well… we all agreed a long time ago that he was our hall pass.”

“Hall pass?”

"Yeah… you know. Like, no matter how serious your relationship is, if you get a chance to sleep with your hall pass, you get to without consequences." Jessi bit her bottom lip as she turned back to Rebecca. "He's one fine-looking man."

Rebecca laughed, then covered her mouth. "I see what you mean."

"You don't have a hall pass?" Jessi asked with a pouty smile.

"Hmm… I never really thought about it." Rebecca put her index finger up to her lips as she looked up at the ceiling, contemplating the question. "Maybe Harry Styles… or… maybe Margot Robbie," she whispered as if almost embarrassed.

"Oh… Margot Robbie," Jessi answered teasingly. "That's a good choice."

Rebecca only grinned as she pushed back into the sofa's cushions. She looked down as she twiddled her thumbs. "What about… I don't know… What's your favorite way to spend a Saturday night?"

Jessi smirked. "Well… not on a sweaty dance floor."

Rebecca chuckled, relief flickering in her eyes. "Same." She hesitated before adding, more carefully: "Do you… Like having people around? Or do you prefer being alone?"

That one lingered. Jessi studied her for a beat. Rebecca wasn't just making small talk anymore; she was circling something, testing the water. She noticed her brown hair, cut just above her shoulders. It had a natural wave that added softness to her features. She had deep brown eyes that reflected quiet curiosity and a softness. Like a lost puppy, Jessi thought. "I guess it depends on the person," Jessi said softly.

Rebecca's fingers fiddled with the hem of her t-shirt sleeve. "Makes sense." She paused, then ventured further, "So… what kind of people do you like having around?"

Jessi tilted her head, warmth tugging at her lips. Rebecca's attempt at subtlety wasn't lost on her; it was awkward, yes, but sweet in its own way. Flirty, even. She didn't want to embarrass her by pointing it out, but she let the moment hang just long enough for Rebecca to squirm before answering.

"The kind who don't try to drag me into nightclubs against my will," she teased gently.

Rebecca laughed, a little too quickly, cheeks coloring. "Well, I guess that makes me safe company then."

She felt a tug of curiosity—what exactly was Rebecca looking for here? "Yeah," Jessi said finally, her voice soft but edged with something Rebecca couldn't quite name. "I think you might be."

The comedy show Jessi had clicked on had ended long ago, the TV screen now cycling through quiet commercials and teasing an upcoming movie. The two had been so engaged in conversation that they didn't even know what had been on. The lamp on the side table next to Jessi cast a soft golden glow, the only light in the room except for the flickering blue light from the screen. Jessi and Rebecca sat with the kind of stillness that only came after hours had slipped by unnoticed.

"You know… I wasn't really excited last time I went out with them," Rebecca said, trying to restart the conversation. "I just… go along with Amy and Traci because it's easier than saying no."

Jessi turned her head, studying her. "Yeah? I figured as much."

Rebecca gave a nervous little laugh. "I guess I'm not good at saying what I really want. Or at least… not most of the time." She paused, twisting the fabric of her sleeve between her fingers. "But tonight… I kind of just wanted to hang out."

Jessi smiled. She wasn't surprised—not really. "That's… sweet," Jessi said gently.

Rebecca's face flushed. She opened her mouth, then closed it again, before finally blurting: "I like being around you. You make it easy for me to… just be myself. I don't get that a lot."

The words hung in the quiet. Jessi's heart twisted. She was finding that she enjoyed Rebecca's company too, in a way that felt safe, uncomplicated, at least on the surface.

"I… don't really do well with relationships," Jessi said as she fiddled with a loop of string.

Rebecca blinked, startled. "Oh. I didn't mean to…"

"No," Jessi cut in softly, shaking her head. "I didn't mean it like that. I just… I've had people in my life who didn't really understand me either. You know what I mean?"

Rebecca leaned closer, cautious but intent. "I do."

Jessi gave Rebecca a small, guarded smile. "Let's just say… I've got a side of me most people wouldn't expect."

Rebecca searched her face, eyes wide but warm. And Jessi saw no judgment there, only curiosity. "Well," Rebecca said softly, "Maybe I'm not like most people."

The words struck Jessi deeper than she expected. She looked away quickly, heart pounding, caught between fear and the tiniest, dangerous spark of hope. "Can I ask you something kind of personal?"

Rebecca blinked, then nodded cautiously. "Sure."

Jessi hesitated. "Do you… consider yourself a lesbian?"

The word hung heavy in the air. Rebecca's face shifted, a flicker of discomfort. She let out a nervous laugh. "I hate that word. It makes me sound like… I don't know, like I'm from somewhere else. Someone from another country."

Jessi tilted her head. "So… what then? Bi?"

Rebecca drew in a breath, twirling the bottom of her shirt. "I like men. But… I've always been more attracted to women. Or… people who get it. I just like people who understand what I'm feeling, even when I can't say it out loud." Her eyes flicked toward Jessi, then away.

As she shifted, pulling the blanket tighter, Jessi chose her words carefully. Her gaze dropped to the floor. "I don't want to pretend to be someone I'm not. I don't want anyone thinking I'm… simple. Easy. I'm not."

The silence between them thickened, not uncomfortable but charged, delicate. Rebecca's hand twitched slightly against her knee, as if she wanted to reach out but wasn't sure if she should.

The silence stretched on until Jessi finally looked at Rebecca, her eyes steady and calm. "You know…" she said quietly, "I like talking with you."

Rebecca's breath caught. Heat rushed to her cheeks, and she immediately dropped her gaze. "I…"

Her voice faltered, words dissolving in the air. She tucked a strand of hair behind her ear, wishing she could melt into the couch.

A faint smile tugged at Jessi's lips as she watched her flush. She tilted her head, studying her. "Tell me something… What thrills you? What makes you feel alive?"

Rebecca blinked, caught completely off guard. The question felt too big, too sudden. Her throat tightened as she searched for an answer, but nothing came. "I… I don't know," she admitted softly, a little embarrassed at her own lack of words.

Jessi didn't press, but the curiosity in her eyes lingered. Rebecca felt it, felt the weight of being seen… really seen… in a way she wasn't used to. It made her nervous, but it also lit something inside her.

"I do like having fun; experiencing new things; thrills," Rebecca said finally, her voice steadier now, even if her hands fidgeted in her lap. "I just… don't always know how to find them."

Jessi leaned back, considering her, then smiled faintly, this time with a hint of mischief. "We might just get along then."

3
Thrill Ride

Over the next couple of weeks, Rebecca kept reaching out, sometimes by phone, other times by dropping by Jessi's apartment. What began as a casual conversation soon grew into lengthy, winding discussions that neither of them ever seemed to tire of.

Jessi discussed her job as a bookkeeper at a small firm, describing the precision and patience it required, although she admitted it wasn't exactly her passion. Rebecca, by contrast, shared stories of her workplace, her cat named 'Bob,' and her love of art; a world of color and imagination, bringing over sketchbooks filled with charcoal figures and vibrant paintings that seemed alive even on the still canvas.

To their surprise, their worlds weren't so different. They both loved classic rock 'n' roll, trading stories of the first time they heard their favorite bands and laughing at how the same songs had carried them through very different moments in life. Jessi's tastes ranged from classic rock to symphonies. Her favorites included "Pretty Tied Up" by Guns N' Roses, "Ich Tu Dir Weh" by Rammstein, and "Bolero" by Ravel. At the same time, Rebecca was a bit more contemporary with "As It Was" by Harry Styles and "Delicate" by Taylor Swift.

The more they talked, the more connections they uncovered, small threads weaving them closer together.

Before long, it felt natural, almost inevitable, that their paths had crossed. While engaged in lengthy phone conversations, each had delved into the other's passions, desires, and even shared a few secrets. Both were guarded, afraid of revealing too much before testing the waters of the other's wants and needs.

Rebecca divulged her favorite food: cheese ravioli with white sauce and garlic bread, and Jessi shared her love for fried shrimp and a baked potato.

Rebecca had also expressed her love of creating new things through her art and exploring new places. She told of her one year in college studying art and her aspirations to return someday to further her knowledge. Sexually, she shared wild fantasies of having a three-way in some scene of raw, unbridled passion, as well as making love on a beach somewhere in the evening with the stars twinkling above. Of course, she played it off as if they were only fantasies to be dreamed of while drifting off to sleep.

Jessi was more cautious when expressing her desires. Her fantasies involved scenes of daring situations and pushing boundaries. To her, the sense of excitement, mixed with a tinge of fear, made her feel alive somehow. She didn't dare share too much with Rebecca without first assessing how far she could go.

***

Another weekend had passed, and on a Sunday evening, Jessi and Rebecca joined Amy and Traci for dinner at a local restaurant. Jessi found herself slipping into a cozy booth, the kind with dim lights and slick vinyl seating, while Rebecca slid in across from her. Amy giggled her way beside Jessi, while Traci slid in beside Rebecca, not sensing the subtle flirtation between the two.

The conversation rolled easily across the table, stories about work mishaps, favorite bands, and the merits of one concert over another. Jessi laughed, joining in, but she couldn't help noticing the way Rebecca's eyes kept finding hers. It wasn't the casual kind of glance you share at a table. Rebecca didn't just look at her; she seemed to see into her, peeling back layers Jessi rarely let anyone glimpse.

Each time it happened, Jessi felt her pulse quicken. She tried to focus on Amy's joke or Traci's story about her dog, but inevitably her gaze drifted back, locking with Rebecca's for a heartbeat too long. There was something magnetic in the way Rebecca carried herself, her posture strong yet relaxed, her smooth, soft-toned complexion catching the low light, the faintest smile tugging at her lips as if she knew precisely what Jessi was feeling.

The attraction stirred quietly at first, then grew harder to ignore. Jessi admired the firmness in Rebecca's figure, the delicate curve of her shoulders, and the way even the smallest gesture seemed intentional, alive.

Still, nothing was said aloud. Amy and Traci remained oblivious, laughing and eating, caught up in their own rhythm. But under the table, in the pauses between stories, Jessi and Rebecca shared glances that spoke louder than words, glances that hinted at something new, fragile, and electric blooming between them.

The night wound down with empty plates and lingering laughter. Outside, the summer air was warm, the street humming with the quiet life of a city as it eased into the midnight hour. Jessi offered Rebecca a ride as they waved goodbye to Amy and Traci. She accepted, slipping into the passenger seat of Jessi's Mustang.

* * *

The drive back to the apartment complex was filled with a comfortable silence, the kind that spoke more than idle chatter could. The radio played softly, a classic rock station spinning familiar riffs that made Jessi smile. She turned her head once, catching Rebecca's profile lit by passing streetlights, and felt that same pull, an ache and a thrill tangled together.

Inside, the apartment was warm and quiet. Jessi set her keys on the counter, suddenly aware of how close they were standing. She offered a Coke, tea, coffee, anything to break the charge in the air, but Rebecca shook her head, eyes never leaving hers.

For a moment, neither spoke. Jessi felt her heart race; her throat tightened. It was Rebecca who closed the space between them, not abruptly, but with a certainty that made Jessi's knees weak. Her gaze softened as though she were memorizing Jessi's face.

"I had a good time tonight," Rebecca said quietly, "I keep feeling like I've known you longer than I have."

Jessi took a deep breath. "I had a good time too," she said softly.

They stood there, the weight of unspoken words thick between them, until Jessi reached out, brushing her fingers against Rebecca's hand. It was a small gesture, yet it felt like the beginning of something much larger, something neither of them could ignore anymore.

Rebecca's fingers curled gently around Jessi's, their touch sparking like a live wire. Jessi's breath caught, and before she could second-guess herself, Rebecca leaned in. Their lips met softly, almost tentatively at first, but the warmth of it spread through Jessi like fire catching on dry kindling. She closed her eyes, letting the kiss linger, savoring the taste of closeness she hadn't realized she'd been craving.

When they pulled back, Jessi felt her face warm, her heart pounding with a tinge of excitement that felt both dangerous and exhilarating. She looked into Rebecca's eyes, a smile tugging at her lips.

"Want to do something?" Jessi asked, her voice barely above a whisper.

Rebecca tilted her head, curious, a playful glint in her gaze. "What do you mean?"

Jessi didn't answer right away. Instead, she slipped her hand free and crossed the room, grabbing her car keys from the counter. Turning back, she dangled them with a mischievous grin.

"Let's go for a ride."

Rebecca's brows lifted, then she laughed softly, a low, surprised sound that made Jessi's pulse race all over again. Whatever the night held, it was clear they were both ready to step into it together.

* * *

The night air still radiated the heat from the day as they stepped outside. The streets were quiet, with only the occasional car rolling by. Jessi's old Mustang sat under a streetlight, paint dull but well-kept. It was much nicer than Rebecca's 20-year-old Honda Civic with 200 thousand miles. She unlocked it with a chirp, and the two of them slid inside.

Rebecca fastened her seatbelt, fingers brushing nervously at the strap. Jessi started the engine, the low hum filling the silence. For a moment, neither spoke. Then Jessi glanced at her, a half-smile tugging at her lips.

"You nervous?"

Rebecca gave a little laugh. "A little."

"Good," Jessi said, shifting into gear. "That's where the thrill starts."

They pulled out onto the empty streets, the glow of street lamps washing over the windshield in slow rhythm. Jessi drove without telling her where they were going, and Rebecca didn't press, though her curiosity buzzed in her chest. She kept sneaking glances at Jessi, at the calm way her hands gripped the wheel, the faint confidence in her posture.

"Where are we going?" Rebecca finally asked, her voice barely above a whisper.

Jessi's eyes stayed on the road. "You'll see."

Rebecca's lips curved into a cautious smile. "That sounds… ominous."

"Only if you don't trust me." Jessi flicked her a look, brief but piercing.

Rebecca felt her stomach twist, a flutter of fear mingling with excitement. She wasn't used to this side of Jessi, the controlled, almost teasing edge to her words. And she liked it more than she expected. She nodded, trying to hide her nerves. She trusted Jessi more than she cared to admit. There was something about her, a certain allure, a magnetism that drew Rebecca in despite her reservations.

The city lights thinned as Jessi guided them onto a darker stretch of road, trees arching overhead silhouetted by the moonlight. Rebecca shifted in her seat. "So, you do this often?"

"Not like this," Jessi replied. Her voice softened. "Usually, it's just me. Sometimes I drive until the road feels like it's mine. Until I'm far enough from everything else that I can breathe."

Rebecca studied her profile, the way the passing light caught the line of her cheek. There was a loneliness in Jessi's words, but also a kind of hunger, something unspoken that pulled at Rebecca.

She hesitated before speaking. "And tonight, you wanted… company?"

Jessi turned her head just slightly, her eyes glinting before returning to the road. "You're here."

The car rolled on into the night, the world outside falling away until it felt like there was only the two of them, suspended in the hum of the engine and the silence of possibilities.

Eventually, the road narrowed, and the trees thinned, giving way to a wide-open expanse of water. Jessi slowed the car as she approached a narrow gravel road, turned, and eventually pulled the vehicle to a stop at the river's edge, next to a concrete picnic table. "Here we are," she said, her voice laced with a hint of mischief.

Rebecca looked out at the dark water, her brow furrowing in confusion. "What are we doing here?" she asked, her voice trembling slightly.

Jessi turned to face her, her hazel eyes glinting with excitement. "Do you have anything in your pockets?" she asked, a playful smile tugging at her lips.

Rebecca's eyes widened, and she swallowed hard. "Just my keys and a little wallet with my ID," she echoed, her mind racing with possibilities.

Jessi nodded, her smile widening. "Leave them in the car. Your shoes too."

Rebecca's jaw dropped, and she stared at Jessi in disbelief. "What? Why? Are we going swimming?" she managed to stammer out.

Jessi jumped out of the car and began pulling her shirt up and over her head. "Strip," Jessi said with a big grin, her eyes looking back at Rebecca's.

"What?" Rebecca asked with a stammer.

"You heard me," Jessi said, her voice soft but firm. "Come on." She unbuttoned her shorts, letting them fall to her ankles, quickly followed by her panties. She slipped out of her shoes and tossed them through the open car window; her clothes were still crumpled in piles on the ground.

Rebecca hesitated as she looked at Jessi standing naked in the moonlight. She had never seen her bare form, and it was beautiful. Her petite frame, her light skin glistening in the moon's blue glow, her small but perky breasts shimmering with small, erect nipples. Her mind was in a whirlwind of thoughts. She had never done anything like this before; she had never even considered it. But there was something in Jessi's eyes, a challenge, a promise, that made her want to take the risk.

She took a deep breath, her hands trembling as she reached for the hem of her shirt. She looked around at the abandoned picnic area and took a deep breath. The air hung heavy in the warm and muggy night. The warmth of the day had baked the mud along the riverbank, releasing a loamy, almost musky scent that mingled with a whiff of nearby honeysuckle. A symphony of crickets and tree frogs serenaded the night as the occasional lightning bug flashed as it hovered in the slight breeze.

Slowly, she pulled her shirt over her head, her eyes locked on Jessi's. Her gaze was intense, her expression unreadable, and it both terrified and thrilled Rebecca. She continued to undress, her movements hesitant and self-conscious. She folded her clothes neatly, her heart pounding in her chest, and laid them on the table. She unlaced her high-tops and, like Jessi, tossed them into the car. When she was finally naked, she stood there, her arms wrapped around herself, feeling vulnerable and exposed.

Jessi stepped closer, her eyes roaming over Rebecca's body with a hunger that made Rebecca's breath catch. Rebecca's body was toned and muscular, and she stood a full two inches taller than herself. Her ass was firm and round, and she had these small breasts that reminded Jessi more of a chubby 12-year-old than a woman in her 20s. "You're beautiful," Jessi murmured, her voice low and husky. Jessi took her hand and slowly led her to the river's edge.

Rebecca looked at the dark water, her stomach churning with nerves. She hesitated, her mind racing with doubts. But then she looked back at Jessi, at the way her eyes were shining with anticipation. As she watched Jessi dip her toes into the water and slowly wade in, she knew she couldn't back down.

Taking a deep breath, Rebecca cautiously stepped into the calm river. She could feel the gravel bottom beneath her feet as she shifted slowly deeper and deeper. Taking a deep breath, she jumped into the depths, joining Jessi as she giggled and splashed.

Jessi had already plunged underneath, her hair wet and clinging to the side of her face. She reached out and took Rebecca's hand, pulling her close. They stood there in the shoulder-deep waters, naked and vulnerable, the warm night air brushing against their wet skin. Rebecca felt a surge of adrenaline, a rush of excitement. She looked at Jessi, her heart pounding, and saw her own emotions reflected in Jessi's eyes.

"You do this a lot?" Rebecca asked, her voice barely above a whisper.

Jessi grinned, her eyes sparkling with playfulness. "Every now and then."

Rebecca turned to Jessi, still breathless, and laughed. She tilted her head back, dipping her hair in the water. Jessi laughed too, the sound ringing across the water. Then, headlights appeared on the roadway in the distance.

"You think they can see us?" Rebecca asked in a worried tone.

"They can't see us," Jessi reassured. "And if they could... so what?"

Rebecca shook her head and laughed. "Oh my God... You're so crazy."

Jessi just grinned as she ducked under the water. She reemerged in front of Rebecca, close, letting her body slide up against hers. She looked into her eyes, then quickly leaned in and gave Rebecca a sudden peck on the lips.

Pulling Jessi closer, Rebecca slipped both legs around her hips. They bobbed in the water, nose to nose, each gazing into the other's eyes. Rebecca tilted her head and leaned in, giving Jessi a deep, passionate kiss. Jessi closed her eyes. She could feel Rebecca's soft, pouty lips; their tongues exploring, her pulse quickening.

Taking Rebecca's hand, Jessi slowly pulled her towards the riverbank. As they stepped out of the water, the night air suddenly felt cool, and goose bumps formed along their bare flesh. Water dripping from their bodies, Jessi guided Rebecca back to the picnic table, having her sit not on the bench seat, but on the broad concrete top. She then eased her way between Rebecca's legs and gently laid her back onto the table.

The concrete was coarse, rough on Rebecca's exposed back, but she didn't care. She was lost in this moment, savoring every second.

Jessi's hands slid up Rebecca's body, starting at her hips, moving gently to her breasts. Her fingers circled slowly around her nipples until they stood erect and hard as stones. She leaned in and let her warm breath waft on Rebecca's shaved mound.

Raising her arms above her head, Rebecca grabbed the edge of the table. Her back arched as she felt Jessi's tongue slowly probe, lightly licking along her vulva. She let out a soft moan, which only made Jessi explore deeper. Rebecca looked upwards to the sky; the moon and stars shimmered through the canopy of the pine trees above her. Her body tingled, and she found her breath quickening.

Moving her head up Rebecca's body, Jessi gave tender kisses until she reached her navel. There, she let her tongue explore again as she slid a hand down and leisurely rubbed along Rebecca's clit. She could feel Rebecca's juices increase, becoming warmer and wetter. She slid one finger inside, then another, and another. She gently curled her fingers back and forth, sensing the pleasure building through Rebecca's winded moans.

Raising, Jessi gazed at Rebecca's expression, increasing her rhythm as she stared into her eyes. Reaching up with her other hand, she placed a firm grip around Rebecca's throat, not pressing to restrict her breath, but a grip of commanding dominance.

To Rebecca's surprise, this sent her over the edge. Her body quivered as her breathing became labored. She reached up and grabbed Jessi's arm as her hips attempted to move to Jessi's rhythm. Her moans, in sync with the motions, grew louder and louder until she pushed her chest upwards and let out a squeal. Her body convulsed and twitched until the sensations left Rebecca breathless and trembling on the table.

Leaning up to meet Rebecca's gaze, Jessi gave Rebecca another deep, adoring kiss. She then leaned over and lay on her back next to her, gazing up at the night sky.

"Oh my God, Jessi," Rebecca said as she gasped for air. "That... that was amazing."

"I'm an amazing person," Jessi replied with a mischievous grin.

"But... what about you?" Rebecca asked as she turned and faced her.

"Oh... the night's not over," Jessi quipped with a laugh. She turned and lay back on the table next to Rebecca, looking up at the twinkling heavens. The two lay there for a long while, holding hands and not speaking a word. As they stared upwards, a streak of light shot across the evening sky, sparkling like a Roman candle before it disappeared into the darkness.

"Did you see that?" Jessi asked, still gazing up.

"I did," Rebecca whispered. "Make a wish."

They lay there, holding hands and lost in the moments, listening to each other's rhythmic breathing.

"Come on," Jessi said suddenly as she lifted and began looking for her and Rebecca's discarded clothes. She jumped off the table and gathered the garments, bunching them in her arms as she fumbled with her keys.

Rebecca leaned up and watched as Jessi pushed a button on her key fob. With a click, the trunk lid popped open. Jessi walked over and threw all of their clothes inside the trunk, then shut the lid.

"Wait. What are you doing?" Rebecca posed as she jumped off the table. She laughed as she looked at Jessi standing naked next to the car, hands on her hips.

"What?" Jessi said with a smirk. "Time to go home. Come on. I'm really horny."

"You... are... insane!" Rebecca exclaimed as she shuffled back to the car.

As Jessi started the car, adrenaline rushed, and laughter spilled out of both of them like they hadn't felt in years. The hum of the tires filled the silence after they left the picnic area, both of them still laughing in bursts as the headlights of a passing car swept along the empty road. Rebecca pressed a hand to her chest, trying to catch her breath.

"Oh my... I can't believe this," Rebecca said, still grinning.

"But you like it," Jessi replied, grinning at the windshield.

Rebecca hesitated, then laughed again. "What if we get pulled over?"

"I guess we'll have to give the cop some head and try to get out of it," Jessi replied, grinning at the road ahead.

Rebecca shook her head, but she couldn't stop smiling. "You're going to get me in trouble."

"Maybe," Jessi teased. "You never know."

As they rewound their way toward the city, every set of headlights made Rebecca tense. She ducked slightly in her seat and tried to cover her exposed chest and private area, laughing nervously as the glow swept over them. "I swear they can see us," she whispered.

"See what?" Jessi asked, smirking.

"That we're naked!"

Jessi chuckled. "Good. Let them." Jessi sat upright in the driver's seat without bother; her eyes locked on the road.

As they traveled, the car passed through increasingly urban areas, with streetlights and well-lit signs illuminating the vehicle's interior. Rebecca squealed as Jessi pulled next to another car at a stoplight, shrinking down until she was nearly in the floorboard.

Jessi just giggled watching Rebecca squirm. She knew that with the tinted windows and the dim evening light, no one would be able to see in.

"I could really go for a milkshake right now," Jessi teased. "Want to stop by McDonald's on the way?"

"Don't you dare!" Rebecca screamed with a snicker. "Oh my God. You are so much trouble!"

By the time they reached the apartment complex, Rebecca's heart was pounding, but her nervousness had shifted into exhilaration. Jessi parked, and on the count of three, they grabbed their shoes and bolted from the car, half-running, half-laughing, stealing glances at the quiet apartment windows around them as if every shadow might hold a curious neighbor.

Rebecca nearly tripped on the steps, grabbing Jessi's arm for balance. Jessi steadied her, their laughter spilling out again as she fumbled with her keys. Finally, the door clicked open, and they rushed inside, slamming it behind them.

They leaned against the door, breathless, their laughter tapering into silence. The apartment felt different now, warmer, alive, as though it had absorbed the charge of the night.

Rebecca brushed her damp hair from her face, still flushed and breathless. "I can't believe we just did that."

Jessi looked at her, eyes gleaming. "You're braver than you think."

For a long moment, neither of them moved. The adrenaline lingered, mixing with something quieter, heavier. The kind of silence that came not from exhaustion, but from standing on the edge of something neither of them had named yet.

Rebecca leaned against the door, her chest heaving with each breath.

Jessi grinned, her hazel eyes sparkling with whimsy.

Rebecca reached out, her fingers tracing the line of Jessi's jaw. "You're wild, you know that?"

Jessi leaned into the touch, her eyes never leaving Rebecca's.

Rebecca felt a surge of desire, a need to be closer, to feel Jessi's body against hers. She closed the distance between them; her lips meeting Jessi's in a passionate kiss. Their tongues danced together, exploring, tasting, as their hands roamed each other's bodies, memorizing every curve and line.

Jessi's hands found their way to Rebecca's small breasts, her thumbs circling the nipples until they were stiff and aching. Rebecca gasped into the kiss, her own hands moving to Jessi's soft curves, squeezing and caressing.

They moved together, their bodies pressed tightly, as they made their way to the bedroom. Jessi's bed was soft and inviting, and they fell onto it with a tangle of limbs and laughter. Rebecca straddled Jessi, her body hovering just above hers, her hands pinning Jessi's wrists to the bed.

"Your turn," Rebecca whispered, a playful smile on her lips. "I want to explore every inch of you."

Jessi's eyes darkened with desire, and she nodded, a soft moan escaping her lips as Rebecca began to trail kisses down her neck, her collarbone, her breasts.

Rebecca took her time, savoring every inch of Jessi's body, her hands and mouth working in tandem to draw out groans and gasps. She moaned softly, threading her fingers through Jessi's hair and pulling her closer.

Jessi's tongue circled Rebecca's nipple, teasing and sucking until it hardened under her touch. She switched to the other breast, giving it the same attention as Rebecca's hips lifted off the bed, seeking friction. Jessi could feel the heat of Rebecca's core, making her own arousal spike.

Rebecca reached between her legs. Her fingers brushed against Jessi's neatly trimmed clit, just a strip of hair shaved smooth on either side. Her motions made her gasp and buckle up into the touch. Rebecca smiled wickedly and began to rub slow circles around the sensitive nub.

Jessi's hips bucked against her, seeking more, and Rebecca obliged, her fingers finding her wet and ready. She circled and teased, her own body aching with need, until Jessi was writhing beneath her, begging for release.

"Jessi," Rebecca breathed, her voice heavy with desire. "I need you." She pushed Jessi back onto the bed and straddled her hips, grinding against her. She moved back up and slipped one leg between hers. She pressed her clit against hers, her hips moving in a slow, sensual rhythm.

Jessi met her thrust for thrust, their bodies moving in perfect sync, their breaths mingling, their hearts pounding. Rebecca's mound was warm and wet as it slid against her own.

The room was filled with the sounds of their passion, their moans and gasps, the soft slapping of skin against skin. Rebecca could feel the tension building, the pleasure coiling tighter and tighter, and she knew Jessi was right there with her.

Their rhythm increased until, with a final, deep thrust, they both tumbled over the edge, their bodies convulsing with pleasure, their voices crying out in unison. They clung to each other, their bodies slick with sweat, their hearts racing, as they rode out the waves of their release.

In the aftermath, they lay on the bed, their bodies still intertwined, their breaths slowly returning to normal. Rebecca rested her head on Jessi's chest, listening to the steady beat of her heart, a contented smile on her lips.

Jessi kissed the top of her head, her arms tightening around her.

Neither spoke. They didn't need to. The silence was thick with everything they couldn't quite say—attraction, relief, the thrill that still crackled between their bodies. And with that, they drifted off to sleep, their bodies still tangled, their hearts full.

4
Hard Memories

Jessi awoke in a sleepy haze and found Rebecca's head lying on her shoulder; her arm wrapped around her chest. One of Rebecca's legs was draped across her belly, and she could feel the warmth of her soft skin pressed against her own.

The memories of the previous night's events slowly popped back into Jessi's mind, and she gradually pulled Rebecca's arm up as she slinked out of the bed, trying not to wake her. She quietly crept out of the room and closed the door.

Jessi made her way to the bathroom and looked in the mirror. She was a mess; mascara smeared, hair tussled and knotted; last night's lipstick still smudged around her mouth. She ran some warm water and, with a cloth, began cleaning last night's adventure off her face.

The morning sun pierced the vertical blinds covering the sliding glass doors to the apartment's balcony. Jessi, now revigorated, sat nude at the kitchen table, her hands wrapped around an empty coffee mug, eyes fixed on the thin line of light spilling through the blinds. The coffee maker burbled, filling the room with its warmth. She felt the buzz of last night still in her chest, half memory, half lingering adrenaline, but it was tempered now by the hush of morning.

The soft creak of the bedroom door broke her thoughts. She looked up to see Rebecca standing there, unclothed, hair tousled, rubbing her eyes.

"Morning," Rebecca said softly, her voice still rough with sleep.

Jessi nodded, forcing a small smile. "Morning. Coffee's almost ready."

Hesitating for just a moment, Rebecca shuffled into the kitchen before sliding into the chair across from Jessi. She folded her arms on the table, leaning forward slightly. There was a quiet awkwardness between them, the kind that only comes after a night that changed something.

"Did you sleep okay?" Jessi glanced at her, then quickly looked away.

"Better than I have in a while," Rebecca said with a little nod.

The coffee maker hissed, and Jessi rose to pour two cups, needing the small task to steady her hands. She slid a mug toward Rebecca, who cradled it with both hands, blowing lightly on the steam. She reached for the sugar bowl in the middle of the table and spooned several scoops into it.

"Thanks," Rebecca murmured.

"You like your coffee in your sugar, I see," Jessi said with a smile.

"Just a little," Rebecca responded as she rubbed her eyes.

They sat in silence for a moment, sipping. The weight of everything unsaid settled between them.

"Well," Jessi said with a subtle grin, "you've seen me without makeup. I guess I'll have to kill you now."

Rebecca laughed, then put her hands up to her face. "You've seen me without makeup, too."

Jessi shook her head and laughed. "No… You are still wearing yours, it's just not where it's supposed to be."

"Oh my God," Rebecca blurted between her palms. "I'm pretty sure we may have ruined your pillow cases."

"I think last night was worth a couple of messed-up pillow cases, don't you?"

Rebecca lifted her hands from her face and giggled.

Jessi rested an elbow on the table as she stared into her mug of coffee. The silence stretched, with neither knowing exactly what to say. Rebecca shifted in her chair, waiting, searching Jessi's face for something, anything.

Finally, Rebecca set her cup down, the clink louder than it should have been. She rubbed her temples with both hands and sighed.

"So… that was a wild night…" Her voice trailed off, and she shook her head with a grin. "Where did that come from?"

Jessi blinked, frowning softly. "I… well… sometimes I just push," she stuttered, trying to find the right words. She took a deep breath and looked down at the coffee. "Sometimes things like that… excites me… the thrill."

She pushed back in her chair, putting space between them. "Maybe… I shouldn't have pushed you like that."

Rebecca tilted her head, cautious. "I thought it was fun. Especially the end part."

Jessi's throat tightened as she looked up at Rebecca's flirty grin.

"To tell you the truth... that was probably the most fun I've had in a very long time," Rebecca whispered as she leaned in and sipped the hot brew. "You do things like that often?"

She rolled her eyes and smiled as she circled a finger around the rim of her mug. "I don't know. Sometimes."

"The thrill… It's kind of like a rollercoaster?" Rebecca queried.

"Yes. Exactly like that," Jessi replied softly as she shook her head.

"What kind of things have you done?" she asked with a roguish smile. "Tell me."

Jessi laid her elbow on the table and rested her palm on her forehead. "Oh God," she sighed. "I don't know."

"Jessica Renee Morgan!" Rebecca answered with a phony pout as she crossed her arms.

Jessi sat upright. She had used her full name, just as her mother would when scolding. "Okay, okay. Geez." She said as she placed both elbows on the table, hands shielding her embarrassment.

"When I was young… like I told you already, my dad left my mom and me. I was an only kid, and I guess, momma being single with a child, did the best she could."

Rebecca tilted her head as she leaned in, listening intently.

Jessi got up and retrieved the loop of string that was sitting on the end table next to the sofa. She twirled the twine around her fingers as she sat back down at the table across from Rebecca. She looped the string around each finger, then pulled it free nervously as she searched for her words.

"Momma had to work two jobs, sometimes three… You know… just to pay the bills. I remember things being tight, especially in those days. Momma couldn't afford a daycare or a sitter. Being afraid child services would get involved, I was told to stay inside, doors locked, and not to answer if anyone knocked."

A look of sadness swept across Rebecca's face as she sat quietly, focused on Jessi's expression; her sense of sorrow.

Jessi bowed her head. "God! I can't believe I'm telling you this."

Rebecca reached out and grabbed Jessi's hand, pulling it towards her. "Hey… you can tell me anything. You don't have to hide anything from me."

She kept her head low as she looked up at Rebecca, the look of concern and caring on her face. Jessi had always kept these memories guarded; sometimes buried deep inside. She took a deep breath.

"As I grew up, I couldn't go out and play with the other kids, or play in the yard," Jessi explained. "I had to remain inside for the most part, so no one would know a child was inside without her mom. I would do my homework, watch old movies on TV, and wait for Momma to come home, which was usually about an hour before I would go to bed. I… I guess…"

"Go on," Rebecca said with a furrowed brow.

"When you're all alone… no friends to play with… I guess I started finding ways to… challenge myself."

"Challenge yourself? Challenge yourself, how?"

Jessi started rubbing her temples nervously. She couldn't believe she was sharing something so intimate and personal, embarrassing, even. She faltered on her words, beginning to speak, then pulling back.

"Tell me," Rebecca whispered as she tightened her grip on Jessi's hand.

With a tilt of her head, Jessi looked into Rebecca's big brown eyes. They were gentle and reassuring. They say the eyes are the window to the soul, and Rebecca's soul was understanding and caring.

"I… I would do these little things," Jessi said with a giggle. "I would tie myself up with some shoelaces and force myself to get free. I would sneak out at night, and ring someone's doorbell, then run away as fast as I could. Just stupid little dares. Back then, I thought they were so audacious, but now I look back, and it was so stupid."

"No," Rebecca said softly. "Sounds like a lonely girl trying to have some excitement."

Jessi rolled her eyes as she tightened the string around her middle and index fingers. She let out another sigh.

"Momma got sick when I was 14, and I got a part-time job to help pay the bills. Back then, I would go to school, then go to work right after, then come home, do my homework, and sleep."

Tears began welling up in Jessi's eyes, while her voice trembled. "When I was 17, momma was really sick, but somehow, she kept working as long as she could. It wasn't long after that that I was having to help take care of her. I managed to get through high school, barely… Momma died not long after."

Rebecca realized that tears were falling down her cheek, and she reached up to wipe them away quickly without Jessi noticing.

"Oh, stop," Jessi said as she stood up and grabbed a napkin. She handed it to Rebecca and placed her hand on her arm. “I’m not telling you this to make you sad. Let’s talk about something else.”

“No, no,” Rebecca responded. “I want to hear everything.”

Jessi leaned back in her chair and took another sip of her coffee. She looked up at Rebecca, her eyes puffy and red.

Rebecca wiped away the tears and attempted a fake smile. “Tell me. You were all alone?”

“Oh… I had some friends. Amy and Traci helped me find this place. People from work. You know.”

“But you didn’t have any family? No one to help you?”

Jessi looked down at the coffee mug, running her finger in circles around the handle. “You know, I hate to say this… but it was a lot easier after she was gone. I’m not saying I wouldn’t give anything to have her back. It’s just… I had to grow up so fast. It was… hard.”

"You never heard from your father? Never tried to find him?"

Looking down at the mug, Jessi shrugged. "I've never heard anything about him. I only have flashes of memories of him. You know... little memories. He's never been a part of my life."

Rebecca listened intently, silently, trying to imagine what it would be like to have no family in her life.

“Anyway,” Jessi laughed, breaking the somber mood. “I started… these little challenges for myself. I think it was a way of… I don't know… breaking free of responsibility somehow. I don't really understand why it makes me feel like it does."

"What kind of challenges?"

"It was silly stuff at first," Jessi laughed. "I'd go out in a skirt with no underwear. Of course, it wasn't like it was a miniskirt or anything, but I thought it was so dangerous back then."

Rebecca let out a giggle, then covered her mouth.

"I remember one time I stripped down naked and dared myself to run to the mailbox and back. Of course, it was 2 a.m., and no one was around. Then, I dared myself to run all the way around the building one time. That was funny, so then I challenged myself to run around the building two times, then three. I was so stupid back then," Jessi snickered.

"I would've liked to have seen that," Rebecca laughed.

"I bet you would," Jessi giggled. "I don't know. I'm just… weird, I guess."

Rebecca let out a mischievous grin. "You're definitely weird. That's why I like you."

Jessi sat, her head lowered as she looked back at Rebecca. "I like you too," she whispered with a sly smile.

"Like I told you, I don't talk with my family. We had this big falling out and they pretty much disowned me, but I can't imagine…" Rebecca's words trailed off as if she were trying to find just the correct expression. She took a deep breath, then her smile bloomed, small but genuine, like a secret only the two of them shared. "I guess I need to get home," she said. "I need to get ready for work, and I need to feed Bob, too."

"So, you need to feed your pussy?" Jessi scoffed. "Bob the cat."

"You don't like cats?" Rebecca asked, sneering and grinning.

"I love cats," Jessi answered. "But, there's something to be said about a big sloppy lick from a mutt with puppy dog eyes."

Rebecca laughed, and the sound eased some of the tightness in Jessi's chest.

"I just have one problem," Rebecca announced.

"Oh?" Jessi asked with a puzzled gaze.

"You have my clothes locked in your trunk," Rebecca quipped as she put her hands on her hips. She stood and spun, highlighting her naked form.

Jessi let out a big chuckle as she put her hand up to her face. "I'm so sorry. Let me find you something." She disappeared into the bedroom and quickly emerged with a t-shirt and a pair of shorts.

Rebecca took the bundle of clothes from Jessi's hands, their fingers brushing briefly. The spark of contact was enough to send a shiver down Jessi's spine, though she tried not to show it.

"Thanks," Rebecca said softly. "For… everything. Last night, this morning… all of it."

Jessi shrugged, feigning lightness. “Don’t thank me yet. You haven’t seen the clothes I just stuck you with.”

She disappeared into the bedroom to change, leaving Jessi alone in the kitchen with her thoughts. The coffee had gone lukewarm on the table, but Jessi didn’t move. She coiled the string around her thumb; her mind caught in a tug-of-war.

In her mind, she again saw the way Rebecca had stood that night, the way her laughter had spilled out in the dark like she was discovering herself for the first time. For Jessi, it was just a mundane act, but seeing it through Rebecca's eyes somehow made Jessi relive the thrill of those little dares.

And for the first time in years, Jessi wondered if maybe, just maybe, she wasn’t as alone as she’d thought.

Rebecca reappeared in the doorway, now dressed in an old gray t-shirt with Tweety Bird on the front and black cotton shorts, holding her shoes in one hand. She lingered for a moment, eyes meeting Jessi’s with quiet intensity.

“I’ll call you,” she said, her voice soft but steady.

Jessi nodded, fighting the urge to say something more. Instead, she smiled. “I’ll be here.”

Rebecca slipped over and gave Jessi a soft kiss, then made her way out the door, leaving the apartment quiet again, except for the echo of her presence that refused to fade.

The morning air was cool against Rebecca's skin as she stepped outside, Jessi's borrowed shorts brushing lightly against her legs. She hugged her shoes to her chest; the pavement was now cool under her bare feet as she walked toward her apartment.

Her heart was still hammering, not from nerves now, but from the residue of everything that had happened. Last night had cracked something open in her, something she hadn't even realized she'd been starving for. That rush, that edge of danger, that strange sense of freedom, she hadn't felt it in years. Maybe ever.

And Jessi…

Rebecca closed her eyes briefly, remembering Jessi's laugh by the water's edge, the way her eyes glowed in the headlights, the way she had pressed so close in the apartment doorway. There was a darkness in her, sure, but there was also light, something magnetic, something she couldn't turn away from.

She would call. And Jessi would answer.

5
Bound Desires

The first call came that evening. Jessi, in the bathroom, nearly missed it, but at the last second swiped her screen and held the phone to her ear.

"Hey," Rebecca's voice said, warm and tentative. "Just got home from work and getting ready for work tomorrow. Uh… cat's fed. How was your day?"

Jessi chuckled despite herself. "Boring as usual. Glad Bob's fed. Wouldn't want you accused of neglect."

There was a pause, then Rebecca's soft laugh. "So… how are you?"

"I'm fine," Jessi answered in a reassuring tone.

Rebecca didn't bring up their morning conversation. It was too personal to be discussed over the phone. She sensed a darkness in Jessi that she was longing to be released from. Instead, she kept the conversations light and playful.

That became the rhythm of their weekdays: small conversations, nothing too heavy, but threaded with undercurrents of curiosity. A text here, a call there. Sometimes Rebecca would send a blurry photo of her cat sprawled across the bed, captioned: *Bob says hi.*

Well, he meowed, but same thing. Other times, she'd tease Jessi about the weird clothes she had lent her, or about how "mysterious" she always sounded when she went quiet for too long.

And Jessi would shoot back little sarcastic comments, or send Rebecca a picture of the mess her car had turned into after a week of neglect, saying: *Bet your cat's cleaner than this.*

The flirting stayed light, but Jessi could feel it building. A heat beneath the words. A challenge in the pauses. Rebecca was careful, but there was always a little edge of daring now, like she wanted Jessi to push her again.

One evening, after a long silence, Jessi finally typed out a message and stared at it for several minutes before hitting send.

Jessi: You ever been to a club that's not exactly mainstream?

Rebecca's reply came quickly.

Rebecca: Depends. You mean like underground music? Or like… something else?

Jessi's lips curved into a faint smile.

Jessi: Something else. A place where people go to forget who they are for a while. Where they can be anything. Or nothing.

There was a long pause this time, long enough that Jessi wondered if she'd said too much. Then…

Rebecca: Sounds dangerous.

Jessi: It can be.

Rebecca: When do we go?

Jessi froze, her heart thudding. She hadn't expected Rebecca to agree so easily. She stared at the glowing screen; her pulse caught between excitement and dread.

Finally, she typed back.

Jessi: Friday night. I'll pick you up. Wear something sexy.

* * *

The workweek seemed to creep along as anticipation for their Friday outing grew. Rebecca tugged at the hem of her new sweater dress for the fifth time since Jessi's car pulled up to the curb. She'd chosen black, safe, simple, but the open shoulders with a turtleneck collar suddenly felt like a noose.

When Jessi stepped out to meet her, Rebecca took a deep breath. The black dress Jessi wore clung to her like a liquid shadow, plunging low in the front and daringly open in the back. Rebecca noticed she wasn't wearing any jewelry except diamond stud earrings and a black choker. Her strappy heels clicked against the pavement as she approached, a small, knowing smile on her lips.

"Wow," Rebecca said before she could stop herself.

Jessi tilted her head, giving her a once-over. "You clean up nice," she said, though there was amusement in her eyes.

Rebecca flushed, tugging again at her collar. "I didn't exactly know what you meant by 'sexy.'"

Jessi smirked, leaning closer as if to share a secret. "Sexy isn't the dress. It's how you wear it." Her voice dipped lower, teasing. "But don't worry… I'll show you."

The words sent a flutter through Rebecca's stomach, half thrill, half nerves.

* * *

The ride was quiet except for the hum of the engine and the occasional brush of Jessi's perfume when she shifted in her seat. Rebecca stared out the window, trying not to second-guess herself. She wasn't used to plunging into dresses and the nightlife, but something about Jessi's confidence made her want to try.

When they pulled up outside, Rebecca realized quickly this wasn't like the downtown dance clubs Amy and Traci had dragged her to. The building was discreet, tucked between two warehouses, its entrance lit only by a red glow spilling out around the heavy doors. There was no flashy sign on the building; no beer advertisements or any blinking spotlights; only a simple address on the door. A pair of well-dressed men stood outside, checking names.

Rebecca swallowed. "This is it?"

"This is it," Jessi confirmed, shutting off the engine. "It's called Secrets." Her smile had shifted, darker now, carrying an edge of anticipation. "Ready?"

Rebecca hesitated, then nodded, her pulse racing. "How do I look?"

"Gorgeous."

As they approached the doors together, Jessi spoke briefly with the man at the entrance. He looked Rebecca over once before letting them through.

Inside, the world changed. The air was heavy with bass and a whiff of leather, shadows and lights flickering in rhythm. Velvet drapes and mirrored walls created a decadent, secretive atmosphere in the space. People drifted through the haze, laughing, leaning too close, dressed in ways that made Rebecca's sweater dress feel suddenly childish.

Rebecca's eyes widened. "What is this place?" she whispered.

Jessi leaned in close, her lips brushing Rebecca's ear as she answered.

"It's where people stop pretending."

Rebecca stepped cautiously inside, her eyes adjusting to the dim glow. The music was low, more a pulse in the air than a melody, vibrating through the floor beneath her boots.

The first thing she noticed was the furniture, or maybe it wasn't furniture at all. Against one wall stood a tall wooden cross, iron eyelets gleaming faintly at each end. Nearby, an X-shaped frame spread across the shadows, built of the same heavy timber, with more rings fastened at strategic points. And in the center of the room, a circular stage sat under a spotlight, a chain hoist hanging from the rafters above it like something industrial, repurposed for a purpose she couldn't yet name. Her mouth went dry.

Around her, the crowd blurred into fragments of color and skin. Some people were wrapped in leather straps and metal buckles, while others were dressed in lace and silk that seemed more suited to a bedroom than a public space. Masks glimmered here and there, hiding eyes but not bodies. The air smelled faintly of candle wax, threaded with the tang of something metallic, something alive.

Jessi walked forward without hesitation, heels clicking softly against the dark floor. She looked entirely at home here, the cut of her dress flashing glimpses of her back and neckline as though she belonged to this dimly lit world.

Rebecca trailed after her, fighting the urge to cling to her arm. She felt like she had wandered into someone else's dream, or someone else's secret.

Jessi glanced back, catching the look on Rebecca's face. A faint smile touched her lips, reassuring, but edged with something daring. She leaned closer, her breath warm at Rebecca's ear.

"Don't be afraid. No one here will touch you unless you want them to. You're safe with me."

Rebecca nodded quickly, though her pulse betrayed her, hammering in her throat. "What… what is this place, really?" she whispered.

Jessi's eyes gleamed in the half-light. "It's a place where control changes hands. Where people stop pretending to be in charge of their lives, even if only for a night."

Rebecca swallowed hard, her gaze flicking again to the cross, the X, the chain. "And you… You've been here before."

"Many times." Jessi's smile deepened, softer now. "I told you, Rebecca. I love a thrill."

"Are there many places like this in the city?" Rebecca asked as she looked around, her eyes wide.

"Well, this is the only club like this that I know of," Jessi answered in a low voice. "But there are many other types of venues around."

"Oh… like what?"

Jessi smiled at the naive query. She patted her arm and then leaned into her ear. "There are a couple of gay nightclubs I know of, and at least two lifestyle clubs."

"Lifestyle clubs?"

Jessi let out a little chuckle. "It's another way of saying a swingers club," she whispered.

"A swingers club? What is that?"

Jessi tried not to laugh as she squeezed Rebecca's hand. "I'll explain that to you later."

Rebecca's chest tightened. Part of her wanted to turn and run back into the night, back to safety. But another part, a louder part, was caught in Jessi's orbit, desperate to see more.

Rebecca followed Jessi deeper into the club, her eyes darting everywhere, wide and unblinking. The smoky haze and low light seemed to thicken the further they walked, the crowd parting here and there to reveal scenes that made Rebecca's stomach flutter.

Near a corner, a shirtless man in black gloves tilted a red candle over a blonde woman's bare stomach. Droplets of hot wax fell in a steady rhythm, each one earning a shuddering moan that twisted between pain and pleasure. Rebecca's hand flew to her mouth, but she couldn't look away. The woman arched toward the wax as if craving it, her face flushed, her lips parted in a look of something close to bliss. Rebecca turned sharply and nearly collided with Jessi, who steadied her with a hand on her arm.

"It's okay," Jessi murmured, her tone gentle but tinged with amusement. "They're here because they want to be."

Rebecca nodded quickly, though her pulse still raced.

They moved on, weaving through the space. On another side of the room, a man in a tailored black shirt held a leather leash. The collar around a young woman's throat glinted in the light as she knelt at his feet, her hands folded neatly in her lap. His hand brushed her black hair back almost tenderly before giving the leash a short tug. She looked up at him with eyes shining, her expression somewhere between obedience and pride.

They next came upon a man on all fours atop what looked like a large leather ottoman. A black-haired woman clad in a black bustier and fishnet stockings stood behind him, holding a handle with many leather strands dangling from one end. She would whip the device at his exposed bottom; a snap echoing around the room. The man would only flinch, holding in any verbal sign of pain.

Rebecca found herself holding her breath. A strange heat stirred inside her, one she didn't fully understand.

"You see? Every story here looks different. Pain, surrender, devotion… It's all part of the same language," Jessi said as she leaned close, her lips brushing against Rebecca's ear.

Rebecca swallowed, words caught in her throat. Before she could speak, Jessi straightened and guided her toward another section of the room. A figure stood there, commanding without even trying, tall, broad, and built like a man carved out of stone. His hair was silver at the temples, his jaw square, his frame filling out the leather pants and open vest he wore with practiced ease.

When he turned, Rebecca felt the weight of his gaze immediately. Dark eyes swept over her with quiet intensity before flicking toward Jessi. A slow smile spread across his face.

"Jessi," he said, his voice deep and roughened by age and confidence. "I see you've brought a friend tonight."

Jessi's hand lingered at the small of Rebecca's back, steadying her. "Becca," she said softly, "this is Marcus."

Marcus's smile widened slightly, though it carried something assessing, as though he were already measuring her. "Welcome," he said, the word carrying more weight than it should have.

Rebecca tried to respond, but her voice caught, and all she could manage was a nervous nod.

Jessi leaned closer, whispering just for her. "Don't worry. He's a friend. I wanted you to meet him."

Rebecca hesitated at the edge of the floor, her hands twisting nervously at the hem of her dress.

Jessi's voice was calm, steady, the way you'd talk someone down from a ledge. Jessi's demeanor seemed more elegant and refined inside the club. Her words were softer and more reserved.

"There's nothing to be afraid of, Becca. Everyone here understands limits. No one crosses a boundary unless they're invited. You're safe. You can do as much or as little as you want."

Rebecca nodded, though her heart was pounding so hard she thought it might echo in the cavernous space.

Jessi leaned close to Marcus, rising on her toes to whisper something in his ear. Whatever she said drew the faintest smirk from him, followed by a curt nod. Then Jessi turned back to Rebecca, her eyes glinting with an intensity that made Rebecca's breath catch.

"Take a seat," Jessi said softly, with a flick of her chin toward the low benches surrounding the stage. "Just watch."

Rebecca's legs felt heavy as she lowered herself into the seat. The leather cushion was cool under her palms as she pressed her hands flat, grounding herself.

Marcus extended an arm, and Jessi slipped her hand into his without hesitation. He guided her to the middle of the circular stage, directly beneath the chain hoist dangling from the rafters. The spotlight caught her black dress, the fabric gleaming against her skin. She looked transformed there, no longer the hesitant, private woman Rebecca had gotten to know over late-night confessions, but someone else entirely, someone who belonged in this world.

Jessi raised both hands to her shoulders and hooked the straps of her dress with her thumbs. She lifted the dress upwards slightly before pulling the straps off her shoulders, slipping it downwards, and letting it fall gently to her ankles.

Rebecca's lips parted as she gazed at Jessi's nude form beneath the spotlight. She hadn't worn underwear, and after she stepped out of her high heels, she stood fully exposed. Marcus took a length of black rope from a stand near the stage. He worked with quiet precision, his movements economical and deliberate. Jessi stood perfectly still, her head bowed slightly, her breathing even, as though she were preparing herself.

Rebecca leaned forward without realizing it, her stomach fluttering with a mix of fascination and fear.

What did she whisper to him? What is she about to show me?

From the corner of her eye, Rebecca noticed others gathering, their gazes turning toward the stage. There was no jeering, no cruelty, only a hush of anticipation, as though the entire room had shifted to bear witness.

Rebecca gripped her knees tighter. She couldn't look away.

The crowd thickened around the stage, shadows gathering at the edges of the dim light. Rebecca shifted in her seat, her knees pressed tight together, trying to ignore the heat creeping into her cheeks.

Marcus moved with slow, deliberate certainty, the kind of confidence that came from long practice. His hands, broad and strong, held the rope as though it were an extension of himself. He began by drawing Jessi's arms gently behind her back. She didn't resist. She yielded.

The rope crossed over itself in neat, geometric knots, starting at her wrists, then winding upward to cradle her shoulders. Each pull tightened the shape, not harsh, not careless, but precise, as though he were building something beautiful instead of binding a woman.

Rebecca's breath hastened, and she found herself biting her nails.

From there, Marcus let the rope fall against Jessi's collarbone. He wove it across her chest, looping, pulling, tightening, until a diamond-shaped pattern emerged just below her throat. His motions were rhythmic, almost hypnotic, the strands crisscrossing like the lines of a web, descending slowly.

Jessi's head tilted back, her eyes closed, lips parted just slightly. She looked at peace. No, more than that. She looked radiant, as if the knots and the ropes were unlocking something in her that had been locked away.

Rebecca pressed a hand to her mouth, watching as the "net" grew around Jessi's body. From her shoulders down across her breasts, from her waist down toward her hips, each strand snug but not brutal, holding her as though the ropes themselves were embracing her.

A hush fell over the gathered crowd. No one laughed, no one whispered. They were watching art unfold.

Rebecca shivered, caught between awe and the tight flutter of nerves in her stomach. *This is who she is… this is what she meant when she said she likes challenging herself.* She'd never seen Jessi like this. Not the cautious, playful woman who'd whispered in her apartment, or the daring trickster who'd dared her to go skinny dipping, but something else entirely. Jessi wasn't hiding here. She was baring herself without shame.

Marcus stepped back for a moment, tugging at the last knot. Jessi stood at the center of the stage, her arms bound behind her, her body wrapped in a lattice of rope that shimmered under the light. The ropes forced her breasts outward, highlighting her gentle curves. The crowd gave a low murmur, reverent, appreciative.

Rebecca couldn't breathe.

And then Jessi opened her eyes, directly at her.

Rebecca's breath hitched when Marcus stepped closer again, another length of rope held in his hand. From above, the chain hoist swayed gently, its iron hook gleaming in the spotlight. With careful precision, Marcus threaded the hook through a sturdy knot at the center of Jessi's back.

For a moment, Jessi stood perfectly still, her eyes still locked on Rebecca's.

Then the chain rattled as Marcus began to pull. Slowly, steadily, Jessi's feet left the ground.

Rebecca's nails dug into the leather cushion beneath her. She couldn't look away. Jessi rose higher, suspended now in the middle of the stage, the rope net tightening against her form, holding her secure. Her body tilted until she was nearly horizontal, the spotlight catching every curve of her body, every careful knot Marcus had placed. He fixed another length of bindings around one of her knees, making what looked to be a sling. With a tug of the rope, her leg was forced upwards, exposing her glistening mound to all.

Slowly, her body rotated, spinning in graceful silence above the crowd. The rope crisscrossed her like a second skin, binding and displaying her all at once. Her long hair draped downward; her eyes shut. She was vulnerable. Exposed. And yet, the serenity in her face, the calm in her closed eyes, spoke of release, not humiliation.

Rebecca's chest tightened. It was beautiful, yes, but it was also raw. The meaning pressed in on her with Jessi's earlier words echoing in her head. This was Jessi's secret. Not a quirk. Not a passing thrill. A truth about who she was.

Jessi opened her eyes again as she spun slowly, her gaze sweeping the crowd before returning to Rebecca. The message was clear, even unspoken: *This is me. If you want me… this is what you must accept.*

Rebecca's throat burned. The crowd remained hushed, reverent, as though watching a ceremony.

And Rebecca realized she wasn't just witnessing Jessi. Jessi was showing her.

Jessi remained there, on display for a while, like a mannequin slowly spinning in a store window. The crowd watched and whispered.

The chain rattled again, slow and deliberate, as Marcus released her leg and began lowering Jessi back toward the stage. Her body descended gracefully, rope glinting under the light like a woven cage. When her bare feet touched the platform again, the crowd gave a low ripple of polite applause before dispersing, murmuring to one another, leaving Rebecca staring, unable to move.

Marcus tugged a knot free, then another, loosening the web. Jessi's arms slid forward, free again, but she didn't rush. She let him unwind the harness as if savoring the ritual, her chin lifted, her gaze never leaving Rebecca.

Rebecca's heart hammered against her ribs. She didn't know what she was feeling: shame for watching, awe at Jessi's courage, fear at what it all meant, or a dangerous thrill curling low in her stomach.

When the last loop of rope fell away, Jessi grabbed her dress and shoes and stepped down from the stage, her bare body glowing in the dim light, hair tumbling over her back. She walked toward Rebecca with quiet confidence, as though nothing in the world were unusual about what had just happened.

Rebecca's lips parted, but her voice stuck. Finally, she managed to whisper, "That was… Jessi, I…"

Jessi sat beside her, close enough that their knees brushed. Her skin still carried faint impressions from the ropes. She didn't speak right away. She just watched Rebecca, waiting.

Rebecca shook her head, struggling for words. "I didn't know this was… who you are. It's so…" She stopped herself, afraid of the wrong word. *Scary. Intense. Beautiful. All of it.*

Jessi's hand brushed hers, light but steady. "It's a small part of me, Becca. Not all of me. But it's real. I can't hide it, not if you want to be in my life."

The truth hit hard, heavier than the dim music thrumming through the walls. Jessi wasn't asking. She was confessing.

Rebecca swallowed, her pulse still wild. The image of Jessi suspended above the stage replayed in her mind, the ropes, the surrender, the strange peace on her face. It both terrified and entranced her.

She looked into Jessi's eyes, searching. "I don't know if I can understand all of it. But… I want to try."

Jessi's lips curved into the faintest smile, as though she had been holding her breath until that moment.

Rebecca twisted her fingers in her lap, her sweater dress suddenly feeling too warm, too tight. She wanted to ask a thousand questions, but each one tangled in her throat. What if she sounded naïve? What if she said the wrong thing and Jessi pulled away?

Finally, her voice slipped out, quieter than the music. "So… is it always like that? With ropes, and…" She trailed off, embarrassed by her own clumsy words.

Jessi smiled gently, her hand still resting close to Rebecca's. "Not always. There are a hundred different ways it can look. Rope is one. Sometimes it's about trust, sometimes it's about giving or taking control. It depends on the people."

Rebecca nodded slowly, though her brows pinched with worry. "But what if… someone takes it too far? What if they hurt you?"

Jessi's eyes softened. "That's why there are safe words. You pick a word that means stop, no questions, no hesitation. When you say it, everything ends right there. It's a safeguard, Becca. A way to keep the edge thrilling without falling off it."

"What's your safe word?'

"Red." Jessi smiled. "My safe word is 'Red,'" she answered as she stepped into her dress and slowly pulled it up to her shoulders.

Rebecca's chest loosened slightly, though her pulse was still racing. "So, you… You talk about it? Beforehand?"

"Always." Jessi leaned back a little, giving her space. "Communication is everything. You have to be clear about what you want, what you don't want, and where the lines are. And you have to listen just as much as you speak. Limits aren't meant to be broken; they're meant to be pushed but respected."

Rebecca lowered her gaze, chewing her lip. *Limits. Communication. Safe words.* The words sounded clinical, but what she'd just seen on the stage was anything but. It was raw, alive, dangerous in a way that made her chest ache with both fear and… something else.

She risked a glance up. Jessi wasn't pushing her. She wasn't demanding. She was there, steady, waiting.

Rebecca whispered, "I've never… I don't know if I could ever… be like you were up there."

Jessi tilted her head, her voice soft. "You don't have to be like me. You only have to be yourself. This isn't about becoming something you're not; it's about finding out what thrills you, what makes you feel alive, who you are. And trusting the right person to hold you through it."

The words sank deep, stirring something fragile inside Rebecca. She wanted to ask what Jessi's limits were, what thrills she craved most, but the question wedged in her throat. *Not yet. Not tonight.*

Instead, she just whispered, "It's a lot to take in."

Jessi nodded, her hand brushing lightly against Rebecca's knuckles. "I know. And I'm not asking you to tonight."

* * *

Later that evening, the apartment felt almost unnaturally quiet when Jessi shut the door behind them. No low music vibrating through the walls, no murmurs of a watching crowd, only the faint hum of the refrigerator and the soft clink as Jessi set her keys on the counter.

Rebecca lowered herself onto the couch, hugging her arms around her middle. The sweater dress that had felt awkward at the club now seemed almost comforting, a shield against the things she'd seen. Still, the images replayed in her head: Jessi bound in ropes, suspended, radiant in surrender.

Jessi strolled barefoot into the kitchen, filling two glasses of sweet tea before joining her. She handed one over, settling close enough that their knees brushed. For a while, they drank in silence.

Rebecca finally set her glass down, staring at the way condensation pooled at the base. "I can't stop seeing you up there," she said softly. "You looked… so at peace. I don't understand it. Weren't you scared?"

Jessi shook her head gently. "Not with Marcus. Not when I know my boundaries are respected. That's where the peace comes from. It's not about the ropes, it's about the trust."

Rebecca chewed her lip, her voice faltering. "I'm trying to picture myself in your place, but all I feel is… panic. Like I'd lose control and never get it back."

Jessi reached over, brushing her knuckles against Rebecca's hand. "That's why communication matters. You don't give away control, you *choose* to hand it over, and you always keep the power to take it back. Safe words, limits, clear conversations… they're what make the risk safe."

She wanted to know how far Jessi had gone before. Rebecca looked down at their hands, her heart aching with questions she was afraid to ask. She wanted to know if Jessi had ever been hurt. She wanted to ask what she desired most, the fantasies that kept her awake at night. But the words stuck in her throat.

Instead, she whispered, "What if I disappoint you? What if I can't give you what you're looking for?"

Jessi's hand covered hers fully now, warm and firm. "You can't disappoint me by being honest. I'd rather know your limits than see you push yourself into something that scares you. This isn't about fitting into a mold; it's about discovering what's right for you. And if you ever want me to share my world with you, it will only ever happen at your pace."

Rebecca blinked quickly, a sting of tears threatening. "I don't know if I'm ready," she admitted, her voice trembling.

Jessi gave her a small, knowing smile. "Then you're not. And that's okay."

The quiet stretched between them, heavier than silence but softer than fear. Rebecca leaned back against the couch, still unsure, still hesitant.

Becca's heart beat unevenly as Jessi's fingers lingered against hers. The touch was so small, so tentative, but it lit something warm inside her chest. She curled her hand slightly, letting her fingertips brush over Jessi's knuckles in return.

For a second, neither of them moved. The silence wasn't heavy anymore; it felt fragile, like glass, as though any wrong word might shatter it.

"I don't know what this is," Becca whispered, her voice muffled against Jessi's skin. "But I want to be here. With you. I don't want you to feel like you're alone anymore."

Jessi took a long breath, and for a heartbeat, she didn't reply. Then, almost imperceptibly, she tilted her head until her cheek rested against Becca's hair.

"Thank you," Jessi murmured. "That means more than you know."

Eventually, Jessi yawned, the weight of the day finally pulling at her. Becca gave a sleepy smile. "You're tired. Come on, let's get ready for bed before you fall asleep on the couch."

They shuffled into the bathroom together and slinked out of their clothes, each standing at the mirror with washcloths and makeup remover in hand. Neither spoke as they squinched their noses and raised their eyebrows, removing the night's warpaint from their faces. The moment felt so natural, like a couple that had done this a hundred times before.

In the bedroom, Jessi slid under the covers first, and Becca hesitated for a moment before following, lying close but not touching.

In the quiet, Jessi turned her head slightly, her voice barely above a whisper. "Thank you for staying."

Becca smiled into the dim light. "I wouldn't want to be anywhere else."

Slowly, carefully, Jessi let her hand rest between them, and Becca's fingers brushed against it. Their hands didn't fully intertwine, but the contact was enough, comforting, unspoken, real.

Within minutes, their breathing slowed, and the night carried them into sleep, side by side. For the first time in years, Jessi dreamed of warmth.

6
Ice Cream, Pizza, and Being Seen

After that night, the days slipped by at a leisurely pace neither of them had expected. Each evening, after the hum of work and the quiet drive home, Jessi's phone would buzz.

At first, it was just small things:

Becca: "Made spaghetti tonight. I'm pretty sure the sauce could strip paint."

Jessi: "Good thing I like paint thinner on pasta. Save me a plate next time."

Or:

Jessi: "Got cornered at work by Linda—she told me about her son's new school for 20 minutes straight."

Becca: "You survived a workplace hostage situation. Proud of you."

* * *

The conversations grew longer, stretching late into the night. There was no pressure, no rush. Just two voices filling the lonely spaces of each other's lives. Trust had settled in, like the glow of a lamp dimly brightening a room. Jessi found herself looking forward to Becca's name lighting up her phone. And Becca, she realized that Jessi's laugh was becoming her favorite sound, the one she'd wait for at the end of the day.

* * *

Days turned to weeks, and their comfortable banter after each workday continued until they could spend their weekends together. Becca almost always came to Jessi's apartment, something that puzzled Jessi until one day Rebecca reluctantly let her into her home.

It was a Friday evening when Jessi walked up to Rebecca's apartment, a brown paper sack of groceries tucked under her arm. She knocked lightly before Rebecca clicked open the lock and let her inside.

The sight of Rebecca's sparse apartment took Jessi by surprise, lawn chairs in place of a sofa, a laptop in place of a television, and Bob winding himself around her ankles as if welcoming her personally.

Shuffling back to her bedroom, Rebecca curled up on a mattress and box springs set on the floor with no frame. The blinds were half-closed, and she draped a heating pad and a blanket across her stomach. She looked up when Jessi stepped into the room, her expression somewhere between sheepish and relieved.

"I know. It's not much," Rebecca said softly. "You didn't have to come over. My monthly visitor showed up today, so I'm not exactly great company."

Jessi set the grocery sack down and walked over, sitting carefully on the edge of the mattress. "Don't be silly. You're always great company."

Rebecca smiled faintly, brushing her hair back from her face. "You're too good to me."

From the bag, Jessi pulled out a pint of chocolate ice cream and a small bottle of Ibuprofen. She set them on the floor next to the bed like offerings. "Emergency supplies," she said with a grin.

Rebecca laughed, the sound low but genuine. "Oh my God. Ice cream. Thank you so much."

Jessi leaned down, brushing a kiss against her forehead.

Rebecca shifted, making room for her. Jessi stretched out beside her on the mattress, the two of them sinking into the simple comfort of being close. The apartment might have been bare, the furniture mismatched, but none of it mattered.

As Bob leapt onto the bed and curled at their feet, Rebecca nestled against Jessi's shoulder with a sigh. "You know… I'm glad you're here."

They lay in the quiet for a while, the soft hum of traffic drifting in from the street outside. Rebecca shifted slightly, her cheek still against Jessi's shoulder. Her voice came gently, almost hesitant.

"I've noticed... you've never mentioned... having a monthly visitor of your own."

Jessi's breath stilled for a beat. She swallowed, her hand pausing in Rebecca's hair. "Yeah… that's because I don't."

Rebecca lifted her head, curiosity in her eyes. "You don't?"

“No,” Jessi said quietly, forcing a slight smile that didn’t quite reach her eyes. “When I was twenty-two, I was diagnosed with a nasty case of endometriosis. It got so bad that… well... a hysterectomy was really the only option.”

Rebecca’s smile faded, her brows drawing together as she took in the weight of Jessi’s words. She sat up a little, her hand brushing Jessi’s arm. “Oh, Jess…”

Jessi kept her gaze on the ceiling as she tried to fake a laugh. “Just don't get me off my hormone therapy.”

For a moment, silence filled the room. Rebecca’s chest ached with a sadness she hadn’t expected. “I don’t even know what to say,” Rebecca admitted softly.

Jessi finally turned to her, eyes gentle but steady. “It's not like I'm mommy material anyway.”

Rebecca reached for her hand, intertwining their fingers. Her voice trembled, but her grip was firm. “Don't say that. You would be an awesome mom.”

Jessi let out a shaky breath, the tension easing in her shoulders. “I think we both know that's not true.”

Rebecca squeezed her hand tighter, her eyes shimmering. "Stop that!"

Rolling over to face Rebecca, Jessi rolled her eyes. "Hey, at least now I don't have to lie in bed with a heating pad on my belly." She made a funny face, then stuck her tongue out before snickering. "How about some ice cream?"

Sensing Jessi was trying to change the subject, Rebecca let out a quiet sigh, then gave a smile. "I thought you would never ask."

As she opened up the container, Jessi jumped up and went to the kitchen to look for a couple of spoons. She opened drawer after drawer, noticing Rebecca had only a couple of dishes and eating utensils. She gazed out at the rest of the apartment. No pictures were hanging on the wall, no knick-knacks on the nonexistent kitchen table. She managed to find a couple of plastic spoons and made her way back to the bedroom.

Her bedroom wasn't much better; beside the mattress and box springs, plastic totes served as a dresser and chest of drawers. Each box was labeled with the corresponding items, such as shirts, pants, dresses, etc. Jessi likened the furnishings to those of a college student's dorm room.

She looked down at Bob, a slightly overweight tom that had taken to her as soon as she entered the apartment. He purred as he wove a figure eight pattern around her ankles and jumped onto her lap when she sat down.

Jessi sat cross-legged on the mattress beside Rebecca as the two dug into the ice cream. The longer Jessi stayed, the more the bare walls and makeshift furniture faded into the background. She could sense the faint embarrassment flicker across Becca's face when Jessi's eyes lingered too long on the plastic totes lined neatly against the wall.

"This is… cozy," Jessi said with a small smile, as Bob purred on her lap, his whiskers brushing against her hand. "Besides, you've got the most important thing covered."

Rebecca raised a brow. "Oh yeah? What's that?"

Jessi stroked Bob's head, smirking. "Clearly, a well-fed roommate."

Rebecca laughed, the sound filling the sparse apartment like sunlight streaming through an open window. Jessi couldn't resist smiling back, watching as Rebecca's shoulders relaxed, the unease dissolving.

Bob eventually curled up between them, snoring softly, but still they talked. Hours slipped past unnoticed, the night outside deepening until silence pressed at the windows.

Jessi looked around at the simple apartment, then back at Becca, her hair falling loose around her face. Somehow, this stripped-down space, bare as it was, felt more honest than anywhere else she'd been. And she realized, it wasn't the furniture or the paint on the walls that made it feel like home. It was Becca.

* * *

The following evening played out like every Saturday before. Amy and Traci showed up at Jessi's apartment, arms full of dresses and heels, their laughter bouncing off the walls as they claimed her bedroom mirror for their ritual of getting ready. The air would smell of perfume and hairspray, the sound of classic rock spilling faintly from the living room stereo.

Rebecca sat on the couch; her legs tucked beneath her and her sketchbook balanced against her knee, as Jessi sat beside her, legs crossed, painting her nails. They giggled and laughed softly at a joke only the two of them had noticed, lost in a world of their own.

When Amy and Traci finally swept into the living room, dressed to the nines and ready for their night out, they stopped short. Neither Jessi nor Rebecca noticed at first. They were too wrapped up in each other, Jessi reaching up absentmindedly to brush a strand of hair from Rebecca's face, Rebecca answering with that quiet smile that always seemed reserved for her. It wasn't dramatic, but it was intimate. Natural. The kind of thing couples did without thinking.

Amy exchanged a look with Traci, eyebrows lifting. Traci, who was rarely at a loss for words, mouthed, *Oh.*

"Uh," Amy said finally, clearing her throat. "So… why don't you two just kiss already? Like, like we don't already know."

Jessi blinked, realizing only then that Amy and Traci had been watching. She straightened a little but didn't pull away from Rebecca, who gave the faintest shrug.

Jessi's cheeks warmed, but she smiled. "What?"

Traci let out a laugh, half disbelief, half delight. "Come on. The way you two look at each other?"

Rebecca chuckled softly, reaching up and covering her face.

Amy grinned, shaking her head.

For a beat, all four women laughed, the tension dissolving into the easy camaraderie that had always existed between them. But now Amy and Traci left with a little more knowing in their eyes, their playful teasing carrying an undercurrent of approval.

There were kisses for Jon, and when the door closed behind them, Jessi leaned into Rebecca again, her smile lingering and somehow, being seen, really seen, made what they had feel even more real. It wasn't glamorous. It wasn't wild. But it was theirs. Both of them realized that these quiet nights and small rituals were becoming the foundation of something lasting.

Jessi turned and looked at Becca. "I'm hungry. What do you want?"

"I don't know. I'm open to whatever. What about a pizza?"

Jessi's eyes lit up. "Oh my gosh, yes. Pizza! What kind do you want?"

"Just pepperoni is fine," Becca answered as she scribbled on her drawing pad.

"Pepperoni?" Jessi asked with a puzzled gaze. "Nothing else? No, peppers or onions, sausage, extra cheese?"

"I just like pepperoni," Becca reacted, shaking her head. "We can do extra cheese if that makes you happy."

"Okay, okay, geez," Jessi said as she slumped her shoulders. She went to a kitchen drawer, pulled out a card, and handed it to Becca. "You have to order. Rosa's. And… ask them if Lavonte is delivering tonight."

"Who?" Becca asked.

"Just ask."

Becca shook her head as she dialed the number and placed the order, a medium pepperoni with extra cheese. She nodded into the phone instinctively, even though the person on the other end couldn't see her motions. She repeated the price over the phone. "$22.50?… that sounds great." Jessi stomped her foot on the floor, motioning at Becca. "Oh… I'm sorry. Is Lavonte delivering tonight?... He is?... That's great. Thank you very much." She looked back at Jessi. "She said it would be 15 minutes."

Jessi just grinned.

"What are you grinning about?"

"You'll see," she answered with a giggle. She looked at the clock, making a mental note. Reaching into her purse, she pulled out a twenty, then looked at Becca. "You got a ten on you?"

Becca reached into her pocket and pulled out a five and a ten, unfolding the bills and handing Jessi the ten.

About five minutes before the pizza was due, Jessi stood up and began stripping out of her clothes. She pulled her shirt over her head, tossing it and her bra to the kitchen counter, then pushed her shorts and panties down, stepping out and kicking them over on the floor beside the kitchen table.

"Jessi! Oh… my… God! What are you doing?" Becca asked as she set her sketchpad down.

Jessi just laughed as she sat down in the armchair beside her, hanging one leg over the arm with her legs spread wide. She gave Becca a playful sneer as she began playing with herself.

Just then, a knock on the door. Becca cupped her hands over her mouth and nose as she watched Jessi pop out of the chair and peer through the peephole of the door. She giggled, clapped her hands, then opened the door.

Eyes wide, Becca sat stunned. Her face turned red when she noticed the black man standing, holding a pizza box, grinning from ear to ear.

"Lavonte!" Jessi shouted. "How are you tonight? Come in."

"I knew when I saw the address, Jess. You always make my evening when you order a pizza." The man continued to grin as he walked into the living room, looking at Jessi from head to toe.

Becca couldn't move, couldn't breathe as she watched the scene play out.

"Just put it on the table," Jessi said as she closed the door.

"Sure thing, Jess." The man almost skipped to the table. "You're looking really fine tonight. Good to see you're still not wearing those pesky clothes."

Jessi put her hands on her hips, her nakedness on full display. "Clothes? Hmm… I've heard about things like that," she said teasingly. She handed him the money, then spun around, letting him get a good look. "Keep the change, sweetie."

Lavonte just laughed as he put the money in a money bag. "Seeing you is all the tip I need, Jess."

She smiled as she walked back to the door and opened it. The man never stopped grinning. He looked over at Becca, still sitting stunned on the couch, and gave her a little salute. "We'll see ya next time, Jess," he said, giving a wink and walking out the door.

Closing the door, Jessi sashayed over to the table, plopped down in a chair, and opened the box. Steam wisped into the air, filling the apartment with the scent of garlic and tomato sauce.

Becca took a deep breath and walked over to the table, not knowing what to say. Jessi slid the box away from her. "You can't have any."

"What? Why?" she asked with her hands on her hips.

"You're still wearing clothes. This… This right here is a naked pizza."

"Is that so?" Becca quipped. She rolled her eyes as she began stripping down to all but her panties. She tossed her garments over to the couch, then turned back to Jessi. "Happy now?"

"Have a seat, baby."

They sat there, giggling and joking, savoring the cheesy pie, until late in the night.

* * *

The following morning, Jessi was stretched out on the couch, watching Rebecca gather her sketchbook and tote bag as she prepared to head home. The dishes from breakfast were still stacked in the sink, the last of the coffee cooling in their mugs on the table.

Something inside Jessi tightened at the sight. The thought of her leaving, of the apartment going quiet again, suddenly felt heavier than usual.

"Becca," Jessi said softly, sitting up.

Rebecca glanced over her shoulder, tucking a strand of hair behind her ear. "Yeah?"

Jessi hesitated, choosing her words carefully. "What if you didn't have to keep packing up every Sunday? What if you just… stayed?"

Rebecca froze, the strap of her tote still in her hand. Her expression flickered, caught somewhere between surprise and unease. "You mean… move in with you?"

Jessi nodded, her heart thumping. "Yeah. I mean, you're here every weekend anyway. And I… I like it when you're here. The place feels different. Better. More like home."

Rebecca let out a slow breath, setting her bag back on the table. "Jess… I don't know. Moving in together is… big."

Jessi crossed the room, taking Rebecca's hands in hers. "It is big. But I'm not asking for perfect, Becca. I just want... Us. You don't have to decide today. I just… needed to say it."

Rebecca studied her, searching her face as though weighing every word. For a long moment, silence stretched between them, broken only by the sound of the TV.

Finally, Rebecca's shoulders softened. "You really want me here?"

Jessi smiled, squeezing her hands. "Yeah."

Rebecca gave a small, uncertain laugh. "You're stubborn, you know that?"

"Only when it matters."

With a sigh that was equal parts nerves and surrender, Rebecca leaned in, resting her forehead against Jessi's. "Alright."

Jessi's grin spread wide, relief and joy crashing together. She kissed Rebecca, sealing the moment with warmth. The move wouldn't happen overnight, and there would be adjustments, compromises, maybe even fights. But for now, it was enough to know they were choosing the same direction, together.

* * *

By the time a month had passed, the apartment looked different. Subtle at first, an extra coffee mug left on the counter; a pile of sketchbooks stacked neatly beside Jessi's laptop on the counter, but then more noticeable, Rebecca's shoes by the door. Her favorite blanket draped across the back of the couch. Bob's food dish was tucked beside the fridge, his soft purrs now part of the nightly soundtrack.

Jessi loved it. The apartment felt fuller, warmer, like a space that finally belonged to two people instead of one. Even the little inconveniences, Rebecca's habit of leaving charcoal pencils scattered across the kitchen table, or Bob clawing at the edge of Jessi's couch cushions, made her smile more often than sigh.

Their weekdays stayed busy, long hours at work draining them both, but coming home meant something different now. Jessi would unlock the door and hear Rebecca humming softly from the kitchen, or see her curled up in sweatpants, sketching by the lamplight. Some nights, Jessi cooked while Rebecca read out loud from a book she'd plucked off the shelf. Other nights, they both collapsed on the couch with takeout, saying little but finding comfort in each other's presence.

Rebecca would work on her drawings, creating whatever whimsy came into her mind, while Jessi would be on her laptop, surfing the web.

One evening, Jessi had shown Becca a website that she was a member of, Fetcom, a fetish site. Jessi had over 30,000 followers on the site and nearly 50,000 on her X account. Apparently, she had been banned from other sites, such as Instagram and Facebook, long ago. On her fetish page, Jessi listed some of her interests, desires, and fantasies. She also posted numerous photos, all with her face blurred, that showed risky and daring behavior.

Becca was both fascinated and horrified. The photos showed Jessi nude on nature trails, flashing in parking lots at shopping centers, and even some daring selfies inside the store themselves. She couldn't imagine herself having the nerve to be so audacious, but there was something about Jessi... that sense of danger and risk, that drew her to her.

The website also listed clubs, parties, and events around the city. It was a schedule for an underworld of sex and desire, a world that Becca didn't even know existed until she met Jessi. Some of the things Becca had seen on the site took her breath. Fantasies, taboos, and cravings were being lived out in the real world. She was mesmerized by it all.

Weekends settled into a ritual of their own. Amy and Traci still came over on Saturdays, bringing their hurricane of energy into the apartment before disappearing into the night. But instead of waiting for them to leave, Jessi and Rebecca had started leaning into the quiet afterward, trading the noise of clubs for old movies, homemade popcorn, and the slow, steady comfort of leaning against one another until sleep won out.

It wasn't flashy. It wasn't dramatic. But it was theirs, a rhythm of life that felt sturdy, steady, and, for the first time in a long while, right. But Becca could sense Jessi stirring; her mind working and planning, restless for excitement.

She had to prepare herself... She was in Jessi's world now.

7
The Club

Another weekend approached, and Jessi found herself fidgeting more than usual, restless despite the quiet comfort of their apartment. She had spent the week buried in spreadsheets, and now the familiar weekend routine of movies and takeout felt… too safe.

She glanced over at Rebecca, who was lounging on the couch with a sketchbook balanced on her knees, Bob curled against her feet. Jessi chewed her lip, then decided to speak.

"Hey… want to do something different tonight?" Jessi asked, her voice hesitant but eager.

Rebecca looked up, arching an eyebrow. "Like what?"

Jessi took a deep breath, feeling the thrill of saying it out loud. "I was thinking… maybe a lifestyles club."

Rebecca blinked. "A… what?"

"A lifestyles club. Remember I told you about them?" Jessi repeated, leaning forward. "It's—uh, it's kind of like a swinger's club. Couples, sometimes singles, come together… You know… explore, try new things."

Rebecca's cheeks warmed slightly, and she laughed nervously.

Jessi shrugged, trying to sound casual, though her pulse was racing. "We haven't been out in a while. I thought… maybe it could be fun. A little adventure. Something new for us." She reached for Rebecca's hand, squeezing it. "But only if you want to. We don't have to do anything we're not comfortable with."

Rebecca studied her, curiosity flickering in her eyes along with a hint of apprehension. "So… people… swap partners?"

Jessi shook her head gently. "Not exactly. It's… safe, consensual, and private. Sometimes you just go there to dance and have fun, sometimes… more. The website says it's *Ladies Night* this Saturday. I just thought… maybe it could be exciting. Something different."

Rebecca leaned back, fingers tracing the edge of her sketchbook. She gave a small, thoughtful laugh. "I'm intrigued."

Jessi's grin widened, a mix of relief and excitement.

Bob, seemingly sensing the energy shift, purred loudly, curling tighter against Rebecca's side. And as the night stretched before them, the sense of anticipation, tinged with nervous curiosity, settled into the apartment like a new, electric rhythm neither of them had felt before.

***

The bass thumped through the pavement outside before they even reached the doors. Neon lights spilled out in sharp pulses, painting the faces of the crowd lined up along the velvet ropes. Becca looked up at the sign, *Velvet Desires*, as Jessi tugged lightly at Becca's wrist. She guided her forward with that easy confidence that always seemed to cut through Becca's hesitation.

"Relax," Jessi murmured as they stepped inside. "You look incredible."

Becca's sweater dress from their previous outing had been replaced by something far bolder—still modest by Jessi's standards, but daring for her: a fitted mid-thigh crimson skirt and a black silk blouse with a neckline that felt much too low. She sported a slim gold bracelet and a simple gold chain necklace with a small heart pendant. She tugged at the hem nervously, but Jessi caught her hand and squeezed.

"Don't," Jessi said firmly, eyes glittering in the club's shifting lights. "You're perfect. Trust me."

The heat and noise wrapped around them as they pushed inside. Bodies swayed under strobes, the scent of sweat, perfume, and liquor hanging thick in the air. Jessi led them toward the bar at one end of the room, handing over the plain paper bag she had carried inside to the bartender. The bartender pulled the liquor bottles from the bag and, with a magic marker in hand, wrote 'Jessi' on the labels. They knew who she was and her routine.

Jessi ordered two Kamikazes as she yelled over the loud music. She clung to her tiny black purse that hung off one shoulder, while gripping Becca's arm with her other hand.

Becca held on to her own purse with one hand and took a cocktail in the other, sipping to have something to do. She stole glances at Jessi—her strapless cobalt blue mini dress clinging to her body like it had been painted on. It had a full front zipper that sparkled in the club lights. Her black leather thigh-high boots clicked as they walked across the wood floor. Silver earrings dangled from her lobes, and a sparkling choker wrapped around her neck. Jessi looked like she belonged here, a dangerous, magnetic presence. Becca… felt like an imposter.

As if sensing her unease, Jessi leaned close, lips brushing against Becca's ear so she could be heard over the music. "Remember… you don't have to do anything you don't want to. But look around. Just have fun."

Becca swallowed hard and let her gaze drift over the room. Men lingered at the bar, prowled the dance floor, and leaned against walls with their drinks. Some looked rougher, others polished, but all of them carried that same restless hunger. Becca's chest tightened.

"Come on," Jessi said as she pulled Becca through the crowd. "Ladies and couples can sit at the tables. All the single guys have to sit at the bar."

Becca looked back over her shoulder at the bar. "They all look…" She struggled for the word.

"Hungry?" Jessi supplied, smirking.

Becca gave a nervous laugh. "Yeah. That."

Jessi rested her hand lightly on the small of Becca's back, guiding her attention to an open table near the dancefloor. "There," Jessi said as she pointed.

The club was packed shoulder to shoulder, heat radiating from the dancers gyrating on the pulsing dancefloor. Streaks of color washed over the crowd with every sweep of the spotlights, and overhead, a disco ball fractured beams of silver light into glittering shards that spun across the walls.

Rebecca clung close to Jessi, her wide eyes darting everywhere. The DJ booth loomed high above the crowd to one side of the dancefloor, its pulsing lights moving in perfect sync with the beat. On either side, circular stages jutted out with brass poles, where women twisted and spun with practiced ease. Their movements were fluid, sensual, almost hypnotic, and Becca couldn't help staring, caught between awe and self-consciousness.

Jessi leaned down, her lips brushing Becca's ear to be heard over the music. "See? This is the energy I told you about." Her voice carried a playful confidence, a smirk tugging at the corner of her lips.

Becca nodded quickly, though her heart hammered. Everywhere she looked, there were flashes of skin and bodies pressed together. Men in crisp suits held women in sequined dresses tight against them. Younger men in tank tops and baggy black pants bounced with wild abandon, grinding with girls in thin straps and glitter, some practically topless, laughing as if the world outside didn't exist.

"This is… a lot," Becca admitted, shouting a little to be heard. Her cheeks burned as her gaze landed on one of the poles again, where a girl arched her back in a slow spin that drew cheers from the crowd.

Jessi took her hand firmly, tugging her through the throng. "Don't think so much. Just feel it," she said, guiding them toward the edge of the dancefloor.

A group of men nearby glanced at them, some of them openly appreciative. Becca stiffened, but Jessi only smirked and met their eyes briefly before turning her focus back to Becca.

"You okay?" Jessi asked, softening her tone as she leaned close again.

Becca swallowed, nodding slowly. "Just… trying to take it all in."

"That's the point." Jessi's eyes glittered with mischief, but underneath it was something gentler, something that reassured Becca that this was a test, but not one she had to face alone. "Stay close."

As the music swelled and the floor vibrated beneath their feet, Becca realized she wasn't sure if her nervous energy came from the crowd or from Jessi's hand gripping hers so tightly it felt like she was tethered in the storm.

Jessi slid into her chair with a languid ease, her purse hanging carelessly on the backrest as though she hadn't a worry in the world. Becca mirrored her, more tentative, setting her small bag down before wrapping both hands tightly around her drink. The condensation from the glass dampened her fingers, giving her something to focus on besides the swirl of bodies moving just beyond their table.

The music thumped in her chest, but here, just a step off the main floor, there was enough space to breathe. Jessi leaned back, crossing her legs, her dress shifting to reveal just a little more of her thighs under the fractured disco ball light. Her eyes roamed the room with that familiar spark, as if she were already scouting possibilities.

Becca sipped her drink quickly; the sweetness was tinged with a sharp alcohol burn. She tried not to fidget, but she couldn't help glancing toward the dancers again, the women sliding down the poles with such control, the men whose eyes followed them excitedly, the couples pressed together in a rhythm that was more than just dancing.

"You're staring," Jessi teased lightly, her voice low, though she had to lean across the small table to be heard over the beat.

Becca's cheeks flushed instantly. "I'm just… watching. Everything."

"That's fine." Jessi's smirk softened, and she reached across the table, brushing her fingers over Becca's hand. "I guess… this place can overwhelm you at first."

Becca's pulse jumped at the touch, the lightness of Jessi's skin on hers, and she nodded, though her voice caught. "I'm just taking it all in."

Jessi leaned back again, eyes catching a tall man across the floor who had been glancing their way. She didn't say anything about him yet, but Becca could tell Jessi was already in her element, letting the night unfold.

Becca tried to follow her lead, sipping again, settling her nerves. The music's relentless beat, the glittering lights, and Jessi's calm, flirtatious presence all swirled together until the anxiety started to blur into something else. Something closer to excitement.

Jessi rose smoothly from her chair, blue dress gleaming under the flashing lights. The hem hugged her curves, the strapless cut leaving her shoulders bare, and her thigh-highs added a sharp edge to her stride. She turned back toward Becca with a smirk, her hand extended.

"Come on," she said, her voice raised just enough to slip over the pulsing bass. "You didn't come here just to watch."

Becca froze for a heartbeat, her skirt hugging her thighs like a vice, the blouse dipping lower at the neckline than she ever would have chosen on her own. She tugged at it instinctively, cheeks burning, but Jessi's eyes never wavered. They glittered with that daring confidence that seemed to push Becca's blood faster through her veins.

"I don't… I don't know if I can dance like that," Becca admitted, her fingers tightening around the stem of her glass.

Jessi leaned closer, her perfume threading through the haze of sweat and alcohol around them. "It's not about dancing," she whispered, her lips grazing Becca's ear. "It's about letting go. Feeling the music. Feeling me."

The words hit with a force Becca wasn't ready for. Her heart pounded as Jessi's outstretched hand waited, patient but insistent. Slowly, almost against her own better judgment, Becca set her drink down, her fingers trembling as she slid them into Jessi's.

The bassline swallowed them whole as they stepped onto the dancefloor. Jessi tugged her gently but firmly toward the writhing crowd. Lights flashed in violent streaks of blue, red, and silver across their bodies. Jessi turned to face her, their hands still linked, and began to move with the rhythm, hips swaying, dress shimmering, boots stamping the beat with predatory grace.

Becca tried to mimic her, feeling stiff, but Jessi leaned in close, one hand gliding to Becca's hip. "Relax," she murmured over the music. "You're already beautiful. Just move with me."

And slowly, Becca did. Her crimson skirt riding higher up her legs with her movements, her silk blouse sliding against her skin, the neckline dipping as her shoulders loosened. Jessi's hand guided her subtly, pulling her closer, until their bodies moved nearly in sync.

Around them, the crowd pressed tighter, men, women, all grinding and swaying. But Becca only saw Jessi: confident, daring, eyes sparkling with challenge and promise.

Becca felt the thrill catch inside her chest, not just nerves, but excitement.

The music swelled, bass reverberating through the floor, shaking Becca down to her bones. Jessi twirled her once, then drew her in close again, their hips brushing under the lights.

So caught in the rush of it, Jessi's smile, the crowd pressing in, Becca barely noticed at first when a shadow drifted close behind her. Then another. A tall man in a loosened tie slid up near Jessi, his body moving in the same rhythm, his eyes openly trailing over her. On Becca's other side, a younger man in a black tank leaned in, letting the beat guide his hips as they ground almost imperceptibly toward hers.

Jessi's grin only widened. She tossed her hair back, her strapless dress shimmering, her hands sliding along Becca's waist as if to claim her. But she didn't push the men away either. If anything, her sway grew more teasing, a dare written in every motion.

Her pulse spiking, Becca could feel the heat of the men's bodies now, one behind, one at her side, their movements synced to the heavy rhythm. Her crimson skirt shifted with every press of her hips, the silk blouse clinging damply to her skin.

Jessi leaned toward her ear, voice low but alive with energy. "They're watching you," she whispered, the words both reassuring and dangerous. "Dancing with you. Doesn't it feel… electric?"

Becca shivered, unsure if it was fear or thrill. The man in the tank top edged closer, his shoulder brushing hers as his hand almost grazed her hip. Behind her, the suited man kept pace, his body close, unmistakable.

The crowd pulsed around them, all sweat and sound, lights glinting off the mirrored disco ball. For the first time, Becca realized how exposed she truly was, on display, in Jessi's world.

And Jessi reveled in it, her eyes never leaving Becca's face as she whispered, "Just breathe. You're safe. With me."

The music finally shifted, the pounding beat giving way to a slower, more sensual rhythm. Jessi let it carry her through one last sway, pressing her back against the man in the loosened tie before spinning away with a mischievous flick of her hair. She caught Becca's hand and tugged her gently toward the edge of the floor.

The two men followed at a distance, smiling, lingering just enough to let them know their attention hadn't vanished with the music. Jessi's dress sparkled as she walked, her boots striking the floor in bold, confident strides. Becca trailed half a step behind, her skirt still clinging too high where the heat of the dance had left her flushed.

Back at their small circular table, Jessi dropped gracefully into her chair, crossing one leg over the other with practiced ease. She scooped up her drink, the ice clinking softly, then leaned back in a way that gave the nearby men every invitation to keep watching.

"You two move well together," the man in the tank top called over the music, flashing a grin.

Jessi smirked, raising her glass in a mock toast. "We have our moments." Her tone was teasing, with a hint of suggestion.

Becca sat beside her, smoothing her skirt with nervous hands, her pulse still racing. She felt the thrill lingering in her skin, the brush of strangers' bodies, the glances heavy with desire. It was exciting, intoxicating even… but at the same time awkward, like she was standing on the edge of something she hadn't yet decided to leap into.

Jessi reached across and brushed her fingers over Becca's wrist, grounding her. Then, turning her head toward the men, she tilted her smile just enough to spark. "Maybe we'll dance again later."

The men lingered a beat longer, exchanging amused looks before melting back into the crowd, leaving behind the echo of possibility.

Becca exhaled slowly, her shoulders tight, her mind whirling. She sipped her drink, trying to calm her nerves, but Jessi's touch still burned warm against her skin.

"See?" Jessi purred softly, leaning close enough that only Becca could hear. "Nothing to be scared of. You were beautiful out there."

The words struck deep, stirring equal parts fluster and pride. Becca bit her lip, unsure what to say, excitement and awkwardness tangling together until she could hardly tell them apart.

The DJ shifted tracks, and suddenly Jessi's eyes lit up. Her favorite dance song, "Buttons" by the Pussycat Dolls, thumped through the speakers, every beat hitting her in the chest like a call she couldn't resist. She grinned at Becca, a spark of mischief dancing in her gaze.

"Watch this," Jessi purred, standing abruptly and brushing her dress smooth. Before Becca could respond, she strode confidently toward one of the circular stages, the brass pole gleaming under the flashing lights.

Becca's stomach knotted, part excitement, part nerves. She set her drink down, holding it in her lap, eyes wide as Jessi climbed onto the stage. The crowd didn't even notice her; she seemed to command the attention all on her own.

Jessi's fingers slid along the pole, her movements fluid and deliberate. She spun, arched her back, pressed her body into the brass with sultry precision. Every motion was teasing, every glance calculated. Becca felt herself flush, her pulse quickening as she watched Jessi twist and grind with perfect rhythm.

Several men gathered around, eyes locked on Jessi. Their attention was magnetic, but Jessi seemed fully aware of Becca. She let her gaze linger, lips curling into that smirk only Becca seemed to understand, honestly.

Becca's knees pressed together, her hands clutching her thighs under the table. She felt caught somewhere between awe and desire, unable to look away. The heat of the club, the pulsing lights, and Jessi's daring energy made her feel as if the world had shrunk to just the stage and her friend.

Jessi spun again, her boots clicking against the stage, hair flying, hips swaying with unapologetic confidence. She reached up and slowly began unzipping the dress, teasingly pulling it to her belly, then even farther downward. The music thumped in time with Becca's racing heart. Around them, the crowd cheered, but Becca only saw the way Jessi's eyes searched for her, teasing and inviting.

In one swift move, Jessi pulled the zipper loose, letting the dress fall to her ankles. She grinded against the pole, throwing her head back and letting her auburn locks fall to the middle of her back. Turning, she leaned back against the pole, spreading her legs wide. Reaching down between her legs, she slowly rubbed her exposed clit, then, bringing her hand up to her lips, she licked the tips of her fingers.

Becca heard the cheers of the onlookers as Jessi turned and twirled on the stage. Finally, the song neared its climax. Jessi leaned against the pole, one hand arching over her head, a sultry smile on her lips. She winked at Becca, and in that instant, the mixture of excitement, awe, and unspoken tension in Becca's chest surged, leaving her breathless.

As the song wound down, Jessi grabbed a towel from next to the stage and wiped down the pole. She leapt down, naked with dress in hand, landing with a graceful sway that drew whistles and murmurs from the surrounding dancers. A few men in the crowd leaned closer as she threaded her way back to the table, offering murmured compliments, casual touches on her arm, and suggestive smiles.

Jessi let them brush against her without breaking stride, her smirk widening. She whispered back, allowing just enough flirtation to slip through to tease, but not enough to promise anything. Her eyes stayed locked on Becca, who had been holding her breath, wide-eyed, fingers clutching her glass as if it were a lifeline.

"Did you like that?" Jessi purred as she slid back into her chair, crossing one leg over the other. She let her dress hang on the back of the chair as her boots gleamed under the fractured disco lights. "Think I got their attention?"

Becca felt her cheeks heat as her pulse raced. The combination of the men lingering around, Jessi's commanding presence, and the way she singled Becca out made her feel both exhilarated and overwhelmed.

One of the men leaned in slightly, low enough that Becca could hear his voice, "You looked amazing up there."

Jessi tilted her head, letting the comment hang. "Thank you," she replied, her tone playful but sharp, her gaze flicking back to Becca with a teasing glimmer. "Happy I could please."

Becca swallowed hard, excitement and nerves twisting together. Jessi's teasing presence, her control of the room, and the subtle, intimate gestures made the crowded club feel like their private stage.

Jessi leaned in slightly toward Becca, her lips brushing her ear over the music. "Relax. Enjoy it. Let them watch, let them wonder."

Becca's knees pressed together as her breath hitched. She wanted to speak, to say something clever or flirtatious, but all she could manage was a slight, stunned nod.

The men around the table began to step back slightly, sensing the invisible line Jessi had drawn, their curiosity mingling with admiration. Jessi's smirk only deepened, a silent promise of more naughtiness to come, as she leaned back, letting Becca feel both the thrill of attention and the intimate pull of her gaze.

Jessi stood, grabbed the dress from the back of the chair, and leaned down close to Becca. Her lips brushed against Becca's ear, just enough for the words to feel like a tease.

"I have to go to the little girls' room. Don't do anything I wouldn't do while I'm gone," she whispered, eyes sparkling with vivacity.

Becca laughed, the tension in her shoulders easing just a little. "Well… what would that be?" she asked, a playful smirk tugging at her lips.

Jessi grinned, straightening up and giving her a teasing glance over her shoulder. She winked as she flung the dress over her shoulder and sauntered through the crowd. Becca watched as Jessi's tight little butt cheeks bounced as she walked.

Becca felt a flutter in her chest, half-excitement, half-nervousness. She watched as Jessi wove through the crowd, hips swaying confidently, the glittering lights reflecting off her bare skin.

Alone at the table, Becca sipped her drink, her mind buzzing. The men who had lingered near the table earlier now shifted their attention slightly toward her. She could feel their eyes, but instead of the initial panic she might have felt, a surprising thrill ran through her.

Jessi's words echoed in her mind: *Don't do anything I wouldn't do.* She smiled to herself, unsure what exactly that meant, but the challenge, the teasing energy, made her pulse race. For the first time, Becca felt like she could explore the edges of her own daring, just enough to match Jessi's playful energy without overstepping.

She leaned back in her chair, letting her skirt brush against her legs, taking in the sights and sounds of the club with new eyes. The tension, the heat, the flirtation, it all made her feel alive in a way she hadn't before. And she knew, as much as she wanted to follow Jessi immediately, that this little tease was precisely the point.

Becca sat back in her chair for a moment, heart still fluttering from Jessi's teasing words. The men lingering nearby shifted closer, drawn by her sudden confidence, and she felt their attention like a tangible pressure. She could feel herself smiling, the nerves in her stomach twisting into something more daring.

One of the men, tall with a trimmed beard and a sharp black shirt, leaned in slightly. His voice was low, carrying over the music. "You're very beautiful," he said, nodding toward the dancefloor. "Care to dance?"

Becca's pulse quickened, part excitement, part hesitation. She glanced down at the way the lights flickered across her skin and felt an impulse to step fully into the thrill of the night. "Alright," she said, a small, confident smile spreading across her lips.

He held out a hand, and she took it, letting him guide her onto the crowded dancefloor. The music swelled again, the bass thumping through her chest, lights flashing across her skin. She moved cautiously at first, shifting her weight to the beat, hips swaying tentatively, but with every step, she felt more daring, more alive.

The man moved closer, hands grazing her waist in time with the music, and Becca caught herself laughing, a sound she hadn't realized she'd been holding back. Around them, dancers pressed and swirled, bodies weaving in and out, but Becca focused on the man in front of her, his energy, his rhythm, and the small thrill of stepping out of the safe space Jessi had created.

She felt a flash of excitement, along with a hint of embarrassment, as she realized just how much she was enjoying this. The initial hesitation melted, replaced by a warm rush of confidence and desire. And even as she danced, her thoughts flickered to Jessi, imagining her watching from somewhere nearby, daring her to push just a little further.

Becca's laugh mingled with the music, and the man leaned in, whispering against her ear, "You're a natural at this." She tilted her head, biting her lip, caught between shyness and the intoxicating freedom of the night.

Just as Becca started to settle into the rhythm, she caught a flash of cobalt-blue cutting through the crowd. Jessi had returned, dressed and striding confidently toward the dancefloor with that magnetic sway, boots clicking against the floor. Her eyes locked onto Becca's immediately, sparkling with devilishness and challenge.

Becca's stomach fluttered, half excitement, half nerves. The man she'd been dancing with leaned in closer, but she barely noticed; her attention was entirely on Jessi. The music shifted again, the beat slower now, more sensual, and Jessi moved through the crowd like she owned every inch of it.

Reaching them, Jessi leaned close to Becca, brushing her fingers along the small of her back. "Not bad," she murmured as she passed by and returned to her seat.

The man she'd been dancing with moved his hands up Becca's waist, encouraging the movement. Becca was moving more fluidly now, hips swaying with the man. Every once in a while, she glanced toward Jessi, her cheeks flushed, a small smile tugging at her lips. The man's hands hovered along her waist, but it was clear Becca's energy and confidence were coming from somewhere deeper, the spark Jessi had ignited.

Jessi leaned back in her chair, one leg crossed over the other, resting her chin lightly on her hand. A small, teasing smile played on her lips as she watched Becca sway, spin, and laugh. Every glance Becca sent her way, every shy flourish of confidence, felt like a thrill just for Jessi.

She could see the nervous tension in Becca's shoulders, slowly giving way to exhilaration. The flush in her skin, the bite of her lip when the man's hands brushed her waist, it all made Jessi's pulse quicken. Even seated, Jessi radiated control and allure, knowing exactly how to stoke the fire she had started without ever touching Becca.

Becca's laughter caught Jessi's attention, a light, breathy sound that made her heart skip. The man dancing with her leaned in closer, trying to match her rhythm, but Becca's focus was already split, half on him, half on the intensity of Jessi's gaze from across the table.

Jessi's smirk deepened, her hand brushing absently along her thigh as she silently challenged Becca: *Show me how far you'll go.*

Becca felt it, the pull, the dare, the unspoken promise. Her confidence grew with every passing beat, yet under it all was a tender thread of nervous excitement, knowing Jessi was watching, judging, guiding.

Jessi sat at the table; her gaze locked on Becca like she was the only one in the room. The intensity of it made Becca's skin prickle, and it was that stare, not the man's hands, that pushed her to be bolder, to sway her hips harder, to grind just a little closer. She wanted Jessi to see. She wanted Jessi to know.

That's when a shadow fell across Jessi's table. A tall, broad man loomed above her, his dark muscles filling out the tight black pullover shirt stretched across his chest. He looked down at her with a confident grin, extending a hand.

"Dance with me," he said, his voice deep enough to cut through the bass.

Jessi arched a brow as she tilted her head, considering him. Then, with a sly smile, she slipped her hand into his. Standing, she barely reached his shoulder, her five-foot-three-inch frame dwarfed by his height. The contrast made her grin widen; she thrived on that imbalance, that raw visual power.

Becca's movements faltered for a beat when she saw Jessi being led toward the dancefloor. Her partner pulled her back into rhythm, but her eyes remained fixed on Jessi.

Jessi melted into the crowd with the towering man, his hand firm at her lower back as he drew her closer. She moved with effortless confidence, every shift of her hips deliberate, every glance back at Becca calculated. Her dress caught the strobes as she pressed herself against him, the man's large hands roaming her sides.

Becca's heart thudded harder. She arched her back, grinding against her own partner with a sudden flare of boldness. Her shyness burned away, replaced with something sharper, something daring. She wanted Jessi to see she could match her energy, that she wasn't afraid.

And Jessi did see. Their eyes locked across the dancefloor, two different partners between them, but an unspoken electricity sparking in the space between.

The beat throbbed heavier, bodies pressing closer as the song shifted into something darker, more primal. Jessi let the tall man pull her in, her back sliding against his chest, her dress clinging tight to her curves. He moved with confidence, one hand locked at her hip while the other roamed upward, gliding over her stomach, skimming the side of her breast before cupping it fully.

Jessi made no move to stop him. Instead, she tilted her head back against his shoulder, lips parting as her eyes sought Becca's across the room. She wanted her to see. To feel the dare in every touch, every shift of her body against this stranger.

Becca's breath caught when their gazes locked. Her own partner spun her lightly, then tugged her back, hands braced at her waist, guiding her into a grind that pressed her skirt tighter against her thighs. The flush spread down her neck, but Becca didn't pull away. She leaned into it, letting herself move more boldly, hips rocking against him as she tried to push past her natural restraint.

Her laugh came out breathless. She lifted her arms around the man's shoulders, arching her back so her chest brushed his. But even as she tried to focus on him, her eyes darted back to Jessi, always Jessi.

Jessi's dance had grown bolder, the man's hands now shameless as they explored her body, squeezing, stroking, claiming space. She swayed with him as if she belonged in his arms, but her smirk, the flicker of teeth catching her lower lip, was aimed only at Becca.

It was intoxicating. Maddening. Becca's heartbeat thundered as she pushed herself harder into her partner's rhythm, her movements less hesitant, more sensual. She wanted Jessi to see her too, not just as the shy girl following along, but as someone who could rise to her fire.

Across the dancefloor, the unspoken challenge burned between them. Each sway of Jessi's hips, each grind of Becca's body, was no longer just dancing; it was a duel, a seduction, a battle to see who would break first under the intensity.

The music throbbed through every inch of the club, heat rising with the sweat and scent of too many bodies pressed close. Jessi's partner gripped her tightly, his hands bold, brazen, as though the rhythm permitted him. But Jessi wasn't dancing for him; every roll of her hips, every languid arch of her back was a weapon aimed at Becca.

Becca, locked in her own partner's arms, tried to match her, her moves growing looser, braver, hips swaying with a rhythm she didn't know she had. Her blouse clung to her skin as her skirt rode higher, but her eyes stayed fixed on Jessi. Their gazes collided again and again, a spark leaping across the crowded floor, daring, taunting, pulling each of them further.

As the song slammed to its final beat, a cheer erupted from the crowd. The DJ's voice then boomed overhead: "Alright, ladies and gentlemen, let's give the guys a break, this next one is for the ladies only!"

Whistles and applause followed, and Becca felt her partner's hands linger a moment too long before he let go. Jessi's tall stranger leaned down to murmur in her ear, but she smiled politely, slipping free of his grasp.

They both turned at once, as if gravity pulled them together through the haze of light and music. No words, just a shared breath, an unspoken relief, as they came face-to-face in the center of the floor.

The opening notes of "Black Velvet" slinked through the speakers, sultry and slow. Jessi slid her arms around Becca's waist, pulling her close with a familiarity that made Becca's skin prickle. Their bodies swayed together, finding the rhythm, a softer connection after the raw duel of moments before.

Becca took a deep breath as Jessi's lips brushed close to her ear, whispering something drowned out by the music, but the heat of it lingered. Jessi moved her hand lower, steady at the small of Becca's back, guiding her closer until their thighs brushed.

They moved together as though they were one body, close and staring into each other's eyes. They spoke no words, only reveling in the intimate moment, their hands gently exploring each other's forms. For a moment, each was lost in a world where only they existed, oblivious to the throng of people around them.

The tempo soon shifted, the crowd cheering as the music morphed seamlessly into a more playful, teasing beat… "You Can Leave Your Hat On" began to play.

Jessi grinned and leaned back just enough to spin Becca around, sliding her hands down Becca's sides with deliberate slowness. Becca gasped, startled, but the thrill of it made her laugh, her body relaxing into Jessi's lead.

They moved together, sultry and bold now, the heat of the dancefloor forgotten in the way they pressed, pulled, and teased each other with every beat. Around them, other women cheered, clapped, and danced with abandon, but for Becca and Jessi, the rest of the club faded until it felt like the music was theirs alone.

Jessi moved, slow, deliberate, sliding her hands up her own body, tilting her head back with a sultry smile. The crowd around them whooped, sensing the change, as a circle began to open, with men and women clapping and whistling.

Becca's heart hammered in her chest, but Jessi's confidence was infectious. When Jessi trailed her fingers along Becca's arm and tugged her close again, Becca gave in, letting her hips roll with the music, allowing her silk blouse to slip dangerously low as Jessi spun her.

Slowly, Becca moved in behind Jessi, as she trailed her fingers along Jessi's hips. Jessi leaned back, resting her head against her shoulder and arching her back. Reaching up, Becca gently tugged at the zipper at the front of Jessi's dress.

Jessi pushed back into Becca, closing her eyes and grinding her hips with the music. Becca grinned as she worked the zipper downward to her belly, then farther until the garment flew open and dropped to the ground.

With a laugh, Jessi spun around and kicked the dress over to their table, then moved close to Becca and gave a pouty smile. The two of them fed off the crowd, off each other, daring further with each movement. Jessi dropped low, sliding her hands along Becca's thighs as she looked up at her, grinning wickedly. Button by button, Jessi worked her way down Becca's blouse until it flung open. Jessi reached up and pulled it off her shoulders and tossed the garment into Becca's chair.

Cheers roared. Someone shouted, "Work it!"

Jessi rose in one fluid motion, pressing flush against Becca, their mouths so close the air between them crackled. The song's playful, striptease rhythm gave Jessi license to tug gently at Becca's skirt, teasing like she might reveal more. Becca gasped, then laughed, leaning into it, running her own hand down Jessi's exposed side, over the curve of her hip.

The crowd loved it: applause, whistles, stomps on the floor. But for Becca and Jessi, all of it blurred, the noise, the flashing lights, until it was just their bodies moving together, reckless, magnetic, daring the room to look away.

As the song swelled toward its climax, Jessi twirled Becca once more, then pulled her in tight, dipping her low with a practiced ease that had the crowd erupting in cheers. Becca's hair brushed the floor, her laugh rising over the music, while Jessi held her like she'd never let her fall.

When the final beat hit, they froze in that pose, Becca arched back in Jessi's arms, Jessi's lips just at her ear, before snapping upright together, breathless and glowing.

As the song ended, Jessi and Becca were left standing close together, still flushed, sweat gleaming on their skin under the club lights. Becca's heart was pounding so hard she thought it might burst, and she could feel every muscle buzzing with adrenaline as her eyes took in her now-exposed form.

Jessi leaned close, her lips brushing the side of Becca's neck. "Not bad, huh?" she whispered, voice teasing but low, intimate. Becca shivered at the contact, a heady mixture of exhilaration and lingering nerves coursing through her.

They stepped back toward their table, the men who had been watching earlier now looking more like observers than participants. Becca felt self-conscious for a moment, realizing how exposed they had been, but Jessi just laughed, slipping back into her dress and into the seat beside her.

Becca sank into the chair, quickly putting her blouse back on and sipping her drink, trying to calm her racing heart. "I… I can't believe we just did that," she admitted, voice barely above the music. Her cheeks burned, partly from the heat, partly from the awareness that every eye in the club had seen them.

Jessi grinned, brushing her fingers lightly over Becca's hand. "Believe it," she said softly. "You were amazing. And… I loved watching you come alive like that."

Becca looked down at their hands, fingers brushing, and a warm wave of connection washed over her. "I was nervous at first," she confessed, "but… it felt… incredible. Like nothing else existed except you and me."

Jessi's smile softened, the teasing edge melting into something tender. "That's exactly how I feel, too," she murmured.

Becca's breath hitched at the intensity in Jessi's gaze. The adrenaline was fading, but the closeness, the shared daring, the intimate thrill of the night, lingered, wrapping around them like a private world.

For a moment, neither spoke, just sitting side by side, letting the heat of the night settle into a quiet, tender afterglow. The club around them buzzed and throbbed, but they existed in a small bubble, their hands still brushing, their hearts racing from the dance they had shared.

As Jessi and Becca were catching their breath, a deep voice cut through the music.

"Hey," the tall, broad-shouldered man said, stepping closer. His eyes locked on Jessi with an easy confidence. "Mind if I get another dance?"

Jessi's lips curved into that teasing smirk that made Becca's stomach flip. "I'm always up for a dance," she said, slipping gracefully from her seat.

Becca's breath hitched. She watched Jessi rise, every movement fluid and magnetic, hips swaying even as she threaded through the crowd. Her pulse pounded, not just from the dance itself, but from the way Jessi commanded attention without trying.

Jessi's fingers brushed Becca's hand as she passed, a fleeting, intimate spark that made Becca shiver.

He led Jessi onto the dancefloor, his hands firm at her hips, guiding her into the rhythm. Becca stayed at the edge, her own heart racing as she watched the same effortless sensuality unfold. Jessi moved with a boldness that made Becca ache. She was daring, teasing, riding the music, pressing herself against him just enough to make the dance electric but still controlled.

Becca's fingers clutched her drink tightly, her body instinctively leaning forward, wanting to be part of it. Every sway, every grind, every glance Jessi threw in her direction made Becca ache to step closer, to join, to mirror her fearlessness.

Even though she wasn't dancing yet, the energy between them pulsed like a current, drawing Becca into the heat, into the thrill. Jessi's laughter rose above the music, playful and intoxicating, and Becca knew that no matter how daring the club felt, nothing had ever made her feel quite like this, watching Jessi dominate the floor while keeping a tether just for her.

The night blurred into a haze of flashing lights, pulsing bass, and sweat-slick bodies moving in rhythm. Becca found herself weaving in and out of the crowd, sometimes dancing with Jessi, with a stranger, and sometimes simply watching as Jessi spun her spell over the floor.

Jessi had that magnetic pull, her laugh was effortless, and every move seemed to demand attention. Becca couldn't help but be proud and uneasy all at once, her heart caught between admiration and a pang of jealousy each time another man's hands lingered too long on Jessi's hips.

Still, there were moments, glimpses across the floor, fleeting brushes of fingers, shared smirks, that anchored Becca. Reminders that, no matter who else hovered near, Jessi's gravity always pulled back toward her.

By the time the DJ slowed the tempo for a sultrier mix, Jessi finally tugged Becca back toward their table. Her cheeks were flushed, her hair slightly mussed from dancing, and her dress glittered faintly in the spotlight's sweep. She collapsed into her chair with a dramatic sigh, fanning herself with one hand.

Becca sat too, her own body warm and aching from the hours of movement. She reached for her drink, but Jessi leaned close before she could take a sip, her breath hot against Becca's ear.

"So…" Jessi murmured, her lips curling into a mischievous grin. "What would you say if I asked Darrion to come home with us tonight?"

Becca froze mid-sip, blinking at her. "So, that's his name?" she grinned. "Like… for a drink or something?" she asked, her voice tilting high with nervous uncertainty.

Jessi tilted her head, eyes glinting. "Well… or something."

The grin that followed was pure challenge, pure dare, the kind that made Becca's stomach flip and her chest tighten.

Becca set her glass down slowly, her mind spinning with the weight of the question, with the thrill of what Jessi was really asking. She chewed her lip, glancing toward the dancefloor where Darrion was still moving with effortless ease, a broad grin plastered on his face. Her stomach twisted, not just with nerves, but with that unfamiliar pull of curiosity and daring.

"I… I don't know," she whispered, her fingers tightening around the stem of her glass. "I mean… I've never…"

Jessi leaned closer, her dress brushing against Becca's arm, voice low and coaxing. "Hey, it's okay," she murmured, eyes locking on Becca's. "It's just one night. Nothing has to happen that you don't want. You can stop at any time."

Becca's chest tightened as she felt Jessi's fingers brush lightly along her wrist. The warmth, the confidence, the teasing glint in Jessi's eyes, it was magnetic. Her own resolve wavered, the combination of the music, the alcohol, and the thrill in the air clouding her judgment.

"I… maybe," Becca breathed, unsure whether it was the alcohol or the gradual loosening of her inhibitions, "maybe… okay."

Jessi's grin widened, triumphant yet gentle. "Yay," she whispered, leaning in to press a quick, playful kiss to Becca's temple. "We're going to have some fun."

Becca's heart was hammering, nerves and excitement intertwining into a dizzying knot. She had no idea what she was letting herself in for, but Jessi's coaxing and that spark in her eyes had stripped away the hesitation.

She glanced briefly at Darrion, who caught her gaze and winked, giving her a nod of encouragement. Becca swallowed hard, her pulse racing. She watched as Jessi motioned him over, and he took a seat at their table.

"This is Becca," Jessi said smoothly, her eyes daring, mischievous. "She's new to… nights like this."

Becca nearly choked on her own breath, shooting Jessi a wide-eyed look. But Jessi's hand pressed reassuringly against her hip, grounding her.

The man extended a hand, polite but deliberate. "Nice to meet you, Becca."

Becca stared for a second too long before realizing she should take it. Her fingers brushed against his, warm, strong, and she managed a small, nervous smile. "Hi."

They sat like that for a while, the three of them drinking, trading glances and minor flirtations. Jessi did most of the talking, teasing, playful, effortlessly pulling Darrion into their orbit. At the same time, Becca found herself caught in the glow of it, sipping her third drink of the night and watching, drawn deeper by the mix of danger and allure that Jessi always carried.

The table became its own little world. The drinks helped, softening edges, loosening laughter, but it was Jessi who steered the energy. She leaned in close when she spoke, fingers brushing over Becca's knee beneath the table, then drifting away as if nothing had happened. Every so often, her gaze would shift to Darrion, her smirk daring, testing.

Becca tried to keep up. She'd chime in here and there; her shyness tangled with the warmth spreading in her chest. The way Jessi's hand would ghost against her thigh gave her courage, though, and she found herself meeting Darrion's eyes longer, smiling more openly.

The banter circled the usual: music, drinks, work, but Jessi shifted it with a sly tilt of her head. She took a slow sip from her glass, then asked, almost casually, "So, Darrion… have you ever had two girls at the same time?"

The question hit the air like a spark. Becca froze, heat rushing to her cheeks, but Darrion didn't answer right away. Instead, he leaned back, eyes glinting as he let a grin spread across his face.

"No comment," he said at first, letting the pause draw out. Then, with a low chuckle, he leaned forward again. "But are you offering?"

Jessi laughed, low and throaty, shooting him a look that was half challenge, half promise. Becca's stomach flipped. She hadn't expected Jessi to be so direct, or herself to be sitting here, flushed and caught in the middle of it.

Jessi's hand found hers under the table, squeezing gently, her thumb brushing over her knuckles. She didn't answer Darrion right away, just let the tension hang, her smile lingering as she held Becca's gaze for a beat longer than usual.

"Maybe," Jessi said finally, her voice low but meant to be heard over the bass thumping through the club. "Depends on whether my friend here thinks you're worth it."

Becca's heart leapt into her throat. Both Jessi and Darrion were looking at her now, expectant, playful. She could feel the flush creeping up her neck, could hear her own pulse thudding louder than the music. She looked at Jessi's mischievous grin and Darrion's raised eyebrow. "I'm with her," Becca let out before staring back at her drink.

Jessi finally leaned back, tugging her hand away only to swirl her drink lazily. She gave Becca a sidelong glance, her smirk curling like smoke. "I think we've had enough of this place," she said, her tone casual but weighted.

Darrion looked up with a playful scowl. "Already? I was just starting to enjoy myself."

Jessi tilted her head, her eyes locking with his. "Oh, I think the night's just starting. Don't you?"

It was so smooth, Becca almost forgot to breathe. Her chair scraped faintly as she stood, following Jessi's lead. Jessi's hand brushed against hers as they moved through the crowd, not quite holding, but enough to ground her. Darrion trailed close behind, his presence looming, protective and intimidating all at once.

The music pounded through the floor, through their bodies, until the bouncer's nod and the swing of the door released them into the warm night air.

The sudden quiet was dizzying. Becca exhaled shakily, realizing only then how tight her chest had been inside. Jessi glanced at her, reading her without words, and gave the faintest squeeze of her hand before letting go.

"So," Darrion said, his voice low and amused, "where to now?"

Jessi turned to Becca, her smile softening, though her eyes still gleamed with mischief. "That depends," she said. "Do you want to keep the night going?"

Becca hesitated. She wanted to run, to say no, to retreat into her shell. But under that urge, deeper, there was another pull, heat, curiosity, the memory of Jessi's hand sliding higher on her thigh. She bit her lip, her voice small but steady.

"Yes."

8
Three's a Crowd

The three of them stood outside the club as their Uber finally arrived, the warm and muggy night air against their flushed skin. Jessi slid into the back seat next to Becca with that easy, practiced grace of hers, Darrion taking the passenger seat and having to move his seat back to fit inside.

With the purr of the engine and headlights cutting through the dark, the trio was on their way. For a few moments, silence ruled, just the hum of tires on asphalt. Then the driver's voice broke. "Did everyone have a good evening tonight?"

Jessi's voice cut in, low and teasing. "Oh, I think it might get better."

Becca slid down in her seat and covered her face. She could see the driver eyeing both of them through the rearview mirror.

"Darrion," Jessi said, glancing sideways at him, "do you always dance like that, or were you just trying to impress me?"

He chuckled. "Depends. Was it working?"

"Oh, it worked," Jessi purred, her lips curving as she gave a smirky grin to Becca. "Becca thought so, too. Didn't you, sweetheart?"

Becca froze, heat rushing into her face. She opened her mouth, then closed it again, unsure what to say. Jessi caught her hesitation, her smirk widening.

"She's shy," Jessi explained, her voice lilting. "But she felt it. I could tell." She noticed their driver smiling and shaking his head.

Darrion glanced back at Becca, his grin easy but curious. "Nothing wrong with shy," he said smoothly. "Sometimes that just means she's saving it all for later."

Becca's stomach fluttered, her breath uneven. Jessi let the words hang, her hand sliding to rest lightly on Becca's thigh, fingers drumming along with the faint music coming from the car radio. She tilted her head just enough to catch Becca's eyes again.

By the time they pulled up to their apartment's lot, the air inside the car was thick, buzzing with unspoken things, heavy with expectation. Jessi thanked the driver, then slipped out smoothly. She didn't ask, didn't check, she extended her arms, linking one through Becca's, the other through Darrion's.

"Come on," she said, her voice warm and commanding all at once. "Let's see what kind of trouble we can get into."

Linked together, their footsteps echoed up the stairwell, laughter spilling in bursts between the tension. At Jessi's door, she paused with the key in her hand, glancing between the two of them. Her smile curved, wicked and knowing, before she turned the lock and pushed the door open wide.

The apartment door clicked shut behind them, muffling the world outside. The hum of the city fell away, leaving only the sound of their breaths and the faint hum of the refrigerator. Jessi leaned against the door for a moment, her eyes flicking from Becca to Darrion, savoring the weight of their attention.

She didn't rush. She let the silence thrum, let the anticipation build. Then, with a deliberate slowness, she reached out and tugged Becca closer, pulling her into the curve of her arm. Becca's pulse jumped, her body stiff at first, but Jessi's warmth, her scent, the steady press of her hand against the small of her back, unraveled the tension bit by bit.

Darrion stood a step away, watching, his smile unreadable but his presence commanding. Jessi's gaze flicked to him, then back to Becca, and she whispered, "See? Nothing to be afraid of."

She tilted Becca's chin upward, holding her eyes. Looking back at Darrion, she smiled. "Make yourself at home. I've got to go to the little girls' room, and I'll be right back."

Darrion took a seat on the sofa as Jessi made her way to the bathroom. Rebecca timidly smiled at Darrion, then trailed behind Jessi, shutting the door behind her.

"You two must really like Bon Jovi," he said as the door shut.

"What's not to like!" Jessi answered back, yelling through the closed door.

Leaning into the mirror, Jessi began freshening up her makeup and fixing her hair. Rebecca leaned back against the door, her heart racing. "I don't know if I can do this," Becca whispered. "I've never been… I," she paused, trying to find the right words. "He's a black man."

Turning with a puzzled look, Jessi grinned. "I'm pretty sure they have the same parts as all the other guys."

Becca shook her head. "I know that, but… they say… well."

Jessi put her hands on her hips and tilted her head. "What?"

Taking a deep breath, Becca leaned in and whispered, "They are supposed to be really big. I don't know if I can handle really big."

Jessi let out a chuckle and turned back to the mirror. "Trust me. That's just a myth. I've seen guys big and small of all races. Just relax."

Then Jessi kissed her, soft at first, teasing, her lips brushing like a promise. Becca gasped against her, startled by the suddenness, by the heat that rushed through her. And when Jessi deepened it, Becca gave in, her arms winding hesitantly around Jessi's waist.

"Now," Jessi said as she raised and looked into her eyes, "go in there with Darrion. I have to pee."

Becca's eyes widened as Jessi opened the door and slowly pushed Becca back into the living room.

She pressed her forehead against the door as Jessi closed it. Bob came bouncing out of the bedroom and twirled around her ankles. She reached down and picked Bob up, opening the bathroom door long enough to pitch him inside. Taking a deep breath, she turned towards Darrion and made her way over to the stereo next to the TV. She turned on some music and turned back to Darrion.

"Would you like something to drink?" Becca asked, her voice cracking.

"No. I'm fine."

Walking to the kitchen, she opened up the refrigerator and pulled out a bottle of water. Her head was still spinning from the alcohol, and she raised the bottle to her temple.

Just then, Jessi popped out of the bathroom, her dress and boots discarded. Her tiny frame bounced fully nude over to the lounge chair, where she plopped down with one leg hanging over the arm. She looked over at Becca, then back at Darrion.

"So, Darrion," she said as she drew a hand up to her lips. "Becca's a little timid. Do you think you could help her get out of her clothes?"

Becca almost dropped her water bottle as she gave Jessi a wide-eyed glare. Jessi motioned her over to Darrion, and, kicking off her shoes, she nervously complied.

"I think I can help with that," Darrion answered as he stood and pulled his black shirt off.

His dark skin glistened in the lamplight, and Becca noticed his short, curly black hair. It was trimmed precisely, a straight line across his forehead. His muscles rippled like he had been carved out of ebony by some Greek sculptor, and she imagined him as some athlete, maybe in football or a boxer.

Becca trembled as she stood before him. He reached down slowly and began unbuttoning her blouse, flinging it open, then gently sliding it off her shoulders. Leaning down, he gave her a soft kiss on the nape of her neck before spinning her around and grasping the zipper on her skirt. She could hear the clicking buzz as he pulled it downward, freeing the garment from her hips and letting it fall to her ankles. She instinctively reached up and covered her exposed breasts as he hooked his fingers at the side of her panties. Slowly, he inched them down until she stood in the room fully exposed.

Jessi watched from the chair as the scene unfolded. Without realizing, she had begun softly rubbing her clit, legs spread wide, and feeling her juices increase with each sultry motion.

Darrion turned Becca until she was facing him, then lightly pushed her shoulders down until she kneeled. Looking back at Jessi, then glancing up at Darrion, she reached up and began unbuttoning his pants. She could feel the bulge underneath the garment, growing and begging to be released. She pulled open the fly, then with a hand at each side of his waist, pulled the trousers free.

He stepped out of his black Nikes, kicking them out to the middle of the room, the pants soon to follow. He stood there, only his gray boxer briefs and his gray ankle socks remaining.

Her head back, Becca looked up at his eyes as she slid the boxers down to his feet. Again, he kicked the garment to the growing pile in the middle of the room. Becca's eyes widened as his long member hung at eye level. He had to be every bit of 10 inches, with a girth that sent tingles down her spine. She quickly looked over at Jessi, her face a shocked *I-told-you-so*.

Jessi reached up with both hands and covered her mouth in an attempt to hide a chuckle. "Holy shit, Darrion!" she said with a laugh. "From now on, we're going to have to call you Safe Word."

"What do you mean?" Darrion asked with a bewildered smile.

"You haven't killed anyone with that cannon, have you? My God, you're huge."

Sensing some genuine fear on Becca's face, Jessi jumped down and joined her, kneeling on the floor. Becca remained silent, with an astonished expression. Jessi took his cock in her dainty hand and slowly began licking it like she would an ice cream cone. She nudged Becca, who leaned in and joined her.

Almost immediately, Darrion's member hardened and stood erect. Jessi opened her mouth and began rubbing her lips along his tip. Becca continued licking along his shaft.

Darrion leaned his head back and closed his eyes, taking in each sensation. Jessi then opened wide and slid his cock deep inside her mouth. Becca could hear her taking a couple of deep breaths through her nose before she pushed her head forward, taking his phallus deep down her throat. She held it there for a few seconds before moving back, coughing and gasping.

Tears welled up in her eyes again. She pushed, taking him as deep as she could physically go.

He placed his hand behind her head and thrust his hips towards her. Becca could only lean back and watch as Jessi gagged and pulled away, gasping for air. Taking a few deep breaths, Jessi again looked up and opened her mouth wide, inviting another deep plunge. Darrion responded, easing his prick to her lips, then pumping back and forth in her mouth.

Becca watched as Jessi endured each thrust, making strange gulping noises as he pumped into her throat. Jessi looked vulnerable, helpless, but Becca noticed her nipples were standing erect and her clit was dripping in anticipation. She was enjoying this assault, relishing it.

Darrion pulled out, and Jessi leaned forward, putting one hand on the floor as she again coughed and wheezed for air. "Come on," he said as he reached for both their hands.

Jessi couldn't speak but reached up and grabbed Darrion's hand. He pulled her up and reached for Becca. She sat bewildered and doe-eyed. She wasn't sure she could handle this. Jessi coughed, then broke in. "I don't think she can handle you, sweetie. Let her watch as you and I have some fun."

Jessi reached down for Becca's hand and pulled her up to her feet. Jessi then took Darrion's arm and led them both to the bedroom. Becca walked in, turned on a lamp on a dresser, and watched as Jessi stood in front of Darrion. His dark figure towered over her pale white body. She looked like a doll next to him, her skin flushed, faint freckles appearing on her shoulders.

Not quite sure what to do, Becca nervously made her way over to the bed where she plopped down on her side, a hand propping up her head as she watched the lustful night unfold.

Hands at her waist, Darrion picked Jessi up like she was made of feathers and pulled her up to his chest. She wrapped her legs around him as she slowly slid down, Darrion guiding his prick to her wanting mound. She was dripping wet, and gently he eased the tip inside. She threw her head back and closed her eyes as he inched deeper and deeper inside. She grimaced and moaned, but continued to encourage more. She was wrapped between pain and ecstasy.

With one deep thrust, Darrion pushed to the limit, Jessi arching back and giving out a muffled scream. Gradually, Darrion bucked his hips back and forth, with Jessi matching each thrust with her own movements.

A series of rhythmic grunts and groans filled the room, as Becca only watched in awe. She found herself torn, enthralled by the lustful scene, reaching down and rubbing herself as she viewed the frenzy, but also with a tinge of jealousy. Jessi was being given something she could not provide. Becca's breath caught. A part of her wanted to look away—but she didn't.

Jessi and Darrion's lips met in a passionate kiss. Becca watched, her breath catching in her throat as she saw Darrion's strong hands grip Jessi's waist, pulling her closer. Jessi's fingers were running across

Darrion's curly black hair, deepening the kiss as their bodies pressed tightly against each other.

Darrion's rhythm was steady and deep, his hips moving in a primal dance as he drove into Jessi. The sound of their bodies meeting filled the room, a symphony of pleasure that only heightened the moment's intensity. Jessi's moans vibrated against Becca, sending shockwaves of ecstasy through her body.

Becca's hands found their way to her own breasts, squeezing and teasing as she watched the waves of pleasure.

Darrion, feeling Jessi's body tighten around him, walked over to the edge of the bed and gently laid Jessi on her back beside Becca. Moving between her legs, he again pushed deep inside Jessi, making her arch her back and reach out behind her, pushing her hands against the headboard.

He increased his pace, his own pleasure building with each thrust. Jessi's moans grew louder, her hips bucking against him as she neared her climax. Becca, feeling the pressure building just next to her, moved her fingers faster and faster along her own clit, her own release just within reach.

The room was filled with the sounds of their combined pleasure, the air thick with the scent of sex. As Darrion's thrusts became more urgent, Jessi's body convulsed, before a fountain of her clear release shot out like a fountain, ripping through her in waves. Becca could feel the bed soaked in the warm, clear fluids, Jessi's body quivering, and her eyes clenched.

Becca had never seen such an explosion of pleasure, and followed soon after, her body shuddering as she cried out, her release washing over her in a flood of sensation.

As the waves of pleasure began to subside, Darrion gently pulled Jessi around, positioning her on her hands and knees. He mounted her from behind, his strong hands gripping her hips as he slowly slid into her. Jessi moaned, her body still sensitive from her previous orgasm, the sensation sending new waves of pleasure through her.

Jessi reached over, her hands roaming over Becca's body. She traced the curve of Becca's breasts, her fingers lingering on each of her nipples before moving lower. Becca shivered, her body responding to Jessi's touch.

Darrion's movements were slow and deliberate, his hips rolling as he drove into Jessi. Jessi's hands explored further, her fingers brushing against Becca's thighs, teasing the sensitive skin. Darrion's breath hitched, his body tensing as he pounded faster and faster, new sensations coursing through him.

Being pushed back and forth with each thrust, Jessi's hands continued their journey, moving between Becca's legs, her fingers lightly grazing her soft skin. Darrion groaned, his thrusts becoming more urgent as he grew closer to the edge.

Becca felt her body building towards another climax. Jessi's hands were everywhere, teasing and exploring; the combination of sensations was overwhelming, her body trembling with anticipation.

Darrion's grip on Jessi's hips tightened, his body tensing as he neared his release. Jessi's fingers danced over Becca's skin, her touch light and teasing, pushing her further. Becca's moans grew louder, her body convulsing as she felt her own orgasm building. Jessi, caught in the whirlwind of pleasure, cried out, her own orgasm ripping through her, her body milking Darrion as she rode the waves of ecstasy. Again, she squirted her warm fluid all over Darrion's hips, Jessi reveling in ecstasy.

With a final, powerful thrust, Darrion pulled out, keeping his climax from exploding. He then slid down and lay on his back, pulling Jessi on top of him. She straddled him, her hips moving in a slow, sensual rhythm as she rode him. Darrion's hands gripped her waist, his fingers digging into her soft skin as he met her thrusts with his own. The room was filled with the sounds of their pleasure, their moans and whispers of encouragement echoing off the walls.

As the night wore on, their movements became more urgent, their bodies slick with sweat as they chased their releases. Jessi's head fell back, her auburn hair cascading down her back as she rode Darrion harder, her body tensing as she neared yet another climax.

Becca felt like a voyeur, watching something forbidden, but unable to turn away.

Darrion, feeling Jessi's body tighten around him, increased his pace, his hips lifting off the bed as he drove into her. With a final, powerful thrust, they both cried out, their orgasms exploding through them, their bodies convulsing with pleasure.

Exhausted, they collapsed onto the soaked bed, their bodies entwined, their breathing ragged. They lay there for a long while, saying nothing, just breathing and staring up at the ceiling. Becca reached over, softly rubbing Jessi's arm.

The exhaustion finally catching up to her, Jessi struggled to stay awake. She watched as Darrion slowly got out of bed and walked into the living room, searching for his clothes. Returning to the bedroom, Darrion reached for his cell phone, his fingers fumbling as he called for a rideshare.

Jessi and Becca lay in the bed; their nude bodies tangled around one another. Neither said anything as they watched him gather himself. Pulling out his wallet, Darrion reached in and pulled out a card. "Here's my number if you two are interested in another night out." Jessi smiled and gave a wink.

"Goodnight," he murmured, his voice hoarse with exhaustion and pleasure. "It's been a night to remember."

Jessi, her eyes heavy, smiled sleepily. "Goodnight, Darrion."

They watched through the bedroom door as he walked out of the apartment, the front door closing behind him. Neither said anything. The night had turned to near dawn, and Jessi could see the dim pink of the clouds as the sun fought its way to daybreak. It would be a sunrise that neither would see, as both, exhausted, drifted off to sleep.

9
A Bridge Too Far

It was midafternoon before either of them stirred. Sunlight cut across the bed in golden stripes, warm against tangled sheets and bare skin. Becca blinked awake slowly, her body heavy, her mind still hazy with fragments of the night before, the music, the blur of lights, Jessi's lips and hands, the heat that still lingered in her skin.

Jessi was already awake. Propped on one elbow, she watched Becca with that half-smile that always carried a spark of mischief.

"Afternoon, sunshine," she murmured, voice low and teasing. "You look adorable. Still trying to figure out if last night was real?"

Becca flushed, tugging the blanket higher over her chest. "I know it was real," she muttered. "It's just…" Her voice trailed off, embarrassed by her own stammer.

Jessi leaned close, brushing a strand of hair from Becca's cheek. "It's okay. I know you had fun."

Becca bit her lip, glancing away. Her heart pounded, but not from memory; it was the afternoon light, the stillness, the clarity pressing in. "I… I don't usually do things like that," she whispered.

Jessi's smile softened, though the glint in her eyes never faded. "That's what made it special. You let go. You trusted me. And I liked it. I liked you." Her fingertip traced slow circles on Becca's arm.

Becca's chest tightened. She wanted to sink into it, to believe it entirely, but uncertainty tugged at her. "I don't know how you can be so calm about it."

Jessi bent close, lips brushing Becca's ear. "Because I like watching you squirm. Almost as much as I liked last night."

Becca groaned, hiding her face in the pillow, and Jessi's laugh filled the room, warm, rich, alive. But when Becca lifted her head, the laughter caught. Her expression was softer, heavier.

"I mean it," she said, voice low. "Last night was… wild. Fun, yes. But that's not what I want all the time. What I want…" She hesitated, hands clutching the blanket like it might keep her grounded. "…is you. Just you."

The words hit harder than Becca expected. Jessi blinked, her teasing faltering. For a long moment, she didn't move, then she pulled back, the sheet twisting in her restless hands.

"Don't say that," she murmured.

"Say what?" Becca sat up, eyes searching hers. "That I don't need anyone else? That I don't need the clubs or strangers? I just want you. I watched you last night. And yes, I was amazed… but I was jealous too. Even hurt."

"Hurt?"

"The way you were with Darrion…" Becca swallowed. "You've never had that kind of reaction with me."

Jessi raked her hand through her hair. "You mean when I squirted? That's not something I control, Becca. It's different… It's not the same as what you and I have. I don't even know how to explain it."

Becca's brow furrowed. "I don't know. I just felt like he got something that should have been ours."

Jessi reached for her hand and squeezed it tight. "It was just sex. You and I… we connect. Last night was… an amusement park ride, that's all."

"I don't want rides, Jessi. I want you."

Jessi's throat tightened. She wanted to believe it, to cling to it. But old memories rose like shadows, lovers who left, nights that ended in silence, times she had been too much or not enough. Her smile returned, brittle around the edges.

"Becca… last night, I did it for you."

"For me? What do you mean?"

"Remember when you told me your fantasies? On the beach… We did that at the picnic table that night. You even told me you liked men too, and fantasized about a three-way? I was trying to give you that."

Becca sat up straighter, the covers clutched around her. "Those were just fantasies, Jessi. Dreams. That doesn't mean I want to live them out. You have to be careful, Jessi. Sometimes, you get what you wish for, and it isn't what you thought it would be."

"Why dream if you don't want to live?" Jessi shot back, her voice rising. "My mom died at forty-two. I'm twenty-six, Becca… twenty-six… I want to live while I can."

Becca reached for her arm. "Jessi… Just because your mom died young doesn't mean you will."

"How do you know that?" Jessi's voice cracked, sharp. "After everything I've been through… tell me how you can possibly know that."

"Jessi…" Becca faltered, searching for words. "Am I one of those terrible things that's happened in your life?"

Jessi rolled her eyes, shoving out of bed. "Of course not. But I thought you understood."

Becca watched her yank on shorts and a t-shirt, stomping around the room. Her voice steadied as she spoke. "I think you do these wild things to be seen."

Jessi froze. "What?"

"You're afraid of being forgotten… left behind. All your life, you've been abandoned or forced to take care of everyone else. You never had the chance to just be young. Now you do these wild things… not because you like hiding, but because you want someone to notice you. To stay."

The words hit raw. Jessi wrapped her arms around herself, her face unreadable. Then, without a word, she turned and slammed the bedroom door.

Becca's chest burned. She jumped from the bed, not caring about her nakedness, and chased her into the living room. "Maybe I don't understand everything," she shouted, "but I know you keep pushing these boundaries. That piece of string you keep twirling around your fingers. It's like a token or something. Something to relieve an obsession; to keep you occupied. I'm here, Jessi!"

For a moment, Jessi only stared at her, keys and purse clutched tight, caught between anger and fear.

"You don't have to pretend with me," Becca whispered, softer now. "I just want you."

Jessi's jaw clenched. She snatched up her shoes, stormed to the door, and slammed it behind her.

The apartment fell silent. Becca stood trembling in the middle of the room, bare and exposed in every way. Wrapping her arms around herself, she sank to the floor. Her sobs echoed through the stillness, the ache of loving someone who kept slipping through her hands.

* * *

The steady hum of the engine filled the silence, the radio long forgotten. Jessi gripped the wheel; eyes locked on the ribbon of asphalt ahead. She wasn't driving anywhere in particular, just moving, as though distance itself might quiet the restless storm inside her. The window was down, and warm summer air whipped strands of hair across her face, tugging at her shirt and stinging her eyes with the heat.

In the rearview, she caught her own reflection, red-rimmed eyes. Mascara smudged faintly at her cheekbones. She barely recognized herself. She hadn't cared how she looked when she left; she never did, not when the crash came.

The city bled away behind her, its noise and neon fading into the hushed greens and browns of the countryside. Tall pines flanked the highway, bending slightly as if to listen. She turned down the gravel road almost by instinct, stones crunching under the tires, until the trees opened onto the river's edge.

She parked by an old, weathered picnic table, the same spot she and Becca had come to that night. She climbed onto the tabletop, lying flat on her back. Her arms sprawled out as if she were surrendering to the sky itself. Above her, sunlight fractured through the canopy, flickering in and out of shadows, the world suspended in that fragile balance between stillness and motion.

Her chest rose and fell too quickly. The familiar weight pressed in, sharp and suffocating. The crash, always sudden, always merciless. Just hours ago, she'd been alive with adrenaline, fueled by danger disguised as freedom. Now it hollowed out, twisting into guilt, into the quiet echo of shame.

The thoughts began, the same merciless chant that had haunted her for years.

You pushed too far. You're too much. Sooner or later, she'll see. They always do.

Her stomach knotted, the ache spreading outward like wildfire. And with it came that old temptation, dark and seductive. The itch to punish herself. To chase danger the way others chased comfort. To throw herself at the edge of something sharp and reckless until the noise inside her finally went quiet.

Jessi leaned back on the table, staring up at the slice of sky through the pines. Her jaw locked hard, as if it might hold back the words she refused to say, even to herself. But the truth pressed in anyway. Sometimes it felt as if she were trying to punish herself. To pay for the pieces of her that never seemed whole, never right.

Her hands came up to her face, fingers pressing deep into her temples until it hurt. *Why can't I just be normal? Why can't I just take what Becca's offering without ruining it?*

Becca's face flickered in her mind, shy, hopeful, so full of a trust Jessi didn't deserve. The thought cinched her chest tight. Jessi wanted to be the woman Becca believed she was, to give her safety instead of chaos. But the darkness inside wouldn't let her. Her breath came quick and shallow, her hands trembling against her skin.

Alone in the woods, she let the words slip out, hoarse and small:

"What the hell is wrong with me?"

Jessi lay there for a long while listening to the river lap against its banks. Birds called in the trees. Children's laughter carried over the water, bright and cruel against her silence.

* * *

The drive home stretched out like penance, every mile thick with what she should have said, should have done. By the time she pulled into her space, tears blurred the windshield, spilling hot down her cheeks. She killed the engine and sat there a long moment, wiping her face with both hands before she forced herself out.

The apartment greeted her with quiet. Only Bob broke the silence, bounding toward her with a plaintive meow. She bent to scratch him absently before her eyes found the couch.

Becca lay curled beneath a pale pink blanket, her chest rising and falling in the soft rhythm of sleep. For a moment, Jessi just stood there, breath caught in her throat. Then, quietly, she crossed the room and knelt at her side. She leaned in, pressing a feather-light kiss to her cheek.

Becca stirred, blinking herself awake, eyes hazy and warm. Jessi's voice came out soft, trembling:

"I'm sorry. I said things I shouldn't have. I shouldn't have treated you that way."

Becca smiled through her sleepiness, lifting a hand to Jessi's cheek. She tugged her close, wrapping her in a hug before brushing a kiss against her lips.

"I'm sorry too," she whispered. "I'm here for you, Jessi. I want you in my life."

Jessi climbed onto the sofa, curling into the warmth of Becca's blanket and arms. They pulled the cover over them both, the silence no longer empty but full of breath, of closeness, of eyes locked together in a wordless promise.

10

Gray Skies on a Sunny Day

The days began to blur… work, home, shower, bed. Jessi moved through it all as if she were underwater. Everything muted, slowed, dulled. The only constant was Becca.

Every evening, Becca was there when Jessi came through the door. She'd smile, kiss her cheek, and ask how her day went. Their conversations drifted gently: work frustrations, Bob's antics, little things that made them laugh. They curled up together on the couch, Bob choosing whichever lap seemed softer that night.

Jessi tried, she laughed when she should, spoke when she could, but she knew the mask was slipping. She saw it in the way Becca sometimes tilted her head, the careful tone in her voice when she asked, "You okay?"

And Jessi always said, "Yeah. Just tired."

But Becca wasn't fooled. The air between them held a hairline crack, fragile but undeniable. Becca feared she had said too much, too bluntly, and that her truth had cut Jessi deeper than she intended.

Something in Jessi seemed dimmer now, still warm, still Jessi, but subdued, as if some flicker inside her had gone quiet.

One evening, Becca surprised her with a gift. A sketch, pencil on paper, every line deliberate, Jessi standing beside her Mustang. It was startling in its precision: the sweep of her hair, the stance of her body, even the shadow in her eyes.

Jessi held it up, studying it with raised brows. "Couldn't you have made me look better?"

Becca's mouth dropped open. She snatched the paper back and frowned at it. "What? You don't think it looks like you?"

"Oh, it looks exactly like me," Jessi said with a crooked smirk. "That's the problem."

Becca huffed, rolling her eyes, but her lips tugged into a smile. "Stop it, silly."

Jessi's gaze softened as she reached to take it back. "No, really… you're amazing."

Color rose in Becca's cheeks. "And you're biased."

"Maybe." Jessi grinned, still staring at the portrait. "But seriously, why are you working at a home improvement store when you can do this?"

Becca shrugged as she sank into a chair at the table. "Because to make a living with art, you need a degree. And I couldn't afford one. My parents wouldn't pay. They always wanted me in law school, like them."

Jessi let out a laugh. "Sorry, I just can't picture you as a lawyer."

"Neither could I." Becca's smile was faint, thoughtful. "It would've made me miserable. With art, it doesn't matter if I make money. It's about creating. About giving something life that didn't exist before."

Jessi folded her arms, tilting her head as she studied her. "Still… it feels wrong that something you love this much can't be your career too."

Becca looked up at her, eyes steady and warm. "Just seeing you smile when I hand you something like this, that's all the payment I need."

Jessi's chest tightened. She crossed the room, leaned down, and kissed her slowly and deeply, letting the warmth of it linger. Pulling back, her grin turned mischievous. "I'll try to give you a big tip… later."

Becca lowered her head bashfully, peeking up at her with a pouty grin. "Promise?"

Jessi searched her eyes, and for the first time in days, the flicker in her own seemed to flare back to life.

"Definitely."

* * *

The dog days of summer settled heavily over the city. Long evenings hummed with cicadas, and nights stayed warm and restless. Jessi and Becca kept their rhythm, working during the week and having lazy weekends together. Saturdays meant Amy and Traci dropping by with their laughter spilling into the night like it always had.

It was a routine that felt safe, familiar. But Becca sometimes caught Jessi staring out the window a little too long, or laughing just a beat too late at one of Traci's jokes. Small things, but they tugged at Becca's heart.

One Wednesday afternoon, Becca got home earlier than usual. She was surprised to see Amy getting out of her car in the parking lot, sipping from a water bottle, as though she had just arrived home herself.

"Hey, stranger," Amy said with an easy grin. "Off early?"

"Yeah, finally," Becca answered, setting her bag on her shoulder. "Jessi's not home yet, though."

Amy nodded, her expression thoughtful. For a moment, she chewed her lip like she was working up to something. "So… how are you two doing?"

Becca smiled instinctively. "Good. I mean… she's wonderful. But she can be… moody sometimes, I guess."

Amy gave a little chuckle, though there was no humor in it. "Yeah. That sounds like Jessi."

Becca tilted her head. "What do you mean?"

Amy glanced toward the apartment buildings, lowering her voice. "Look… I'm not trying to scare you off or anything. But I've known Jessi since high school. She's always been like that. Peaks and valleys. Highs and lows. She can go months on top of the world, unstoppable, magnetic. Then, like a switch, she'll crash. Fall into a dark place."

Becca swallowed, shifting her weight uncomfortably. "Depression?"

Amy nodded slowly. "Yeah. Big time. She hides it well until she can't. And then it's like she punishes herself for being happy, or for letting anyone close. I just… I've seen it before. I care about her, and I know you do too. She's been through a lot. Why do you think we always come over to Jessi's to get ready on Saturday nights? It's our way of trying to—I don't know… check in with her. I'm not saying run. Just… be ready. Because when the crash comes, it can be rough."

The words hung between them, heavy in the humid air.

Becca forced a little smile, though her chest felt tight. "Thanks… I think?"

Amy reached out and squeezed her arm, her eyes softening. "Don't take it the wrong way. Jessi's amazing… You know that better than anyone. Just promise me you'll look out for yourself, too."

Becca nodded, though unease settled deep in her stomach. She'd already felt the edges of Jessi's shadows. Now she wondered how far down they went.

11
Loss and Loneliness

The week moved in slow, syrupy pulses. Each day blended into the next, work, home, shower, bed, but the rhythm felt hollow, dulled. Becca tried to bring life into it, little deliberate touches: a favorite snack on the counter, soft music humming through the apartment, Bob bouncing happily between them. She hoped her presence might anchor Jessi, even just a little.

Jessi went through the motions, quiet, subdued, occasionally laughing at a joke, but always with a faint shadow behind her eyes. Becca noticed the small tells Amy had described: Jessi obsessively twisting a loop of string around her fingers and letting it go, over and over; staring out the window for long minutes, lost in thought; subtle shifts from animated to flat, as if a switch had been flipped.

Every evening, Becca settled beside her, offering warmth, gentle touches, and conversation meant to tether Jessi to the present. Sometimes it worked, a smile, a laugh, but other times Jessi retreated, curling up with Bob under a blanket, eyes distant, unreachable. Becca learned to watch, never to push, and just be there.

On Wednesday, as Becca tidied the apartment and fed Bob, her phone rang. The caller ID flashed her mother's name. She froze. It had been nearly a year since she last spoke to her parents. After a long pause, she answered.

"Becca?" Her mother's voice trembled, softer than Becca remembered.

"Hi," Becca said cautiously, keeping her tone neutral.

"I… I'm calling about your aunt Sharon. She passed away last night." The words landed heavy, tighter than she expected, squeezing her chest and knotting her throat.

Becca swallowed hard. "Oh… what happened?"

"They think it was a heart attack," her mother replied, sadness threading through her tone.

Tears stung Becca's eyes. "I'm… I'm so sorry, Mom. When's the funeral?"

"Visitation is tomorrow in Atlanta. The funeral is Friday. Your father and I… we'd like you to come. We want to try to mend things, Becca. It's been too long."

Becca nodded, though her mother couldn't see. "Okay, momma. I'll be there," she said softly, heart thumping with a mix of sorrow and hesitation.

* * *

That evening, when Jessi returned, Becca waited until they were both settled on the couch. Her voice was quiet but firm.

"Jessi… I need to tell you something," she said, sinking back into the cushions. "I got a call today… My aunt passed away."

Jessi's eyes softened as she reached for Becca's hand. "Oh, Becca… I'm so sorry."

"I'll have to go to Atlanta for the funeral tomorrow, and… I'll stay until Sunday. My parents… they want to try to mend fences."

Jessi's eyes flickered with an unspoken tension. She shifted on the couch, resting her chin in her hands. "Atlanta… that's far," she murmured, voice tight. "These are the same people who… that disowned you? The ones who wouldn't pay for your college?"

Becca lowered her head, pressing her palm against her eyes. "I'll be back Sunday. Please understand."

Jessi stayed quiet, the tension in her shoulders rigid, jaw tight. Becca reached out, brushing her hand along Jessi's arm. "They're my parents, Jessi. No matter what's happened, I still love them."

"Becca…" Jessi said, finally, in a low voice. She paused, searching Becca's eyes. "I understand. Of course, you should go… try to reconnect. Do you… Want me to come with you?"

Becca squeezed her hand gently. "I don't… I think it's better if I tell them about us gradually. Just… four days. I'll be back Sunday."

Jessi exhaled slowly, a subtle nod, though her eyes betrayed the storm beneath. The apartment was quiet, save for Bob's occasional soft meows. Becca leaned her head against Jessi's shoulder, feeling the warmth, aware of the restlessness simmering beneath it.

For Jessi, the thought of Becca hiding their relationship stung more than she expected. And now, with Becca leaving, a latent compulsion stirred, a whisper urging escape, risk, chaos, wrapped tightly with sadness and longing. Jessi was a master at masking it, but Becca sensed it anyway, in the twitch of her hand, the pause before she spoke, the tension behind her smile.

***

The hours until Thursday stretched long, each one a careful balance. Becca tried to tether Jessi to the present, keeping shadows at bay. She'd alerted Amy and Traci, asking them to check in and be her eyes and ears. But every time she looked at Jessi, she saw the flicker of something she couldn't reach. A dark undercurrent that made the coming week feel like walking a tightrope over stormy waters.

Thursday morning arrived in a muted haze. The apartment smelled faintly of coffee and had the lingering warmth of sleep. Becca tiptoed, packing her small suitcase with deliberate care, trying to be mindful not to wake Jessi. She left folded notes, little reminders tucked into drawers and counters, gentle ways of saying she would be back soon.

But Jessi woke and hovered near the doorway, silent. She tried to mask the tightness in her chest with a smile, to act casual as Becca zipped her bag. But the glance she gave Becca, lingering, betraying both longing and fear, was more honest than any words could be.

"Becca…" Jessi said softly, the syllable heavy. "Drive safe, okay?"

Becca smiled, trying to hide the weight in her own chest. "I will. I'll be back Sunday. I promise." She stepped forward and pressed a soft kiss to Jessi's lips, lingering just long enough to anchor them both.

Jessi nodded, swallowing a lump in her throat. "Sunday," she repeated, almost to herself.

The car pulled away, leaving the apartment quieter than it had been in years. Jessi leaned against the doorframe, watching the taillights disappear. Silence pressed in, thick and suffocating. Bob wandered by, nudging her leg to get attention. She patted his head absently, but her thoughts had already turned inward.

* * *

By late afternoon, the first edges of restlessness began to creep in. Jessi came home from work and wandered the apartment, opening cabinets, shifting cushions, doing small tasks without purpose. Each sound outside the apartment, cars passing, voices echoing from the street, felt like it might pull her into action. She could feel the familiar compulsion stirring, that old itch in her mind that demanded movement, risk, and escape.

She tried to distract herself by scrolling on her phone, turning on music, and watching old shows. But her thoughts kept circling back, spinning dark patterns in the quiet apartment. Her pulse quickened. She could almost feel the scenarios playing out in vivid detail: streets, strangers, darkness, danger. Every fiber of her being screamed for action.

* * *

Night fell, and with it, the compulsion grew sharper. Jessi sat on the couch, Bob in her lap, staring at the window. Her hands twitched, her jaw clenched, her breathing shallow. She whispered to herself, almost inaudibly, "I need it… I need it." The words felt like both confession and curse.

Hours passed. With each passing moment, the internal tension intensified. Jessi knew the danger, knew the line she shouldn't cross, but the compulsion was relentless. The apartment felt too small, the night too quiet. She paced, sometimes running her hands through her hair, sometimes pressing her face into her palms. The isolation gnawed at her, her body humming with adrenaline she didn't know how to release.

* * *

By Friday, the edges of panic had sharpened. Becca's small notes for her reminded her to breathe and stay calm. But even as she wrote, her mind plotted, rehearsing scenarios that grew more daring, more reckless with each passing hour. The compulsion was a storm she couldn't control, a whisper that had grown into a roar.

She called Becca once, in the late evening. Her voice was tight, guarded. "Hey… just checking in. How are things going?"

Becca's warm voice came over the line, full of concern and gentle humor. "It's as good as can be expected. How are you holding up?"

Jessi hesitated, a crack in the practiced armor. "I'm… fine. Just tired."

"I can tell when you're not, Jessi," Becca said softly. "I wish I could be there."

Jessi swallowed the truth that she couldn't admit aloud. "You'll be back soon," she murmured instead. "Sunday."

The line went quiet after that. Jessi set her phone aside and stared out the window. The city lights blurred in the distance. The compulsion was still there, strong and demanding. And the weekend stretched ahead, empty, quiet, and full of perilous temptation.

The city at night felt sharper, the air cooler against Jessi's bare arms as she stepped from her apartment building. The black dress clung to her curves, soft and sleek, its daring neckline both armor and invitation. Her high heels clicked against the pavement with each step; each echo carrying a mix of anticipation and fear she couldn't quite quell.

Secrets loomed ahead, its dark façade unassuming, but the muffled thrum of music spilling into the street promised a different world inside. Jessi paused in the shadowed alley by the entrance, inhaling slowly. The silence of her apartment, the empty weight of Becca's absence, all pressed down on her chest. Tonight, she needed release. Somewhere controlled, somewhere intense… somewhere she could be undone safely.

Inside, the club pulsed with life. Spotlights traced the edges of the dance floor, bouncing off leather, silk, and polished metal. Patrons moved with abandon and purpose, some watching, some performing, some lost entirely in their own worlds of sensation. Jessi's pulse quickened as she weaved through the crowd, scanning for the one person she'd come to see.

Marcus sat in his private booth, a velvet-draped alcove with subdued lighting and a large round table, toward the back. To his right, a woman knelt, nude, wrists and ankles cuffed, a black collar encircling her neck. A silver leash ran from the collar to Marcus's lap. He ran a hand gently over her long black hair, an owner's ease in every motion.

Wealth clung to him like a second skin. Tailored shirts, gleaming watches, cufflinks, and an aura of control that didn't need announcing. But it wasn't the money that drew Jessi; it was the way he observed, careful, predatory, almost clinical. She felt the pull immediately, the familiar thrill coiling in her chest.

He noticed her, too. "Jessi," he murmured, a faint smile brushing his lips. "It's been a while."

"I was hoping you'd be here tonight," she said, letting the words linger. Her fingers brushed the edge of the table, the energy of the club pressing against her like electricity.

Marcus's eyes scanned her carefully, noting the subtle tension in her posture and the restless flicker behind her gaze. "What brings you here tonight?" His voice was smooth, calm, and deliberate. The kneeling woman remained still, head bowed, hands folded in her lap, her body entirely under Marcus' control.

Jessi hesitated. The compulsion within her stirred, tugging her forward into the edge of the thrill she both craved and feared. "I… wanted to see if you'd be interested in some rope play tonight," she whispered.

Marcus' gaze softened slightly but remained commanding. "I wish I had known you were coming. I brought Number Four tonight," he said, nodding to the kneeling woman. Her stillness and total surrender sparked something in Jessi, a mixture of envy and fascination. She imagined herself in the woman's place, the sensation of yielding completely, the loss of control, both terrifying and intoxicating.

"I understand, Sir," Jessi said, composed, respectful. The way he carried himself, the precision of his command, demanded it. She began to turn away but paused, spinning slightly to face him again.

"There's… a place near the lake. A parking lot," she started, her cheeks warming. "I've heard… perhaps… some things happen there?" She dared not meet his eyes fully, letting the question hang between them.

Marcus exhaled a puff of cigar smoke, the rich, expensive scent curling in the dim light. "Jessi," he said, voice low, measured, "are you venturing into dark fantasies tonight?"

She shuffled her feet, embarrassed but defiant. "I… I was just curious. I'd heard rumors," she admitted, voice quieter now, her pulse hammering in her throat.

Marcus' gaze lingered on her, sharp and knowing, weighing every movement, every hesitation. Jessi felt the heat of anticipation and fear swirl together, a storm of desire she had no intention of taming, not tonight.

Marcus leaned back slightly in his booth, cigar smoke wisping lazily around him, his gaze never leaving Jessi. "You're exploring dangerous territory tonight," he said, voice low, smooth, and deliberate.

Jessi's eyes darted back out to the club, her face flushed.

"This isn't just play, Jessi. If you're looking for true submission, real, total release, I could help. I've always admired your beauty. If you're willing to serve, you could be a sister to Number Four. Arrangements could be made."

Jessi's breath hitched slightly. She had never considered this level of commitment, not like this. "What? I'd be… Number Five?" she asked with a smile.

Marcus shifted the cigar in his mouth. "Number Seven."

Jessi blinked, then looked down at the table, almost afraid to make eye contact with him. "Arrangements?" she asked cautiously, her fingers brushing the edge of the table, trying to ground herself.

Marcus nodded. "Yes. Contracts, agreements, compensation for your service. One year, if you wish. I find that to be the right amount of time before renegotiations. Total obedience, structured rules, and guidance." His tone was measured and businesslike, yet there was an unmistakable edge of expectation and challenge.

Jessi swallowed, processing the words. "Compensation?"

"That depends," Marcus replied. "Length of service, the limits you set… and the way you handle yourself under training. It would be 24/7. No job, no bills… just pure submission."

"I have no limits," Jessi said, almost defiantly. She wasn't lying, at least, she didn't think so.

He raised a brow, a faint smile tugging at the corners of his mouth. "So," he said with a chuckle, "you're that elusive unicorn we've all been searching for. Everyone has limits, Jessi."

The comment made Jessi flush, a mix of humility and apprehension swelling inside her chest. Her mind raced, secretly intrigued, but undeniably fearful. A year? Total submission? It was exhilarating and terrifying in equal measure. "That's… a big decision," she murmured, voice tight. "I… I would certainly think about your offer."

Marcus leaned back, exhaling another stream of cigar smoke, his eyes never leaving her. "Take your time, little one. It's not a choice to make lightly. But if you decide, I'll ensure everything is structured, safe, and respected. You wouldn't be stepping in blind."

Jessi nodded, still feeling the magnetic pull of possibility, but also the weight of responsibility and risk. Marcus studied her a moment longer, then leaned closer, lowering his voice further.

"There's also… that place you asked about. A small parking lot near the lake. People go there late at night for random encounters, spontaneous moments."

He pulled out a pen from his coat pocket and began scribbling an address on a business card. "Be careful, Jessi. You just might find what you're looking for."

Jessi's pulse quickened as she took the card from his hand. The idea sparked a thrill inside her, but it was tempered by caution. She knew her compulsion, knew the dangerous edges she flirted with, and part of her recoiled. Yet another part, a darker, daring part, leaned forward, whispering possibilities she could hardly admit even to herself.

"I'll think about everything," she said finally, voice steadying as she forced a calm over her racing thoughts. "I… I appreciate the offer."

Marcus gave her a knowing smile, the kind that made her pulse jump, and tilted his head slightly. "I'll be here, Jessi. Take the time you need. And… remember that curiosity is natural. Just respect the risks."

As Jessi looked down at Number Four, letting her gaze linger a little too long. She sat nude obediently, silent, and a wave tingled across Jessi's body. She stepped back from the booth, her heels clicking against the floor. She felt the tension coil tighter in her chest, equal parts fear, thrill, and irresistible pull toward something she couldn't yet name.

12
Growing Urges

The small parking lot almost looked deserted; the asphalt bathed in the harsh yellow glow of a single streetlight. Beyond the edge of the lot, the lake stretched dark and still, the trees casting long, trembling shadows across the ground. Jessi eased her Mustang in, engine humming low, and parked at the far end, the soft click of her keys echoing in the quiet night.

Several cars were scattered haphazardly under the light, their occupants moving slowly, purposefully. On a grassy patch just beyond the asphalt, a group of men loitered, talking and chuckling, their faces silhouetted by the harsh sodium street light. Another pair lingered near a sleek black sedan, watching the lot with keen interest. Jessi kept her seatbelt on, hands gripping the wheel, her pulse spiking with a cocktail of thrill and fear.

She breathed in slowly, trying to steady herself, her eyes flicking from the men to the darkness beyond. For a few moments, she just watched, feeling the rush of anticipation curl through her body. Her chest tightened, her skin hot in places she couldn't control. The compulsion, always lurking, always pushing, began whispering, urging her closer.

A few men wandered over toward her car, lingering just out of reach. Their glances felt heavy and loaded, and Jessi felt her heart hammering in her chest. Her fingers tightened around the steering wheel, and her mind spun in both directions, thrill and dread, excitement and fear.

And then, as her pulse raced and her breath came in short bursts, a single thought pierced through the haze: Becca.

The image of Becca's wide eyes, her gentle smile, the way she trusted her… it cut through the lust and the dark adrenaline like a cold blade. The room in her mind, the fantasies that had been pulling her forward, began to collapse under the weight of guilt and longing.

Jessi exhaled sharply, her hands trembling. She started the car and shifted into drive, staring for a moment longer at the men lingering nearby, their presence a siren call she couldn't answer. Her stomach churned with frustration and shame. She couldn't do it, not tonight, not like this.

The Mustang's engine rumbled as she eased back onto the road, the city lights of her neighborhood shimmering ahead. Her body buzzed with unsatisfied tension, her chest tight with guilt, and a sinking, helpless ache settled in her gut. She had chased the thrill, the darkness she craved, only to find herself undone by the one tether she couldn't break: Becca.

By the time she pulled into the apartment parking lot, the adrenaline had faded into a hollow ache. Jessi rested her forehead against the steering wheel for a long moment, tasting the bitterness of defeat. She hadn't failed because she was weak, she told herself, but because she still cared. And that, she realized with a pang, was both her anchor and her curse.

Inside the apartment, the quiet wrapped around her. The muffled hum of the air conditioning system, the soft ticking of the clock, even Bob's gentle purr as he padded around her legs, it all felt heavy with a weight she couldn't name. She had almost crossed a line, but she hadn't. And yet, the devastation lingered, a gnawing reminder that the thrill of her compulsion wasn't enough to silence the voice of what, and who, she truly cared about.

* * *

Saturday stretched long and heavy. The apartment felt emptier than usual, the sunlight through the blinds too bright, too sharp, cutting across the worn furniture. Jessi moved through the day like a shadow, restless, pacing between the kitchen and the living room, absently stroking Bob as he curled up beside her.

Her mind churned, looping over the night before, the lake, the men, the pull of the compulsion she'd nearly succumbed to, and the sharp, piercing thought of Becca. The guilt burned hotter than the thrill, yet the compulsion tugged at her chest like an insistent pulse she couldn't ignore.

When the phone rang that evening, she jumped slightly. Becca's name flashed on the screen, and Jessi hesitated for only a moment before answering.

"Hey," Jessi said, her voice tighter than she intended.

"Hey, you," Becca's warm, familiar tone drifted through the speaker. "How are you holding up?"

Jessi exhaled, trying to sound calm. "I'm… okay. Just, you know… keeping busy."

Becca laughed softly. "Busy being the mysterious temptress again?"

Jessi smirked faintly. "Something like that," she muttered.

They talked briefly, exchanging small snippets. Becca inquired about lunch, the weather, and how Bob was behaving. At one point, Becca even spoke with Amy and Traci when the girls stopped by to get ready for their Saturday party ritual, laughing as the three shared some playful teasing over the phone. Jessi listened quietly, the laughter washing over her like a temporary balm. Then there was the goodbye.

Pretending to be busy on her laptop, Jessi hid her mood from Amy and Traci. They joked and, as always, prodded her to come along, but Jessi just smiled and told them to have fun. When the girls finally left, the apartment was quiet again. Too quiet. The stillness pressed against Jessi, stoking that dark, insistent pulse she both feared and craved. Last night would have been cheating, but there were other ways to satisfy her urges.

Her hands trembled slightly as she opened the closet, sifting through clothes with no real thought. She grabbed the first things that felt easy to move in: an old white t-shirt, worn thin at the collar; a cheap pair of jogging shorts; and her flip-flops. No underwear, no bra, as usual. Everything else was forgotten as her mind raced with the familiar cocktail of risk and longing.

Keys and purse in hand, she paused at the door, her pulse quickening as the silence behind her grew heavier. The city beyond the apartment called to her, the empty streets, the unseen corners, the thrill of doing something she knew was reckless.

She swallowed, a hard knot in her stomach, but the compulsion was louder than fear now. It was almost unbearable, a tension that demanded release, a hunger that could only be sated by testing the edge.

Stepping out, the summer night air hit her skin, rustling her hair. The quiet of the early evening enveloped her, and for a moment, she froze on the sidewalk, the weight of what she was about to do pressing down.

Then, she exhaled sharply, slid into the Mustang, and started the engine. The dashboard lights glimmered in the darkness, and the low rumble of the engine beneath her legs was like a heartbeat she could sync with. Her heart pounded, not from fear alone, but from the adrenaline of the unknown, the dangerous path she was about to tread.

Tonight, there would be no Becca. No safety net. Just Jessi, the city, and whatever boundaries she dared to cross.

13
Twenty-Eight Blocks

Jessi's Mustang rolled to a stop a short distance from the strip club, the faint yellow glow of two street lamps casting long shadows across the gravel lot. The rest of the street was swallowed by darkness, and she preferred it that way. She parked along the roadside, just across from the building, leaving herself an easy exit if she needed it.

She sat gripping the steering wheel, heartbeat loud in her ears. "What is wrong with me?" she whispered to herself. "What the hell am I doing?" Butterflies churned in her stomach, her pulse quickened, and her fingers trembled. She reached for her phone and dialed the number scrawled on a scrap of paper.

"Hello? Yes… I need a cab. 102 East 4th Street… Tommy's… My name? Pam Martin." She ended the call, giggling at the ridiculous alias she'd chosen. Her plan was in motion.

The club was a plain cinder-block building, with neon signs flickering weakly and a handful of people moving in and out. Jessi strained to make out their silhouettes, but only shadows shifted behind the glass. She reached into her purse, pulled out a twenty-dollar bill, and tucked it into the waistband of her shorts. Then she retrieved a small black metal box from the glove compartment, detached her car key, and clicked it inside. After tucking her small purse under the seat, she gave a glance around. Stepping out of the car, she knelt at the front wheel well and attached the magnetized box to the underside of her vehicle. Locked doors, slam—done.

The warm summer night pressed around her. The faint sulfur scent of nearby factories lingered in the air, blending with the distant thrum of machinery and the muffled beats from inside the bar. This part of town was rough, always alive with late-night wanderers, and Jessi had mapped every angle in her mind.

This was a new level of risk, not like anything she had dared before. She had driven through the area several times months before, surveying the streets and the routes. This was not a midnight nature trail or an abandoned swimming area under the moonlight. This was urban; raw.

She adjusted her shorts and stepped closer to the club. A row of motorcycles gleamed under the light outside, Harleys, unmistakably, men loitering around them, beer in hand. Hard, dangerous types. She noted three men in particular: one perched on a bike, the other two leaning against it, laughing and nudging each other. Jessi's stomach fluttered.

Under the porch light, she kept her arms crossed, chin tucked, eyes darting. The bikers had noticed her.

Their laughter carried, sharp and hungry, and she felt naked under their gaze. Leather chaps, heavy jackets, tattoos partially hidden, symbols of a life she didn't belong in.

"Where's that damn taxi?" she whispered, heart hammering. Headlights cut across the street, but the first car passed by, disappearing into the night. The three men's attention sharpened.

"Hey! Come over here, honey!" one yelled, grinning.

She kept her head down, forcing a polite smile. The man stepped toward her, with long hair, a goatee, and a tattoo peeking from under his dirty t-shirt.

"Hey! I'm talking to you! Can't you hear me?"

"I'm just waiting on a taxi," she said, voice trembling.

"Well, hell, baby, we can take you wherever you want," he replied, laughter in his tone. His friends smirked and nodded.

Jessi's chest tightened. Her shirt was thin, almost see-through in the dim light. She considered slipping inside the club if things went too far. "I… I think I'll just wait," she stammered.

"Oh, come on, baby. You ever felt a 1200cc vibrator between your legs?"

Jessi gave a nervous laugh, then shuffled her feet.

"You should come inside. We'll have a little fun," he said with a grin.

Jessi turned and peered through the iron-barred doorway, through the haze of cigarette smoke and neon lights. She could see several other bikers, clad in various leather attire, holding pool cues, drinking beer, and laughing at something one of them said.

She turned back to the biker outside. "It looks like I might get eaten alive in there."

The biker laughed. "Yeah, that might be true, sugar pants. I bet you taste just like candy."

Jessi gave a nervous grin, then stepped back, not sure of what she should say or how to act. Then, headlights. Another vehicle turned onto the street, slowed, and pulled into the lot. Relief washed over her. She tried to hurry to the cab, but the biker stepped over and grabbed her wrist.

Shocked, Jessi just stood there. The biker then reached into his vest and pulled out a pen. He pulled Jessi's arm out and wrote his phone number across her skin. "Name's Spike. You ever get brave, little girl; you just give me a call."

Jessi just smiled and nodded. He let go of her wrist, and she quickly opened the door and slid into the backseat.

"Aww!" the men called after her, feigning heartbreak.

"203 East 28th Street. And let's get out of here quickly, please," Jessi said, voice shaking but firm.

"No problem," the driver replied.

As the cab pulled away, she watched the bikers laughing and gesturing after her. Jessi let out a heavy breath, tension slowly leaving her body. She smiled faintly, knowing this was only the beginning.

***

"Are you sure this is the place, ma'am?" the cab driver asked, his voice carrying a note of concern.

Jessi glanced at the abandoned factory buildings around her, dark and silent, their windows blacked out and broken. "Yes," she said firmly. "This is it. Thank you. How much do I owe you?"

"$8.50, ma'am. Are you really sure this is right? I can wait if you want."

She smiled faintly at him. He was an older man, with graying hair at his temples, eyes warm and cautious. "No, this is fine," she said, fishing the twenty-dollar bill from her shorts and handing it to him. "Keep the change." She opened the door and stepped out, shutting it behind her.

"Have a good evening," he said, shaking his head as he watched her walk toward the darkened street, disappearing into the shadows.

Jessi paused, surveying her surroundings. She watched as the taillights from the cab disappeared down the darkened road. The street was nearly deserted, lit only by distant factory lights and the occasional flicker from a cracked window. The night was eerily quiet, no barking dogs, no distant voices, just the hum of an unseen brook nearby. She had been here before, during the day on one of her scouting trips, but tonight everything felt sharper, alive. She kicked off her flip flops and moved slowly toward a bridge spanning a small flowing creek, the next step in her game.

The concrete beneath her bare feet radiated the heat of the day. She set her footwear on the railing, then lifted her shirt up and over her head. Her shorts next slipped from her body, leaving her exposed to the night air. Wrapping the garments around her footwear, she looked down at the dark water below.

She cursed her devious imagination. Her mind didn't have to push her to complete some daring tasks; it only needed to move her to the point of no return. It was the fear, the risk, the danger that made her feel something; made her feel desired somehow; alive.

There would be no going back if she went through with it. Her heart was pounding in her chest; goose bumps formed on her naked flesh; her nipples were erect and hard. In one swift motion, she tossed the bundle into the dark waters below.

Grabbing hold of the railing, Jessi suddenly began to hyperventilate. As she gasped for air, she watched the white cloth float swiftly down the murky stream and out of view. She felt as though she were about to be sick. She closed her eyes and worked to control her breathing. Her heart pounded so hard she could hear her pulse inside her head.

It was always the same: the thrill and anticipation, followed by fear, regret, and even guilt. Her mind pushed her schemes so there would be no turning back, forcing her to face her challenge head-on. As tears began to form in her eyes, she stood upright and tried to regain her composure. "That's it," she said. "I have no choice now."

She looked down the empty street. Nearly three miles, or twenty-four blocks, separated her from her car, and though the area around the bridge was deserted, she knew the blocks ahead would be lined with homes, businesses, and who knows what else. She cursed herself; one wrong step, one encounter, and she could be in real danger.

But, while she cursed her perverted mind, she also felt a sense of euphoria. The fear made her feel alive, and she had never felt as alive as she did right now. Every sense was on fire. To her, it was as intoxicating as any drug could ever be.

Jessi took a deep breath and started down the roadway again. She walked down the sidewalk for the first five blocks, holding her arms up to her chest, shielding her breast from the night air. There had been no streetlights on her path, and she merely strolled down the walkway as if she were walking to the store or was out for an exercise.

She gazed at the row of empty buildings to either side of the road as she walked, wondering what might have been made in the factories back in the day. She thought there would be more traffic on the road at that time of night, but had yet to see a vehicle. She was constantly looking for places to hide in case she saw an oncoming car, but there were no headlights in sight.

Her luck quickly changed, however, as she soon found herself approaching a fairly well-lit section of the road. She slowed her pace as she approached the area. The streetlights were bright, bathing the boulevard and sidewalk in a sickly yellow glow. She knew this was a part of her path where there were homes on both sides of the street, and she stopped to survey the passage.

As she looked down the street, she was again beginning to feel that rush of exhilaration that she had craved for several weeks. She couldn't help but feel her body tingling all over. Reaching down between her legs, she began rubbing her slit. It was warm, and her excitement made it drip between her fingers. Reaching up with her other hand, she gently rolled one of her nipples between finger and thumb. She had no idea why it took this type of situation for her to feel this way, but it did. She felt shame and ecstasy all at the same time.

Steeling herself, she again started down the sidewalk. Jessi slowed, scanning the houses and front yards. They were poor homes, run-down and shabby, but she could tell they were occupied, with the occasional lamp or television light emanating from their windows. She could also see that several front yards had hedgerows or fences lining their borders.

She crouched and turned her head slightly, listening intently for any sound to be heard. Hearing nothing, Jessi stood upright and whispered, "Damn." She could either move forward down the sidewalk, or maybe she could make her way through the backyards of the homes. Jessi reached up and ran her fingers through her hair as she thought. *If I go through the backyards, it will be dark, but I might run into a dog or something,* she thought to herself. She also thought there may be fences she would have to cross, and being totally naked, she was in no condition to jump a chain-link fence.

Giving a heavy sigh, she looked forward. She had made her decision; she would walk down the sidewalk as if nothing was wrong. If she were to notice someone, she would dash to the nearest hiding spot. As she strolled into the light, Jessi felt a rush. Here she was, out in the open, and totally exposed to anyone who might happen upon her. *My God, I can't believe this,* she thought.

She was beginning to regret her decision to discard her shoes, as she could see broken bottles and glass sparkling in the light on the sidewalk. Jessi had even noticed a used syringe lying on the walkway, near a telephone pole. She now kept her eyes on the concrete, keeping a close eye on where she stepped as she walked at a steady pace.

For another three blocks, Jessi walked in the basking yellow light without seeing a soul or hearing so much as a bark. She was beginning to think her challenge had once again been too easy. She now walked with her hands to her side at a casual pace, but still scanning the sidewalk for any sharp obstacles.

It was then that she heard the shout. "Woo hoo!" echoed throughout the neighborhood.

In an instant, Jessi stepped into a darkened lawn and crouched down behind a bush. She looked in all directions, desperately searching for where the voice had come from. Her body trembled, and her heart raced. In all her outings, this was the first time that she knew someone had seen her.

"Did you see that?" the voice yelled again.

Jessi could hear other voices, but the sounds were unintelligible to her. Nevertheless, it was apparent there was more than one. Almost in a frenzy, she scanned all around. Just then, she saw where the voices were coming from. It was behind her, a couple of houses down. There, she could make out the shape of five boys coming out from the shadows of the front porch of one of the homes. She had obviously walked right in front of them.

Damn it, she thought. She had been paying so much attention to where she stepped that she had let her guard down.

"Yo man, she was naked, I tell you!" one of the boys yelled. "Dat bitch was buck ass naked, I swear to God!"

"Naw," another said. "You're a crazy mother fucker."

Jessi looked on as they emerged from the darkness. She could tell they were all Hispanic. They were all young, well-built boys, maybe in their late teens or early twenties. She could see that two of the boys were wearing white tank tops with dew rags on top of their heads. The others were wearing plaid shirts unbuttoned over T-shirts; one had a bandana around his head, while the others wore ball caps turned backwards.

"Shit," she blurted. She knew these were not the kind of boys who needed to find a naked white girl in their neighborhood. She watched as they argued. It was evident that only one of them had actually seen her, and he was trying to convince the others of his discovery.

"I'll prove it to you, God damn it!" the boy screamed. "Bitch walked right down here."

She could see that the boy yelling was muscular, with intricate tattoos displayed from both wrists to his shoulders.

"You're full of shit," another boy laughed. "Ain't no bitch walking around here naked, less she some crack ho."

Again, Jessi's heart was racing. She stood motionless as the young men drew nearer. Another decision had to be made; either she stayed at her hiding spot, hoping they didn't find her, or she could make a run for it. If she did decide to run, it was apparent she wouldn't be able to continue down the street she was on. She would have to run one or two streets over, then continue her way towards 4th Street. She looked down the roadway, and to her right, she could see a cross street about three houses down. She tried to peer through the darkness at the yards between her and the road, but the large trees on the lawns blocked the light.

The boys were jumping into the yards behind her, hooting and hollering as they swept around every tree and bush. She was going to have to run for it. She decided she would run through the darkened front lawns in front of her, hoping none had a fence or any other obstacle to block her way. With a bit of luck, they wouldn't see her. It was the only chance she had of getting away. Slowly she counted, "One …. two … three," and she was off.

"There she is! There she is!" one of the boys screamed. "Holy shit, get her!"

Jessi never looked back. She darted through the first yard like a gazelle with a cheetah behind it. She could hear the gang in pursuit behind her, yelling and screaming along the way. Reaching the second yard, she noticed trim hedgerows lining both sides of the sidewalk leading to the front door of the house. She kept her pace as she leapt across, hurdling both hedges and sidewalk in one stride.

Bolting through the shadowy third yard, she zigzagged around several shrubs and made her way to the far corner of the house. There she tried to turn and head for the adjacent cross street, but it was then that she felt her feet come out from under her. The humid air had left the grass heavy with dew, and Jessi found her bare feet had little traction. She slid on her butt for several feet before coming to a stop.

Quickly, she looked back. She could see three of the boys barreling their way through the bushes, coming straight for her. They were laughing and yelling as they neared the frightened auburn-haired daredevil.

In an instant, Jessi had jumped to her feet and was once again on her way to the street. The road was not lit, and she found the warm pavement more reassuring than the wet grass beneath her bare feet. Not wanting to wear herself out, she tried to pace herself, controlling her breathing and speed. She could hear the steps of her pursuers closing in behind her. She had always been a good runner and knew if she could keep in front of them, she could probably outlast them.

But they were gaining on her quickly, and she had to move as fast as she could. Jessi could hear the footsteps draw closer and closer, and she dared to look over her shoulder. One of the boys was now only a car length behind her. He was a muscular youth with a shaved head. She could tell he was one of the boys who had been wearing a dew rag, but he had obviously lost the item somewhere during the chase.

She could see that the other two, who had been close, were now fading and losing distance. They were shouting and urging their friend on as he closed in. He was fast and still gaining ground, and her legs began to ache as she pushed herself. Her bare breasts bounced as she ran and began to hurt. She grunted with every stride, mixing with her heavy panting breaths.

Jessi continued as fast as she could and made a quick turn onto a road that paralleled the one that she had first been on when she started her trek. The street was darker than the previous route, and she could tell she was once again running through a row of older homes. The boy was now right behind her as he chased her. She could hear him breathing heavy and groaning as he pushed forward. No longer was he yelling and screaming; he was trying to take in every ounce of air he could manage.

Suddenly Jessi could feel his fingers on her back. He was reaching out, trying to grab her, his fingertips just within reach, grasping at her dark red locks. Letting out a yelp, she pushed as hard as she could. *Oh my God*, she thought. *He's going to catch me.*

She imagined her fate, chained in some basement and taken over and over again for days. Tears began to well up in her eyes. Her feet were raw. She couldn't keep this pace much longer.

Just then, she could hear the boy's footsteps fading. She kept her fast stride for another fifty yards before looking back. She could see him, stopped, hands on his knees, and gasping for air. She could also see him pointing at her, trying to make some sly remark, but his lack of breath kept him from uttering a word. He only stood, bent over, with labored breaths.

She continued to run until she was well away from the boy. Slowing her pace, she continued for another block before she made her way to the side of a house at the corner of a side street. There, she collapsed in the murky shadows of the driveway near the home's garage. She sat up, bringing her hands up to her face, trying to muffle her uncontrollable huffing and puffing. She had never run so hard in all her life. Her muscles ached, and her legs were on fire. She could feel the heat of her body and the beads of sweat that had formed across her bare flesh.

Jessi lay there trying to regain her breath and ease her racing heart. She knew if she were found at that moment, she would not be able to get away. She reached up and cupped her hands over her mouth, trying to muffle her gasps. Reaching back, she rubbed her butt, caressing the spot she had fallen on earlier. There would definitely be a big bruise there in the morning. As her breathing became more controlled, her heartbeat slowing, Jessi covered her face and began to sob.

Jessi sat alone in the darkness for what seemed like an eternity. Her mouth was parched from the dash, and she believed she could kill for just a glass of water. Keeping low and listening intently, she surveyed her surroundings.

Several times, she had noticed a low-ride car pass down the street, driving slowly as if the occupants were looking for something. She could only guess that it was the Latino gang, now mobile and searching for their intended prey. She looked around, knowing she was going to have to move eventually. She couldn't stay where she was all night. Slowly, she rose to her feet and cautiously made her way back to the side of the roadway.

She was cursing her mind for deciding not to wear shoes. Her feet were raw from her recent scamper, and her legs were sore and throbbing. Her hair was hot and damp, and she could feel the perspiration on her bare body dripping down her back and chest.

Keeping to the side of the road, she stayed in the shadows of the large oaks and maples that bordered the street. She walked just on the edge of the yards, the cool dew on the grass now feeling good on the bottom of her feet. She was one street over from the route she had previously been on, but was still traveling in the right direction. She had lost track of exactly where she was, but surmised that she was more than halfway to her car. But she had to be careful. With another incident like the one before, she would probably give up and hope for the best.

From yard to yard, Jessi crept down the street, passing one block, then another. Looking at the street signs, she gained her bearings. She was on the corner of Robinson Road and 11th Street; there were still seven blocks to go. Suddenly, she heard a dog barking from behind a home up ahead of her. The sound instantly aroused the other dogs in the neighborhood, prompting a chorus of barking in all directions.

She sneaked behind a tree and watched for any movement in front of her. It was then that she noticed a set of headlights approaching from behind. It was the same automobile she had seen several times before. She turned and made her way to the other side of the tree, where she carefully peered out and spied the vehicle.

It was a four-door car that sat low to the ground. She could see its large chrome wheels, with their thin-profiled tires wrapped around them. The car seemed to change color as it passed from one streetlight to another. It was moving slowly, and she could hear rap music blaring from within. She knew there were at least four people inside the vehicle as she could see one arm hanging out of each open window. She tried in vain to see who was inside, with the vehicle's dash lights only faintly highlighting the faces inside.

Jessi shook uncontrollably as she continued to look on. She knew in her heart that it was the boys who had been chasing her. "They're not going to give up," she said to herself. "My God. I have to make it to my car." She looked down the roadway. "I will never do this again," she swore to herself. "Just let me get to my car and go home."

She watched as the car leisurely traveled past her. She could hear the men laughing inside. *This is fun to them,* she thought. *They are enjoying this little chase.* But she wasn't going to make it easy. If she could make it maybe one more mile, she would be free. As the car's taillights faded out of sight, Jessi pushed herself onward. The dogs were still barking, but not just one; several could be heard, and all around her. She believed that as long as several animals were carrying on, her position wouldn't be revealed.

Again, she sneaked from yard to yard, block by block, taking shelter beneath the shadows of the trees. Occasionally, she found herself making a mad dash beneath the light of the street lamps as she came to a lawn blocked by a fence or wall. At one point, she watched as a front porch light was turned on in front of her. She had hunched down behind a parked car, in an adjacent driveway, and watched as the homeowner walked outside and lit a cigarette. She guessed she was delayed for eight or nine minutes as she watched the man puff and blow smoke from between his lips. She sat silently watching the man, biting her bottom lip to make sure she didn't utter a sound. She then noticed the man drop the cigarette on the ground and stomp it out. He then casually walked inside and turned off the light.

With a heavy sigh, she gathered herself and, after traveling a couple more blocks, soon found herself in another predicament. Standing at the corner of Robinson and 7th Street, she could see that the next leg of her journey took her past a small park. To her left stood several basketball courts, surrounded by very tall chain link fences. On her right was an enormous security wall that spanned several hundred feet down the road.

At first, she thought she might be able to travel through the ball courts and reemerge somewhere on the other side. But, after a closer look, she realized the gates to the courts were chained and padlocked. Her only advantage was that the park didn't seem to have any lights, and with the gates locked, it was likely no one was inside.

Jessi sat in the darkness for several minutes, assessing the path in front of her. She wanted to be careful; gang members were searching for her, and she didn't need any more people on her trail or alerting them to her whereabouts. But she could see no other route. She decided she would have to make another hard run until she reached the next block. She hadn't scouted this street during the planning of her dare, and she wasn't sure what lay beyond her newest obstacles. She could only hope there were trees or bushes to hide behind.

In the shadows, she crouched on all fours as if she were prepared for some race. Taking a deep breath, she came to her feet and sprinted across the road, into the unwelcomed illumination of the streetlights.

Her fists clenched tight, Jessi swung her arms as she raced down the sidewalk. The night air now felt cool on her damp skin, her nipples tight and erect. She concentrated hard on controlling her breathing as she darted past one telephone pole to the next. In the distance, she could hear the sound of a loud car engine and tires squealing, one or two streets over.

The noise had scared her, and her mind wondered if it had anything to do with her. She kept her focus. She had to make it to the next block.

For a moment, she had to dart into the middle of the roadway as she dodged a couple of metal garbage cans that blocked the sidewalk. But in an instant, she was back on the concrete path and could see the next street in the distance, another row of houses just beyond. She also noticed she was now running next to a baseball field. She was at the outfield end of the field and thought that if she had to, she could climb this smaller fence to find an escape route.

It was then that she thought she heard voices coming from near the dark baseball diamond. She tried to listen over the sounds of her regulated gasps, but she couldn't be sure if it was voices or just the night playing tricks on her. If there was someone there, perhaps she was too far away to see that she wasn't wearing clothes. She really didn't care at this point; it was too late to worry about. She had to make it to the safety of the trees ahead of her.

It took only a few more seconds before she reached the next cross street and the homes beyond. She jogged past the first house, which was on a corner lot and had few trees, and took refuge in the lawn of the next home. There she jaunted behind a set of hydrangea bushes. She lay down in the grass, flat on her back, and again attempted to slow her pulse and breathing.

As she rested, she gazed up at the stars. She was deep in the city, and the surrounding lights illuminated the sky, drowning out the light from the smaller celestial bodies. But she could easily make out the larger stars and even noticed a shooting star as it streaked across the sky. She closed her eyes and made a wish, thinking of that night with Rebecca. She thought to herself, *I'm almost home.*

Jessi continued on her stealthy journey, darting here and there and hiding at points along the way. After a few minutes, she found herself on another side street. The sign read, 5th Street. *I'm almost at the club*, she thought. Across the street, she could see a vacant lot. There were no more houses or buildings in front of her, and she could see the rear of the bar in the distance. There were no streetlights either, but another problem had arisen. She could see that the lot was bare, with no trees, no bushes, and no places to hide if anyone were to spot her. But there was no other way, and her need to reach her destination outweighed her need for stealth at the moment.

She had already planned what she was going to do. She would dart across the lot and make her way to the back of the club. Once there, she would make a mad dash for her car and not worry whether anyone saw her. The surprise she would give any onlooker would surely buy her enough time to reach the key and unlock her car. She would then speed away as fast as she could.

Hurriedly, Jessi jogged across the empty land. It was a gravel lot, and the tiny rocks cut into the souls of her already raw feet. But the adrenaline was flowing through her body, and it masked her pain with determination. She had made it three-quarters of the way across the lot when, once again, she noticed headlights on the road behind her.

Quickly, she dropped down, spread-eagled on her belly. She could feel the gravel and grime stick to her body. She looked behind her and could see the same car, slowly rolling down the road on the other side of the lot. She could hear the muted rumble coming from the vehicle's exhaust. She felt as though her heart would burst from her chest. *I'm so close, they can't catch me now.*

Again, the car slowly rolled down the roadway. *They didn't see me*, she thought. Not waiting for the car to drive out of sight, Jessi swiftly sprang to her feet and sprinted for the building. She ran with all the strength that she had left, pushing her body to the brink of its limits.

Suddenly, she could hear the thunder coming from the car's mufflers. As she looked back, she could see the car speeding down the street, away from her, in the opposite direction. She wasn't sure if they had seen her, and she didn't care. In just a few moments, she could reach her vehicle.

Reaching the back of the club, Jessi crouched next to a dumpster. A sour and putrid smell permeated the air around her, and it almost made her gag. Quickly, she ran around the corner of the building and made her way to the front edge of the business. She leaned back against the cinderblock wall, taking a moment to catch her breath, then peered around the corner to where her car was parked.

The night pressed in around her, the faint buzz of a neon sign, the distant laughter from inside the bar. She needed to move. Quickly. Her green Mustang shimmered under the streetlight, like a beacon calling her to it. She glanced to the front of the bar. A couple of bikers were outside, sitting on their bikes and engaged in deep conversation. She had to make it to her car without being seen by them.

Her stomach churned inside her. "Oh my God! Oh my God! Oh my God!" she repeated softly over and over. "What am I going to do now?" Slowly, she arose to her feet, letting her back slide its way up the painted block wall. She turned, looking out over the parking lot, where numerous cars, trucks, and motorcycles were parked all around.

Jessi froze, watching the bikers' every move, calculating how she could cross the lot unseen. She pressed her palms flat against the wall, grounding herself, willing her breathing to slow. The adrenaline buzzed in her veins, almost dizzying. Every nerve screamed for her to run, but any movement would draw attention.

She looked again toward the car, her one safe place, and made herself a promise. One deep breath. One clean shot across the lot. If she timed it right, she could make it before anyone noticed.

The bikers' laughter rose again, then died down. One of them flicked a cigarette into the street and turned toward the door.

Now or never.

Jessi exhaled, pushed off the wall, and bolted for the car.

Jessi sprinted across the gravel lot, her bare feet stinging with each stride. Every sound felt magnified, the grunts she found herself making, the thud of her heartbeat in her ears. She reached under the wheel well and quickly grabbed the keyholder. Popping it open, she grabbed the key and struggled to fit it into the keyhole of the door. She hadn't even noticed the shouts coming from the bikers outside the bar. She yanked the car door open and slid inside, slamming it shut behind her as if she could lock the whole world out.

For a second, she just sat there, gripping the steering wheel, chest heaving. The Mustang's interior smelled faintly of vinyl and her perfume, but the safety she expected to feel didn't come. Instead, her hands were shaking so badly she could barely fit the key into the ignition.

When the engine roared to life, she let out a strangled laugh that was half-sigh, half-sob. "What am I doing?" she whispered. She threw the car into drive and peeled out, the neon of the bar shrinking in the mirror until it vanished into the dark.

The road home blurred. She didn't care that she was still nude. She didn't try to avoid any routes. Streetlights smeared across her windshield, and her thoughts tangled with them, Marcus's voice, the memory of his calm certainty, the look in his eyes when he called her dangerous. He was right. She was drifting somewhere she didn't understand.

By the time she reached her apartment, the adrenaline had burned away, leaving her hollow and trembling. Sneaking in the darkness, she stumbled inside, locked the door, and slid down against it until she was sitting on the floor. The silence hit her like a wave.

Her throat tightened. The whole night replayed in her mind; each moment had felt like standing on the edge of a cliff. She pressed her face into her hands. *You're losing it, Jess*, she thought. *You're chasing something that's going to eat you alive.*

But even through the shame and fear, a small, treacherous part of her still hummed with the memory of that rush, the heartbeat of danger, the nearness of surrender. It terrified her how much she wanted to feel it again.

She sat there in the dark for a long time, her feet raw, muscles burning; the abrasion on her butt aching. Eventually, she whispered, "Becca, please come home," though she knew Becca couldn't hear her.

The tears came then, slow and exhausted, and when they finally stopped, Jessi felt wrung out, empty, and no closer to understanding the darkness that kept calling her name.

14
Hiding Within

The apartment was still when Becca turned her key in the lock. She eased the door open, suitcase rolling softly over the threshold. The faint smell of Jessi's perfume soap in the air, something floral.

"Jessi?" Becca called quietly.

A muffled sound came from the couch. Jessi sat up, hair tangled and flat, eyes puffy and red. She smiled quickly, too quickly. "Hey, you're home."

Becca set down her bag and studied her. Jessi was still wearing the same white t-shirt from Thursday night, the hem wrinkled and twisted around her legs. The coffee table in front of her was littered with an empty Coke bottle, a half-burned candle, and her phone facedown.

"Hey," Becca said softly, trying to sound casual. "You look… tired."

"Didn't sleep great," Jessi said with a shrug, forcing a small laugh. "You know me."

Becca smiled, but it didn't reach her eyes. "Rough weekend?"

"Nah. Amy and Traci came over last night for a bit. Nothing major."

Becca sat down beside her on the couch, brushing a few stray crumbs off the cushion before she did. Jessi's knee bounced slightly, just enough to betray the edge beneath her words. Becca reached out and stilled it with a hand.

"Your hair… It's a mess."

"Yeah," Jessi said as she ran her fingers through the mop. "I took a bath last night and must have fallen asleep before drying it."

Becca nodded, still watching her. There was something brittle in Jessi's voice, a hollow cheerfulness that rang false. Her eyes darted toward the window, avoiding Becca's gaze.

Becca leaned back and sighed. "Mom and Dad were… actually decent. I didn't expect that."

"Really?" Jessi perked up slightly, eager for the change of subject. "That's great, Bec."

"Yeah," Becca said, though she didn't sound convinced. She reached for the remote, turned off the TV that had been silently looping through a screensaver of glowing fish. "Feels weird, though. Like they were trying too hard."

"People change," Jessi said softly, almost as if to herself.

Becca looked at her, really looked at her, and saw something flicker behind her friend's eyes. Fatigue. Shame, maybe. Or something darker she couldn't name.

"Did you eat?" Becca asked.

"Yeah," Jessi lied.

Becca stood, walked to the kitchen, and returned with a banana and a granola bar, setting them on the table. Jessi smiled faintly.

"Thanks, Mom," she teased weakly.

Becca managed a small laugh, but inside, unease coiled tight. She didn't know what Jessi had done while she was gone, but she could feel it in the air, like static before a storm.

She'd seen this before, pieces of it, after certain nights, certain moods. Whatever Jessi had been chasing, Becca could tell it had left her emptier than before.

Jessi leaned back against the couch, her legs still sore, rubbing her arms absently. "How was the funeral?" she asked.

Becca's voice carried a quiet warmth. "It was sad, Jessi… really sad. But it went well. I saw so many people I hadn't seen in years, friends, family… it was overwhelming in a way, but good to reconnect."

Jessi exhaled slowly. "And… your parents? How did that go?"

"They took me out to dinner afterward," Becca said, a note of relief in her tone. "We had a long talk. They… tried to put some things behind us, Jessi. We even discussed… maybe… helping me go back to college. It feels like there's a possibility now, you know?"

Jessi shifted on the couch, her stomach tightening. "And… did you… Tell them about us? About you and me?" Her voice was careful, probing.

Becca hesitated, a faint pause stretching across the line. "I… alluded to it," she said finally. "I didn't exactly come out and say it. I wanted to ease into it; not throw them into a conversation they weren't ready for."

Jessi's chest constricted. She tried to mask the unease in her voice. "I see."

"I know it worries you," Becca continued gently. "I promise, I'll tell them eventually. I just… wanted to make sure the moment was right. I didn't want to force it or make things worse than they already are."

Jessi nodded. "Yeah… I get it," she murmured, her mind turning over the implications. The thought of Becca softening her parents, while also holding back the truth about them, left her restless. The worry gnawed at her, tugging at the edge of that darker, impulsive side she had been struggling to contain.

By late morning, Becca had begun tidying the apartment, putting away her suitcase and straightening the cushions. She glanced over at Jessi, who was perched on the couch with her legs tucked beneath her, absently rubbing at her calves.

"Your legs," Becca said softly, approaching her. "You're… sore?"

Jessi's head snapped up, and she gave a quick, easy laugh. "Ah, it's nothing. Just… slipped yesterday." She tried to brush it off with a casual wave, but Becca noticed the way her thighs tensed as she shifted.

Becca knelt slightly to get a closer look. The skin on the back of Jessi's legs was reddened, with minor abrasions catching the morning light. Her eyes flicked to Jessi's rear as she adjusted on the couch, and she noticed a faint scrape on the upper curve of her butt, raw and pink.

"Jessi…" Becca said, her voice careful now. "This looks worse than just a slip. Turn over."

Jessi shrugged, trying to hide the pain with a smile. "Really, it's fine. I slipped on some wet grass. No big deal."

"Turn over," Becca commanded with her hands on her hips.

Jessi huffed and rolled her eyes before turning over on her belly.

Becca reached out and pulled her shorts down slightly, brushing her fingertips lightly over the tender spots. "Jessi! That has to hurt. Oh my gosh." Becca rushed into the bathroom and returned with a tube of Neosporin. Dabbing a glob onto her fingers, she gently rubbed the wound.

Jessi sucked in air and held her breath, her muscles tensing with the touch.

"Why didn't you say something?" Becca asked.

Jessi swallowed, a flicker of guilt passing over her features. "I… I just didn't want to worry you. You've been gone, and I didn't want to ruin the weekend you were trying to mend with your parents. It's not that big a deal."

Becca's expression softened, but concern lingered. "Jessi… I need you to be honest with me. You're scaring me a little here. I can tell something happened, or maybe more than one thing. You don't have to explain everything, but… Jessi."

Jessi exhaled, a mixture of relief and frustration. "I slipped. I swear. I'm fine, really. I'll tell you more about it later, but right now let's just have a nice day." She turned over and tried to shift her position to hide the scrape more, but Becca's eyes followed her, unwavering.

Becca sighed and gave her shoulder a gentle squeeze. "Okay."

Jessi nodded, forcing another small smile, but inside, a storm of shame, excitement, and lingering guilt churned. She hadn't lied entirely, but Becca's worry had touched the raw nerve of her secret weekend. And even as she nodded, part of her ached for the thrill she had chased, the one she could never admit to anyone, not even Becca.

* * *

The rest of the morning passed slowly. Becca moved around the apartment, putting things away from her trip, and talked to Jessi about everyday topics. Jessi nodded, answered, laughed lightly at the right moments, but her mind was elsewhere, on the surge of adrenaline she had felt, the thrill she had sought, and the guilt that now pressed heavily against her. Every slight touch from Becca, every gentle glance, reminded her of what she had risked, and of the dark desire still simmering beneath her skin.

***

By late afternoon, Becca went into the kitchen to start prepping lunch. Jessi stayed on the couch, curling up slightly, absently rubbing her sore legs. When Becca called out that lunch was ready, Jessi forced herself upright, smiling faintly. "Coming."

They ate in silence for a while, the normalcy of the routine contrasting sharply with the chaos brewing inside Jessi. Afterward, Becca washed the dishes while Jessi lingered at the window, staring out at the street. She tried to focus on the sunlight, the mundane rhythm of cars and pedestrians passing by, but her thoughts kept drifting to the previous night, the danger, the thrill, the escape.

As the evening approached, Becca suggested they relax on the couch with Bob. Jessi nodded, curling up beside her, resting her head against Becca's shoulder. Together, side by side, they lay there watching *An Affair to Remember* on the TV. "That's Cary Grant," Jessi said as she let out a quiet sigh.

Becca turned and smiled, giving Jessi a quick peck on the lips.

The quiet settled around them, but Jessi knew it was only a matter of time before her compulsion stirred again. And deep down, part of her feared that when it did, there might be no turning back.

15
Confessions

Monday evening settled in quietly; the air filled with the faint aroma of soy sauce and garlic from the steaming Chinese takeout boxes spread across the kitchen table. Jessi and Becca had both come home from work, each tired but carrying the invisible weight of their separate days.

Becca poured herself some sweet tea while Jessi carefully unwrapped her chopsticks, her fingers trembling slightly, not from fatigue, but from the words she had been turning over in her mind all day.

"So… I got us some General Tso's and fried rice," Becca said, trying to infuse cheerfulness into the quiet kitchen. "Thought it might be nice to just… relax for a little while."

Jessi nodded, giving a small smile she hoped looked natural. "Yeah… sounds good."

They ate in a rhythm that was easy but quiet, the clatter of takeout containers and the soft scraping of chopsticks filling the spaces where conversation might have gone. Jessi's thoughts, however, were anything but calm. She had rehearsed the confession in her mind, twisted it, softened it, and delayed it, but now, sitting across from Becca, the words felt impossibly heavy.

Finally, she lowered her chopsticks, exhaling through her nose. "Becca… I… um…" Her voice faltered. She clenched her fists on the table, willing the courage to form the sentence. "There's something I need to tell you."

The weight in her tone made Becca's stomach knot. "Okay," she said carefully.

Jessi looked down, her chopsticks nervously rearranging her food. "Last Saturday… I… went somewhere."

Becca's heart thudded. "Where?"

Jessi inhaled sharply, the words rushing out before she could stop them. "I drove into the city, a rough part of town, and then…" She shut her eyes. "I made a little challenge for myself."

Becca blinked, not sure she'd heard right. "You what?"

Jessi went through the entire story, the bikers, the cab, standing on the bridge, and throwing her clothes in. She took a deep breath, then told of the boys who chased her and how she had slipped trying to get away. Jessi kept her head low, as if she were a child confessing to her parent.

"I managed to outrun them," Jessi said quickly, her words tumbling in a desperate rush. "I ducked behind a dumpster, then made a run for it back to my car." She broke off, her hands trembling. "That was what I did. That's how I was injured."

Becca's breath caught in her throat, horrified. The silence between them was thick, suffocating. Her eyes filled, but not with tears this time, with fury. Her voice shook, raw and sharp: "You lied to me!"

Jessi flinched. "I didn't…

"No!" Becca's hand slammed against the table, rattling the dishes. "You lied, Jessi! And not just that, you put yourself in insane danger! Do you even realize what could have happened? You could've been beaten, assaulted, or killed. And I would've been there, waiting by my phone, thinking you just needed sleep."

Jessi's lips parted, her breath shallow, but no defense came.

Becca pushed back from the table, pacing, her voice breaking with anger and fear all at once. "Do you think this is fair? To me? To anyone who cares about you? You don't just risk your own life when you do this; you drag me into it. You make me sit here, powerless, while you run around like you're trying to get hurt."

Jessi swallowed hard, her guilt plain on her face.

Becca's hands clenched at her sides. "I'm angry because I care, Jessi. Because I can't stand the thought of losing you. And you…" Her voice faltered, softer now, almost pleading. "You keep throwing yourself to the wolves like you want to sacrifice yourself."

The room was still, but charged; Jessi trembled in her chair, Becca standing rigid with emotion she could barely contain.

"I'm sorry," Jessi whispered, tears pricking at the corners of her eyes. "I didn't tell you… I didn't want you to worry. But I couldn't… I just couldn't stop myself." She swallowed and looked up at Becca. "The thing is… I was scared, really scared… and… I liked it. It makes me feel… alive. I know that sounds weird. It's hard to explain. I think back to that night, and now I keep thinking to myself… what if they had caught me? What would they have done?" She took another breath, "My mind… it fantasizes about what would have happened."

Becca's voice was quiet but firm, carrying both concern and steadiness. "Jessi… we need to talk about this… about how far you pushed yourself, and how dangerous it got. Jessi… baby… maybe you need help."

Jessi shook her head, shame and relief mingling in her chest. "I don't know… I just… I can't stop it. Things get in my head and they… just grow. I just… it makes me feel alive."

Becca squeezed her hand. "You don't have to put yourself at risk like that. We'll figure out another way to… cope with it. Together."

Jessi exhaled, leaning slightly into Becca's hand, feeling both guilty and comforted. For the first time since Saturday, the tension in her chest eased just a little. The takeout sat between them, untouched now, but in that quiet moment, it didn't matter.

"I think… I need another bath," Jessi said after a pause, glancing toward the bathroom. "To… just soak."

She rose slowly, moving toward the bathroom. Becca sat at the table with a reassuring gaze. The water ran hot, steam curling around her like a soft shield, and Jessi closed her eyes, letting herself sink into the warmth. The shame, fear, and guilt still lingered, but for the first time since the incident, she felt a thread of control returning. She didn't need to be perfect; she just needed to be safe, for now.

Becca sat at the table, lost in thought, the plates of takeout pushed aside. She reached up and rubbed her temples, not knowing if her words had reached Jessi. She wasn't sure how to help, but she knew she had to try.

"What do I even do?" Becca muttered to herself, barely audible. She took a slow breath, trying to steady the rising panic. "I can't just… tell her not to do it. That won't work. She's too… complicated. Too strong-willed. But if I let her keep going… I don't know if she'll survive it next time."

She leaned back in her chair, head resting in her hands. Her gaze drifted to the counter, where Jessi had left her things scattered: her laptop, a loop of string, and her car keys. Each one was a reminder that Jessi had her routines, her coping mechanisms, and a world Becca could never fully enter.

She glanced toward the couch, where Bob had curled up for a nap, and his quiet presence gave her a fraction of comfort. Becca's jaw clenched. "I can't fix this with a pat on the head and an 'I need you.' She needs more… more than I can give sometimes. But I'll try. She's worth it. She's worth everything."

* * *

The week unfolded with a rhythm both familiar and fragile. Jessi seemed… lighter, almost radiant. She laughed more freely, spoke with warmth and enthusiasm, and even lingered longer in the kitchen while making tea, humming a tune she hadn't sung in months.

Becca watched her closely, a careful observer of the fragile joy that danced across Jessi's features. She knew the signs, the sudden bursts of energy, the impulsive plans, the way Jessi's eyes seemed to sparkle with an almost reckless delight. It was intoxicating to be around, but also terrifying, because Becca knew the other side would eventually come. Amy's warning echoed in her mind: Jessi's highs always ended in lows.

At work, Jessi called or texted often, sending little jokes, snippets of her day, and even teasing photos of her standing naked in front of the bathroom mirror, or a playful video of her doing a striptease and telling her to get home soon because of how horny she was. Becca smiled at each one, feeling flushed as she snuck a peek at work. This was the side of Jessi she fell in love with, but she knew it wouldn't last forever.

* * *

By Thursday, Jessi's energy had become almost electric. She suggested impromptu plans, taking a shopping trip for some new clothes, trying a new Thai restaurant, and even suggesting posing nude for a small home art project with Becca. Every moment seemed vibrant, seductive, every glance and touch charged with an almost manic delight.

"You're in a really good mood," Becca said one evening as they sat on the couch, Bob nestled between them. Jessi beamed, spinning the cat gently in her lap.

"I'm happy," Jessi said, eyes shining. "Like… everything is right." She laughed softly, almost to herself, as she played with Bob.

Becca forced a light smile, though her concern gnawed at her. "That's great, Jessi," she said, reaching over to brush a stray curl from Jessi's face.

Jessi's grin softened, leaning into Becca's touch.

Yet Becca's intuition was unrelenting. She could sense the undercurrent beneath Jessi's exuberance, the restless energy, the compulsion humming quietly beneath the surface, waiting for the high to falter. Becca's mind ran ahead, imagining the eventual crash, the sudden withdrawal into shadows, the self-destructive temptations Jessi had tried to resist just days before.

For now, she let the week play out, holding onto the light of Jessi's joy, savoring the warmth and laughter. They both deserved some happiness.

* * *

The weeks that followed were unexpectedly golden, an almost fragile stretch of calm and laughter that felt like spring after a long, gray winter. Jessi remained on her high, a steady current of light running through everything she did. Her energy was contagious. Becca, cautious but grateful, did everything she could to keep her girlfriend's mind occupied and her hands busy.

They went to farmers' markets on Saturday mornings, spent lazy Sundays walking through art fairs, and even took day trips to nearby parks. Jessi seemed genuinely happy, her laughter unforced, her eyes bright again. Every moment together felt like a brief miracle that Becca didn't dare question.

* * *

As September rolled in, the hot summer days gradually broke to warm afternoons and cooler nights. One Saturday afternoon, while the rain pattered softly outside, Becca set up her easel in the living room. She'd been sketching again lately, first absentminded doodles, then more serious pieces. Jessi noticed.

"You should draw me," Jessi said suddenly, flopping back on the couch with a mischievous smile. "Like, really draw me."

Becca looked up from her sketchpad, eyebrow raised. "You're kidding."

"No, I'm not," Jessi said, grinning. "Come on, you've drawn me by my car, a fruit bowl, and, what, three buildings? Let's do something interesting."

Becca chuckled softly. "You just want an excuse to take your clothes off."

"Maybe," Jessi teased, slipping one shoulder from her t-shirt with an exaggerated flourish.

Becca tried to protest, but her cheeks flushed pink. "You're impossible," she murmured.

Within minutes, Jessi stood in the soft glow of lamplight, nude, poised against the neutral backdrop of the wall. The air was still, intimate, charged. She wasn't self-conscious; if anything, she seemed perfectly at ease, her confidence and serenity drawing Becca in.

Becca worked in silence, pencil gliding across paper, capturing every curve, every line, every shadow. Time seemed to dissolve around them.

Hours passed. Jessi dozed lightly under a blanket while Becca continued, the scratch of graphite the only sound in the apartment. When she finally finished, Becca stood back and stared at her work, heart pounding.

"Can I see it?" Jessi's voice broke the silence.

Becca hesitated, then turned the easel around.

Jessi's breath caught. The drawing was breathtaking, delicate yet powerful, and startlingly realistic. Becca had captured not just Jessi's body, but her essence, the mix of strength and vulnerability, her eyes closed in peaceful surrender.

"Oh my God, Becca…" Jessi whispered. "It's… incredible."

Becca's cheeks burned. "You really think so?"

"Think so? It's… Becca, this looks like something you'd see in a gallery. Why don't you do this professionally, instead of working at that boring store?"

Becca gave a small, wistful laugh. "Because school is expensive. Art programs even more so. And I can't exactly afford to take out a loan just to chase a dream."

"What about what your parents said?" Jessi pressed. "You told me they mentioned helping you."

"They did," Becca said softly, her gaze drifting. "But… I don't know. They want me to be someone I'm not. I haven't heard any more about it."

Jessi frowned, glancing back at the drawing. "You're wasting your talent, Becca. I mean it."

Becca smiled gently, though her eyes were sad. "Maybe someday. For now, I'm happy where I am. With you."

Jessi moved to her, wrapping an arm around her shoulders. "Well, if I ever win the lottery, you're going back to school. Deal?"

Becca laughed, leaning into her. "Deal."

As the rain continued outside, the two sat together in quiet contentment, the sketch propped nearby, a perfect reflection of Jessi's radiance in that fleeting, beautiful season of calm neither of them quite trusted to last.

16
Rock 'n' Roll and Shopping

Things between them stayed bright for a while, surprisingly, wonderfully bright. Jessi's energy stayed up, steady and buoyant, and Becca let herself exhale into the good stretch, the easy laughter, the unguarded smiles.

One weekend, Becca surprised her with movie tickets downtown for a showing of the classic *The Shop Around the Corner*, starring Jimmy Stewart and Margaret Sullivan. Jessi couldn't stop smiling the whole drive there, her hand resting on Becca's thigh as they sang along to old songs on the radio. The theater was small and artsy, the kind that played independent films and served lattes instead of fountain sodas. They shared popcorn and whispered commentary to each other in the dark, Jessi occasionally leaning over to press a kiss to Becca's temple.

Afterward, they strolled hand-in-hand through the cool night air, neon signs flickering above the old storefronts. The city felt alive in a way Jessi loved, so many people, so much motion.

"Let's go shopping," Jessi said impulsively as they passed a boutique.

Becca laughed. "Now? It's almost ten o'clock."

"They're still open," Jessi said, tugging her inside before Becca could protest. The store was loud with music, racks filled with tight jeans, sheer tops, and lace. Jessi immediately started pulling things off hangers: denim shorts, a low-cut top, and a short black dress.

Becca watched her dart from rack to rack, amused. "You know you don't need half of that."

"Maybe not," Jessi said, holding the dress against her body and turning in the mirror. "But imagine this with my boots. You wouldn't be able to take your eyes off me."

"I already can't," Becca murmured.

Jessi grinned and kissed her. "Flatterer."

By the time they left, Jessi had two shopping bags swinging from her arm and a glow that Becca couldn't help but love.

***

The next night, they tried out the new alternative rock club downtown, a place called *The Hinge*, tucked between a tattoo parlor and a vintage record shop.

"107 17th Avenue," Jessi told the cab driver as she and Becca slid into the back seat.

"No!" Becca interrupted. "It's 701 17th Avenue, not 107."

Jessi turned to Becca with a puzzled look. "Is it?"

"Yeah, silly. You transposed the address."

"Okay," Jessi said with a laugh as she turned back to the driver. "What she said."

The club was in an edgier part of town; not quite dangerous, but still a place to keep their guard up. Inside, the place was dim and crowded, the air thick with the scent of beer, sweat, and guitar feedback.

Jessi was in her element. She wore the black dress from the night before, her hair loose and wild, eyes glittering in the strobe lights. Becca stood beside her, watching her sway to the music.

The band, three guys and a girl on bass, played loud and rough, full of life. Jessi moved closer to the stage, pulling Becca with her until they were right up front, close enough to feel the vibrations through their shoes.

Becca found herself laughing, head tipped back as Jessi danced, unselfconscious and fearless. Becca had all but forgotten the darkness that had hung over them for so long. Jessi was glowing, alive, radiant in a way Becca hadn't seen in months.

Later, after the band's encore, they stumbled out into the cool night air, ears ringing and adrenaline still coursing. Jessi turned to Becca and kissed her hard, right there on the sidewalk under the streetlight.

"God, that was awesome," Jessi breathed. "Didn't you think so?"

Becca smiled against her lips. "It was."

* * *

The ride back to the apartment seemed premature, as if the evening had only reached its second act and was waiting for an encore. As the cab dropped them off in the apartment parking lot, Jessi looked at her car, then back to Becca.

"Let's not go home yet," Jessi said suddenly. "Let's just drive. No destination. Just… go."

Becca hesitated, then nodded. "Okay."

And they did, windows down, music up, the city lights blurring past them as if the world was something they could hold together by momentum alone. They drove aimlessly through the city, weaving from one glowing district to the next. The streets shimmered with neon and rain slick, the late-night air humming with life. Jessi leaned back in her seat, one hand on the wheel, the other resting loosely over Becca's on the console.

"Feels good, doesn't it?" she said softly, smiling toward her.

Becca nodded. "Yeah… it really does."

They didn't talk much after that. The silence wasn't empty; it was charged, alive. Streetlights flicked across their faces in quick, golden flashes as they passed beneath them, Jessi glancing over now and then with that bright, unrestrained grin that always made Becca's chest ache.

Eventually, the city began to thin, the blocks giving way to quieter neighborhoods, then the familiar stretch that led home. Neither wanted to end the night, but when Jessi finally pulled into their parking space, there was still that same electricity hanging between them, soft, fragile, but pulsing like a heartbeat.

* * *

Inside, the apartment was dim and still. They left the lights off. The sound of the door closing behind them felt heavy, intimate. For a moment, they stood there, two outlines in the low glow spilling from the street through the blinds.

Jessi stepped closer, her expression softening. "Tonight was perfect," she whispered.

Becca smiled faintly, her pulse quickening. "Yeah. It was."

The distance between them disappeared. The laughter, the dancing, the thrill of the drive, all of it found its quiet echo in that closeness. There were no words left to say; only the warmth of skin and the slow rhythm of breath, two hearts syncing after a night that had carried them so high. The throws of passion took them to the bedroom: no words, just raw emotions, bare skin, and the sounds of desire.

When at last they drifted to sleep, their naked bodies intertwined, the city outside had fallen silent. Becca thought, just before slipping under, this was what peace felt like.

* * *

The week slipped by in a blur of routine. Work felt endless, emails, meetings, and the hum of fluorescent lights that seemed to drain every bit of color from the day. Both women found themselves counting down to Friday, holding onto the memory of that perfect weekend, the laughter, the music, the easy warmth between them.

Late Thursday afternoon, while she was at work, Becca's cell phone rang. She almost didn't answer when she saw the caller ID. Her stomach fluttered uneasily.

"Hey, Mom," she said, forcing cheer into her voice.

The conversation was brief but heavy. Her parents wanted her to visit that weekend. "We have something important to talk about," her mother had said, no other details, no hint of what it might be.

After she hung up, Becca sat at her desk for a long time, staring blankly at the computer screen. The loudspeaker of the store echoed across the building, "Plumbing, line two… Plumbing, line two." She looked at the screen, the cursor blinking in rhythm with her thoughts. She knew she couldn't avoid it; she had to go. But the idea of leaving Jessi again filled her with a vague, uneasy dread.

* * *

That night, she finally told her. Jessi was sitting cross-legged on the couch, flipping through her laptop when Becca spoke.

"They called again," Becca began quietly. "My parents. They want me to come up this weekend. There's… something they want to talk about."

Jessi looked up, expression unreadable. "Something important?"

"That's what they said." Becca hesitated, twisting the edge of a cushion in her hands. "I don't know what it's about, but… they sounded serious."

Jessi gave a slight nod; her eyes fixed somewhere beyond Becca. "So, you're going?"

"I think I have to."

Silence stretched between them for a moment. Then Becca leaned closer. "Just… promise me you'll be careful while I'm gone, okay? No more… lone outings. No wandering off at night. I mean it, Jess."

Jessi smiled, soft but distant. "I promise," she said.

Becca missed the flicker of something behind her eyes, something sharp and unsettled. She reached out and squeezed Jessi's hand. "I'll only be gone a couple of days."

"I know," Jessi replied, her voice calm, almost gentle. "You don't have to worry about me."

But after Becca turned away, Jessi's smile faded. A cold, hollow feeling settled somewhere beneath her ribs. She didn't like the idea of Becca going back again—to that house, to those people who didn't even know she existed in Becca's life.

She told herself she was being silly, that she'd be fine. Still, as Becca disappeared into the bedroom, Jessi sat alone on the couch, her eyes fixed on nothing, her pulse quietly quickening.

She whispered to herself, barely audible…

"Yeah. Everything will be fine."

***

The sun had just begun to set, its last gold spilling across the apartment as Becca zipped up her overnight bag. Jessi sat on the edge of the bed, watching her fold a few more clothes into the duffel. Now and then, Becca would glance over her shoulder, her eyes lingering on Jessi a little too long.

"You sure you'll be okay?" Becca asked again, her tone light but edged with worry.

Jessi smiled faintly. "You've asked me that three times already."

"Well, yeah," Becca said, pausing with a shirt in her hands. "The last time I left town, you didn't exactly… rest easy."

Jessi's lips twitched into a half-smile. "That was different."

"Different how?"

"I don't know," Jessi said, avoiding her gaze. "I'm fine now. Really."

Becca didn't answer right away. She folded the shirt, tucked it in, then sat down beside Jessi on the bed. "You've been doing great," she said softly. "I just—Jess, I don't want you slipping back into that dark place again."

Jessi looked up, meeting her eyes. "I won't."

"Promise me," Becca said. Her voice was gentle but firm, her fingers finding Jessi's. "No dangerous dares. No late-night adventures. Just… be safe, okay?"

"I promise," Jessi said, her thumb brushing against Becca's. "I might go hang out with Amy and Traci tomorrow. They're always bugging me to go out with them again."

Becca's shoulders seemed to ease a little at that. "Good. They'll keep you out of trouble."

"Exactly."

Becca smiled, though the worry didn't leave her eyes completely. She reached up and tucked a strand of Jessi's hair behind her ear. "You know I hate leaving you."

"I know," Jessi murmured. "But it's your parents. You should go. I'll be here when you get back."

They kissed, softly and tenderly, with a warmth tinged with reluctance. When Becca finally pulled away, she stood for a moment by the doorway, her bag slung over her shoulder, her gaze still on Jessi as if trying to memorize her.

"Text me when you get there," Jessi said.

"I will," Becca replied. Then, after a pause, she closed the door behind her.

The apartment fell silent. Jessi sat there a long moment, staring at the space where Becca had been. The ticking of the clock seemed suddenly louder, the air heavier. She exhaled slowly, her lips tightening into something that wasn't quite a smile.

* * *

Friday night crawled by, each hour stretching longer than the last. Jessi had drifted from one episode on TV to a few mindless games on her laptop, her thoughts wandering, circling Becca's absence and the gnawing restlessness she couldn't shake. The apartment felt emptier than usual, every creak of the floorboards and flicker of the overhead light exaggerating her solitude.

Saturday evening arrived with its usual chaos. Amy and Traci barreled in, laughing loudly, their energy spilling into the apartment like wildfire. Jessi looked up from her laptop, a small, almost shy smile tugging at her lips.

"How are you, Jessi?" Amy asked as she set her bag down on the lounge chair.

"I'm good. How are the party twins tonight?"

The girls just laughed as they rummaged through their bags trying to find the night's outfits.

"You know… I thought I might actually come along with y'all tonight," she said softly.

Amy and Traci froze mid-motion, exchanging glances. "Wait—what?" Amy said, raising an eyebrow. "You? You actually want to go out? Tonight?"

Jessi nodded with a smile, tucking a loose strand of hair behind her ear. "Yeah. Why not? You two keep asking, and since Becca's gone, I thought it might be fun."

Traci leaned against the doorframe, smirking. "You mean you're actually tired of staying home and watching your exciting TV?"

"Exactly," Jessi said, shrugging. "Get out and see how the party twins live. A little… fun."

Amy exchanged a hesitant glance with Traci. "Well… Jessi… I wish we'd known. We actually have dates tonight," Amy finally said, her tone apologetic. "A couple of guys we met a few weeks back. You know…"

Jessi's brow furrowed slightly. "Oh."

Traci grinned. "So… you could totally come along with us."

Amy cut in. "Yeah. Definitely. We'll all have fun."

Jessi shook her head firmly. "Oh, no way. I don't want to be a third, or I guess, a fifth wheel tonight. Seriously. I'll be fine."

Amy hesitated, biting her lip, then shrugged. "I guess we could cancel our dates…"

Traci nodded. "Yeah. We can always go out with them another night. I mean… It's not always that you say yes to going out with us."

"Hell no," Jessi said, waving her hand. "Nope. I'll be fine. Really. I was thinking… I might check out that new rock club Becca and I discovered. Something loud, something with a live band. Keep me occupied."

Traci looked at Jessi. "I feel bad now. Really, Jessi, it's not a big deal."

Jessi just shrugged them off and laughed. "You two go have fun… but not too much fun."

The girls smiled as they looked at Jessi. She looked confident and at ease, like not a bother in the world. Jessi was good at hiding her feelings.

"Well, I guess we'd better get ready. Next weekend. Let's all go out somewhere… okay?"

"Sounds awesome," Jessi said with an excited grin. The grin faded as the girls made their way to the bathroom to start applying the night's warpaint.

Later, as the girls blew kisses to Jon and dashed off to start their night, Jessi felt the pulse of anticipation, somewhere where she could safely disappear into the music and the night. Rummaging through her clothes in the bedroom, Jessi searched for just the right outfit for a night of rock'n'roll. She chose a little sequin, deep-V neck, backless halter top, paired with a leather miniskirt with an elastic waist. The top hung loosely across her chest, exposing the sides of her breasts provocatively.

For a moment, she thought of forgoing a pair of panties. It would be so daring with the miniskirt, but she decided against it. She was being a good girl for Becca as promised. The clothes were already daring enough. But a pair of black thongs never hurt anyone. A pair of strappy black heels completed the ensemble, making her legs look long and lean.

Punching her fingers on her cell phone, Jessi called for a cab. Her tiny black purse was barely big enough to hold her phone, ID, and some cash, and she struggled to fit the phone inside. She glanced at the clock. "Alright, let's see how loud the world can get tonight," she whispered to herself, stepping out into the evening as the city lights beckoned.

* * *

Jessi settled into the cab, sliding the door shut behind her with a soft click. The leather seat felt warm beneath her, and the hum of the engine quickly began to lull her thoughts. "107 17th Avenue, please," she told the driver, her voice calm, almost casual. The man nodded and pulled smoothly into the street, the city lights flickering past the windows.

Jessi leaned back, letting herself sink into the ride. Her mind drifted to the music, the crowd, and the lights of the club she was heading toward. For a moment, the buzz of anticipation and the lingering restlessness from the week kept her from noticing anything else.

The cab slowed, the driver indicating the turn, and soon the car came to a stop. Jessi hardly registered the exact location as she slipped out, dropping a couple of bills on the seat. The cab pulled away almost immediately, leaving her alone on the bustling street.

As she looked around, she realized that all the buildings in the block had identical dull brick façades, windows barred and dark, with streetlights casting long shadows across the sidewalks. The familiar sense of anticipation hit her again—and then a slight, sinking dread. She had given the driver the wrong address. Her stomach fluttered. "Oh… crap," she muttered under her breath.

The club wasn't far, only a few blocks further up the street. She could see the faint glow of neon in the distance. The thought of walking alone through the unfamiliar, shadowed streets sent a thrill through her chest—a mix of excitement and nerves she couldn't quite separate.

Jessi squared her shoulders, tucked a strand of hair behind her ear, and started down the sidewalk.

The asphalt was cool under her shoes, the night air still and tinged with the faint scent of rain from earlier in the evening. With each step, her pulse quickened, her mind oscillating between the lure of the music ahead and the sharp awareness of how exposed she was in the empty street.

She told herself it was just a few more blocks, a simple walk. The club was right there. And with that, she picked up her pace, her eyes fixed on the faint neon glow that promised music, lights, and a temporary escape from everything else.

17
The Alley

There was a nip in the night air, and Jessi regretted not bringing a jacket along. She had not intended to be walking around in the outdoors, and hadn't wanted to drag a jacket along in the hot club. The buzz of neon signs still lit over corner bodegas, the faint thump of bass from a car creeping past, the murmurs of figures clustered in shadows. She pulled her halter top tighter around her frame, as if it could somehow shield her from the cool air.

Her heels slapped against the cracked sidewalk, each step a little faster than the last. She didn't really know where she was going, not really. Just that the club was a few blocks up. One block, then another, then she came upon an unlit stretch, the brick facades dark and seemingly abandoned.

The air grew heavier as she approached. She could see the lights of stirring businesses up ahead. She crossed a corner where a group of men leaned against a shuttered shop. Their voices dropped as she passed, then rose again with laughter and words she didn't catch, didn't need to see.

Her stomach flipped. *Just a little further. Just one more block.*

Her heart hammered as she glanced down side streets, half hoping to see someone, half praying she wouldn't. She imagined Becca's voice in her head, angry and worried: "You promised." Jessi whispered back to the memory: "I didn't do this. This is a mistake."

Just then, Jessi realized there was someone a car-length behind her, walking, keeping her pace. Her heart raced. She didn't know who they were or what they were doing. Were they just walking like she was, or was it something else? She quickened her stride.

Ahead, in the shadows, she noticed two more figures. Jessi couldn't see their faces, just silhouettes, trailing long shadows. She turned down an alley without thinking, the stench of old trash and damp concrete rising. Maybe she could disappear; lose them in the darkness. The walls pressed closer here, graffiti crawling like scars across brick. Jessi's chest ached with adrenaline. She couldn't tell if she wanted to scream or laugh.

Then came a sound, a low whistle, sharp, deliberate.

Her steps faltered. Voices followed, closer now, echoing in the narrow space. She couldn't see them yet, but she didn't have to. Her hands trembled at her sides. She should run. She wanted to run. But she froze instead, caught in unbearable terror, men in front of her, men behind her.

The shadow of a figure spilled across the wall ahead of her, then another. Jessi's breath quickened.

Every nerve in her body screamed with danger, but still, she didn't move. Her breath hitched as the first man stepped into view. Tall, broad-shouldered, his hoodie pulled low. Another followed, leaner, wiry, smirking. Their eyes locked onto her like she was already caught prey.

"Well, look what wandered in," the wiry one said, his voice echoing off the brick.

Jessi's pulse roared in her ears. Her legs begged her to bolt, but the rest of her was frozen, held her rooted. The fear sharpened every sensation: the chill of night air clinging to her skin, the damp grit of concrete beneath her shoes, the heat flooding her chest.

"Are you one of Dee's girls?" the tall one asked, his tone both mocking and curious. He took a step closer. Jessi's back brushed the rough brick wall behind her.

Her throat went dry. She opened her mouth to speak, but nothing came.

The wiry one laughed. "Did you hear me? You one of Dee's girls?"

They were both closer now, boxing her in without even touching her. Jessi's breath came in quick bursts, her heart thudding so violently she thought it might crack her ribs. She wanted to scream, but another part of her whispered *This is what you deserve.*

Her fingernails dug into her palms. She tried to remember all the things she'd told Becca about boundaries, about safe words, about control, but there was no safe word here. No rope stage. No dim, curated club where everyone played by the rules. This was raw. This was real.

The tall one leaned in, his breath hot with smoke. "Are you fucking deaf?"

Jessi's lips parted. She was… terrified. She swallowed hard, finally forcing out a whisper. "I… I was just walking up to a club."

The wiry one's grin widened. "Ain't no clubs back here, baby."

Jessi's back pressed hard against the wall as the tall man planted his hand beside her head. The wiry one lingered just a step away, his laughter sharp in the night air.

Her chest rose and fell in quick, uneven breaths. She should scream; she knew it. She should shove past them and run. But her legs felt like lead, her body locked in place, humming with terror. She knew they would catch her. She needed to talk her way out.

The tall one tilted his head, studying her. "You ain't one of Dee's girls. Bitch, you in the wrong neighborhood."

His words scraped against her skin like a dare. Jessi's lips parted, her voice shaky: "I'm sorry. I… just want to be on my way. I'm leaving."

That made the wiry one laugh again, louder this time. "Did we say you could leave? Look at her, Jay."

Her knees wobbled, heat flushing her face and chest. For a dizzying second, Jessi thought about kicking her shoes off and just sprinting. She looked down to the end of the alley at the street. Three shadows now lurked on the corner.

The tall man leaned in closer, so close she could smell the smoke and sweat on him. He looked at the other man. "You wanna fuck her here, or take her inside?" His hand brushed her shoulder, sliding toward her arm.

"Please!" Jessi pleaded. "Look… I have money. I can pay you. I… just want to…" The wiry man cut her off midsentence.

"Aw, baby. You ain't gotta pay us to fuck you. We'll do it for free."

Jessi shook her head as tears began to stream down her cheeks. "No!" she yelled as Jay grabbed her arm and started dragging her towards a doorway in the darkened building. Jessi dropped her purse as the wiry man slapped her on the top of her head. "Shut up bitch. Get in there!"

Jessi began to kick and thrash. She could hear the other three men running down the alley towards them. "Please stop!" she begged as they pulled her to the door. Then a slap, hard against the side of her head. Jessi perceived a flash of light, then the haze of darkness.

She fell limp as the men dragged her into a dimly lit storeroom, with four bare brick walls, no furnishings or shelves, and only a couple of support beams jutting up along the centerline of the room. The floor was littered with old papers and wrappers, and next to one beam, an old, stained twin-bed mattress.

In her haze, Jessi could hear the men laughing and hollering. The room smelled stale and musky. She could feel her top ripping as they pulled it from her body, her leather skirt being yanked down to her ankle. There were already several hands pawing at her breasts, pinching and tugging at her nipples, and someone had torn her thongs away, leaving her bare and exposed.

Jessi pulled out of her fog, and the realization of what was happening quickly set in. Again, she screamed, which only seemed to amuse the five men who now surrounded her. She lay on the floor, naked and vulnerable, with only one shoe remaining on her feet. Three of the men had already stripped out of their pants and stood erect, looking down at her.

One man kicked her in her side, and again on the side of her hips as he commanded her to kneel. She just lay there covering her face and sobbing uncontrollably. Another man reached down, grabbing her by the hair of the head, and yanked her upright to her knees.

"Open your mouth," Jay yelled as he slapped her hands away from her face.

Jessi could only look around, darting her eyes as she looked up between the men. Their faces were a blur from her swollen eyes and tears.

"I said, open your fucking mouth whore," Jay yelled again, rapping his palm across the top of her head.

Tears flowing down her face, Jessi sat back up, hair tousled, mascara smeared across her cheeks. She gasped for a breath between sobs, then slowly opened her mouth, looking up at Jay.

His cock was hard and standing erect, and he guided it down to Jessi's mouth, rubbing the tip along her lips. Jessi kept her mouth open wide, her eyes closed, not wanting to watch.

With a quick thrust, Jay plunged his member down her throat, causing her to choke and gag. He didn't care. He grabbed the back of her head, forcing it as deep as it would reach.

Jessi instinctively reached up and tried pushing away at Jay's hips, but the other men grabbed her wrists and pulled her hands to their own hardened cocks.

Jay held Jessi's head for a long moment, until Jessi thought she would pass out from lack of air. Suddenly, he pulled out, allowing her to gulp and gasp for breath. Her reprieve didn't last long, as almost as soon as she took a deep, labored breath, another cock took its place in her mouth. Jessi could feel the others pressing their cocks on her forehead, her eyes, and her cheek. Each man took turns pumping furiously back and forth in her mouth, then pulling out, only to be immediately followed by another.

To Jessi, it was a blur of tears and body parts. She didn't have time to react or beg. Her cries were only weird gurgles and slurps as she struggled for air between assaults. Someone was smacking her tits hard, and another was slapping her exposed ass. The stings sent electric jolts across her body, but she could do nothing. She was at their will; their mercy.

"I want some of that pussy," Jessi heard one man say, and she felt a hand grab a handful of hair as she was dragged backward and thrown onto the mattress. She was still coughing and choking from the throat assault, gagging like she was about to throw up, when she felt someone push her legs open before falling on top of her. She could tell he was big and muscular, a black man by his short curly hair on the top of his head.

She could feel his hand reaching down, guiding his prick along her slit. With one deep thrust, he pushed deep inside her, and Jessi reached up, trying to push him away. His weight pressed her down, pinning her to the mattress. She felt each stroke as he pumped his hips back and forth. Jessi groaned and grunted with each movement. She was helpless, powerless to stop anything. Her sobs soon fell to a quiet shock, her eyes wide with disbelief, as though this were happening to someone else and she was just an observer.

Jessi heard the other men yell, "Come on. My turn. My turn." She lay there, her body rocking back and forth with each deep drive.

The man then rolled over without pulling out, positioning Jessi on top of him. He held on to her ass as he kept rolling his hips, pumping harder and harder. Men to each side of her had each grabbed one of her hands and were guiding her palms across their dicks, already slick with precum.

Then, Jessi felt someone behind her, his cock probing her exposed ass as it shook with the motion of the man beneath her. The sudden realization hit

Jessi, and she turned and tried to push him away and cover her anus. "Please no," she found herself begging. The words seemed hollow, somehow echoing in her mind. "Not my ass. Please. I'll give you some more head."

The man slapped her hand away. "Shut the fuck up bitch." His prick guided its way to the button, and gradually he forced his way inside her, each thrust driving deeper and sending electric pain through Jessi's body. He pushed his way inside, making her feel as though she were about to be ripped apart.

Jessi arched her head back and let out a high-pitched shriek. A hand quickly covered her mouth, muffling her whining screams, as the two men stroked inside her in rhythm.

Jay had walked around in front of Jessi, again pushing his cock to her lips. As Jessi let out another yell, he pushed down her throat and began pumping.

Bewildered and stunned at everything that was happening around her, Jessi now realized she had three cocks inside her, and one in each hand. She had stopped crying, stopped begging. She let them do whatever they wanted without a word or resistance. She was just a piece of meat to them; a toy to be used for their pleasure. She closed her eyes and thought of Becca.

Jessi could feel the man in her ass pumping harder, the heat building with imminent release. With a loud groan, he pushed deep inside, and she could feel his body convulsing and throbbing. He held there for nearly half a minute before pulling out and collapsing to the side.

Almost immediately, another man took his place. He was smaller than the first, or maybe Jessi thought she was stretched bigger. It didn't matter. She opened her eyes and looked up at the man they called Jay. He was grinning as he watched her torment. His actions told her that he loved being in her mouth. No longer did she gag and choke; she was taking in breath when she could and letting him slide deep down her throat. He pumped furiously, letting out quick gasps with each thrust, until again she felt his cock throb and shudder, the hot liquid streaming into her stomach. He pulled out breathless as he walked to the center of the room, zipping up his pants.

Jessi looked down at the face of the man beneath her, unshaven, with a broad nose, and rows of braids on his head. His eyes glared at her, like he was willing hate into her. His motions increased to a frenzy, before his eyes rolled back and he filled her with his hot come. Sliding out beneath them, he left with Jessi on all fours, the man behind her reaching around and tugging at her nipples as he continued his battering.

The last man came around to Jessi's face, plopping his hard member into her mouth. She opened almost like she had been commanded to, letting him slide inside. She lapped her tongue around it as he entered, surprising him at first. Her head jolted back and forth with each pump of the man behind her, forcing her mouth along the cock like a rhythmic machine.

With a loud cry, Jessi felt the man's body behind her tense up and release inside her. He slapped her ass hard as he pulled out, leaving only her and the man in her mouth. Reaching down, the man pulled out of

Jessi's mouth and turned her around, laying her on her back. Still on his knees, he slid up between her legs while grabbing at her hips. Lifting her, he slid deep inside and made slow, long strides. He reached up and put his hand on Jessi's throat, squeezing tightly.

Jessi grabbed the man's arm. He was strong, his muscles like stone, and she closed her eyes as she struggled for air. To the man's surprise, Jessi's hips began to roll with his motion. Her nipples stood erect, and he could feel her moist mound become hot and wet. She started bucking her hips as the man clutched tighter at her neck. Then a gush of warm, clear fluid flowed from Jessi. She grunted as her body tensed and her back arched.

The warm sensation overcame the man thrusting inside her. He pumped faster and faster, until with a great cry, Jessi felt him filling her pussy with his pearly come. He let go of Jessi and collapsed on the mattress beside her, limp and satisfied.

Jessi, gasping for air, clutched at her throat as she just stared up at the ceiling. There was an overwhelming sense of shame. Not for what they had done to her, but because her body had betrayed her and let out a release she did not expect.

She lay in the bed, naked, legs spread wide, and dripping with sweat and come. Her hair was wet and stuck to the side of her cheeks, and her butt and tits showed the red handprints from punishing licks she had endured. She stared up at the ceiling stoically. There were no more tears; no pleas or whimpers. She could hear the men, still in the room, laughing and talking.

It was then that the one they called Jay bent down and whispered in her ear. "You tell whoever you're working for that this is Dee's territory. Ain't no hos coming up here and working these streets without his say so. Understand?"

Jessi looked at him side-eyed, not knowing what he was talking about. She nodded without saying anything.

Jay just smiled as he stood up and stared at her ravaged body. He gave her a wink as the men walked towards the doorway. "If you ever want to continue our little fun, just let us know. We'll be right here."

The others laughed as they walked into the night. The room fell silent, with Jessi hearing only the sound of her own ragged breathing. She lay there for what seemed like forever. No words, just the ache of her body inside and out.

Slowly, she raised and looked around the room. She couldn't see any remnants of her tattered clothes. Looking down in amazement, she realized she was still wearing one black heel, the other shoe nowhere to be seen. Reaching up, she raked her fingers through her tangled hair. Her ass stung with each move, and her thighs and arms ached. It felt like she had just fallen off a cliff. Every muscle seemed to cry out.

Standing, Jessi slowly made her way to the doorway. Come and blood dripped from her pussy and her ass. Each step hurt, like her legs might give out at any second. She stepped outside and surveyed each end of the alley. No one was around, at least no one she could see.

Jessi felt the muck and grime from her attack all over her body. She felt unclean, dirty. Looking down, she noticed a water spigot on the side of the building. She turned the handle, but not a drop of water came out. Looking over to the middle of the alley, she noticed a puddle of water, and she gradually shuffled over, wading into the ankle-deep pool. Squatting down, she began splashing her legs and butt, using a tattered newspaper as a washcloth to clean herself. The water was dingy, but she didn't care. The cool water soothed her; eased the pain. She cupped the water in her hands and splashed her face, then sprinkled her tousled mane, running her fingers through it like a comb.

Back towards the doorway, she noticed her small purse still lying on the ground where she had dropped it. For some reason, the men had either not seen it or not cared about it. Jessi struggled to bend over to retrieve the bag from the ground. Quickly, she popped it open. Her phone was still inside. She swiped the screen, then paused. Who could she call? She certainly couldn't call a cab or a rideshare; she hadn't found her clothes. Becca was out of town, and she didn't want her to know what had happened. She couldn't call Amy or Traci; they would want her to call the police, and would surely tell Becca as well.

She rummaged through her purse, then found a small scrap of paper with a phone number scribbled on it. It was the biker, Spike, she had been so afraid of that night at Tommy's Bar. He had inked his number on her arm, and for a reason she could not explain, she had kept it. Perhaps the danger she felt that night compelled her to keep a memento, or maybe it was something else.

Jessi looked around the ground for something, an old rag, a bag, anything to cover herself. She found another old scrap of newspaper that she used to wipe herself off with, but there was nothing to shield her nakedness. She looked down at the phone number, then to her cell phone. She dialed the number.

"Hello. Spike?... This is Jessi, the girl you met at Tommy's a few weeks ago. Do you remember me?"

"Well, of course I do, sweet thang. The little redhead. You ready to go for that ride?"

Jessi paused for a second and took a deep breath. "I know you don't really know me, but I kind of need your help. Can you come pick me up?"

"That depends on where you're at, sweet thang." The crowd noise and background music muffled Spike's voice.

Jessi looked down both ends of the alley. "I'm at the 500 block of 17th Avenue. There are these old buildings, and I'm in the alley beside them."

"I think I know where you're talking about. I'm about five minutes away, babydoll."

"Spike," Jessi said excitedly. "Do you have a jacket or something I can wear?"

"Hmm, not sure about that, sweetie. I'm on a hog. Not exactly a lot of trunk space if you know what I mean."

Just then, Jessi heard something down at the back end of the alley; a bottle or something rolling across the pavement. She ducked down and back up beside a dumpster. "Never mind about that then," she whispered. "Just come get me quick, please."

Spike could sense the urgency in Jessi's voice, and he answered in a more serious tone. "Don't you worry, sweetheart. I'm on my way."

As the call ended, Jessi quickly shut off her phone's screen. She hunched down, bringing her knees up to her chest, wrapping her arms around them. She glanced back and forth down one end of the alley to the other, but could see no one. She listened intently, but could only hear the traffic on the nearby road and the faint thump of music from the nearby club.

She waited for what seemed an eternity before she finally heard the distant thunder of the Harley's open exhaust. It echoed down the alley as it came closer, until Jessi saw the single headlight, and the street vibrated with the boom of the engine.

Jessi quickly stood up and waved her arms, and Spike pulled to a stop. "God damn babydoll. Are you alright? What happened?"

"I'm fine, Spike. Can you just get me out of here? Anywhere but here?"

Spike reached back with his leg and kicked down a footrest on each side of the bike. He twisted the throttle a couple of times, the engine revving in a rumbling harmony. "Hop on, sweetheart. I don't have nothing for you to wear. Just don't touch the exhaust and wrap around my big ole belly."

Jessi stepped one bare foot on the footpeg closest to her, then swung her leg over the bike and plopped down on the small padded seat. She could smell the leather of his vest, mingled with the scent of beer.

"Hang on, baby," he said as he kicked the cycle in gear. The bike lurched forward, and Jessi grabbed hold of Spike's thick leather belt at his waist. She was ready... ready to be anywhere but here.

18
Knights on Steel Horses

Once on the road, the night air became almost frigid. Jessi's hair whipped around in the wind, and she felt goosebumps form all along her skin. She lay the side of her head against his back and just watched as the road whizzed by them. The bike roared down the streets like an angry monster, letting all know to get out of its way.

Jessi noticed as Spiked passed a few cars, some not even noticing the naked girl riding on the back. She pressed close to Spike, the warmth of his husky body almost comforting, but from behind, she was exposed for all the world to see. One car, full of several young men, honked and yelled as the motorcycle passed by. Jessi could only hold on and watch.

The traffic slowed as Spike neared a stoplight. Several cars and pickups were stopped in both lanes as the bike eased to a stop behind them. The car full of young men then pulled up beside Spike, hooting and hollering. "Hell yeah!" she heard one voice say. "Turn around, baby, show us your tits!" another yelled.

Spike turned and looked at the men. "You fuckers looking at my old lady?" he yelled in a deep, almost demonic pitch. The men looked back, startled, and rolled up their windows. Jessi just grinned and squeezed Spike tighter.

It was then that the blue lights behind them lit up. A police car, a couple of vehicles back, its searchlight zeroing in on the motorcycle.

"Ah, oh. Hang on, sugar britches," Spike yelled as the bike again lurched forward. The deep grumble of the motor flooded the streets as Spike weaved between vehicles, running the red light. A few shifts of the gears, and Jessi watched as the pavement seemed to blur, the streetlights passing like strobes. 90, 100---120 miles per hour, the wind howling past them, Jessi's eyes watering as the cool air blasted her face. The blue lights slowly faded into the distance as the vehicle was caught in the entangled evening traffic.

***

It was only a few more minutes before Spike turned down a neighborhood street, then turned to another. A few driveways down, he slowly pulled onto a gravel drive, easing into the backyard of a small white house. There were several other bikes and choppers parked outside, leaning in a row in unison.

He cut the motor and turned off the lights. Jessi could hear several people inside the house, as if a party was going on. "You stay right here, babydoll. I'll be right back." She watched as he climbed off the bike and walked through the back door of the home.

Jessi just sat on the bike, one arm across her chest with the other hand down, trying to cover between her legs. Her body trembled from the cold, and she felt her teeth chattering.

Spike reemerged from the back door, carrying a couple of garments in his hands. "Here," he said as he tossed an oversized black t-shirt over to Jessi. She caught it and opened it up. Black Sabbath… perfect. She smiled as she slid it over her head. He then tossed over a pair of oversized shorts. They were way too big for Jessi, but she thanked him as she stepped off the bike and stepped into them. She pulled them up to her hips and bunched the loose waistband up in her hand, holding them up.

"Sorry. That's the closest thing I could find that would fit you."

"Thank you, Spike. Thank you so much."

"You're welcome to come inside and meet the boys."

Jessi smiled as she looked at the house. "Thank you, but… I've had… I think I just want to go home. Can you take me home, please?"

Spike was no longer the vulgar, teasing partygoer he had been before. He looked at her with a serious gaze. He nodded. "Of course, I will, babydoll. Just tell me where to."

Jessi looked at him and gave a sad smile. She felt like crying, like screaming, like just lying down where she was and going to sleep. She told Spike her address, and once again, they were on their way.

***

The parking lot at Jessi's apartment echoed with the thunderous claps of the Harley. It was well past 1 am, but Jessi just wanted to get home. "Thank you, Spike. I know I don't know you, but I can't thank you enough. I promise I'll make it up to you somehow."

Spike's grin was wide under his thick goggles; his graying goatee hung from his chin. "Think nothing of it. You decide you want to go for a real ride; you just let me know, sweet thang."

Jessi smiled as she climbed off the bike. She leaned over and gave him a peck on the cheek before turning and running to her door. She turned and watched as the bike made its way down the road and off into the night.

***

The door clicked shut behind her, and the sound seemed to echo through the quiet apartment. Jessi stood there for a moment in the dim entryway, barely breathing. Spike's oversized black T-shirt hung loose on her frame, brushing against her thighs. The borrowed gym shorts bunched awkwardly at her waist. She could still feel the chill of the night air on her skin, the scent of motorcycle exhaust clinging to the fabric.

She didn't turn on any lights. Her body ached, deep, hot bruises blooming beneath the fabric, and every step sent a pulse of pain through her legs. Her hair was tangled and matted, her face streaked with dried tears and city grime. All she wanted was to disappear into something warm, something clean.

As Jessi walked to the bathroom, she looked at the poster hanging on the door. She screamed as she reached out, ripped the poster down, wadded it up, and threw it in the trash. She collapsed on the floor and began to sob, the shame and guilt overwhelming her.

After a few moments, she walked into the bathroom, closing the door behind her with a soft click. She turned the water on as hot as she could stand, the sound filling the tiny room. Steam curled upward, fogging the mirror. Tears streaming down her cheeks, she stripped silently, peeling the borrowed clothes from her bruised skin. When she stepped into the tub, the water burned at first, but she welcomed it. It was something she could control.

As the grime of the night swirled away in the bath, Jessi sank deeper into the water, hugging her knees to her chest. The ache in her muscles throbbed beneath the surface, and she could feel the raw sting of a few cuts she hadn't dared to look at yet.

She tried to steady her breathing, but her chest was tight. Her mind replayed flashes she didn't want. Her jaw trembled. Another sob slipped out before she could stop it, quiet, strangled. Then another. And then it was like something inside her cracked wide open.

Jessi buried her face in her knees and cried, deep, shaking, uncontrollable weeping that filled the steamy bathroom. She pressed her hand over her mouth to muffle the sound, but it only made the tears come harder.

She wanted Becca. She craved the safety of being in someone's arms. But at the same time, she couldn't imagine telling her. Not this. Not yet. The thought of Becca seeing her like this, broken, ashamed, bruised, made her stomach knot.

So, she sat alone in the tub as the water slowly cooled around her, tears soaking her skin, whispering to herself through clenched teeth, "Don't fall apart. Not now."

The water had long since gone lukewarm before Jessi finally pulled herself to move. Her skin was pale and wrinkled, the steam having faded to a thin mist on the mirror. She reached for a towel, wincing at every motion, and patted herself dry with careful, trembling hands.

In the mirror, she caught her reflection and froze. The bruises were starting to show, blue and purple blooms on her thigh, the faint scrape along her hip. She felt the air leave her lungs. For a long time, she just stood there, gripping the edge of the counter until her knuckles turned white.

She couldn't let Becca see.

She rummaged through the cabinet beneath the sink, pulling out a first-aid kit, rubbing alcohol, and a tube of antiseptic cream. Sitting on the closed lid of the toilet, she cleaned what she could, quickly, mechanically. Every sting made her flinch, but she forced herself to stay silent. Then she pulled on an oversized sweatshirt and tossed the borrowed clothes into a trash bag. She tied the bag tight, pressing it down into the bottom of the bin under the sink.

When she stepped out of the bathroom, the apartment felt oppressively still. The clock in the kitchen ticked steadily, too loud. Bob lay on the couch, curled in a ball. She checked her phone; there were no messages or missed calls. Becca had texted earlier: Plan on being home tomorrow afternoon, safe and sound. Call you in the morning.

Jessi stared at the message until the words blurred. Then she typed back, Good. Be careful. She deleted the thread immediately after sending it.

She curled up on the couch, pulling a blanket tight around her shoulders. The ache in her body wouldn't stop; it lived somewhere beneath her skin, an echo she couldn't shake. But worse was the silence, the way her thoughts circled and collided until they made no sense at all.

She focused on small, simple things: breathing evenly, counting seconds, watching the glow of the streetlight move across the wall. She told herself that when Becca got home, everything would go back to normal. That she could bury this deep enough that it would never surface.

But when she finally drifted into a fitful sleep, the sound of the men's laughter echoed faintly in her mind.

19
Things Best Left Unsaid

The next morning came gray and muted. Light seeped through the blinds in thin, dusty stripes, cutting across the coffee table and the blanket Jessi hadn't realized she'd fallen asleep under. Her body ached in places she hadn't known could ache. When she moved, the pain caught her off guard, sharp at first, then dull and deep.

She sat up slowly, wincing as the blanket brushed against her skin. Her head felt heavy, as if she hadn't really slept at all.

The apartment was still. Too still. She turned on the TV, not to watch, but to fill the silence with something that didn't sound like her own thoughts. Morning news chatter spilled into the room, voices that meant nothing but were easier than the quiet.

In the kitchen, she poured herself a glass of orange juice. Her hand trembled just enough to make the glass clink against the counter. She pressed her lips together, took a small sip, and then set it down again. Even that simple act made her stomach twist.

She caught sight of herself reflected in the microwave door, her hair still a tangled mess, faint shadows under her eyes. She looked like someone who hadn't been sleeping well, nothing more. That was good. That she could explain.

Jessi forced herself to move through her morning routine as though it were any other Sunday, dishes from the night before into the sink. Blanket folded neatly. Couch cushions straightened. The motions were small, mechanical, something to keep her mind occupied.

When her phone finally buzzed on the counter, her heart jumped. She wiped her hands on her shirt and answered quickly, trying to steady her voice.

"Hey, babe," Becca's voice came through, soft and bright, familiar. "Did I wake you?"

"No," Jessi said quickly. "Been up a while. Just… doing some cleaning." She smiled even though no one could see it, because it made her voice sound lighter.

"Everything okay?" Becca asked. "Did you go out with Amy and Traci last night? You sound tired."

Jessi thought for a second, then took a deep breath. "Oh, I was cleaning out Bob's litter box and dropped it. Just flustered, I guess." She laughed faintly, forcing the sound out. "Amy and Traci had dates, so I didn't want to intrude. Thought about going to that rock club, but never made it. Just ended up here on the couch. How's your morning?"

Becca started talking about her parents, about breakfast, about how they'd stayed up late reminiscing. Jessi nodded along, saying uh-huh and that's nice in the right places, her voice soft and even. But her mind felt like it was behind glass, listening from somewhere else entirely.

Becca's laughter carried through the phone, light and warm. "I miss you," she said finally. "I can't wait to be home."

Jessi swallowed hard. "Yeah," she whispered. "I miss you too."

There was a pause. Jessi could hear Becca breathing on the other end. "Are… you okay?" Jessi asked.

"Oh, I'm fine. Just miss you. We'll talk later."

Jessi sensed some unease in Becca's voice. "Promise?" she asked softly.

"Promise."

After they hung up, Jessi stood there for a long time, phone still in hand, staring at the blank screen. The apartment felt smaller somehow, the air heavy again.

She took a long, shaky breath and whispered to herself, "It's fine. You're fine."

But even she didn't believe it.

* * *

By the time Becca's car pulled into the lot that evening, Jessi was curled up on the couch, wrapped in her old gray sweatshirt and loose sweats. The lamp beside her threw a dim circle of light across the coffee table, where an untouched glass of sweet tea sat.

The door opened, and Becca stepped in, dragging her small duffel behind her. The air outside carried a damp chill, and Jessi used it as her excuse before Becca could even comment.

"Hey," Jessi said, smiling faintly. "You're back."

"Yeah," Becca answered, closing the door behind her. "God, it's cold out there. I didn't expect it to drop this much."

"Yeah, I felt it earlier," Jessi said quickly. "Couldn't get warm, so… sweatshirt weather, I guess." She tugged at her sleeve, making it look casual. But even that small motion made her wince, her sore muscles tightening beneath the soft fabric.

Becca didn't notice. "You're all bundled up. You cold?"

Jessi nodded fast. "I don't know. I think I may be catching a cold or something."

Becca gave a little half-smile and crossed the room to sit beside her. She smelled faintly of the lavender shampoo Jessi loved. "Well, I'm glad you didn't go out and party with Amy and Traci then," she said teasingly.

Jessi laughed softly, relief fluttering through her chest. "Yeah, I decided to just stay in. Watch movies. Be boring."

"Sometimes boring's good."

They sat there for a long moment in comfortable quiet. Becca leaned her head against Jessi's shoulder, and Jessi felt both warmth and pain radiate through her body. She wanted so badly to melt into her, to let the safety of that simple touch erase everything that had happened, but she couldn't relax. Every shift of weight reminded her of bruises she was desperate to hide.

After a while, Becca sighed and sat up. Her hands fidgeted in her lap. "There's… something I need to tell you," she said softly.

Jessi felt her stomach twist. "What's wrong?"

Becca looked down at her hands. "When I was… visiting, I told them about us."

Jessi froze. "You… told them?"

"Yeah." Becca's voice cracked slightly. "I just… I couldn't keep avoiding it. They kept talking about me finding a nice boy and getting serious about my life. I just… I said it. I told them about you. About us."

Jessi's chest tightened. "And… What did they say?"

Becca gave a small, bitter laugh. "They laughed and said it was a phase. An infatuation."

Jessi reached for her hand, hesitating only a second before lacing their fingers together.

"There's something else," Becca said without looking up.

"What?"

They… offered to pay for college again," Becca whispered. "Full tuition."

Jessi smiled and clenched her hand. "That's great. I said you really need to continue college and do what you love," she said excitedly.

Becca rolled her eyes and drew her hand back. "Only if I moved back home. If I…" she swallowed hard. "If I agreed to move back to Atlanta."

The words hung heavy in the air. Jessi's breath caught. "Oh… and… what did you tell them?"

"I told them no," Becca said quietly. "I told them this is my life. You're my life."

Jessi felt a rush of emotion that almost undid her: a mix of pride and guilt. Her throat ached. "You didn't have to do that," she murmured, guilt threading through her voice.

"I did." Becca looked at her then, eyes red-rimmed but steady. "Jess, I told you, I have my art, I don't need anything else but you. They'll just have to live with it."

Jessi smiled faintly through the ache building behind her ribs. "It's your dream, Becca."

Becca leaned in and kissed her softly. Jessi kissed back, gentle and careful, afraid of betraying the soreness she carried beneath her clothes.

When Becca finally pulled away, she whispered, "I'm where I want to be."

Jessi met her gaze and forced a small smile. "I'm glad you're home."

Becca studied her for another heartbeat, then nodded, resting her head once more on Jessi's shoulder. It was then that Becca noticed the bathroom door. "Hey! What happened to the poster?"

Jessi looked over her shoulder, then shrugged. "It got ripped, so I threw it away."

"Aww... I'm sorry," Becca lamented. "We'll see if we can find another."

Jessi exhaled slowly, holding her close, hiding her pain, her fear, and her guilt beneath the soft rhythm of Becca's breathing.

As the night wore on, the apartment grew quiet. Becca yawned and stretched, her head still resting against Jessi's shoulder. Jessi shifted slightly, forcing another weak cough.

“Hey,” Jessi murmured, “why don't you take the bed tonight? I think I'm coming down with something. Don't want you catching whatever this is.”

Becca frowned, blinking the sleep from her eyes. “You sure?”

“Yeah,” Jessi said quickly. “I'll crash out here. The couch is fine.”

Becca turned toward her, concern softening her features. She reached out and pressed the back of her hand to Jessi's forehead. “You feel warm,” she said softly. “You might actually be sick.”

Jessi gave a small laugh, trying to play it off. “Just a little fever, probably. I'll be okay.”

Becca leaned in and kissed her gently, the kind of kiss that was more reassurance than passion. “I'll grab some medicine,” she said, disappearing into the bathroom.

When she returned, she was carrying a small plastic cup with a couple of pills and a glass of water. “Here,” she said. “This should help you sleep.”

Jessi took them obediently, her hands trembling just slightly as she swallowed the tablets. "Thanks, babe."

Becca smiled faintly. "You'd better not be dying on me," she joked.

"I'll survive," Jessi said, forcing another smile.

"Good." Becca brushed a stray lock of hair from Jessi's face and stood. "Try to get some rest. I'll see you in the morning."

Jessi nodded and watched her disappear into the bedroom. Only when the door closed did she let the mask slip—her face tightening in pain as she slowly lay down on the couch. Every muscle protested. Her ribs ached when she drew in a breath. She pulled the blanket up around her shoulders, biting back tears.

When sleep finally came, it was shallow and uneasy.

* * *

The next morning came too soon. The sunlight through the blinds cut pale stripes across the living room. Jessi stirred awake with a groan, her body stiff and sore, but she pushed herself upright. She had to act normal… had to.

By the time Becca emerged from the bedroom, Jessi had already started the coffee. The smell filled the small apartment, warm and familiar.

"Morning," Becca mumbled, tying her hair back.

"Morning," Jessi echoed, her voice faint but steady. "How'd you sleep?"

"Like a rock." Becca gave her a small smile. "You?"

"Better," Jessi lied. "The medicine helped."

Becca looked relieved. "Good. I was worried." She leaned against the counter, sipping from her mug. "I dread going to work today."

Jessi chuckled softly. "Ditto."

They shared a quiet breakfast, toast, scrambled eggs, coffee, and light conversation about nothing important. It almost felt normal again, nearly as if Saturday night hadn't happened.

When it was time to leave, Becca kissed her goodbye at the door. Jessi stood there for a long moment after the sound of Becca's car faded, her smile falling away completely. The silence of the apartment felt heavier than usual.

She touched her ribs and winced, whispering under her breath, "You're okay. You're okay."

Then she turned toward the bathroom mirror and caught sight of herself, tired eyes, a faint purple shadow blooming just above her collarbone. Her reflection stared back at her, hollow and unrecognizable.

Jessi dressed more conservatively than her usual work clothes, a button-up blouse and slacks, carefully arranging her hair to conceal any marks from the previous day. Every movement reminded her of the bruises on her legs and the dull ache in her ribs, but she forced herself to move as if nothing was wrong.

* * *

By the time she arrived at the office, her heart was still racing from the morning commute, and the fluorescent lights overhead made her feel exposed and tense. She waved halfheartedly to a few colleagues as she settled at her desk, but her usual cheerful energy was muted.

As she sorted through emails, her hand shook slightly as she reached for the stapler. She cursed under her breath, blinking hard to steady herself. Each ping of the incoming messages felt louder than usual, each interruption jarring.

Her phone buzzed. A notification from Becca, but she ignored it, not ready to answer and reveal even a hint of what had happened. Instead, she buried herself in work, focusing on numbers and reports, anything to drown out the memories.

By mid-morning, a coworker, Jenna, leaned over her desk. "Jessi, you okay? You look… off."

Jessi smiled tightly, forcing a laugh. "Yeah, I'm fine. Just didn't sleep well, I guess."

Jenna frowned but didn't press further. Jessi returned to her screen, trying to concentrate, but every time she shifted in her chair or reached for a paper, a twinge of pain reminded her of the assault. She flinched whenever someone walked too close behind her, her body reacting before her mind could catch up.

During a brief meeting in the afternoon, Jessi struggled to maintain eye contact, her attention drifting as she felt her pulse spike at the memory of someone's hands on her throat. She forced herself to answer questions, nodding along, but her voice was quieter than usual, and she caught herself trembling slightly when asked for input on a spreadsheet.

By mid-afternoon, she excused herself to the bathroom, locking the stall door behind her. She leaned against the cool tile wall, taking deep, shuddering breaths as she tried to calm the rising panic in her chest. She ran her hands along her thighs, feeling the bruises there, remembering the raw ache from running barefoot through an unfamiliar alley. She pressed a hand to her mouth, stifling the sound of a sob, and stared at her reflection in the mirror.

"No one can know," she whispered. "You're fine. Just get through today."

When she returned to her desk, she tried to smile and act normal, but the edges of her composure were fraying. She caught herself flinching at a loud laugh from a nearby colleague, and the ache in her legs made sitting still a test of willpower.

By the time the clock finally reached five, Jessi practically bolted from her chair, muttering excuses and avoiding eye contact. Her commute home felt longer, each stoplight casting shadows that reminded her of what she had endured. By the time she reached the apartment building, her hands were clammy, her stomach was tight with anxiety, and her legs still ached from the bruises and scrapes she could barely hide.

***

Inside the apartment, she collapsed onto the couch, hugging a pillow to her chest. She had made it through the day, but only barely. Her mind raced with the thought of Becca coming home later, and she steeled herself to hide everything, the bruises, the pain, the fear, behind the mask she had perfected over the past week.

The sound of the key turning in the lock made Jessi sit a little straighter on the couch. She had been curled into a ball, trying to make herself small, trying to ground herself before Becca arrived.

Becca stepped inside, shrugging off her jacket and loosening her bag strap. Her eyes immediately scanned the room, taking in Jessi's posture, the way her fingers clutched the pillow, the faint tension in her shoulders. Small things, easily overlooked by anyone else, but Becca had learned to notice the signs, the slight tremor of her hands, the tightness in her jaw, the distant look in her eyes.

"Hey," Becca said softly, stepping closer. "Long day?"

Jessi forced a smile, tilting her head and nodding. "Yeah… just… long." Her voice was steady, but her throat felt raw. She wanted to tell Becca everything, to spill the weight of the past few nights, but a tighter knot of fear tightened in her chest. She knew Becca would panic or, worse, think she'd done something reckless on purpose.

Becca crouched slightly to be level with her, her hand brushing a stray lock of hair behind Jessi's ear. "You're tense. Did something happen today?"

Jessi shook her head quickly. "No, nothing. Really." Her eyes flicked away, scanning the floorboards, anything but Becca's penetrating gaze. She could feel the truth pressing at the edges of her chest, ready to burst, but she clenched her jaw, forcing it down.

Becca reached out, gently taking Jessi's hand in hers. The touch was warm, familiar, grounding, but also a reminder of what she wanted to confess. Jessi's fingers curled around Becca's, holding the act together just a little longer.

"You sure?" Becca asked, her voice soft but insistent. "You're shaking a little. And your eyes… they're kind of distant."

"I'm fine," Jessi said, keeping her tone light, almost teasing. "Just… tired, I guess. Work was… work." She shifted on the couch, smoothing the fabric of her sweatshirt over her sore legs, careful to hide any sign of bruising or abrasion.

Becca didn't press further, though her brow furrowed with concern. Instead, she leaned back slightly and placed a hand on Jessi's shoulder, giving it a reassuring squeeze. "Okay… just know you can tell me anything, yeah? Anything at all."

Jessi nodded, swallowing hard. Inside, she was shaking, not just from the day, but from the weight of holding herself together, from the secret she bore. She desperately wanted to confide in Becca, lean on her, cry, and be held, but she also feared the fallout. Becca's disapproval, worry, disappointment… it felt like a risk too high to take.

So, she smiled, small and brittle, and nodded again. "I know… thanks."

Becca gave her another quick squeeze before heading toward the kitchen to start dinner. Jessi watched her go, the pang of guilt and shame twisting in her stomach. Every laugh, every word she exchanged over the meal, was carefully measured, a delicate act of deception.

As the night wore on, Jessi's mind kept replaying the events of the past few nights, the assault, the bruises, the fear, and yet, outwardly, she remained calm. She laughed at Becca's little jokes, commented on the food, and even helped clear the dishes afterward. But beneath it all, her heart thumped with the secret she carried alone, and the small cracks Becca had noticed, and that she herself knew were widening, pressed heavier with every passing minute.

20
Break Down

Over the next few days, Becca started to notice little things. Nothing glaring, nothing she could point to and say this is wrong, just fragments of unease that didn't fit the version of Jessi she knew so well.

When Jessi moved around the apartment, she was slower than usual and more careful about how she sat or leaned against the counters. Sometimes she winced as if from a sharp twinge, though she quickly masked it behind a nervous laugh or a sudden cough.

Becca would catch her zoning out, her gaze unfocused, her expression distant, like she was somewhere else entirely. And when Becca would call her name, Jessi would blink and look up with a forced, lopsided smile.

"Sorry," she'd say. "Just tired." Jessi, meanwhile, was barely holding it together.

At work, she made minor mistakes, misplaced files, snapped at a coworker for no reason, and forgot to return a call. She avoided mirrors and flinched when someone brushed past her in the hallway. When

Becca came home, Jessi would force a smile, desperate to appear okay, but the mask was beginning to slip.

* * *

Late one night, Becca woke to the sound of the bathroom door clicking shut. The faint rush of water followed, then silence.

Inside, Jessi sat on the floor beside the tub, wrapped in a towel, staring at the bruises fading along her thighs and ribs. She wanted to tell Becca everything, to break down and let her hold her, to say *it wasn't my fault.*

But she couldn't. Not yet. Because a part of her still believed Becca would look at her differently… or worse, that Becca would think she let it happen, something Jessi even wasn't sure of.

So she dried her eyes, pulled on her sweatshirt, and went back to bed, careful not to wake Becca.

By morning, Becca would act as if nothing were wrong, and Jessi would follow her lead.

Two women circling a secret neither of them could quite name.

* * *

By midweek, Becca couldn't ignore it anymore. The distance. The half-smiles. The quiet pain flickering in Jessi's eyes was like a light trying not to go out.

They were sitting on the couch after dinner, a soft conversation from the TV filling the silence. Jessi had tucked herself into the corner with a blanket, pretending to scroll through her laptop. Becca watched her for a while, how she flinched when she shifted, how she rubbed absently at her shoulder, how she smiled without ever really looking up.

Finally, Becca set her drink down and said quietly, "Jess… what's going on?"

Jessi didn't look up. "What do you mean?"

Becca sighed. "Don't do that. You've been… off. Since I got back. You say you're fine, but you're not. You barely sleep. You jump if I touch you."

"I am fine, Becca," Jessi snapped, too sharply. The words came out brittle, cracking under pressure.

Becca blinked, startled, then softened her voice. "I'm not trying to corner you. I just… I'm worried. Talk to me. Please."

Jessi's throat tightened. For a second, she almost did. Almost let it all spill out, going to the club, the wrong address, the alley, the bruises, the way she'd frozen. But then she saw Becca's face, open and trusting, and the words turned to ash in her mouth.

If Becca knew, she'd think Jessi had gone looking for it, that she'd made one of her reckless choices and paid the price. Maybe she'd even start to resent her for it, for the chaos, for the pain, for being a weight Becca had to keep carrying.

Jessi forced a laugh instead, a hollow sound. "You worry too much. I'm fine. I swear."

Becca studied her for a long moment. "You're not fine."

Jessi met her gaze then, tears stinging at the corners of her eyes. "I just… I'm tired, okay? You shouldn't have to deal with all my moods and screwups. You should be painting, going back to school, doing something that actually matters."

Becca frowned. "What are you talking about?"

Jessi looked down at her hands. "Your parents offered to help, right? To pay for you to finish school? And you said no… because of me."

"Because I wanted to stay here," Becca said firmly. "With you."

But Jessi shook her head. "No, Becca. I'm holding you back. You know it, and I know it."

Her voice broke on the last word. She pressed her palms to her eyes, trying to keep herself from unraveling completely. The scream was there, somewhere deep inside her chest, raw, shaking, desperate to get out, but she swallowed it down until it became another knot of guilt in her stomach.

Becca reached over, laying a hand gently on her knee. "Jess," she whispered. "Hey. Look at me."

Jessi did, reluctantly.

"You're not holding me back," Becca said. "But you are shutting me out. And that hurts a lot more than anything else could."

Jessi nodded, eyes glistening. She wanted to say, 'I'm sorry.' She tried to tell her everything, but the words wouldn't come.

So, she just whispered, "I know."

And Becca, sensing the limits of what Jessi could bear, didn't press further. She just pulled her close and held her, even as Jessi stayed rigid in her arms, trembling, the secret still burning between them.

* * *

Later that evening, Becca woke from her sleep and paused by the bathroom door, the faint sound of running water drawing her to it. The door was cracked open just enough for a sliver of light to spill across the carpet. She knocked gently.

"Jess? You okay in there?"

No answer. Only the quiet hum of water and the occasional ripple, soft and uneven.

Becca eased the door open, the humid air washing over her face. Jessi sat in the tub, her back slumped against the porcelain, eyes half-closed. She startled when she saw Becca, instinctively reaching for a towel that floated near the edge of the bath.

"Hey, it's just me," Becca said softly, crouching beside the tub. "You scared me for a second."

Jessie turned her face away, wiping quickly at her eyes. "Sorry. I just… needed to soak."

Becca frowned, her gaze catching the faint discoloration along Jessi's thigh, another along her shoulder. "Jess, what happened?"

"It's nothing," Jessi whispered, her voice cracking as she covered herself with the towel.

She wanted to give another lie of reassurance, but the words tangled in her throat. She clutched the towel tighter against her skin, trembling. Her chin quivered, and then all at once, the dam broke. She began to bawl, pushing her hands to her face to hide her eyes.

"Jess..." Becca murmured, reaching for her hand.

Jessi shook her head, tears spilling freely now. "I can't, Becca, I feel like I've ruined everything. You're supposed to have this whole future ahead of you, and I'm just... dragging you down."

Becca sat on the edge of the tub and gathered Jessi into her arms, water sloshing gently against the sides. "No," she said firmly. "Don't you ever say that. You haven't ruined anything. You don't have to explain. You don't have to tell me yet. Just... let me hold you."

For a long time, Jessi cried into Becca's shoulder, her sobs quiet but deep, like something finally giving way after being held back too long. Becca stroked her damp hair, whispering soft reassurances, nothing forced, nothing demanding, only the steady promise that she wasn't alone.

Jessi just sobbed; nothing was said, no false looks. When she finally began to still, Becca reached for a towel and wrapped it around her. "Come on," she said gently. "Let's get you warm."

Jessi nodded weakly, her face red and swollen from tears, but there was the slightest flicker of relief in her eyes, a fragile thread of safety, woven through the quiet between them.

* * *

As the morning light crept through the blinds, Becca was already awake, lying on her side with her arm draped lightly over Jessi. She'd barely slept, her mind looping through the night before, Jessi's trembling, her tear-streaked face, the faint bruises she hadn't been able to hide.

Now, Jessi slept curled against her, still wearing one of Becca's oversized shirts. Her breathing was shallow but even, her face peaceful in a way it hadn't been in days. Becca wanted to keep her there, suspended in that small moment of calm before the world could touch her again.

When Jessi stirred, Becca feigned sleep. She didn't want to startle her or crowd her. She listened as Jessi shifted quietly out of bed, padding toward the kitchen.

A few minutes later, the faint scent of bacon and eggs cooking drifted through the apartment. Becca finally sat up, rubbing her eyes and pulling on her robe before joining her.

Jessi stood by the counter, holding her mug in both hands as if it were an anchor. Her hair was pulled back, her eyes still a little puffy, but she offered Becca a faint smile.

"Morning," she said softly.

Becca returned the smile and crossed to her. "Morning." She poured herself some coffee and leaned against the counter next to Jessi, spooning in some sugar. Neither of them spoke for a long moment. The silence wasn't uncomfortable, just careful.

"How are you feeling?" Becca asked, finally.

Jessi took a slow breath. "Sore," she admitted. "But better, I think."

Becca nodded, studying her profile. Jessi's shoulders were drawn tight, her knuckles white against the ceramic mug. "You don't have to pretend for me," Becca said quietly. "You don't have to be okay yet."

Jessi blinked, her mouth opening as if to say something, then closing again. She nodded faintly, eyes glistening. "I know. I just…" She exhaled shakily. "I don't know if I can... I..." She just shook her head and stared off into space.

Becca reached out, brushing her fingers over Jessi's wrist. "We'll just take today. One piece at a time. You don't have to tell me until you're ready, Jessi."

Jessi's eyes lingered on her, searching, then softening. She nodded again, setting her mug down and stepping closer. Becca wrapped her arms around her, feeling the faint tremor still running through Jessi's body.

"I love you," Jessi whispered into her hair.

Becca blinked, then gave a wide grin. "You love me?"

Jessi clung to her for a long time before whispering back, "I do."

"I love you too, Jessi. I don't think you know how much."

Outside, a light rain began to fall, tapping gently against the windows. The two stood in the small kitchen, holding each other, uncertain, but for the first time in a long while, together.

21
New Beginnings

Two weeks passed in a rhythm that was both comforting and fragile. Jessi tried to weave herself back into the routines of their lives, work, meals, and the small rituals she and Becca shared, but each step carried a shadow she couldn't quite shake. She laughed at the right moments, contributed to conversations, and even joined Becca for late-night walks around the neighborhood. On the surface, it was the Jessi everyone remembered: bright, mischievous, full of life.

Becca watched her closely, though she didn't push. She saw the subtle tics, Jessi flinching at sudden noises, a hasty glance over her shoulder, or holding herself more rigidly than necessary. Becca didn't mention it. Instead, she offered small gestures: a hand brushing Jessi's hair out of her eyes, a cold glass of tea waiting when she came home from work, a quiet presence on the couch when Jessi curled up with a book.

One evening, they cooked dinner together. Jessi chopped vegetables, her hands steady, her smile easy. Becca noticed the faint yellowing bruise on Jessi's wrist and the lingering tension in her shoulders. She said nothing, only moved closer, sliding an arm around her as they stirred the simmering sauce. Jessi leaned into her, grateful for the warmth and support, and for a moment, it was enough.

* * *

On another afternoon, they curled up in the living room, watching a movie. Jessi's head rested against Becca's shoulder; her fingers entwined with hers. Every time a suspenseful scene flickered on the screen, Jessi's body tensed, but Becca's hand on her back was steady and reassuring. She didn't speak of the assault; she didn't need to. Jessi felt seen, even without words, and it gave her a strange kind of strength.

At night, when they lay together, Jessi would sometimes wake in the dark, haunted by memories she didn't voice. Becca's presence, warm and unwavering, let her breathe, allowed her to ride out the tremors of panic that sometimes shook her.

They existed in this delicate balance: life carrying forward, trauma lingering beneath the surface, and love steady enough to provide a fragile, protective cocoon. Becca sensed the fractures in Jessi, but she also sensed resilience, a tiny flame that refused to be extinguished, even in the shadow of what had happened.

And slowly, imperceptibly, Jessi began to trust that she could lean on someone again, that the world didn't have to be faced alone.

* * *

Monday morning arrived in a haze of unease. Jessi sat at her desk, staring at the screen, her mind half on the spreadsheet in front of her and half on the tight coil of dread twisting in her stomach. The last few weeks, weeks of scattered focus, impulsive choices, and sleepless nights, had left marks she couldn't hide.

When her manager, Mr. Caldwell, called her into his office, her chest tightened. The office smelled faintly of doughnuts and stale paperwork. He gestured for her to sit.

"Jessi… I don't envy saying this," he began slowly. "But over the past month, we've noticed... well, a decline in your work. There have been repeated errors, missed deadlines, and… frankly, it's affecting the team. I'm sorry to have to say this, but I'm afraid we have to let you go."

The words hit Jessi like a punch she hadn't expected. For a heartbeat, she couldn't breathe, her mind scrambling for some protest, an excuse. Then a strange, almost guilty relief swept over her.

She hated this job; hated the small cubicle that made her feel trapped, hated staring at the computer screen for hours while her body and mind screamed for movement, for freedom, for… something more. And now, the cage had been opened for her, whether she wanted it or not.

"I… I understand," she said, her voice soft but steady. She stood, gathering her things, each movement heavy with a strange mixture of shame and liberation.

* * *

Back in the apartment, Jessi sank onto the couch, letting the weight of the day settle over her. When Becca arrived, her eyes immediately searched Jessi's face. She noticed the tired set of her shoulders, the faraway look in her eyes.

"What happened?" Becca asked, concern threading her tone.

Jessi took a deep breath, forcing a smile that didn't reach her eyes. "Glad to see you too," she said with a smile.

Becca smiled back. "I'm sorry. I really am glad to be home with you."

"I got fired," Jessi admitted with a laugh. "I… I guess I've not been at the top of my game at work. Honestly… I hated it anyway. But now... how am I going to pay the bills?"

Becca moved closer, sitting beside her and taking her hand. "I'm sorry, Jess. I know you've been trying. But... look at it this way. Now you can find something you enjoy. Something better. I'll keep us afloat. Don't worry."

Jessi nodded, squeezing Becca's hand. "Yeah… maybe. I'm not sure what I could do that I'd enjoy. And, I don't want to put a burden on you. I'll be looking for... something… something better, I hope." She paused, letting the words linger.

Becca leaned her head on Jessi's shoulder, offering comfort without pressing for details. Jessi allowed herself a small sigh, the tension in her body loosening just a fraction. The future was uncertain, but she felt a tiny spark of possibility flicker inside her.

* * *

Jessi sank into the couch, the morning paper spread across her lap, the bright glow of her laptop casting a soft light on her face. She scrolled through online listings, flipping through classified ads. Still, nearly every position required a college degree, sales, marketing, and administrative work, and the frustration built like a tightening coil in her chest.

She closed the laptop with a soft sigh and leaned back, staring at the ceiling. Her thoughts drifted to Becca—Becca and her art. She wanted Becca to chase her passions. *If only…* Jessi shook her head, pushing the idea away. She needed something practical, something to pay the bills. "God, I don't want to be a waitress," she said to herself under her breath.

Not finding anything, she decided to take the car and drive around, scanning neighborhoods, small shops, and any business that might have a help-wanted sign. The city passed by in a blur, sun glinting off buildings, the hum of traffic filling the quiet moments.

As she turned a corner near the old factory district, her stomach gave a slight lurch. There it was: Tommy's. The memories of that night, the leering bikers, Spike's quiet, unexpected help, came rushing back. She slowed the car and parked at the far edge of the parking lot, keeping her distance.

Through the dusty, barred windows, she could see the neon sign still flickering faintly: *Girls, Girls,*

Girls. And taped to one of the doors, a help-wanted sign. *Strippers wanted.*

Her mind raced. How hard could it be? She thought about the money, the freedom, the raw, chaotic thrill of the work. She'd done things before that she wasn't proud of. This… this might just be manageable.

Jessi hesitated at the doorway, taking a deep breath. The sunlight streaming through the barred windows made the interior feel cavernous and muted, the faint scent of alcohol and smoke lingering in the air. There were two sections inside: a large room with pool tables and a bar to one side, and, at the other end of the building, an ample space opening onto a stage, tables, and booths. The stage sat at the far end, a couple of brass poles shining under a spotlight. A short catwalk jutted out from the main stage, with chairs lining each side. Along the wall, a long bar stretched, glasses and liquor bottles lining the shelves behind it. On the opposite side, a DJ booth sat on an elevated pedestal.

The club was nearly empty; chairs turned upside-down and placed on tables scattered around the main floor, a polished stage gleaming under the dimmed ceiling lights.

A large man with broad shoulders and a husky frame lounged behind the bar, polishing a glass with a rag that looked like it had seen better days. His eyes lifted as Jessi approached, and he gave a slow, appraising nod.

"How can I help you, girlie?" he asked in a low, gruff voice.

Jessi felt her stomach tighten. "Yeah… I was wondering about... the help wanted sign."

The man set the glass down and leaned forward slightly. "You wanting to dance?"

Jessi looked back with a shy grin. "I was thinking about it."

He nodded as he continued to clean glasses on the bar top. "House fees thirty to fifty bucks during the week," he said, motioning toward a worn ledger on the bar. "Zero on Mondays, that's your only free day. You'd charge five per lap dance, fifty for fifteen-minute VIPs, a hundred for thirty, and two hundred for an hour. Don't forget to tip the DJ, he runs the music."

Jessi blinked, letting the numbers sink in. "Okay… okay, I think I understand." She tucked a strand of hair behind her ear, trying to appear confident despite the fluttering in her chest.

"You can work the pool room too. Get them to buy you a drink, and I'll give you half the price."

Jessi blinked and looked at the alcohol on the shelves. "Well, I'm not sure I can handle too many drinks."

The man let out a half-laugh and shook his head. "You get the guys to buy you a Jack and Coke. It's $10 a drink. I give you just a Coke, and you get five dollars. No one knows any better, and everyone's happy."

Jessi smiled and rolled her eyes. "Oh... I understand."

The man shrugged, leaning back against the bar. "That's the deal. You want to try it, you show up, do your thing, and keep the money that comes in. Simple enough."

Jessi nodded again, her mind racing. It wasn't glamorous, but it was a start, and, for her restless compulsion, it promised a thrill she hadn't felt in weeks. She took another deep breath and straightened her shoulders. "Alright… Thank you. Your name is... ?"

"I'm the owner, Tommy."

"Oh. Nice to meet you, Tommy."

He gave a short grunt, like he approved of the determination in her tone, then went back to his glass. Jessi lingered for a moment, taking in the empty stage and quiet club. It was surreal, trying to imagine being up there, performing, commanding attention, making her own money… and pushing her limits at the same time.

When she stepped back out into the sunlight, her heart was racing, a strange mixture of fear, anticipation, and exhilaration swirling through her. This was a different kind of risk, but for the first time in weeks, she felt something ignite inside her again.

22
Taking the Stage

Tuesday afternoon, Jessi felt an unfamiliar mix of anticipation and nerves. She slipped into a cropped gray t-shirt that barely reached below her breasts, the soft fabric clinging lightly to her skin, paired with tight, frayed Daisy Duke shorts. Her legs looked long and lean, accentuated by the high-heeled ankle boots she'd chosen. She glanced at herself in the mirror, fidgeting with her hair, before grabbing her keys and heading out. She left a note on the counter for Becca. *Going to check on a new job. Will be back later.*

The street outside was quiet as she drove. The club's neon sign buzzed softly in the night air: *Girls, Girls, Girls*. It cast a pinkish glow over the worn sidewalks. As she stepped through the door, the scent of perfume, sweat, and alcohol washed over her. The place was empty compared to the weekend rush; only a handful of patrons sat at the bar or at small tables near the stage.

A few dancers were on the stage, their movements fluid, practiced, and mesmerizing. Jessi watched, fascinated, as one girl twisted and arched under the spotlight, a glittering bra and tiny shorts catching the dim light. Another leaned against the pole with effortless confidence, spinning and sliding her body in ways Jessi hadn't realized required such precise control. The music thumped through the floor, a pulsing rhythm that seemed to sync with her heartbeat.

Jessi noted the small details: the way the girls held their weight on the balls of their feet, how they moved their hips just so, how they used their hands to emphasize curves or tease the crowd. Their outfits varied, from lace bras to leather bodices, bikinis, and lingerie, each girl owning her own edgy version of allure.

She edged closer to the stage, leaning on the rail as she observed, trying to memorize every move, every subtle shift in posture, every glance thrown to the patrons. Her pulse quickened. The room was quiet, but she felt alive, energized by the performance and the possibilities it suggested for her own future on the stage.

A small smile tugged at her lips. She could do this, she could learn to move like that, to command attention with just a glance, to turn her nervous energy into power. For now, she would watch, take notes in her mind, and imagine herself in those outfits, under those lights, performing for a crowd that hung on every movement.

* * *

As night fell, the club felt electric, and as the music carried through, Jessi knew this was more than curiosity. This was the spark of something dangerous and thrilling, a path that might let her reclaim herself, piece by piece, through dance and control, even as her life outside the club felt uncertain.

Jessi drove home with the idea gnawing at her, her mind a mixture of fear, excitement, and guilt. The apartment smelled faintly of Becca's lavender candle, a small comfort. She found Becca in the living room, sketching quietly at the coffee table.

"Hey," Jessi said, trying to keep her tone casual.

"Hi, baby," Becca answered without looking up. When she did, her eyes widened. "What are you wearing?"

Jessi looked down and giggled, "Oh… I saw a sign the other day. Help wanted… at this place I know, Tommy's." She paused, watching Becca's eyes lift, curiosity flickering. "I was... thinking about.... maybe dancing there," she added, almost in a whisper.

Becca set down her pencil, tilting her head, unsure how to respond. "You're… thinking about... dancing? Like, being a stripper?" she asked carefully, the concern in her voice unmistakable.

"Maybe," Jessi admitted, shrugging, trying to make it sound light, casual. "I mean… It's good money. At least I think guys would pay to see me. And I need a job, right? How hard could it be?"

Becca studied her for a long moment, her gaze sharp but gentle. She didn't say anything immediately, just let Jessi's words hang in the air. There was worry there, yes, but also the faintest trace of understanding.

Jessi watched her, waiting for a reaction, and wondered if Becca knew more than she let on about the dangerous edge she sometimes teetered on.

Becca leaned back in her chair, her sketchpad forgotten for the moment. She could feel the tension in the room, the way Jessi's voice had wavered, trying to make the idea sound casual, harmless. She thought of the first time she'd watched Jessi on stage at the swingers' club, graceful, confident, owning the room in a way Becca could never quite imagine. She could do it, that much was undeniable.

But the memory was sharp-edged. Her stomach tightened at the thought. Safety… that was her first, instinctive reaction. Could she really let Jessi go back into that world, this time fully on her own?

Yet she also understood something else, something she had never fully acknowledged before. Jessi had needs, compulsions that weren't going to disappear just because they weren't convenient. There was a hunger in her, a restlessness, a thrill-seeking drive that could either be destructive or… channeled. Maybe this could be that channel.

Becca ran her fingers through her hair and let out a slow breath. "I… I don't know, Jess," she said finally, her voice soft but layered with conflict. "There might be other jobs… something safer. I know you can do it. I just… I worry, that's all."

Jessi watched her, reading the worry behind Becca's words, but also the hesitant understanding. "I know, Becca," she said quietly. "I'll be careful. There are bouncers there that protect the girls. And, I can work my own hours, maybe just a couple of nights a week. I just… I need this. I need to feel alive again. I'll figure it out, okay?"

Becca's eyes lingered on her, torn between the instinct to protect and the realization that shielding Jessi completely might do more harm than good. "I don't want to be someone who tries to control you, Jessi. Just… promise me you'll watch your back. Always," she murmured.

Jessi smiled faintly, reaching out to squeeze Becca's hand. "I promise," she said, though both of them knew that it was a promise of effort, not certainty.

For a long moment, they sat in silence, the apartment quiet. Becca's thoughts were a jumble of fear, hope, and resignation, while Jessi felt the spark of something dangerous, thrilling, and necessary stirring inside her again.

It was a fragile truce with the night, with their lives, with each other, but for now, it was enough.

* * *

Jessi decided her first night would be on Thursday, and it arrived with an electric kind of tension for her. Her hands shook slightly as she grabbed her purse, the nerves coiling in her stomach like a live thing.

When she walked through the club's doors, the interior looked different at night. The bar was still polished, the stage gleaming under a soft wash of overhead lighting, but there were only a handful of other dancers scattered around, practicing routines or chatting quietly. The air smelled faintly of cleaning supplies, mixed with the lingering aroma of cigarette smoke and alcohol.

Tommy was behind the bar, giving her a nod as she approached. "You ready, kid?" he asked.

Jessi swallowed hard and nodded. "Yeah. I… I think I am."

He grunted. "First time's always rough. Stick to the rules, don't let anyone touch you, and keep your wits about you. Money comes after that. You aren't allowed to let them touch you, but what happens in the private rooms, I don't want to know about. You get caught, that's on you."

Somewhere deep down, she knew that this new life she had stepped into wasn't safe. It was risky, thrilling, and a little reckless, but for now, it was exactly what she needed to keep herself from sinking back into despair.

She had met bouncers at the club, alternating nights. Dan was a husky, mountainous man with a long beard. She had tried to flirt with him a couple of times, but she couldn't even crack a smile with him. Duncan was a man with bulging muscles, clean-shaven, including his head. Everyone at the club referred to him as Mr. Clean, and tonight he stood at the front entrance like a sentinel.

Jessi's heart thudded in her chest as she stood in the dimly lit dressing area of the club. She had spent hours preparing, curling her dark red locks into ringlets that draped across her face and shoulders, down to the middle of her back. Diamond studs sparkled in her earlobes, but she had forgone any other jewelry, afraid of losing them as she danced.

She had shopped for a daring outfit, a micro bikini in emerald green that made her skin tingle with both excitement and nerves. The top barely covered her nipples, and the thong, tied delicately at each hip, left almost nothing to the imagination. Her thigh-high leather boots hugged her legs like a second skin, the sharp heels clicking against the floor as she moved. She layered a skimpy green top over it that tied at the chest.

Each step toward the main room quickened her pulse. The club was alive, though still lightly populated for a weekday night. The music thumped in her chest, a deep, steady rhythm that seemed to sync with her own heartbeat. She talked with the DJ for just a bit, setting up her playlist for when she planned to be onstage.

She met most of the other dancers that night, each with some erotic stage name. There was Candy, Veronica, Crystal, Jasmine, Destiny, Tiffany, Cherry, Honey, Rose, Asia, and Blaze. Each of them had their own niche and routine.

Asia was a beautiful Chinese American girl who played up her Asian heritage on stage, dancing with oriental fans in a mesmerizing, seductive performance. Blaze was a demure African beauty who twerked and shook her ass in a powerful hip-hop-themed presentation.

Jessi had thought about what her onstage forte would be. She decided to be herself. No fancy stage name or themed dance. She would just let the music guide her in her own seductive way. She didn't want to perform so much as just let herself go.

Behind the velvet curtain, she took a deep breath, adjusting her top and tugging the bottoms into place. Her hands trembled slightly, but she forced herself to stand tall. This was her choice. She wanted this. She briefly talked with a couple of the other dancers; most were nice, while a few acted indifferent to her presence.

"This your first time, sweetie?" one dancer asked as she chewed gum while looking Jessi over. She was a buxom blonde with large breasts that she constantly adjusted in her lacey black bra.

"Uh... yeah. I guess it is," Jessi answered timidly.

"Don't worry, honey. You look great. My name's Candy."

"Nice to meet you, Candy. Jessi."

Candy grinned. "Well, go knock 'em dead, sugar."

A glance at the other dancers gave her a mixture of inspiration and intimidation. They moved with fluid confidence, hips rolling, eyes teasing the small crowd that lingered near the stage. Their bodies shimmered under the stage lights, every curve exaggerated by glittering fabrics and the sparkle of sweat. Jessi felt the electric pulse of possibility, imagining herself owning the stage.

When the music shifted, the DJ signaling her turn, she stepped through the curtain, feeling the heat of the spotlight on her skin. He played "Buttons" at her request. Every eye in the room seemed to fall on her instantly. She tightened her core, lifted her chin, and began to move.

Her first steps were cautious, almost tentative, as she adjusted to the slickness of the stage under her boots. But the music pulsed through her, and her confidence grew with each sway of her hips. She reached for the pole, gripping it, spinning carefully at first, then with more fluidity as her body remembered lessons she'd observed in the other dancers.

Jessi's heart raced, a cocktail of fear and exhilaration. She let herself lean into the performance, teasing the audience with glances, arching her back, letting her hands trace over her body as if the stage itself responded to her movements. She reached up and untied the top, letting it fall to the floor.

She could hear the crowd clap and cheer as she teased with a tug at her micro top. Each second on the floor, she felt more herself than she had in weeks, alive, daring, and in control in a way that nothing outside this room could replicate. She could see a couple of men standing in front of the stage, waving five-dollar bills in their hands. She seductively danced up to them, lifting her top to expose her tits and bucking her hips slowly as she hooked a thumb underneath the string of her thong. She pulled it away from her body as she smiled at the men. Each tucked a bill under the string, one of them giving a wolf whistle.

By the end of her first song, she was panting, flushed, but exhilarated. The small crowd clapped, a few whistles piercing through. She stood in the spotlight, breathing hard, and tasting the rush of danger and desire mingled together. For the first time in a long while, Jessi felt an intoxicating sense of power, and the thrill was addicting.

Jessi felt the heat from the stage lights burn against her bare skin as she stepped back, letting the next song carry her into a rhythm that was all her own. "Pussy Liquor" was her following selection. She noticed a few patrons leaning closer to the stage, eyes following every curve of her body. Their attention was intense but not threatening, giving her a thrill that made her chest tighten and her stomach flutter.

As she moved through her routine, she spotted a man near the back who seemed more interested than the rest of the casual crowd. He was sharply dressed, exuding confidence, and he nodded at the DJ, who immediately picked up on it. The DJ's signal was subtle, a quick tap on the console, then a flick of his wrist toward the VIP room.

Jessi's pulse quickened. She'd read about the VIP rooms, small, private areas where clients could pay for lap dances or extended time. Her mind raced with a mix of anticipation and nervousness. Could she handle it? She had to. Her body, still alive with the adrenaline from the stage, seemed to demand it.

The DJ waved her over with a grin. "Looks like we've got a VIP request. You in?"

She swallowed, feeling the lump of both fear and excitement in her throat. She gave a thumbs up despite the tingling in her limbs.

The VIP room was located a short distance down a dimly lit hallway. The air smelled faintly of incense and alcohol, warmer than the main floor. A man sat in the leather armchair, watching her with intent curiosity. Jessi paused at the doorway, letting herself assess him. He was clearly a regular, relaxed, confident, but not predatory. That helped her take the first step forward.

"Hello, baby. How are you tonight?" she teased with a seductive smile.

"I'm wonderful. You're new here, aren't you?" the man said as he took a sip from the drink in his hand.

"I am sugar. My first night. I guess you could say you're taking my VIP cherry."

The man let out a laugh as he sat back in the chair. He opened his wallet and pulled out a $50 bill. "Let's start with this."

She grinned and started with subtle movements, teasing with her hips, letting her hands trace lightly along her own body. He reached out once, lightly touching her hip, and she responded with a tilt of her head, meeting his gaze. She wagged her finger. "No touching. You wouldn't want me to get in trouble on my first night, would you?"

He smiled. "Well, we can't have you in trouble now, can we?"

The tension between control and surrender was electric. She knew she had to navigate it carefully, playful, enticing, but never unsafe. The man signaled for her to come closer, and she stepped in, feeling her confidence swell. She reached up and pulled her top off, then slowly turned and gently eased her bottoms down, bending down until they were at her ankles. She stepped out of the garment, then turned, putting one finger to her bottom lip with a pouty tease.

Each motion she made, the lean, the sway, the touch of her hands along his thighs, was deliberate.

She let herself feel the power of the moment: her body, her choice, her control. She seductively worked her way up his body, keeping her boobs close to his face. She could feel his hot breath on her exposed skin. She turned and sat in his lap, leaning back with her head against his cheek. Rocking her hips back and forth, she could feel the bulge in his pants grow, aching to be set free. This made her smile. He wanted her, and she loved it.

After a few minutes, the man leaned back and nodded appreciatively, handing her the $50 with a smile. "You've got talent," he said. "That was very good."

Jessi took the money, her hands steady, feeling a mix of pride and exhilaration. This wasn't just money—it was proof that she could reclaim control, find pleasure in her own terms, and navigate a space that had once seemed intimidating. She bent over, grabbed her small outfit, and struggled to put it back on. She blew him a kiss as she opened the door. "Thank you, baby."

As she returned to the main room, the lights and music wrapping around her, she felt a heady mix of empowerment and thrill. The night was still young, and Jessi felt not only alive but in charge of her life, even if just for this hour, under these lights.

Her second lap dance came quickly. A middle-aged man slid into a chair near the stage, discreetly flashing a fifty-dollar bill. Jessi walked up to the man and ran her hands through his hair. She reached out and took his hand, guiding him back to the private rooms. Her hands trembled slightly as she performed, but she forced herself to keep her movements smooth and confident, feeling the warmth of her own power and control. Each small act of performance ignited the adrenaline she craved.

By the third VIP request, she felt a strange, dizzying mix of fear and exhilaration. Another man had requested fifteen minutes, and she kept her distance, following the rules Tommy had given her. She smiled, letting her movements flow; the gnawing sense of helplessness that had haunted her was replaced by control, control over the room, over her body, and over the chaos within herself.

Later, she wandered the room, making eyes with customers and offering small talk. She flirted and joked, asking each man if they would like to buy her a drink. Almost all did; she waved over one of the waitresses and told her that the gentleman would like to buy her a Jack and Coke. Just as promised, the drink returned to Jessi, missing the alcohol, but she played along with the charade. She feigned the harshness of the whiskey before downing the drink.

By the time she was counting her earnings at the end of the night, Jessi was exhausted, but alive in a way she hadn't felt in months. The faint bruises from past traumas ached, a dull reminder of her fragility, but her mind buzzed with a sense of accomplishment. She tucked her tips into her purse, straightened her hair, and glanced at the stage.

She felt alive… she felt… at home.

23
Naked Purpose

It was nearly midnight when Jessi slipped through the apartment door, easing it closed behind her. The faint scent of alcohol and cigarette smoke clung to her hair and her coat, drifting into the darkened living room. Only the kitchen light, deliberately left on, cast a soft glow through the space.

Rebecca was already in bed, though sleep had been impossible. She'd spent the earlier part of the evening parked across from the club, watching the line of Harleys glitter under the streetlamp, the gravel lot full of trucks and strangers. She had gripped the steering wheel, torn between going inside and calling her name… or staying invisible.

She had chosen invisible.

Jessi needed space. She needed to feel capable. And Rebecca refused to become another person who told her what she could or couldn't do.

Still, the unease gnawed at her.

Now, as the bedroom door creaked open, she looked up.

"You're back," she said softly, unsure whether she sounded relieved or still worried. "How was your night?"

Jessi paused, as if gauging how much truth she could safely reveal, then dropped her purse onto the floor and leaned back against the bed. "It was pretty good." Her voice wavered almost imperceptibly, but she smiled, a tired, shaky smile that didn't quite reach her eyes. "I made three hundred seventy-five dollars."

Rebecca blinked. "In one night? How long were you there?"

"Uh… five hours." Jessi shrugged lightly. "And it wasn't even busy. The owner said weekends are way better."

Rebecca pushed herself up on her elbows. She didn't know what she was supposed to feel. Impressed? Proud? Terrified? Jessi had gone out and done something undeniably brave, but the flashing neon, the unfamiliar men, the motorcycles lined like a wall of warning signs, those images still flickered in her mind. "That's… a lot of money," she said carefully.

Jessi gave a breathy laugh, sinking into the small chair beside the bed. She pulled off her overcoat, revealing the micro bikini beneath, and began unzipping her thigh-high boots. "Yeah. Crazy, right? I mean… I was amazed."

Rebecca studied the bikini, the glitter, the way Jessi's skin still held the faint flush of adrenaline. "Did you wear that?" she asked quietly.

Jessi smirked. "Well… yeah." She wiggled her eyebrows. "Guess I'm gonna need more sexy outfits."

Rebecca recognized that spark, the bright, volatile light that meant Jessi felt alive again… sometimes too alive. "Did you… enjoy it?" she asked softly. "Are you okay? Really, okay?"

Jessi hesitated, the question landing harder than she expected. For a moment, her façade faltered. Then she reached out and took Rebecca's hand, giving her a reassuring squeeze.

"Yeah," she said. "I think I did. I feel great."

Rebecca squeezed back. "Just promise me you'll be careful, okay?"

"I will," Jessi answered. Her tone was steady, but the shimmer in her eyes, restless, searching, made Rebecca's heart twist. It was the same look Jessi wore every time she stood at the edge of something she couldn't fully control.

The room grew quiet. Jessi slipped out of her bikini and let it fall onto the bed beside Rebecca, her movements slowing with exhaustion. She shuffled into the bathroom, leaving the door open as she removed her makeup.

"You worry too much."

Rebecca only smiled, not saying a word.

A few minutes later, Jessi climbed onto the mattress and rested her head against Rebecca's shoulder. When she spoke, her voice was barely a whisper. "I just want to keep feeling like I matter."

Rebecca closed her eyes, kissed the top of her head, and whispered back, "You matter to me."

* * *

The next morning, Jessi stirred with a low, satisfied hum. The sound of Becca moving around in the bathroom, the faint clink of her makeup case, the rush of running water, carried through the small apartment. Jessi stretched, her body still loose from sleep, then rolled out of bed and slipped toward the bathroom, still naked.

Becca stood at the sink, her hair pulled back, brushing a touch of color onto her cheeks when Jessi appeared in the doorway.

"Morning, sunshine," Becca said with a faint grin.

"Morning, you gorgeous thing," Jessi replied with mock dramatics, slipping past her for her morning pee. She reached out to start the shower. Steam began to rise as she stepped in, her voice lifting over the noise of the water. "I've decided I'm going shopping today!"

Becca raised an eyebrow at the mirror. "Shopping, huh? For what?"

"Work clothes." Jessi laughed, the sound bright, maybe too bright. "I mean… I can't exactly wear the same green bikini every night, right? I need variety. Something sparkly, maybe something leather. Ooh, maybe even a red one, you think I could pull off red?"

Becca couldn't help but smile at her enthusiasm, but there was an ache behind it, too. Jessi's highs always glowed like this, so full of life they almost blinded her. "You can pull off anything," Becca said quietly, meeting Jessi's reflection in the fogged mirror. "Just don't go overboard, okay?"

"Me? Overboard?" Jessi giggled, pressing her wet hands to the shower curtain to pull it back a bit. "Never. I'm being practical."

"Right," Becca said with a teasing grin that didn't quite mask her concern.

Jessi's voice softened then, her words rolling out through the steam. "You know, for the first time in a long while I didn't think about..." She paused, and Becca could sense her trying to find her words. They never came.

Becca froze mid-motion, toothbrush in hand. She wanted to ask what she was thinking about, but she didn't want to reopen a wound that had obviously not healed. "You are something beautiful, Jess."

Jessi smiled faintly, though Becca couldn't see it through the shower curtain. "You're sweet."

Becca didn't reply right away. She only listened to the hiss of the water, the faint, uneven tremor that had crept into Jessi's voice beneath the cheerfulness.

When the water stopped, Jessi peeked out from the shower, dripping and grinning, her hair slicked back. "I'll be gone before you get home tonight," she said. "Friday nights are supposed to be wild."

Rebecca smiled, gentle but tight around the edges. "I'm glad you feel good about it."

Jessi paused. "You… sure?"

Rebecca hesitated, only a heartbeat, but long enough for the air between them to shift.

"Jessi," she said softly, "I want you to do what feels right for you. Truly. But I also want you to be safe. That place…" She trailed off, choosing her words carefully. "There are other jobs out there. Ones where you don't have to worry about the wrong kind of attention."

Jessi frowned, setting the towel down. "You think I can't handle it?"

"That's not what I'm saying."

"Then what are you saying?"

Rebecca folded her hands, steadying herself. "I'm saying I care about you. And I don't want to lose you to something dangerous just because it feels empowering at first."

Silence settled between them. Jessi looked down as she stepped out of the shower.

Rebecca watched her, saw the conflict tighten her jaw, saw the familiar flicker of defiance and hurt. She resisted the urge to reach out, to guide her, to shield her. Jessi needed autonomy. She needed to heal in her own way.

"So…" Jessi murmured, "you don't want me doing it?"

Rebecca swallowed hard. "I want you to choose what's best for you. I just… Hope you stay open to other options too."

Jessi nodded slowly, not entirely convinced but not shutting the door.

Rebecca didn't mention the Harleys, the gravel lot, or the shadowed door she'd watched men walk through. She kept that worry to herself. Not out of secrecy, but because Jessi deserved the chance to stand on her own feet, even if the ground was uneven.

And Rebecca stayed close, quietly, ready to catch her if she slipped. "I'm going to miss our Fridays and Saturdays together."

"It won't be all the time. We'll still have time together."

“Okay. Just… text me when you get there tonight?”

Jessi leaned over and kissed her on the cheek, quick and playful, then disappeared into the bedroom, humming to herself as she got dressed.

Becca stood there for a moment longer, staring at the foggy mirror, the condensation dripping slowly down. The sound of Jessi’s bright humming carried through the apartment, beautiful, alive, and somehow heartbreaking.

* * *

That evening, Becca came home to an apartment that felt too quiet. The lights were low, Bob's purring the only sound greeting her. Jessi’s perfume still lingered faintly in the air, a sweet, musky scent layered with something sharper, like expensive body spray. It clung to the bedroom door, left half-open, to the faint trace of glitter on the bathroom counter.

Becca dropped her keys in the bowl on the counter and exhaled. “Jessi?” she called out softly, though she already knew there wouldn’t be an answer.

She walked through the apartment, the click of her heels echoing against the tile. On the bed lay the discarded overcoat Jessi sometimes wore to the club, its collar turned up, a smear of foundation on the inside of the lapel. The kitchen table held the remnants of her morning chaos, a half-drunk cup of coffee, a crumpled receipt from a store, and a small paper bag with a new tag that read "Wild Siren Boutique."

Becca peeked inside. Only the photo of the garment remained: a deep-red satin and black lace. The new "work clothes."

She sighed, sitting on the edge of the bed, running her thumb along the tag. Jessi had looked so alive that morning, eyes sparkling, words tumbling out like a stream that couldn't be stopped. And now, as the apartment swallowed Becca's quiet, she felt that familiar ache creeping in again, the worry, the helplessness, the knowledge that Jessi's highs never lasted forever.

Becca slipped out of her shoes and lay back on the bed, staring at the ceiling fan spinning lazily above. She could almost picture Jessi now, that same energy spilling out of her under neon lights, laughter too bright, maybe a little desperate.

She picked up her phone, thumb hovering over Jessi's name. The clock on the screen read 9:42 PM. Becca typed:

Hope you're having a good night. Be safe. Love you.

She hesitated, reading the words twice before hitting send.

A moment later, the phone buzzed, Jessi's reply flashing across the screen:

I'm fine, babe, don't worry.

Becca smiled faintly, but her chest tightened. It was too cheerful, too rehearsed.

She turned off the lamp, rolled onto her side, and listened to the silence fill in around her again. Outside, traffic murmured in the distance. The city continued to live, laugh, and sing. But the apartment, their small, imperfect home, felt like it was holding its breath, waiting for something Becca couldn't name.

* * *

At the club, Jessi stepped onto the stage, the spotlights throwing everything into stark contrasts of color and shadow. The room was alive with Friday night patrons, and the low hum of the music made her pulse race. She could feel the heat of the lights against her skin and the energy of the packed audience.

She moved with confidence, letting the rhythm guide her. However, her mind was half elsewhere, calculating tips, watching the reactions, thinking about the money she could make, and about the strange mix of exhilaration and vulnerability that came with being on stage. She teased the crowd with her new lacey outfit, turning and thrusting her hips in a seductive ballet. Every step of her strappy red heels, every turn, made her heart beat faster, and though she felt exposed, there was a thrill in claiming control over the attention she drew. She saw the dollar bills being tossed to the stage, while others leaned over, bills in hand, waiting for her attention. She would lean over, flashing her boobs in their face as they tucked the money along the thin string of her thong.

From the corner of her eye, she noticed the other dancers. They were experienced, fluid in their movements, and she observed them quietly, learning what worked and what didn't. The way they handled the crowd and created a persona larger than themselves fascinated her. She realized that this wasn't just about money; it was about crafting a performance, a presence, a way to channel her energy that had been so chaotic lately.

By the time her set ended, she gathered up her tips and stepped off the stage. Her legs were tired, her palms slightly sweaty, but her mind was buzzing. She stuffed the tips into her purse, then made her way through the crowd. This was a world she hadn't expected to navigate, and yet, she was finding her footing.

Almost immediately, she had a fifteen-minute VIP session, then a thirty-minute session. She was new to the crowd and found herself popular amongst the regulars. She ate up the attention, savoring the infatuated stares and longing looks. The more she performed, the better and more daring she became.

Again, she shuffled along the main room, flirting and smiling at the throng of men. A couple of the more experienced dancers nodded at her as she passed, giving her small, encouraging smiles. They didn't say much, but the recognition alone gave her a little boost.

A few patrons, curious, wandered over and asked questions about her performances or complimented her outfit. Jessi handled it with a practiced smile, keeping the conversation light, careful to remain in control. She realized quickly that this environment rewarded confidence and poise as much as anything else. Every word, every gesture, mattered. She would ask them to buy her a drink, and they were happy to oblige.

Tommy came over, wiping his hands on a rag. "You're doing well," he said, low and rough. "Keep it up, and the tips'll get better as people start remembering you." Jessi nodded, smiling, letting herself feel the validation. She knew she had a long way to go to really understand the business, but for now, she felt capable.

She decided to wander over to the pool hall area of the club to measure the crowd. Jessi pushed through the dimly lit room, the low hum of conversation and clinking balls filling the air, the smell of stale beer mixed with the faint scent of leather jackets and cigarette smoke. The room was alive in a subdued way, not as intense as the main room, but vibrant in its own right.

Her eyes quickly scanned the crowd, and there he was, Spike. Leaning casually against a pool table, cue in hand, he laughed at something one of his friends said. His presence instantly brought a mix of familiarity and nerves. She hadn't expected to see anyone from that night, and now he was here, watching, aware.

"Spike," she said, stepping closer, trying to keep her voice casual.

He looked up, surprised, and then his eyes widened. “Jessi? Is that really you?” His voice carried a mix of disbelief and relief. “I didn’t expect to see you… here.”

Jessi suddenly felt self-conscious in her skimpy, barely-there outfit. Even though she knew Spike had seen her completely naked, standing in front of him now seemed out of place somehow.

"God damn little girl. That's some sexy outfit. You working here?"

She smiled, a little nervously, leaning against a nearby table. “Yeah, I… I started working here this week.” She gestured vaguely toward the main stage area. “Just for a bit, seeing how it goes.”

Spike shook his head slowly, still leaning on the table. “Damn… I wondered about you. I didn’t think I’d ever see you here, and certainly not working the stage.” His tone was light, but she could catch the undercurrent of concern. “How are you doing?”

Jessi hesitated, brushing a strand of hair from her face. “I’m fine,” she said, trying to sound casual. “It’s… actually kind of fun. I make decent money, and it’s… different.” She laughed softly, though the edges of it didn’t quite reach her eyes.

Spike nodded slowly, his eyes scanning her face. “Different, huh?” he said. “Just… be careful, alright? There’s a lot going on here.”

“I know,” Jessi said, her voice firmer now. She appreciated his concern. “Thanks, Spike. I just wanted to tell you thank you. You know... for... that night.” She looked down at her feet and shuffled nervously.

He gave her a half-smile, tipping his cue slightly in acknowledgment. "You ain't gotta thank me, sweet thang. Just… remember you've got people who've got your back, yeah?"

Jessi nodded, feeling a small surge of reassurance. "No, I needed to tell you how much... well, you helped me out. A lot." She looked back at the main room. "Listen... if you want... maybe I could... I don't know... give you a dance. If you want."

"Aww, thank you, honey bun, but I ain't got that kind of money to spend."

"Oh... no. It would be... on the house. You know?" She gave a wink and a sly smile.

Spike grinned. "Well, if you put it that way. Hell yeah."

Jessi smiled and looked back at the room. "Okay. Give me a few minutes."

"Will do sweet thang. See ya in a bit."

Jessi giggled as she slinked back into the stripper room. She went to the bar and looked at the bartender. "Hey... can you give me a Jack and Coke? A real one this time," she laughed as she leaned over the bar top.

The bartender laughed. "Of course."

She took the glass and smiled. "Thank you," she said as she took a quick sip. The Coke was sweet, followed by the bourbon's slow burn. She took a deep breath, then, throwing her head back, downed the drink in a quick motion.

Turning back to the crowd, Jessi could see Spike looking around before noticing Jessi at the bar. She met him on the floor before he reached her, and she took his hand, guiding him back to the private room area.

A dim red light illuminated the small space; the music from the main room was muffled but still pulsing in her chest. She closed the door and pushed him back into the padded armchair. She began slowly, letting the rhythm guide her, moving with deliberate sensuality. Reaching up, she set her top free, then let her thong fall to the floor. Spike watched, captivated, his hands resting casually on his knees as she circled him, swaying, teasing with just the right touches of proximity.

She leaned close, letting her fingers brush his shoulders, then his chest, letting the music dictate the pace. Spike remained still, his expression a mixture of fascination and respect. She could feel the heat of his gaze, but he didn't cross any boundaries; he watched, absorbed in her performance. She leaned toward his ear. "I'll let you touch me if you want."

Spike's eyes widened as he looked at Jessi's grinning face. He reached out and cupped her breasts, one in each hand. She let out a soft moan as her body slinked from side to side with the rhythm of the music. She turned and eased her naked ass into his lap. She could tell he was hard and ready. Bucking her hips in and out, she grinded in his lap, as he reached around, fondling her nipples.

Jessi reached down, unbuttoning Spike's jeans and sliding the zipper down. She slipped her hand in, grasping his hard member, guiding it out. She pushed her butt up and guided his prick to her warm and wet pussy. She slid it back and forth along the slit, letting out a breath she had been holding in. She inched down, sliding his prick inside.

His cock was long, and she rode him deep inside her, rocking back and forth, grinding her hips as she leaned back against his husky chest. He smelled of cigarettes and motor oil, and she could feel his scruffy goatee and unshaven cheek against her face. He said nothing, only taking long, deep breaths.

Her motions increased. She reached up and grabbed one of his hands that was at her chest, and guided it down between her legs. She rocked her hips and let out a long moan. She could feel his rod grow, the heat building within him. "Give it to me, baby," she whispered between labored breaths, her rhythm increasing. She pushed him deep inside as she felt him pulse and quiver. His body tensed as his hot come filled her and eased out onto her thigh.

They both fell silent and lay in the moment, unmoving. She leaned toward his ear. "Thank you, baby."

"No, thank you, sweetheart. God damn, that's the best thanks I've ever received."

Jessi let out a little laugh as she pulled off of him. She reached for a box of tissues in the corner of the room, pulling out several and wiping herself.

“You’ve… really got it,” he said, voice low. “I didn’t think you’d be this… damn good.”

Jessi smiled, slightly flushed, her heart still racing. "Thanks," she said as she slipped back into her outfit. She stepped back, letting herself breathe, feeling a rush of empowerment and control that she hadn't expected to feel so intensely.

Spike nodded, tipping an imaginary hat. "You ever need help again, just call baby doll."

"Tell me something," Jessi said as she leaned back against the door. "What's your name… your real name?"

Spike leaned back in the chair and rubbed his goatee. "Howard. Howard Butler."

"Howard?" Jessi said with a funny grimace.

"That's what my momma told me," Spike answered as he leaned back with his hands behind his head.

"Okay," Jessi laughed. "I'm just going to keep calling you Spike."

"Honey. After that, you can call me whatever the fuck you wanna call me."

Jessi grinned as she leaned in and gave him a peck on the lips. "I better get back to work. Our secret, okay?"

"Sure thing, sugar pants."

As she left the private area, she felt a thrill in her chest, not just from the thrill or the attention, but from the realization that she could hold her own, even in a space that once had felt intimidating.

Jessi returned to the stage with renewed energy. Her body moved confidently to the pulsing music, every sway of her hips and toss of her hair commanding attention. The new lacey red-and-black outfit hugged her curves perfectly, making her feel powerful, seductive, and in control. She danced through a few more sets, each lap drawing appreciative glances and tips from the crowd.

After her set, she stepped down and mingled among the patrons. She laughed softly at their flirtations, twirled a strand of hair, and accepted drinks with a charming smile. A few men requested VIP sessions, and she negotiated smoothly, 15 minutes here, 30 minutes there, always keeping the energy high without overextending herself.

The thrill wasn't just in the money; it was being desired, the confidence, and the way she could command attention while remaining her own person. Every interaction, every dance, reaffirmed something she hadn't felt in a long time: alive, daring, and desired.

By the time the night began winding down, she felt a satisfying exhaustion, a mix of accomplishment, adrenaline, and sensual energy. Jessi knew she had found a place where she could safely channel her urges, feel her own power, and maintain some semblance of control over the chaos of her emotions.

24
A Bright Future

When she got home, the apartment was silent, and Jessi eased the door shut behind her, careful not to let the lock click too loudly. The clock on the stove glowed 3:37 a.m., later than she meant to be home, but time had blurred at the club, swept away in flashing lights and pulsing bass.

She kicked off her heels by the door, setting her purse down softly beside a pair of Becca's sneakers. Two glossy shopping bags swung from her wrist, new things she wasn't sure how to explain yet, and one that she was excited about.

The place was dim, with only the streetlight filtering through the blinds. Becca's old coat hung on the back of a chair; her sketchbook sat open on the kitchen counter, a half-drawn figure paused mid-line. Jessi paused too, watching the shadow of that outline, her outline, and feeling something twist inside her chest.

She tiptoed to the bathroom and turned on the shower, letting the noise cover the quiet. Steam filled the air quickly, curling around her as she washed away the scent of smoke and cheap perfume. Her reflection in the mirror afterward was both familiar and not: eyes bright but tired, mouth set somewhere between pride and guilt.

When she finally glided into the bedroom, naked, Becca was asleep on her side, wearing an oversized football jersey, the covers tangled around her legs, hair spilling across the pillow. Jessi stood there for a long moment, just watching her breathe. Then she slipped under the blanket, careful not to wake her, and pressed close until she could feel the warmth of Becca's back against her chest.

Jessi slid her hand along Becca's outer thigh, inching underneath the jersey to the side of her hip. She realized she wasn't wearing any panties, something that sent a tingle across Jessi's body. She moved her body down, positioning her head between Becca's legs, where she gently ran her tongue along her exposed slit.

Still in a deep slumber, Becca let out a soft moan as if she were having some erotic dream. Jessi continued, sliding her head under the sports shirt and giving smooth, gentle kisses across her belly. She reached up, slipping her hands across Becca's chest, and began tenderly pinching at her hardening nipples.

Becca slowly began to rouse, her eyes barely open, her hands reaching down to caress Jessi's head. "Jessi?" she said, her voice barely above a whisper.

"Shh…" Jessi answered. "I'm horny."

Becca pulled the shirt up and away from Jessi's head, watching her as she ran her tongue along her belly button. The sensation tickled Becca, and she began to giggle. "Oh my gosh, Jessi," she said as she tried to focus on the digital clock on the nightstand. "What time is it?"

"Playtime," Jessi said under her breath, her lips now suckling one of Becca's nipples.

Becca wiped her eyes and tried to sit up, but Jessi scooted up to face her and met her lips with a deep, passionate kiss. Their tongues danced around in their mouths; Jessi's eyes met Becca's, full of lust and desire.

"Baby," Becca said in a mock protest, reaching for the lamp on the nightstand.

Jessi only gave a sultry grin, then reached out and softly pulled the jersey up and over Becca's head. She tossed the garment across the room onto the floor, then pressed close to Becca, kissing the nape of her neck.

"Where did all this energy come from? Aren't you tired?" Becca queried.

Sitting up, Jessi continued to fondle Becca's tits. They were small but firm and perky. Suddenly, she leaned back and put a finger to her bottom lip, giving a pouty smile. "I almost forgot. I'll be right back."

Becca watched as Jessi jumped out of bed and made her way to the living room, her tiny butt bouncing with each stride. She returned carrying a large shopping bag. Jessi giggled as she tossed the package onto the bed and sat back in front of Becca.

"What's this?" Becca asked, a puzzled furrow on her brow.

"Presents," Jessi answered with a mischievous grin. She rummaged through the bag, the plastic crackling and popping with each movement. She pulled out a plastic container with a large purple dildo inside. The device was attached to a black harness, and Jessi held it up, laughing. "Now… do you want me to fuck you, or do you want to fuck me?"

Wide-eyed, Becca grabbed the package and held it up. "Oh my God, Jessi," her voice breaking with a giggle. "Where did you get this?"

"I went shopping for some new outfits before work. I saw this and thought, 'Maybe this would be fun.' You didn't answer. You or me?"

Becca let out a loud laugh as she leaned back in bed. She shook her head. "I don't know… how about both?"

Jessi's eyes lit up, and she chuckled as she rummaged through the bag again. "Oh, both? I got that covered, too." She pulled out a long pink object that Becca struggled to understand at first. She then realized it was a double dildo, a molded, veiny penis at both ends.

"Oh my God, Jessi. You are insane." She grabbed the item and twirled it above her head. "Your mind has been working overtime, hasn't it?"

Jessi grinned and bit her bottom lip. "I have one more thing, baby. Be right back."

Once again, Jessi's butt wiggled as she bounced into the living room, almost skipping in delight. She returned with another bag, this one containing a large cardboard box. She slid the box out of the bag and laid it in Becca's lap.

"What's this?" she asked.

"Open it and see."

Becca gave Jessi a side-eye and a grin as she opened up the box. Inside, a tailored black leather coat. The item gave off a rich, earthy smell as she pulled it from the box and held it up to the light. "Very nice. You'll look great in this."

"It ain't for me, dummy. I bought it for you."

She looked back at Jessi; her arms crossed with a teasing smirk. "Oh Jess… you… I mean… this had to be expensive."

"I wanted to get you something. That old quilted coat you wear… I think it's seen better days. Try it on."

Becca stepped out of bed and slid her arms through the coat. She pulled it across her shoulders and straightened it. It felt cool, the leather giving off a musky aroma. She pulled it tight across her chest.

Jessi looked at Becca, the smile on her face, her little ass peeking out below the coat. "Do you like it?"

Becca looked back at Jessi, tears forming in her eyes. "I love it, Jessi. I absolutely love it."

"I love you, Becca," Jessi answered, her eyes serious and her voice low. She stepped over and gave Becca a long hug, then kissed her cheek. She leaned in and whispered in her ear. "I guess this means you're fucking me then."

Becca laughed as she planted a big, long kiss on Jessi's lips. She pushed Jessi back as they both plopped back down into bed. She reached over and turned off the lamp. "I guess it does."

* * *

The light filtering through the blinds was thin and gold by the time Becca stirred. Jessi was already awake beside her, lying on her stomach, hair spilling across the pillow, scrolling through her phone, and humming along to a song only she could hear.

Becca stretched, feeling that soft, heavy stillness that came after a night of closeness. She smiled sleepily, but there was something new in Jessi's energy, restless, bright, electric. Her eyes were sharp, her laugh a little too quick. The expensive-smelling leather coat hung from the closet door, the one Jessi had insisted was for her, a gift.

Becca traced the collar absentmindedly and said, "You didn't have to do that."

Jessi beamed. "I wanted to. I just… wanted to do something nice for you." She reached out, brushing her fingers along Becca's cheek, her smile wide and almost radiant.

It was infectious, this mood. Becca found herself smiling back despite the unease twisting somewhere low in her chest. She knew these highs; she'd seen them before. Jessi's voice was bright and full of plans, what she could cook for lunch, and the new outfits she wanted to try on for her. It was like the past few dark months had never happened.

But Becca noticed the small things: the way Jessi's hands trembled slightly when she poured coffee, how quickly her voice shifted from laughter to intensity, and the way she avoided meeting Becca's eyes when asked about work at the club.

Still, it was good to see her like this, to see the light back in her eyes, even if it burned a little too hot.

Becca wrapped her arms around her from behind as Jessi stood at the window, sunlight catching in her auburn hair. "You seem happy," she said softly.

"I am," Jessi replied, with a smile that was too bright to doubt but too fragile to believe. "I feel like things are finally turning around, you know?"

Becca kissed her shoulder, nodding. "I hope they are," she murmured, but her eyes lingered on the city beyond the glass, wondering how long this light would last before it dimmed again.

* * *

That evening, Becca sat on the edge of the bed, watching as Jessi stood in front of the full-length mirror by the dresser, finishing her makeup. The apartment smelled faintly of vanilla body spray and hair product, mixed with the subtle tang of leather from the coat hanging on the chair.

Jessi's outfit tonight was even bolder than before, a silver micro bikini that shimmered in the light like it was made of metal. Becca thought she looked terrific in the "barely there" outfit. The cloth on the top just covered her nipples, and the small strip of fabric on the bottoms only hid her shaved clit. Her black heels, strapped around her ankles, made her legs look long and sultry. Jessi had opted to cover with a man's white button-up dress shirt, something she could slink out of on stage to work the crowd up.

She watched as she curled her auburn hair, falling in perfect ringlets over her shoulders. She looked radiant, alive. But to Becca, that brightness carried something fragile underneath it, like glass under pressure.

Jessi adjusted her top in the mirror, then turned with that confident, restless smile.

"It's just one more night," she said lightly, slipping into a pair of jogging shorts until she got to the club. "Then I don't work again till Thursday. We'll have all day tomorrow, and I'll be home when you get off work this week."

Running her fingers along the hem of the bed sheet, Becca let out a faint smile. "I know," she said. "It's just… weird not having you here on weekends."

"Bec, I know," Jessi answered softly. "But it's good money, and honestly…" she hesitated, eyes flicking away before adding, "I kind of like it. The lights, the music, the energy… it's… freeing, in a way."

Becca looked up at her, the slight smile fading into concern. "I just don't want you to get hurt again. That place…" she trailed off, unsure how much to say.

Kneeling in front of her, Jessi took her hands. "Hey," she said, voice gentle. "I'm careful, I promise. Tommy looks out for the girls, and I stay in control, okay? You don't have to worry. They have bouncers there the size of mountains."

Becca nodded, but her eyes didn't quite meet Jessi's. "Just don't lose yourself in it," she whispered.

Jessi smiled, leaning in to kiss her. "How could I? I'm coming home to you, remember?"

She tried to smile back, but the words didn't comfort her the way they used to. Becca watched Jessi grab her jacket, her purse, and her keys. As Jessi turned to leave, the door closing softly behind her, the apartment felt too quiet, like all the light had followed her out.

Becca stood there for a long moment, listening to the muffled hum of traffic below, the faint echo of a siren in the distance. She knew Jessi was chasing something she couldn't quite name, something thrilling and dangerous and alive.

And Becca, for all her love, wasn't sure if she could ever compete with that.

* * *

Jessi arrived at the club just as the neon lights flickered on, bathing the street in pink and blue. The bass from the speakers thumped against the sidewalk as she walked inside. She had slipped off her leather coat in the car, not wanting to deal with storing it somewhere in the club. She walked to the dressing room behind the stage, slipping off her jogging pants to reveal her shimmering silver outfit beneath.

After walking out to mingle in the sparse early crowd, Tommy gave her a nod. "Lookin' good tonight, Jessi. Should be a good night since it's Saturday."

Jessi grinned. "Thanks, Tommy. I'll make it worth it." She slipped onto one of the side stages, letting the music move her, the lights tracing her curves. Her confidence was high tonight as she unbuttoned her shirt just to the top of her belly, each step precise. She would tease them, opening the shirt and dropping it to the floor, each sway exaggerated, drawing the few early patrons' eyes immediately.

The crowd was sparse at first, but as the night grew, so did the energy. She danced with purpose, letting the music take her as she collected tips from the audience. The small VIP area was quiet, but she already knew she'd have a few requests for private dances later. Her mind buzzed with excitement and adrenaline, the stage lights casting a halo over her like she was untouchable.

Spike was leaning against a pool table, a grin breaking across his face when he spotted her. Jessi caught his eye and gave him a small wave as she continued to dance.

She looked toward the main stage and saw Candy dancing. The buxom blonde was bubbly, and her routine was filled with mischievous humor. The crowds ate it up. It was her personality, and they loved it. Jessi was sultrier in her routine; a serious sexiness, enticing and teasing.

After a set of dances, she stepped down and moved into the crowd, charming patrons with a light laugh, coaxing drinks, and booking a couple of VIP sessions. Each interaction was electric, and with every tip slid across the stage or table, she felt the intoxicating pull of control, desire, and attention.

By the time she stepped off for a brief water break, her pulse was still racing. Her reflection in the mirrored wall caught her eye; her flushed face, glittering eyes, and the curve of her body in the lights made her pause. She saw a hint of vulnerability there, too, the thrill, yes, but also a fragile edge, a need she couldn't completely name.

A man at the bar, older, with a quiet intensity, caught her gaze. She smiled, and he tipped his drink. Tonight, she was the center of her own world, and no one could pull her down.

Jessi headed back to the stage for the next set, the music swelling around her. The adrenaline, the attention, the freedom, it was addictive. She knew she had to go home eventually, to Becca, to everyday life. But for these hours, this stage, this spotlight… she was untouchable, alive in ways the world outside the club could never understand.

A young man across the room caught her attention, waving a couple of twenties and a ten with a tentative, almost shy gesture. Jessi approached him, noticing the nervous energy radiating off him. "Would you like a private dance?" she asked, her voice low and inviting.

He nodded quickly, barely able to meet her eyes.

Jessi smiled as she led him through the dimly lit hallway to a small private room. She closed the door behind them, the dim red light of the private room casting a soft glow over the small space. His eyes were wide as he watched her, and she could sense every bit of nervous energy radiating off him. She gave a teasing smile and let the music from the small speaker hum through the room, filling the silence.

"What's your name?" she asked softly.

"Richard," he replied, his voice barely above a whisper.

She tilted her head, a playful smile curving her lips. "Can I call you Richie?" she purred. He nodded, a slight tremor running through him. "I hope you're ready for this. It's going to be… fun." She ran a hand down her arm, letting her fingers brush across her body in a slow, deliberate tease.

"First time here?" she asked, her tone gentle, reassuring.

He swallowed, nodded again, and murmured, "Yes… I just turned 21 last week."

Jessi's smile softened. "Don't worry," she said, brushing a strand of hair from her face. "You're in good hands."

Richie let out a quiet laugh, half nervous, half excited, and Jessi saw his tension begin to melt. She leaned back, spinning slowly on her heel, letting the curves of her body flow naturally with the music. She knew the power she had in this moment, the way she could coax his hesitancy into trust, and she played with it gently. He watched wide-eyed and anxious.

She looked down at his astonished gaze, the sweat forming on his forehead. "Have you… Ever seen a girl before?" she asked as she twisted her hips back and forth.

"Oh, of course, I've seen a girl before," the man laughed awkwardly.

Jessi reached out and ran her fingers through his short-cropped hair. "I mean a naked girl."

The man stuttered for a bit. "In movies, magazines."

A grin formed across Jessi's face. She reached up, hooking her thumbs underneath the straps of her top. With a slow, deliberate motion, she pulled the top free, exposing her firm tits.

His breath quickened, and his hands trembled. Jessi was loving every second. She turned, bending over to expose her ass as she slipped her bottoms to her knees, then ankles. She kicked them over to the corner, then looked over her shoulder with one finger to her lips. "Do you like what you see?"

Richie nodded, his face filled with astonishment. Sweat dripped from his temples.

Jessi turned and straddled his lap, grabbing the back of the chair and sliding her bare chest lightly across his face; her hardened nipple grazing his cheek and brow. She rocked her hips back and forth in his lap until she noticed him closing his eyes and letting out a deep groan. His lower body twitched, then relaxed.

Jessi pushed herself back and looked into his eyes. "Did you… Just come, baby?"

Richie's eyes darted back and forth, his face flushed red as a ruby. "I'm so sorry. I… I didn't…"

Jessi put a finger up to his lips. “Shh… It’s okay, baby.” She looked at him and realized the embarrassment growing. “Oh, this happens all the time,” she said in a reassuring tone.

“Really?” Richie asked as he looked up.

“Yep. Usually, it’s the big, tough-looking guys that do it. I think it’s a compliment... that I get you so excited, you just can’t wait.”

Jessi looked up at the small clock behind him. “So… you have thirteen minutes left. You want me to keep dancing?”

“Can… we just talk a bit?” Richie asked, fidgeting in the chair.

“Sure thing, baby.” Jessi relaxed and eased her naked body down onto his lap. “Tell me, Richie, what do you do?”

“Me? I’m a student.”

“Oh? Where at? What are you studying?”

“I go to the Southern Art Institute downtown. I’m studying graphic design and digital media.”

Jessi’s ears perked up. “You go to an arts college?”

Richie shook his head.

“What classes do they have there? Like… are there drawing and painting classes? Other stuff?”

“Um… yeah. They have all kinds of art classes. Media, filmmaking, sculpting… all kinds of stuff.”

"Really?" Jessi said with a chuckle. "Can I ask you something… something personal?"

Richie nodded and smiled. "I guess so."

"How much does it cost to go there?"

"Oh… well," Richie rubbed his chin and thought for a moment. "I think I pay around $25,000 a year."

Jessi leaned back and sighed. "That much, huh?"

"Are… you thinking about going to college?" Richie asked.

"Me? No. I was wondering about a friend of mine. She's really good at drawing and stuff."

"Oh, too bad," Richie responded with a bit of disappointment. "I was thinking I could show you around if you did."

Jessi grinned and cupped his cheeks with both hands. "You're sweet." She leaned in and gave him a quick kiss on the lips.

* * *

Jessi quietly unlocked the apartment door well past 3 a.m., careful not to wake Becca, though this time, the rustle of her coat and the clatter of her heels on the floor stirred her from sleep. Becca blinked groggily, pulling herself upright in the bed, a faint frown of concern on her face.

"Hey," Jessi whispered, giving a sleepy grin. "Don't worry, I'm just home."

She set her purse down beside the bed and, without a word, slipped into the bathroom for a quick shower, the warm water washing away the sweat and grime from the night. She emerged minutes later, damp hair falling in loose curls, and slid under the covers beside Becca. She nuzzled close, letting her warmth seep in, then propped herself up on an elbow.

"So," Becca murmured, voice thick with sleep, "how was your night?"

Jessi reached over to her purse and tipped it onto the bed. A cascade of bills tumbled out, forming a neat, impressive pile. "Take a look," she said, eyes gleaming with excitement. "Three nights… $1,755 total."

Becca's eyes widened, and her jaw dropped slightly. "You… you made how much?!"

Jessi shrugged casually, though a triumphant smile played on her lips. "Of course, it's missing the money I paid for new outfits and your coat. It's good money," she said simply. "I told you, the weekends are the big earners."

Becca shook her head, a mix of awe and worry in her expression. "I… I don't even know what to say. That's… that's incredible, Jessi. Hell, maybe I should start working there," she said with a chuckle.

Jessi's eyes widened. "Oh, could you imagine both of us on stage together?" she said excitedly. "A two-woman show. We'd make all kinds of money."

"Jessi! I was only kidding," Becca responded with a scowl.

"But couldn't you just picture us on stage?"

"I could picture me screaming in terror," Becca laughed. "It was a joke. There's no way I could ever be as bold as you."

Jessi reached out, taking Becca's hand in hers. "Yeah. I guess it's not really your thing, is it?" she said, her tone light, almost teasing.

Becca sighed, still stunned but unable to argue with the look of exhilaration in Jessi's eyes. She leaned back into the pillows, letting Jessi curl up against her. For now, the money, the adrenaline, and the thrill were just another part of Jessi's high, and Becca could only watch, a little anxious but quietly supportive.

Running her fingers through the pile of bills, Jessi grinned. "You know… with all this I'm making now, I was thinking maybe we could finally make your college classes happen," she said, her voice hopeful.

Becca blinked, shaking her head. "Jess… that costs a lot of money."

Scooting closer, Jessi rested her head on Becca's shoulder. "No, really. I think we could make it happen. If I had to, I could add another night. It's not that hard."

Becca let out a soft laugh, a mix of disbelief and affection. "Jessi… that's sweet, but I don't want you working your ass off, literally, for my sake."

Jessi's grin didn't falter. "It's not work for me, not really. And besides, I'm good at it. Look at it this way, I get to do what I love, and you get to do what you love. Everyone wins."

"I don't know, Jessi," Becca murmured. She exhaled slowly, trailing her fingers over Jessi's arm. "I just… I worry, that's all. I… I want you to be happy."

Jessi tilted her head up, meeting Becca's eyes. "I am happy," she whispered. "Especially knowing that maybe, I can help you be happy too."

Becca smiled, a mixture of pride, worry, and warmth washing over her. "We'll think about it… together. Okay?"

Jessi let out a contented sigh, snuggling closer. For a moment, the world outside didn't exist, just the two of them, the money stacked between them, and the promise of dreams becoming real.

25
Freedom, Thrills, and Independence

The next few days passed in a warm, almost ordinary rhythm, though both of them carried an unspoken awareness of the change in their lives. Sunday stretched luxuriously before them, a full day just for each other. Jessi woke early, curling up beside Becca for a slow morning. They made coffee together, laughed over breakfast, and lounged on the couch for hours, letting time drift by as they talked about everything and nothing. Becca painted while Jessi watched, occasionally offering suggestions or teasing her about the way she held her brush. They listened to a newly discovered band, letting the music thread through the apartment's quiet, punctuated only by their shared smiles and small touches.

Monday evening, Jessi had dinner ready when Becca walked through the door. The smell of garlic and herbs filled the apartment, and Becca was genuinely touched. They ate slowly, savoring both the food and the rare tranquility of the week. The night stretched lazily afterward, with the two of them curling up on the couch to watch old movies. Jessi's head rested against Becca's shoulder, her fingers occasionally brushing across her arm, enjoying the comfort and normalcy of their shared space.

The following nights were similarly calm, punctuated by small, meaningful routines, Jessi listening as Becca sketched, and the music that became their quiet soundtrack. Jessi reveled in these hours, letting herself feel safe and connected, while Becca couldn't help but notice the lingering glimmers of excitement in Jessi's eyes, the memory of the stage, the music, the thrill she carried with her.

* * *

By Thursday, the weekend glow had faded, and it was back to the club for Jessi. She moved through her routines with growing confidence, her sultriness now natural and almost effortless. Halloween came, and she arrived dressed as a sexy nurse, which drew cheers from onlookers. Each step on the stage, each sway of her hips, was measured, practiced, and commanding. The crowd took notice of her, tipping generously, and she began to understand the subtle power she wielded over the room.

Even from across the floor, she could feel Becca's presence in her mind, soft, comforting, worried, proud. Jessi carried both sensations with her as she danced, letting them fuel her performance. Each night, she returned home with the same mixture of adrenaline and warmth, holding onto Becca in the quiet aftermath, their nights together a refuge from the glittering chaos she had embraced outside the apartment walls.

The weeks slipped by with the rhythm of Jessi's new life at the club, the leaves turning fiery shades of orange and red as November settled in. Chilly air seeped into the city streets, and the approaching holidays added a sense of urgency and reflection to everything.

Jessi's confidence on stage had blossomed. She moved with fluid grace, her emerald-green outfit now replaced by a rotating wardrobe of daring costumes, every piece chosen to maximize her allure and impact. The regulars noticed, and the tips reflected it: she had become the third-highest-grossing performer at the club, behind the buxom Candy, whose commanding presence drew consistent high-spending clients, and Veronica, the raven-haired, leather-clad woman whose commanding, edgy style held the room in thrall.

Jessi thrived on the freedom, the thrill, and the independence the job afforded her. Each night, she felt a rush she could never find in a cubicle, in the monotony of a desk job. She returned home each morning with a pocketbook full of cash and a quiet sense of accomplishment, though Becca noticed the fatigue behind her smiles, the subtle shadows beneath her eyes.

Becca, meanwhile, balanced her pride with worry. She had looked seriously into college tuition, and the numbers were daunting: $22,600 per year, not counting supplies and fees, a total that made her chest tighten. She had longed to return to art school, and Jessi's generosity could make it possible. Still, Becca couldn't stop wondering about the safety, the physical and emotional toll, and the long-term sustainability of Jessi's work at the club.

"You know," Becca said one evening, after Jessi had counted her nightly earnings and gazed at the pile of bills on the table, "I looked into the tuition for school. I've crunched the numbers. We might can do it, if you really think we should."

Jessi's eyes sparkled. "I know we should. Look at what I made last week. We just have to keep this up for a little while, and we can make it real. No loans, no worrying about whether we can cover books or supplies. We don't have to rely on your parents."

Becca reached across the table, hesitating for just a moment before taking Jessi's hand. "I'm proud of you… But if I went to school, I wouldn't be able to work my full-time job. I worry. I can't stop thinking about… the burden on you."

Jessi leaned forward, brushing a strand of hair from Becca's face. "I know you worry. There's no burden. I can handle it. I love you, Becca, and want to make you happy. It's for us. For your future."

Becca's lips pressed into a tight line. She wanted to argue, to insist there had to be a safer way, but looking into Jessi's determined, sparkling eyes, she realized there was no stopping this energy. All she could do was stay close, support, and try to manage her own fears.

* * *

The apartment felt warmer that night than the November chill outside, as they sat together planning, dreaming, and calculating. The holidays were coming, and they thought of celebrating without financial worry. Jessi's success at the club, her boldness, her freedom, all fed into a single, unstoppable force, one that Becca couldn't help but admire while quietly guarding her heart.

As November deepened, the first breath of winter rolled in, cold mornings, long shadows, and the faint smell of the leaves falling to the ground. The apartment's old heater hummed constantly, its metallic clicks filling the quiet between Jessi's late mornings and Becca's early returns from work.

The holiday lights began appearing around town, storefronts glowing with reds and golds, garlands draped across downtown lampposts. Jessi noticed them on her way home from the club each morning, the world half-asleep, her windshield fogging as the heater struggled to keep up.

Her life had shifted into this nocturnal rhythm: sleeping through the day, rising at sunset, transforming herself in front of the mirror, lashes, perfume, hair. She had grown into her role at the club with confidence that surprised even her. Her name, whispered among regulars now, carried weight. Her dances had evolved, more deliberate, fluid, magnetic. The crowd responded. The money flowed.

But Becca watched all of this with a quiet ache that she couldn't quite name.

She'd stay up late sometimes, sketching by lamplight, waiting for Jessi's return. She told herself it was to keep her company, to hear about her night, but sometimes it was to make sure Jessi came home at all. When Jessi finally slipped in through the door, smelling faintly of alcohol and cigarettes and something darker, Becca would greet her with sleepy eyes and a smile, trying not to let her worry show.

"Busy night?" she'd ask.

"Always busy," Jessi would grin, dropping her purse with a soft thud before showering, humming off-key through the running water.

Some mornings, they'd sit together on the couch afterward, Jessi wrapped in a towel, hair damp and curling around her face. She'd count her money, fives, tens, twenties, stacked in neat little piles on the coffee table.

Becca would sip her coffee, gaze half-lidded. "You're making a small fortune," she'd murmur.

"See? Told you it'd pay off," Jessi said one morning, brushing damp hair from her eyes. "If we keep this up, we'll be ahead by spring. You could be enrolled by next fall."

Becca nodded, but her expression lingered somewhere between admiration and unease. "You make it sound so easy."

Jessi smiled softly. "Nothing about it's easy. But it feels… worth it."

There was pride in her tone, but also something else, something that worried Becca more than she let on. A hunger that wasn't about money or stability: Jessi seemed to crave the rush, the lights, the attention, the control she felt when she danced.

It felt real. It felt like she had found herself.

26

A Face from the Past

By mid-November, the club had decked itself out in tinsel and neon ornaments. Holiday parties brought in larger crowds, and Jessi's earnings grew with every weekend. Candy had taken her under her wing, teaching her tricks about the regulars and how to "work the floor" without ever looking desperate. She had also given Jessi warnings on how to spot undercover cops that might be looking for code violations. "Only trust the ones you know," she would tell her.

Veronica, always aloof, had warmed up slightly, offering cool, quiet nods of approval when Jessi pulled in big nights. Chumminess wasn't Veronica's style, but she sensed a mutual respect from the performer.

At home, the apartment took on its own kind of glow. They had spent Thanksgiving Day together, cooking, laughing, and enjoying each other's company. Becca had turned down the invitation to spend the holiday at her parents' house, something that deeply touched Jessi.

Jessi surprised Becca one night with a tiny, cheap, slightly crooked artificial tree, lit with small white lights. "Our first Christmas tree," she'd said, laughing as she set it up on the table by the window. Becca drew and colored paper ornaments to hang from its branches, while Jessi strung popcorn around as garland.

Becca hugged her from behind, chin resting on her shoulder. "You're full of surprises lately."

Jessi turned and kissed her cheek. "Just wait till you open your presents."

Becca laughed, but in the back of her mind, a shadow lingered. The more Jessi thrived in that world, the louder the applause, the thicker the envelopes of cash, the more Becca feared losing the gentle, insecure girl who once hid behind her own quiet shyness.

Still, when Jessi wrapped her arms around her at night, whispering dreams about paying off debts and walking across a college campus together, Becca let herself believe in it, if only for a moment.

The chill of November didn't touch the inside of Tommy's. Jessi had learned how to move with the room's pulse. The nerves that once made her hands tremble were gone, replaced by a confidence that turned every eye in her direction.

She was wearing a red-and-silver sequined outfit that caught the lights like sparks. Her boots clicked across the stage, her hair tumbling in wild auburn waves that shimmered under the colored beams. The regulars knew her by now. They shouted her name as she climbed the pole, spinning slowly, deliberately, like she owned the place.

Candy watched from the side with a playful smirk. Veronica, draped in her usual black leather and chains, gave Jessi a respectful nod. There was no rivalry anymore, just recognition. Jessi had found her rhythm.

She'd learned the tricks, how to flirt without promise, how to make every man in the room think he had her attention. When she smiled, it was magnetic. When she danced, she made the music part of her, every note flowing through her hips and legs. She could see the hunger in the crowd's eyes and used it, shaping it into tips and VIP sessions.

Spike was there some nights, leaning against the bar, giving her a subtle nod that said he was watching out for her. But Jessi didn't feel like she needed anyone's protection anymore. She was the one in control. The money rolled in, hundreds a night, sometimes over a thousand when the crowd was right.

By midnight, she'd already made enough to cover another week's rent. By one-thirty, she was taking a break backstage, sipping bottled water, counting folded bills. The other girls laughed and smoked, teasing each other about the customers. Jessi leaned back, breathing deep, the thrum of bass still vibrating through the floor beneath her heels.

She thought briefly of Becca, probably asleep, sketchbook on her lap, the TV murmuring low. Jessi smiled faintly. When her next song cue hit, she stood, adjusted her top, and walked out into the glow. The cheers rose again. The world outside the club, the cold, its weight, didn't exist here.

Here, she was fire.

The music thumped through the floor, a steady, hypnotic pulse Jessi could usually ride like a wave. Her body knew the rhythm instinctively by now: the slow turn, the flick of her hair, the deliberate roll of her hips under the strobing lights.

But halfway through the song, something changed.

She caught sight of a man near the edge of the stage, dark eyes, cornrows gleaming under the colored lights, a smile that seemed too familiar. Her breath hitched mid-movement. For a heartbeat, she froze, the rhythm faltering.

It wasn't him.

It couldn't be.

Still, her pulse started to pound faster than the bass. The edges of the room blurred, and the humid air of the club felt suddenly heavy and thin all at once. Her knees wobbled. A flicker of memory, streetlights, pavement, a voice too close, pushed its way into her mind before she forced it back down.

Someone cheered, snapping her back. Jessi clutched the pole, forcing herself to smile. She could feel the sweat prickling at her neck, the way her heartbeat fought against the music. Her hands trembled slightly, but she moved, she had to move, turning, bending, making the motion into part of the act.

When the song ended, she stepped offstage, her chest heaving. The man was gone. Or maybe he hadn't even been there, perhaps just someone who looked like him.

In the dressing room, Jessi leaned against the mirror. The bright bulbs around the glass stabbed at her eyes. She pressed a towel to her neck, trying to breathe through the trembling.

Candy passed by, humming, dropping a stack of ones onto the counter. "You okay, babe?"

Jessi nodded quickly, forcing a grin that didn't quite reach her eyes. "Yeah. Just... stage lights. Hot tonight."

Candy shrugged and moved on, but Jessi stayed there, staring at her reflection, her mascara slightly smudged, her pupils too wide.

She whispered, barely audible over the music seeping through the walls, "You're fine. You're fine. You're fine."

Then, as if on autopilot, she reapplied her lipstick, squared her shoulders, and went back out, her body ready to perform, even if her mind still echoed with ghosts she couldn't silence.

Jessi's heels clicked softly against the worn floorboards as she retreated from the stage, forcing herself to keep her head high. The man, the one with the cornrows, the wide nose, the smile that had haunted her for months, was still there, lingering at the edge of the crowd. He didn't glance her way, oblivious to the storm of memories boiling inside her.

Her pulse surged violently as she forced a smile, trying to convince herself it was just another customer, just another night. He dropped a $5 bill onto the stage at her feet. Jessi froze for a moment, staring down at it, the past flashing like a film behind her eyes: the streetlight, the darkness, the fear that had gripped her body that night. He didn't remember her, but she could never forget. Tears pricked at the corners of her eyes, unbidden.

She picked up the bill and, without looking back, placed it in the tip jar of another dancer who had just stepped off stage. Her hands shook as she adjusted her outfit, the tiny swimwear now feeling heavy and suffocating. She eased herself down from the stage and walked toward the pool room, her steps small and careful, trying to act casual, but the knot in her chest only tightened.

Spike was leaning against the bar, nursing a mug of beer, his biker instinct sharp enough to notice her immediately.

"Jessi?" he asked softly, his tone carrying concern rather than accusation. He didn't need to see the tears welling in her eyes to know something was wrong.

She forced a shaky laugh, tucking a strand of hair behind her ear. "Hey… Spike. Just… tired, I guess. Long night."

Spike set the mug down and stepped closer, lowering his voice. "You sure, kid? You don't look fine. You look… like you've seen a ghost."

Jessi swallowed hard, clenching her fists at her sides to stop them from shaking. She wanted to tell him, to spill everything, but she didn't know how.

"I'm okay," she whispered, but it sounded hollow, even to her own ears.

Spike didn't press, just nodded, keeping a hand near her shoulder but not touching. "Alright. But if you need to get outta here, just say the word. I've got your back, alright?"

Jessi nodded again, barely able to trust her voice. She forced a smile and moved toward the pool tables, leaning in, trying to bury the panic. Her hands still trembled slightly, and the music of the club felt distant, almost cruel. She watched two men play, the small clack of the cue ball against the racked balls grounding her.

She couldn't shake the image of him. He *was* the one; the one who clenched her throat so tight she couldn't breathe; the one who grinned as she suffered the humiliation, the memory of fear, but having Spike nearby, sensing without judging, gave her the tiniest anchor. She could breathe again, just enough to make it through the night.

Jessi's hands fidgeted with the edge of the pool table, tapping her fingers as she finally let the words tumble out. "Spike… that man… he's one of the guys from that night," she whispered, her voice barely above the din of the club. "One of the ones that… you know… the ones who…" She choked, unable to finish the sentence, her stomach knotting.

Spike's eyes narrowed instantly, sharp and furious. His jaw clenched as he scanned the room, then his gaze landed on the man she had described. The hair, the nose, the smug smile. "That son of a…" Spike muttered under his breath, fists tightening.

Jessi reached out, trying to grab his arm. "Spike! Wait… don't! Please!" she begged, panic flaring. "You don't know what… he's not aware I know him. I just…"

But Spike was already moving. He barked a quick order to two of his biker friends who had been lingering near the bar, and within moments, they were striding toward the man with purposeful aggression.

Jessi's heart dropped. Her stomach twisted in a mixture of fear and regret. "Oh God… Spike, stop! Please, don't…" Her voice trailed off as she watched them approach, realizing she had unleashed something she couldn't control.

The man looked up from his drink, sensing the change in the air. Spike and his friends loomed over him in seconds, the room suddenly tense with the threat of confrontation.

Jessi's chest tightened, every nerve screaming that she'd made a terrible mistake. "Why did I say anything?" she whispered to herself, hiding behind a pool table as her pulse raced. She had wanted comfort, someone to understand, but now she feared she had just put herself and the situation in even more danger.

The tension in the air was thick, almost suffocating, as Spike and his friends closed in on the man. Voices rose, heated words exchanged, and before Jessi could fully register what was happening, the bouncer's efforts to intervene were too little, too late. Spike's fists struck with precision, and the man went down hard, groaning.

The scuffle spilled toward the exit, the room buzzing with shocked patrons who instinctively moved out of the way. Chairs scraped, drinks spilled, and the lights of the club seemed to flicker in rhythm with the chaos. Spike's friends were kicking the man as he lay on the floor, as the bouncers tried to drag Spike away. Jessi's chest tightened, her knuckles white as she gripped the edge of the bar and watched the brawl spill outside. *I shouldn't have said anything…* she thought, heart hammering.

Minutes dragged on, each one stretching longer than the last. She didn't dare move from her spot, peering toward the doorway, straining to see if it was over. The noise outside, muffled shouts, a thud, then silence, left her trembling.

Finally, Spike stepped back in, his leather jacket rumpled, knuckles still slightly bruised. His expression was a mix of grim satisfaction and reassurance. He saw Jessi at the bar, pale and tense, and offered a slight nod.

"Relax," he said softly, his voice carrying over the hum of the club. "He won't be coming around again. You don't have to worry about him."

Jessi exhaled shakily, letting the tension in her shoulders drain just a little. Her lips quivered as tears threatened to spill, but she blinked them back, swallowing hard. "Thank… thank you," she whispered, voice barely audible.

Spike leaned closer, lowering his tone. "You're safe. That's all that matters. No one… I mean, no one is going to mess with you, Jessi, alright?"

Jessi nodded, still trembling, feeling both relief and lingering shock. For the first time since that night, a small piece of her terror eased, replaced by the raw gratitude for the bikers, even if it had escalated far beyond anything she had imagined. The music thumped around her, but it felt distant, almost unreal.

Other dancers drifted over, concern etched on their faces.

"What happened?" Candy asked, tilting her head, her usual confident grin replaced by genuine worry.

Jessi forced a small smile, trying to sound casual. "It's nothing," she said, though her voice wavered. "Just a disrespectful customer. Spike… and the bouncers handled it."

A few of the girls nodded, murmuring their sympathy, but the curiosity lingered. Veronica leaned closer. "Handled it how?"

Jessi shook her head, brushing a loose strand of hair behind her ear. "I don't want to get into it. He won't be back. That's all that matters."

Before the conversation could drift further, Tommy emerged from the back, his bulk filling the doorway. His eyes scanned Jessi, noting her flushed face and the slight tremor in her hands.

"What happened in here?" he asked, his voice low but firm. He stepped closer, hands on his hips.

Jessi took a deep breath. "A customer just crossed the line. Spike stepped in."

Tommy's gaze hardened slightly, though he didn't look angry at her. "I don't care what happened," he said firmly. "I don't want any trouble at this club. Understood? You do your work, stay safe, and leave the rest to me."

Jessi nodded quickly. "Understood, Tommy."

He gave her a curt nod, then turned and walked back to the office. She exhaled, feeling some of the tension in her chest loosen, though the adrenaline still coursed through her veins. She stayed at the bar, swirling a glass of water in her hand, taking deep breaths, and letting the thrum of the music slowly ground her back into the present.

The other dancers, sensing she wasn't ready to talk, slowly drifted back to their routines. Jessi felt a small surge of gratitude for the club, for Spike, and for the walls that contained the chaos, even if just for tonight. She knew she'd replay the night in her mind later, but for now, she focused on steadying herself and finishing out her shift.

* * *

As the night wound down, the crowd thinned, leaving the neon glow of the bar casting long, empty shadows across the floor. Jessi wiped down the stage one last time, her movements slow, deliberate—almost meditative. The adrenaline from earlier had faded, leaving her body buzzing in a strange, hollow mix of relief and exhaustion.

She slipped out from behind the curtains, checking the club one final time. Spike was leaning against the pool table. Their eyes met, and he gave her a subtle nod, the unspoken reassurance carrying more weight than words. Jessi forced a smile, feeling both comforted and still fragile.

Outside at closing time, the night air hit her like a cold splash. She pulled her overcoat tighter around herself and took a deep breath, the mix of chilly wind and city smells grounding her. The streets were mostly empty, the late hour leaving only a few lingering cars and scattered pedestrians in the parking lot. Her heels clicked on the sidewalk as she made her way toward her Mustang at the corner.

Sliding into the driver's seat, she sank into the cushions and let herself exhale fully for the first time since the confrontation. She watched the city pass by, the neon lights and streetlamps blending into a blur as she drove. Thoughts of the night's events lingered, but she kept them contained, telling herself she was safe now.

* * *

By the time she pulled up to her apartment, it was again well past 3:30 a.m. Jessi hurried inside, careful not to make a sound. Becca stirred slightly in bed but didn't wake. Jessi shed her coat and heels, then headed to the bathroom for her routine shower. The warm water washed over her, calming her body and mind, though the memory of the man, the fear, and the violence still gnawed at her edges.

Finally, she climbed into bed beside Becca, snuggling close. Becca murmured in her sleep, and Jessi let herself relax just enough to drift toward a fitful, dream-laden sleep, holding onto the fragile thread of safety she felt in Becca's arms.

27
Cracks in the Dam

The next morning, Jessi and Becca lay entwined. Jessi stirred first, pulling the blankets around her as if shielding herself from more than just the cool November air. She forced a quiet smile as Becca stirred, greeting her with a soft "Morning," but inside, her thoughts kept returning to last night, the man, the fear, and Spike's violence.

Becca noticed the tension immediately. Jessi's smile didn't reach her eyes, and the way she held herself seemed tighter, more controlled than usual. "You okay?" Becca asked gently, touching the side of Jessi's face. Jessi nodded quickly, muttering something about needing coffee.

They moved through the morning routine with the usual banter, but Becca's worry grew with each subtle sign, the tense posture at the kitchen counter, the way she avoided eye contact when certain memories might have flashed across her mind. Becca had learned to read these cracks in Jessi's composure, and her heart ached to see the girl she loved carrying so much on her own.

Jessi kept the events of the night locked tightly inside. She didn't mention the man, the fear, or even Spike's intervention. She couldn't, she didn't want Becca to know about that night months ago. Instead, she laughed lightly at Becca's jokes, poured coffee, and made a show of normalcy.

Yet underneath the surface, something had shifted. A small, fragile part of her that had once embraced her work at the club with thrilling abandon now felt the weight of memory pressing down. She shook it off with practiced ease, but Becca, watching silently, knew that night had left a mark. And though Jessi refused to speak, the worry in Becca's eyes silently promised that she would be there, no matter what, to help Jessi rebuild that part of herself that had been chipped away.

Jessi finished her coffee, standing to clear the dishes, forcing herself to move through the morning as if nothing had happened. But deep inside, the memory lingered, a quiet reminder that even in her high and her freedom, there were nights she would not soon forget.

* * *

That week, Jessi returned to the club with her usual flair, her daring outfits catching the dim lights as she moved across the stage. But beneath the confident sway of her hips, a subtle tension lingered. Her body remembered the fear, the darkened streets, and the man who had triggered those memories. Each step and twirl carried a tiny shadow of caution, an instinctive awareness of the space around her.

As she mingled with the crowd, flirting and laughing, she noticed a man at the edge of the room, nervously clutching a crisp $100 bill. His gaze was fixed on her, and the weight of the money in his hand was both an invitation and a test. Jessi approached with a practiced smile, letting the familiar thrill of negotiation wash over her, masking the residual anxiety from her earlier encounter.

"Would you like a private dance?" she asked, her voice soft but commanding. The man's hesitation was palpable, a mix of excitement and nerves. He nodded quickly, almost spilling the bill in his haste.

"Follow me," Jessi said, leading him toward the private rooms tucked away in the corner of the club. Her strides were measured, each step carefully maintaining control of her composure. The echo of her heels on the floor reminded her of how easily control could slip, and she caught herself scanning the room instinctively, a shadow of last week's fear flaring briefly before she shoved it back.

As the door to the private room clicked shut behind them, Jessi let herself exhale quietly. The man fumbled for his seat while she began to move with practiced seduction, teasing and guiding him into the experience. He was an older, well-built man with a mustache. "So… you want an entire 30 minutes with me?" she said with a sultry smile. "Think you can handle me that long?"

The man smiled and pushed back in his chair. "Tell you what. I'll give you $200 if you give me something a little… extra." He plucked another bill from his wallet and waved it in front of her.

Jessi smiled as she leaned back against the door. She gazed at the bills hanging from his fingers. *A quick $200,* she thought. "It's against the rules… You know?" she said timidly.

"Oh, come on. I've watched you all night. How about I add another $50?"

Jessi bit her bottom lip and then took a deep breath. She wanted to reach out and take the money from his hand. It would be easy money for her, but she pushed him back into the chair. "I'm sorry, baby. I can't. But I can give you a really nice dance."

She began swaying to the music and tugged at the knot on her top, loosening the garment. Just then, the man flipped open his wallet and revealed the shiny gold-colored badge.

Jessi jumped back as the man stood. "Okay. How about we just call that solicitation, little girl? You want to put your hands behind your back for me?"

Stunned, Jessi just stood there a moment, her heart racing in her chest. "What do you mean? I was just dancing!" she said excitedly.

The man reached out and turned Jessi around. He then pulled out a set of cuffs and clicked them around her wrists.

"What are you doing?" Jessi pleaded. "I'm sorry. I… I didn't do anything!"

The officer grinned as he pushed her forward against the door. He reached around and began fondling her breasts, squeezing them hard and pinching at her nipples. She could feel his hot breath on her neck as he inhaled her scent.

“Wait… what are you doing?” Jessi asked as she tried to turn her head. "This is bullshit!"

The officer pushed her hard against the door, holding her fast at the back of her neck. “I need to check and see if you have any weapons on you.”

She stood there, clad in only the skimpy micro bikini bottoms as his hands ran down her back, then curved in between her legs. “Spread your legs,” he commanded.

“Please don’t,” Jessi begged. She began to tremble as one finger slid under her bottoms and rubbed along her clit.

“Spread… them,” he repeated slowly with a deep growling command.

Slowly, she spread her legs, his hands running between her butt cheeks. His fingers probed her ass and back to her slit, sticking in one, two, then three fingers. He hooked her with his fingers and pulled her ass back until she was leaning forward against the door.

The tears began to stream down her cheeks. “Please, please, please,” she repeated. Her body trembled as she heard him unzip his pants. She could feel his hardened cock, sliding up and down the crack of her butt, searching for the right opening. He found her pussy, and he slid deep inside.

Her arms fastened behind her back; Jessi could do nothing but let it happen. He pumped in and out, grabbing a bunch of Jessi’s curls and holding her head like the reins of an animal. His other hand tugged at a nipple, stretching it out and making her wince. He was rough; his thrusts were deep and fast. He grunted with each motion, and he continued to slam Jessi against the door as he pumped inside her.

Finally, he let out a deep groan and pushed deep inside her. He held it for a long time; Jessi could feel his dick throbbing and pumping inside her; the hot liquid dripping out of her pussy and down her thigh. With a gasp, he pulled out of her and flung himself back into the chair.

Jessi stood there, trembling, frozen against the door.

The policeman stood up, fastening his trousers and tugging Jessi back against his chest. He cupped one hand under her chin and pulled her head up. "I've been watching you… Jessi. You've got a pretty good act. Bet you're making a lot of money up there… huh?"

Jessi only nodded, her heart racing; tears blurring her eyes.

"Let me tell you something. I had one of my associates in here the other night. He got roughed up pretty bad. Only after did he remember who you were. He said you were out pretending to be one of my girls."

Trembling, Jessi looked over her shoulder. "That's.... not what happened," she said, her voice shuddering.

The cop just shook his head. "If you want to continue to keep making money, you're going to have to go through me. This is my area. Do you understand?"

Jessi nodded again, sniffling through her nose.

"Of course, I could put a girl as pretty as you to good use. You give me half your earnings, and maybe some more of that sweet pussy of yours. I tell you what. If you want to keep working this shit hole, that's fine too. You give me... say, $200 a week."

Jessi's hands trembled. Her mind raced; she could barely believe this was happening. Sweat prickled at her temples, her chest tight with panic. "I… I can't," she whispered, almost to herself. "I can't do that…"

He leaned forward, voice dropping into a dangerous whisper. "You don't have a choice. I really hope there's not any drugs in your purse back stage. Would be a shame… a sweet girl like you getting busted for something major like that."

Jessi didn't argue. She knew his hypothetical scenario wasn't a warning, it was a threat. She didn't do drugs and barely drank, but a planted bag of something would be all the ammo he would need. Who would believe her anyway.

"You want to keep your freedom? Keep your job? Or you go to jail. Your call."

"I didn't do anything," she whispered.

He just laughed. "It doesn't matter," he said with a smile. "I have judges, DAs, other officers, all in my pocket. I'll have you tied up with so many charges that you won't see the light for over a year. Plus... There are a lot more bad things that can happen out there in the world. Really... bad... things."

Jessi didn't say anything; she just stood there shaking. He pushed her against the door again. "I didn't hear an answer."

"Yes.... Okay. Yes," she whispered, her voice trembling.

He stood there a minute, looking at Jessi shaking. He reached into his pocket and pulled out a set of keys. Jessi could hear the clink and click of the lock being released, and she pulled her arms in front of her, beginning to rub each wrist. She turned to see him smirking as he eased past her and opened the door. "You can consider tonight audition night," he quipped as he tossed the bills on the floor.

As the door clicked shut behind the officer, Jessi slumped to the floor, her body shaking with a mix of fear, humiliation, and anger. The weight of what had just happened pressed down on her, threatening to crush her. Again, she felt violated, used, and utterly powerless.

Her mind raced, trying to process the events of the night. The initial assault, the threat, the forced sexual act, then her mind raced back to the alley; it was all too much. She wrapped her arms around herself, trying to find some semblance of comfort, but the memory of his hands, his touch, lingered like a stain on her skin.

Jessi stayed on the floor for what felt like an eternity, her thoughts a whirlwind of confusion and despair. She knew she had to get out of there, to escape the club and the man who had just turned her world upside down. But her body felt heavy, her limbs leaden with exhaustion and shock.

Slowly, she managed to pull herself up, her legs trembling beneath her. She glanced around the room, her eyes landing on the crumpled bills on the floor. The money that had once seemed like an easy way out now felt tainted, a mockery of her situation.

With a deep breath, Jessi put her top back on and adjusted her bottoms, trying to regain some semblance of dignity. She opened the door cautiously, peering out into the hallway. The club was still buzzing with life, oblivious to the horror that had just unfolded in one of its private rooms.

Jessi made her way back to the main area, her steps unsteady. She scanned the crowd, her eyes landing on Candy, who was still mingling with the patrons, her laughter and smiles a stark contrast to the turmoil Jessi felt inside.

As if sensing her presence, Candy turned, her eyes meeting Jessi's. The concern in her gaze was immediate, and she excused herself from the group she was with, making her way to Jessi's side.

"Jessi, what's wrong?" Candy asked, her voice low and urgent. "You look like you've seen a ghost."

Jessi shook her head, her eyes filling with tears. "I can't... I can't talk about it here," she managed to whisper.

Candy nodded, understanding. "Let's get out of here."

They made their way off the club's main floor, back to the dressing room, Jessi leaning on Candy for support. As they entered the dimly lit dressing room, Jessi felt a sense of safety wash over her. The room was quiet, a stark contrast to the club's throbbing energy. She sat down on a plush chair, her body still trembling with the aftershocks of the night's events.

Candy sat beside her, her presence a comforting anchor. "Tell me what happened, Jessi," she said softly, her voice filled with genuine concern.

Jessi took a deep, shuddering breath, trying to find the words to describe the horror she had just endured. "It was a cop," she began, her voice barely above a whisper. "He was in one of the private rooms. He said he wanted a dance, but then... he flashed some money and asked for more. I told him I couldn't, then he pulled out his badge."

Candy's eyes widened in shock, but she remained silent, letting Jessi continue.

"He cuffed me," Jessi said, her voice trembling. "He said it was for solicitation. But I didn't... I said no... then... he started touching me. He fondled me, and then... he raped me."

Tears streamed down Jessi's cheeks as she relived the trauma. Candy reached out, pulling her into a tight embrace, letting her cry on her shoulder.

"I'm so sorry, Jessi," Candy murmured, her voice filled with emotion. "That's... that's terrible. It was Decarlo wasn't it? He harasses all the girls in some way. I've dealt with him before, but never anything like this. What a fucking monster."

"The guy who was beat up the other night," Jessi said, looking up at Candy. "That was one of his guys. I think he's... angry about it."

Jessi looked back at Candy and pulled away, wiping at her tears. "It gets worse," she said, her voice hoarse. "He said if I want to keep working here, I have to go through him and pay him. He wants some of my earnings and... and more."

Candy's expression darkened with anger. "That bastard," she hissed. "He can't do this to you. We won't let him."

Jessi shook her head, a bitter laugh escaping her lips. "He can, and he will. He's a cop, Candy. Who's going to believe me over him? He told me he has judges, DAs, and other cops. He said he'd make sure I go to jail, that he'd hit me with so many charges I wouldn't see daylight for over a year."

Candy's grip on Jessi's hand tightened. "We'll figure something out," she said, her voice filled with determination. "We'll tell Tommy and the guys. They'll help figure something out."

Jessi pulled back from Candy's embrace. "We can't! You don't know what would happen. If Spike and the boys find out, there's no telling what they'll do. And then what? They go to prison? I don't know what to do," she admitted, her voice small and vulnerable. "I'm so scared, Candy."

Candy held her tightly, rocking her gently. "You're not alone, Jessi."

"You have to promise you won't tell anyone, Candy. Promise me!"

Candy looked at her, the uncertainty displayed in her eyes. "Maybe you should take the rest of the night off, Jess."

Jessi nodded and started gathering her things. She left the dressing room feeling hollow. Every time the cop's face flashed through her mind, she shivered, imagining him watching her from the shadows, keeping his threat alive in every step she took.

She made her way over to the bar, where Spike approached, noticing the tension in her posture. "You okay, Jessi?" he asked, concern furrowing his brow.

She forced a small smile, shaking her head slightly. "Yeah… just tired tonight. Long week."

But the fear was there, nagging at her with every thought. She realized she couldn't let anyone else, not even Becca, know. She ducked out into the cool night air and climbed into her car, where she sat for a long moment, gripping the steering wheel, breathing heavily. Her mind raced through scenarios—pay the cop… but how would she protect herself? What more will he want? Those old feelings came rushing back. The freedom the club had provided her now seemed to be stripped away.

By the time she pulled into the apartment parking lot, her hands were numb from clutching the wheel. She carried her bag inside silently, avoiding waking Becca, and stripped off the skimpy club for a warm bath. She washed off the glitter and makeup mechanically, the water doing nothing to wash away the anxiety that clung to her.

Later, in bed beside Becca, she pressed herself close, feeling the warmth of her partner but knowing she couldn't confide the truth. She held back the tears, the anger, the fear, forcing herself to smile and whisper goodnight.

* * *

A week had passed since that night, and Jessi was back on stage, trying to lose herself in the familiar rhythm of her dance. The lights were low, the music pulsing, and the crowd was a blur of faces and voices. Clad in only a tiny leather top and bottom outfit, with heels, she moved with grace, her body fluid and seductive grinding on the dance pole, but her mind was elsewhere, haunted by the memories of her ordeal.

As she danced, her eyes scanned the crowd, and there, in the shadows, she saw him. Detective DeCarlo, his eyes locked onto her, a cruel smile playing on his lips. He waved a bill in his hands, a silent command, a reminder of the power he held over her.

Jessi's heart raced as she finished her set, the applause of the crowd fading into the background. She gathered her tips and jumped off the stage, her mind screaming at her to run, to escape, but her feet moved of their own accord, carrying her towards the private rooms.

She tried to avoid him, weaving through the crowd, pretending she didn't see him, but it was no use. He was there, a dark presence, a looming threat. And when he caught her arm, his grip tight and unyielding, she knew she had no choice but to follow.

He led her to a private room, the door clicking shut behind them with a finality that sent a shiver down her spine. The room was dimly lit, the air thick with tension and the lingering scent of lust and sweat.

Jessi stood there, her body trembling, her mind racing with fear and uncertainty. She knew what was coming, what he expected, and the thought filled her with dread and helplessness.

DeCarlo leaned against the door, his eyes roaming over her body with a hunger that made her skin crawl. "Looking good up there again, Jessi," he said, his voice low and mocking. "Real good. But you know what I like even better?"

Jessi shook her head, her voice barely a whisper. "Please, just leave me alone."

He chuckled, a sound devoid of humor. "Oh, I don't think so. How much did you make this week? $1,000? $1,500? Let's say you pay $600, or would you like to work out something different?" He smiled. "You know exactly what I'm talking about."

Jessi's heart pounded in her chest as he stepped closer, his presence overwhelming, suffocating. "You told me $200," she answered back. She pulled away, her hands clenched into fists at her sides, but there was nowhere to go, no escape from the nightmare that had become her reality.

"We can do $200. With... a little extra added in," he said with a smirking grin.

"Please," she whispered again, her voice trembling. "Don't do this."

But he just smiled, a slow, predatory smile, and reached out, his hands gripping her shoulders as he pulled her close. Jessi closed her eyes, bracing herself for what was to come, her body tensing with a mix of fear and revulsion.

And as he leaned in, his breath hot on her neck, she knew that this was just the beginning, that her nightmare was far from over, and that she was utterly, entirely at his mercy.

DeCarlo's eyes gleamed with a predatory hunger. He grabbed the string of Jessi's leather top, pulling it forcefully over her head, exposing her small tits. The cool air of the room made her skin prickle with goosebumps, but it was nothing compared to the chill that ran down her spine as she anticipated what was to come.

He then grabbed her by the shoulders and spun her around, facing the chair, pushing her roughly into it. Jessi's heart raced as she felt the cold, unyielding vinyl against her chest. She tried to push herself up, to resist, but his strong hands pressed down on her shoulders, holding her in place.

With a cruel smile, DeCarlo reached down and grabbed the ties of her bottoms at each side of her hips. He pulled them loose, letting them drop down to her knees. Jessi's breath hitched as the fabric slid down her thighs, leaving her vulnerable and exposed. She tried to cover herself, but he slapped her hands away, his grip unyielding.

"Please," Jessi pleaded, her voice trembling with fear and desperation. "Don't do this again."

DeCarlo just chuckled, a sound devoid of any warmth or humanity. "I can do whatever I want, Jessi. You're going to like it."

Jessi felt tears welling up in her eyes as she realized the full extent of her helplessness. She was at his mercy, and there was nothing she could do to stop what was about to happen. The room seemed to close in around her, the dim light and the stale air suffocating her senses. All she could think about was the inevitable assault that was to come, and the knowledge that she was utterly powerless to prevent it.

From behind, she felt him probing his cock until he felt her wet opening. Tears were welling in Jessi's eyes as she felt him slide deep inside. He pumped in and out, sliding faster with each thrust. Jessi's breasts swung back and forth with each plunge, and she could feel his balls slapping against her exposed mound. She kept quiet, not letting out a cry or a moan; she didn't want to give him any satisfaction.

Reaching down, Decarlo grabbed each of Jessi's shoulders, leveraging her body, and he attempted to plunge as deep as he could go. Jessi closed her eyes, resting her forehead on the back of the chair, her body being violently thrashed with his attack.

To Jessi, the attack seemed to last an eternity. Her body was simply a device for him to use as he wished. Finally, she felt his body tense. He pushed deep, then let out a deep grunt. She felt him pulse inside her, her pussy filling with his vileness. He pulled out and slapped her ass hard, leaving a red handprint.

Jessi didn't move as she heard the familiar sounds of DeCarlo pulling up his pants and buckling his belt. The metallic clink of the buckle echoed in the small room, each sound a mocking reminder of her helplessness. She kept her head down, her eyes tightly shut, as if by not looking, she could somehow escape the reality of what had just happened.

A rough hand gripped her chin, forcing her to look up at him. DeCarlo's face was a mask of cruel satisfaction, his eyes gleaming with a perverse sense of triumph. "I'll be back for the money," he said, his voice laced with a mocking grin. "That's some sweet pussy you have there."

Jessi's throat constricted, and she felt a wave of nausea wash over her. She wanted to scream, to lash out, but her body remained frozen, trapped in a state of shocked paralysis. She didn't answer, her silence a small act of defiance against the monster who had just violated her.

As DeCarlo's footsteps receded and the door clicked shut behind him, Jessi turned around in the chair, pulling her knees up to her chest. She sat there, bewildered and stunned, her mind a whirlwind of conflicting emotions. Her body ached, a physical reminder of the trauma she had just endured, but it was the emotional toll that left her feeling utterly shattered.

Her tears were dry, but the sting of them lingered on her cheeks. Jessi reached down and gathered her clothes, her movements slow and mechanical. She dressed with a stoic detachment; her mind disconnected from her actions. Each small piece of clothing felt like a layer of armor, a fragile shield against the world outside.

As she made her way back to the main room, the booming music and the chatter of the crowd washed over her, a cacophony of sounds that seemed to come from a different reality. She scanned the room, her eyes landing on Candy, who was engaged in a heated argument with DeCarlo. Candy's finger was pointed accusingly at the detective's face, her expression a mix of anger and concern.

Jessi turned away, her heart heavy with a mix of fear and resignation. She made her way back to the dressing room without a word, her steps leaden with the weight of her ordeal. The door clicked shut behind her, and she leaned against it, her body sliding down to the floor as the full force of her emotions finally broke through.

In the relative safety of the dressing room, Jessi allowed herself to crumble, her sobs racking her body as she curled up into a ball. The tears came in waves, each one a release of the pain and humiliation she had been forced to endure. She knew she couldn't continue living like this; she had to find a way to fight back and reclaim her power and dignity.

But for now, all she could do was cry, to let the tears wash away the filth of the night, and to hope that tomorrow would bring a glimmer of light in the darkness that had consumed her.

The sound of the dressing room door creaking open pulled Jessi from her sobs. She looked up, her eyes red and swollen, to see Candy standing in the doorway, wearing only frilly red panties and red pasties with black tassels covering the nipples of her huge breasts. She had an expression of determination and concern.

"Jessi, are you okay?" Candy asked, her voice soft but firm. She crossed the room and knelt beside Jessi, pulling her into a tight embrace.

Jessi leaned into the comfort of Candy's arms, her body shaking with residual sobs. "I... I don't know," she managed to whisper. "He was here."

Candy's grip tightened, and Jessi could feel the anger radiating from her friend. "I know, Jessi. I saw him. I told him to leave you alone and never come back."

Jessi pulled back, her eyes wide with alarm. "Candy, no! You shouldn't have done that. He's dangerous. He could…"

Candy cut her off, her voice filled with a fierce resolve. "I don't care, Jessi. Someone had to do something. You can't keep living like this, in fear and pain. It's not right, and I won't stand by and watch you suffer."

Jessi shook her head, her voice trembling. "But what if he hurts you, too? Or worse, what if he hurts someone else because of what you said?"

Candy's expression softened, and she cupped Jessi's face in her hands, gently wiping away the tears with her thumbs. "I'm not afraid of him, Jessi. And I won't let him hurt you or anyone else. We're in this together. We're a family, and we protect our own."

Jessi leaned into Candy's touch, feeling a glimmer of hope amidst the darkness. "I'm so scared."

Candy pulled her into another tight embrace, holding her close as if she could shield Jessi from the world and all its cruelties.

As they sat there, entwined in each other's arms, Jessi felt a small sense of security, but she knew it was fragile. The fear would return soon.

***

The days that followed Saturday were a blur for Jessi. She spent most of her time with Becca, trying to mask her fear behind a facade of normality. Becca, ever perceptive, sensed the turmoil simmering beneath Jessi's surface, but Jessi brushed off her concerns with reassurances that everything was fine.

"Jessi, I can tell something's wrong," Becca said one evening as they sat on the couch, the television playing softly in the background. "You don't have to hide it from me. I'm here for you, remember?"

Jessi forced a smile, her eyes avoiding Becca's gaze. "Work has been crazy, and I think I'm coming down with something. Don't worry about me, okay? I'll be fine."

Becca looked at her with a mix of worry and disbelief, but didn't press the issue. Jessi was grateful for her understanding, even as she felt a pang of guilt for not being more honest.

* * *

As Thursday rolled around, Jessi found herself back at the club, her heart heavy with dread. The familiar surroundings, once a source of comfort and escape, now felt tainted and unsafe. She changed into her costume, her movements mechanical and detached.

As she made her way to the main floor, she noticed an unusual quietness in the air. The usual banter and laughter seemed subdued, and a palpable tension set her on edge. Jessi approached Tommy and asked about Candy.

"Tommy, have you seen Candy? I haven't seen her around lately," Jessi said, trying to keep her voice casual.

Tommy shook his head, his expression serious. "Yeah, about that. Candy called up and said she was leaving town. She quit, Jessi. She won't be coming back."

Jessi's heart sank, and a wave of panic rose within her. "Leaving town? But... why? Did she say anything else?"

Tommy shrugged, his brow furrowed in confusion. "No, just that she had to go. Spike and I tried to get more out of her, but she was pretty insistent. Said she had to leave and that was that."

Jessi nodded, her mind racing with thoughts of DeCarlo and the consequences of his actions. She knew, without a doubt, that Candy's sudden departure was connected to him. The terror she had been trying to suppress surged to the surface, threatening to consume her.

As she stood there, trying to process the news, Spike approached, his expression equally concerned. "Jessi, you okay?"

Jessi managed a weak smile, her voice trembling slightly. "I'm fine, Spike. Just... just a bit shocked about Candy. I had no idea she was planning on leaving."

Spike nodded, his eyes filled with a mix of empathy and confusion. "Yeah, it's weird. But you know, Candy, always a bit of a wild card. Maybe she just needed a change of scenery, you know?"

Jessi forced a nod, even as her mind screamed with the truth. As she made her way back to the dressing room, Jessi's steps were heavy with the weight of her fears. She knew that she had to find a way to protect herself, to fight back against the monster who had turned her life upside down. But with Candy gone and the full force of DeCarlo's power looming over her, Jessi felt utterly alone and terrified of what the future might hold.

Jessi forced herself to go through her routines at the club, but the weight of the cop's threat clung to her every step. Her once-confident movements on the stage had begun to falter—hesitations in her spins, slight missteps in her routines, a nervous flicker in her smile. Patrons noticed, and tips began to shrink.

Even Spike had commented one night, "You're off tonight, Jessi… something's on your mind." She'd brushed him off with a tight-lipped smile, afraid to let anyone glimpse the fear she carried.

Tommy pulled her aside in the dimly lit back office. His bulk cast a shadow over her as he spoke quietly but firmly. "Jessi… maybe you need to step away for a while. You're not yourself out there."

"I'm fine. Just having an off night. I'll get through it." Her stomach knotted. She knew he was right, but thoughts of Becca's tuition, of the dreams she had been holding close to her chest for both of them, refused to let her back down. "I… I can handle it," she whispered, her voice tight. "I just need… a little more time."

***

It was later that evening when DeCarlo made his presence known. Jessi made her way through the crowd and handed him an envelope.

"You don't want to go back to a private room?" he asked with a sneering grin.

Jessi didn't respond and just turned and tried to walk back to the stage, but he grabbed her arm and pulled her close.

"Saturday night, after you get done here. I have some high rollers coming into town. I want you on the hospitality team. You know what I mean?"

Jessi pulled her arm free and just looked at him.

He smiled and gave a wink as he walked away. "I'll pick you up."

She wanted to scream. She wanted to run. No matter how hard she tried, the stress began to overwhelm her. The once-thrilling rush of performing was replaced with dread.

The cop's shadow haunted her every dance. Her confidence eroded further until she fell from a pole with a thud onto the stage. She jumped up, embarrassed, and tried to resume her dance, but her timing was shattered. She broke down, covering her face and running back to the dressing room.

Tommy had noticed, and he shook his head, his tone tinged with frustration and concern. "Jessi… I can't keep you on like this. You're gonna hurt yourself. Maybe you need to take some time off for a while."

The words hit her like a punch to the gut. Christmas was only a couple of weeks away. She felt the icy squeeze of panic, her chest tightening. How was she going to keep her promise to Becca? DeCarlo's expectations loomed.

* * *

Driving home that night, Jessi gripped the steering wheel as tears pricked her eyes. The city lights blurred past, but she couldn't focus. Her thoughts swirled—Becca, the tuition, the money she had promised. She felt like she was failing the one person who mattered more than anyone.

When she stepped inside their apartment, the glow of the living room greeted her. Becca was perched on the couch, a stack of brochures and enrollment papers spread around her, excitement radiating from her. "I finally got it all sorted!" Becca said, beaming. "Next semester, I start back at school, art classes, Jessi! Can you believe it?"

Jessi forced a smile, her throat tight, her heart pounding. "That's… amazing, Becca. I'm so proud of you," she said, her voice careful, hiding the storm inside. She pressed her lips together, willing herself not to crumble in front of her.

As Becca chattered about schedules and class projects, Jessi felt a pang of despair. She was failing her, and Becca had no idea how close she was to the edge. The high she had once felt from performing and making money was gone, replaced with guilt, fear, and the creeping realization that she had no clear way forward.

She sank beside Becca on the couch, letting her laughter wash over her, masking the truth that she couldn't yet tell—the truth that she was broken, and scared, and utterly unsure of how to fix what she had promised.

The apartment was warm and cozy, the city outside a soft glow, but inside, Jessi felt the icy weight of failure pressing down on her chest.

28
Desperation

Jessi spent the following day scouring newspapers, online listings, and temp agencies, hoping against hope to find something, anything, that could bring in enough money for Becca's tuition. She thought of dancing at another club, but the cop would find her there, too. Every promising posting evaporated quickly: positions requiring degrees she didn't have, internships that paid next to nothing, part-time work that barely covered a month's rent.

Each dead end gnawed at her confidence and stoked the guilt she carried. She even considered turning tricks, but there was no way she could make the kind of money she needed.

She even thought about DeCarlo's arrangement, but he would use her. He would bleed her dry for his own profit. The thought of working for him made her feel physically ill.

* * *

By the time Saturday night rolled around, Jessi had no choice but to pretend. She would go through the motions, getting dressed and leaving the apartment at the time she usually went to the club, though in reality she just drove around town. It became routine.

Each evening, she would text Becca little updates, vague and cheerful, about her "night at the club," careful never to mention that she hadn't gone. She watched Becca's happiness grow, felt the warmth of her laughter, and hated herself a little more each time.

But Jessi also worried. Worried DeCarlo would find her. She had bailed on his proposed high rollers. She had to keep low. She couldn't enter that world again.

* * *

Finally, Christmas arrived. The apartment glowed with the soft light of a small tree; ornaments twinkled, and presents were stacked underneath. Jessi had splurged on a few gifts, pooling her last savings, but she had kept a tight lid on the real struggle behind her smile. Becca was radiant, tearing into her presents with wide-eyed delight, laughing at everything, genuinely happy. Jessi's heart ached as she watched her, the warmth of the moment cutting sharply against the icy guilt clutching her chest.

"I got you the brushes you wanted," Jessi said softly, handing over a neatly wrapped package. Becca's eyes lit up, and she embraced Jessi tightly.

"And the computer drawing pad!" she cried, holding up another gift. "You remembered!"

Jessi hugged her back, swallowing hard. "Of course. I… I wanted you to have a good Christmas."

Jessi's gifts were more suited towards her: a Metallica CD, a velvety black button-up shirt, and a box containing a naughty schoolgirl outfit. Becca blushed when Jessi opened it, and Jessi told her they would play school later in the evening.

Becca's laughter and joy were a balm and a torment all at once. She spoke of her hopes for the future… returning to college, building a portfolio, and painting full-time. Jessi nodded, smiling, but inside, the weight of her secret pressed harder than ever. She had promised her support, and yet here she was, unable to fulfill it.

As they settled in, sitting close on the couch and sipping hot chocolate, Becca's head resting on Jessi's shoulder, Jessi felt tears welling again. She let them slide quietly, hidden against Becca's warmth. Becca was utterly happy, her future seemingly bright, and Jessi felt she had ruined it.

She made a silent vow: she would figure something out, anything, to make it right. But for now, she allowed herself to enjoy the Christmas magic, hiding the storm inside, even as it raged fiercely behind her eyes.

* * *

The week after the New Year, Jessi found herself continuing her charade of dancing at the club. Her savings had all but withered, and she was on her last leg before having to stand before Becca and break her heart, crush her dreams. The nights often found her parked by the river, just watching the moonlight shimmer along the waves, or parked at a department store, just waiting for the clock to tick by so she could go home.

One night, Jessi decided to visit an old haunt. Her pulse quickened as she stepped into the dimly lit interior of Secrets. The familiar scents of leather, candle wax, and incense enveloped her like a cloak, triggering memories she had tucked away for months. Her feet, tucked inside soft boots, carried her silently across the polished floor, past the observing eyes of those engaged in their own games of power and surrender.

Marcus was in his usual private corner, seated on the low throne-like chair that marked his dominion over this corner of the club. The ambient light caught the angles of his face, his eyes scanning the room with the calm authority she remembered. Jessi hesitated for a heartbeat, then squared her shoulders and approached him.

"Marcus," she began, her voice quiet but deliberate. "So glad to see you. It's been a while."

Marcus's eyes widened. "Miss Jessi," he said in a low tone. "It's so good to see you. I've missed our little play sessions."

"Me too, Sir," she answered with a subtle smile.

"Come, Jessi. Join me," he said, motioning into his private booth. He raised his arm to offer her his hand.

She reached out, placing her fingers in his palm as he guided her to a seat.

"I… I wanted to ask again about the agreement we discussed months ago." She kept her gaze low, aware of her nervous tremor, but she made sure her tone carried the respect and caution necessary.

He looked up slowly, his dark eyes assessing her as if weighing her intentions. "Jessi," he said, in a low, even tone. "Are you considering… an arrangement?"

She nodded. "I'm considering it. Can I ask… what the arrangement would… entail?" Her voice faltered slightly, betraying the mixture of fear and desire she was trying to mask with composure.

Marcus leaned forward slightly, resting his forearms on his knees. "It's not something entered into lightly," he said. "Total submission for a year. Compensation is guaranteed, but the rules are absolute. You would be under my guidance and control every day we engage, whether at my home or here at the club, if needed. Are you sure you understand what that means?"

Jessi swallowed hard. The thought of giving herself entirely, even in small ways, was terrifying. "I understand," she whispered, though her chest tightened with anticipation and nerves. "What… what would the compensation be?"

Marcus studied her for a long moment. "You would give up your life… entirely for the time of the contract. That means no job, no socializing… total devotion. The terms would depend on what level of involvement you would agree to." He puffed on a cigar, the smoke swirling above his head.

"What level?" Jessi asked.

Marcus looked at her. "What are you willing to do? Your limits, hard and soft. Your level of dedication. We would go over those issues, discuss what is off limits, what limits can be pushed, and from there, we would negotiate terms."

"Negotiate terms?" Jessi queried. "It sounds so… technical… legal."

"The contract would not be legally binding; however, the money would. Renege on the agreement, and you would lose any financial compensation."

Jessi nodded as she listened.

"But Jessi, this shouldn't be about money. It should be about whether you're ready to embark on the journey of submission. Letting go of your life and every aspect of control. Is this something you truly seek?"

Looking down at the table, Jessi lost herself in thought. "I think… I've always wanted that on some level. I'm tired of the responsibilities; trying to hide myself."

Marcus nodded. "If you're ready, and your mind is clear, we can draft the terms. But Jessi… this is serious. It will test you, push you. You'll have to be honest about what you can endure, and trust that I will guide, protect, and hold you accountable. Are you ready for that?"

Her throat tightened, and she took a deep breath. "I… would need to see what the compensation would be. But… if we agree, I think I am."

Marcus's lips curved slightly, a small, approving smile. "Very well, Jessi, but remember, it's your choice to submit. Total submission is not for the faint of heart." He snapped his fingers at a man standing outside his booth. Marcus whispered something in his ear, and the man walked away to the other side of the club.

Jessi felt a strange mix of relief, fear, and excitement. For the first time in weeks, she felt like she had a possible path forward, a way to regain control over the spiraling tension between her guilt, her fear, and her desire to support Becca.

Marcus studied her a moment, then motioned toward the man who had returned with a folder in his hand, clearly an assistant of sorts. He stood and handed Marcus a black folder. Marcus opened it, glanced at the pages, then slid it across the table toward Jessi.

"This isn't a contract," he said carefully. "Not yet. It's a framework. It outlines expectations, procedures, and, most importantly, boundaries. No one proceeds until both parties are clear about what they want and what they don't."

Jessi looked down at the papers. Her hands trembled slightly as she turned a page. There were forms for consent, a section for health verification, psychological screening, and physical fitness, and a checklist that made it all seem alarmingly real.

"You'll need a medical evaluation," Marcus continued. "I require that of everyone. It protects both of us. You'll also fill out a questionnaire, your limits, both hard and soft, and the areas you believe you want to explore."

She didn't answer right away. Her eyes kept flicking over the sterile language: submission, duration, boundaries, control. Every word felt like a mirror reflecting something she wasn't sure she wanted to see.

Marcus must have seen the hesitation in her face. "You don't have to decide now," he said quietly. "Most people don't. They think. They process. They come back if they still feel the same."

Jessi nodded, clutching the folder against her chest as though it might steady her heart. "I'll think about it," she murmured.

He gave a slight nod of acknowledgment. "Good. If you do, we'll move carefully. Intentionally. No surprises."

* * *

When she stepped back out into the night, the air was cold and damp. She hugged the folder tighter as she walked toward her car. Her breath trembled as it left her lungs.

Inside, she sat behind the wheel, staring at the paperwork on the passenger seat. Becca's smile flashed across her mind, her warmth, her laughter, the way she looked at Jessi like she could still see something whole beneath the cracks.

And yet… something inside Jessi whispered that maybe this was what she deserved, a purgatory of sorts, to redeem herself and give Becca the future she deserved. She hadn't been truthful with Becca; she was unfaithful, maybe even pushing her into things she didn't understand or want to do. She was the corruption in Becca's life.

She didn't start the car for a long time. Just sat there, the night pressing in around her, the folder waiting like a question she didn't yet have the strength to answer.

Jessi parked on a quiet street near the river, the winter wind rattling the branches overhead. The glow from the dashboard lit the stack of papers in her lap, the agreement Marcus had given her. Each page seemed to breathe with a kind of gravity she wasn't ready for.

Her fingers trembled as she flipped through the forms, reading questions about boundaries, limits, and permissions. The language was clinical, almost cold, yet the implications ran deep. It wasn't just about signing a contract; it was about surrendering something far more personal.

The checkboxes for things she was willing to explore were huge, and some of the acronyms she didn't understand. CNC, ENF, GB, etc., they were things she honestly didn't recognize. She spent the next few hours looking up the acronyms and checking nearly all of them on the form. If she were to be compensated enough to take care of Becca, she would have to open herself to Marcus's will. In the end, she checked her hard limits as blood, bathroom play, and permanent marks or injury.

She felt small in that moment, alone in the car with the sound of the wind and the soft hum of the heater. Her reflection in the window looked almost like a stranger's: eyes wide, mouth tight, trying to be brave.

What am I doing? she thought. She had thought about going to another club to dance, but the cop would find her there, too. She couldn't go through that again.

The money, the security, Becca's tuition, it all flashed through her mind. Becca's laughter on Christmas morning, the way she'd hugged Jessi and said, "Next year's going to be amazing." Jessi wanted to believe that. She needed to believe it, but her mind always fell back to disappointment in her eyes; disappointment in her.

But here she was, considering something she didn't fully understand, something that scared her. She knew what Marcus represented: control, power, structure. A world where she would no longer be the one deciding who she was.

And maybe that was part of the pull.

She drew in a long, unsteady breath. The papers sat in her lap like a test she wasn't sure she could pass. Her heart said no, but her guilt whispered yes. If it meant Becca's dreams could stay alive… maybe she could find a way to bear it.

She folded the packet carefully, pressing it flat as though trying to smooth her doubts away, and whispered into the quiet: "I have to do this."

***

The following week moved in a quiet blur of half-truths. Jessi made her appointments as instructed, a complete physical on Monday, bloodwork, vitals, and even a psychological evaluation with an assigned, sharp-eyed woman who asked more questions about why she was doing this than what she expected to happen. Jessi had smiled through it, giving answers that sounded rational enough. "Financial stability," "trust," "a sense of purpose." All true in their own way.

But underneath, she couldn't admit the rest, that it was about penance. About letting go of control. About the illusion of saving someone else when she couldn't save herself.

* * *

By Thursday, the tests were done. "All clear," the doctor said, handing her a neat packet of results. Healthy. Stable. Fit. On the outside, at least.

The psychologist labeled her obsessive-compulsive, with tendencies toward exhibitionism, which suggests traumatic childhood experiences. "The subject also shows signs of impulsivity, a strong need for sensation-seeking, and a low level of self-control. This can manifest in behaviors such as reckless driving, unsafe sex, gambling, or substance abuse."

She resented the diagnosis and wondered if it might kill the deal with Marcus, though, deep down, she felt how sharp it had been. She began to think that maybe she had been, on some level, trying to punish herself for the pain she had caused.

To her, her father had left most likely because he couldn't handle being a parent, leaving her as a burden to her mother. Because of her, Jessi believed she had robbed her mother of happiness and eventually health. *Maybe*, Jessi thought, *I should be punished for what I've done.*

And why not? She had driven everyone in her life away. All had abandoned her in one way or another...

that is, except for Becca. Throughout her life, there had been one-night stands or month-long flings, but there had never been anyone serious; no one she could lean on and share her desires or her darkest thoughts; who had been there even though they should have been running away screaming... except for Becca.

* * *

That morning, after Becca left for work, Jessi drove to a downtown office, anonymous, glass-fronted, with no sign but a single suite number. She handed the folder to a receptionist who barely looked up. "Thank you," the woman said, sliding it into a drawer. It was all so... impersonal.

* * *

For the next few days, Jessi went through the motions. Pretending to go to the club. Pretending everything was fine. Becca noticed the distance but chalked it up to exhaustion, and Jessi let her believe that. Each lie pressed heavier on her chest.

Then, on a cold Thursday night, her phone buzzed. A simple message, no greeting:

Meet me at Secrets. Midnight. M.

She read it three times before responding with a single *Okay.*

When she arrived, the club was quieter than usual… low music, faint laughter from the back rooms. Marcus waited in his private booth, sitting on the edge of a leather chair with his usual measured calm. A folder rested beside him.

“Jessi,” he said, rising as she entered. “Happy to see you.”

She nodded. Her palms were slick with nervous sweat.

He motioned for her to sit. “I'll ask you this once more. Are you sure you want to go through with this?"

Jessi fidgeted, then nodded. "Yes, Sir."

"Then we can discuss terms.”

The folder opened with a soft click. Pages rustled.

Marcus explained things carefully, what he expected, what the arrangement entailed, and what she would receive. The tone was businesslike, yet there was an edge of gravity in his words, the sense that once she agreed, the balance of her world would tilt permanently.

When he was done, he slid an envelope across the table toward her. The white paper gleamed faintly under the low light. She opened the envelope and looked at the figure inside.

"I hope this compensation would be agreeable," he said in a low, deliberate tone. He puffed on a cigar as she looked at the paper. The money was more than she expected, and her hand shook as she closed it back up.

“Take your time,” he said. “Understand what you’re agreeing to. Because once this begins, Jessi… it won’t be a game.”

Her throat tightened, but she managed a slight nod. "The terms are wonderful," she answered. “I understand," she said softly. "But, can I ask you something?"

"Of course, Jessi. Anything."

Though her voice was steady, her heart beat like it knew the truth. Once she signed, nothing would ever quite be the same. Jessi shifted slightly in the leather seat, hands clasped tightly in her lap. "Do you… know any of the board members at the Southern Arts Institute?" she asked, her voice barely above a whisper.

Marcus leaned back, one arm draped over the back of the chair. "Perhaps. I might know one or two," he said slowly, his gaze assessing.

She hesitated, then pushed forward. "Could you… Maybe help get a scholarship for my friend, Becca? She's brilliant, she deserves to go back to school, to study art. I want to make that possible for her."

Marcus's eyes narrowed slightly. "And you… You want to do this for her?"

Jessi swallowed hard. "I love her," she admitted. "But... I'm broken, Marcus. I want you to know... I'm damaged goods."

She leaned forward, looking into Marcus's eyes. "She is... innocence... light... love... she is everything good that I'm not. I have lied to her, hid things from her; I've been unfaithful. I don't deserve her, and she definitely didn't deserve what I've done to her."

Jessi realized tears were streaming down her cheeks. "I've made promises to her, Marcus, and I don't want to let her down."

Marcus nodded slowly, leaning forward now, his expression unreadable. "I see," he said. "That's a rare kind of devotion. Dangerous, but rare."

Jessi's stomach tightened, but she met his gaze. "I just… I need to do this. I have to do this. For her."

He studied her for a long moment, then finally said, "Very well. But understand something, Jessi… this isn't a gift. This is a contract. Every choice, every boundary, every limit you set… will define how far this goes. If you want me to leverage connections or help with your… other goal, you need to understand the stakes. You are free to cancel this contract at any time, but the compensation will also end."

Jessi nodded, a shiver running down her spine. "I understand," she said firmly. "I just… I will do anything you want me to."

Marcus's lips curved into a small, knowing smile. "Then we'll begin," he said.

Jessi sat at the sleek, black table, the folder open before her. Her hand hovered over the pen as a knot of anxiety twisted in her stomach. "Can… can it start Saturday?" she asked, her voice tight. "I need a few days to… get things in order."

Marcus leaned back, studying her carefully. After a long moment, he nodded. "That's acceptable. The start date can be adjusted. But understand this… once it begins, there is no turning back. You will be fully committed, and every term of the contract applies."

Jessi swallowed hard, the weight of the agreement pressing down on her chest. She took a deep breath. "And… the scholarship for Becca?"

Marcus's gaze sharpened. "Contingent. I'll pursue it, but it must be tied to your adherence to the contract. You understand this?"

"I do," she said, the determination in her voice battling with the fear twisting inside her.

Finally, she picked up the pen and signed her name. The ink dried like a seal on a future she wasn't sure she was ready for, but she told herself she had no choice. This was to help Becca lead a happy life and fulfill her dreams.

She slid the folder back to Marcus. "Good. We'll meet on Saturday to go over the final instructions. Until then, prepare yourself, mentally, physically, and emotionally. This is not a game, Jessi. This is your life."

Jessi nodded, her pulse racing. The decision was made. The weight of what she had agreed to both terrified and exhilarated her.

As she left the club, the city lights blurred past, and she tried to imagine herself walking into the next chapter, one she had chosen, yet feared more than anything.

29
Redemption

Friday evening, flickering candles cast a warm glow over the apartment, bouncing off the walls and casting long shadows. The table was set with simple elegance, two wine glasses, cloth napkins, and a small vase holding a single rose. Jessi had gone all out, and the scent of garlic and cheese drifted from the takeout containers, promising the comfort of Becca's favorite meal.

Becca stepped inside from her workday, her eyes widening. "Jessi… what is all this?" she asked, her voice tinged with surprise and emotion.

"I wanted to do something special for you," Jessi said, her grin bright and uncontainable. "Just thought that tonight… you're the queen."

Becca felt her chest tighten. She had been worried about Jessi for weeks, but seeing her like this, so full of life, energy, and love, stirred a warmth in her heart. "You didn't have to. Oh my, Jessi. Is that...?" she whispered.

“It is,” Jessi said, sitting down across from her. "Your favorite, from Rosa's. You said you loved it that time we were there." She reached out and took Becca’s hand. “I… I love you, Becca."

She looked into Becca's eyes, tears forming in her own. "I wanted you to know that I love you more than I’ve ever loved anyone in the world. I’m sorry for worrying you. I know I can be… a lot sometimes, and I feel like I’m a burden.”

Becca’s eyes welled with tears. She squeezed Jessi’s hand tightly. “You’re not a burden,” she said softly. “You’re… everything to me. I love you too, Jessi. More than you know.”

Jessi’s grin faltered for a brief moment as the raw vulnerability passed between them. Then she chuckled softly, a little embarrassed by her own emotion. “I just want you to be happy. That’s all that matters.”

Becca reached across the table, brushing a strand of Jessi’s hair away from her eyes. “We are happy,” she whispered, her own tears slipping down her cheeks. “Tonight… right now… we are.”

They shared a long, quiet moment as the world outside faded away. The flicker of candlelight mirrored the spark between them, a warmth that neither money, fear, nor circumstance could extinguish.

Dinner that night was more than just food; it was laughter, whispered promises, and soft touches across the table. Jessi fed Becca bites of ravioli, and Becca returned the gesture with garlic bread, and with every mouthful, the weight of the world seemed to lift.

By the time the candles had burned low, Jessi had poured them both glasses of wine. She raised hers with a mischievous smile. "To us," she said.

"To us," Becca echoed, clinking her glass gently against Jessi's.

There had not been a more perfect night together. For a few hours, the apartment was filled with nothing but love, warmth, and the unspoken understanding. Jessi gazed deep into Rebecca's big brown eyes, the eyes that had lured her in so long ago, and in them she saw her bright future.

She kissed her deeply, passionately. Their fervor didn't end until they were each sated with their entwined naked bodies wrapped in a lustful embrace. They would drift off to sleep, each holding the other in their arms.

* * *

Becca woke slowly, the soft light of a chilly Saturday morning filtering through the blinds. She stretched, expecting to feel Jessi curled up beside her, but the bed was empty. The apartment was quiet, too quiet, and her heart gave a slight, uneasy flutter.

"Jessi!" she called out, but there was no answer. She rose and shuffled to the window, peering out at the gray morning streets, hoping to catch a glimpse of Jessi's familiar form. Nothing.

A cold wind rattled the trees outside as Becca stepped out into the parking lot. Jessi's Mustang sat parked beside her Honda. She shivered… not from the chill, but from the sudden emptiness.

Returning inside, she noticed a large brown envelope propped against the kitchen counter. Her name was scrawled across it in Jessi's distinctive handwriting. With a mix of curiosity and trepidation, Becca picked it up and slit it open.

Inside were several documents: a letter, official-looking papers, a set of keys, and a thick packet from the Southern Arts Institute. Her eyes fell on the first line of the packet: Congratulations, Rebecca Lynn Taylor, you have been selected for a full four-year scholarship to the Southern Arts Institute.

Becca's heart fluttered. Was this real? She looked at the papers again... her name clearly printed in the type.

She sorted through the papers when she found the letter from Jessi:

Becca,

I want you to know how much you mean to me. For the first time in my life, I have had someone who cares for me, listens to me, and loves me. I don't think I've had that in my life in a very long time. You are everything to me, Becca, and I'm sorry for all the things I've put you through.

I know when you read this, you will be calling me a coward, and the truth is, I am a coward. I've been running all my life. You were right when you said that I wanted to be seen. I think, deep down, I've been running from my demons while begging to be noticed.

Becca, when I look at you, I see light, goodness, innocence, faith, and hope. When I look in the mirror, I see deceit, guilt, fear, and shame. I'm broken, Becca. You know it and I know it. I've lied to you, kept things from you, and I've been unfaithful physically, but never mentally or emotionally. I told myself I was trying to shield you from my pain, but the truth is I was trying to protect myself from my own guilt. I can never forgive myself for hurting you.

I lost my job, Becca, and with it, my promise to you is lost. I don't know what else I can do. I've made an agreement, an arrangement, to secure your future and allow you to pursue your passion. I'm leaving for a while, a year. Don't look for me, baby. You won't find me. I want you to live for you, and live for your art, your creativity.

Jessi's words poured out onto the page, each sentence carrying her heart and her sacrifice. And Becca began bawling before she could finish. She sank to the floor, clutching the letter to her chest. Tears streamed freely down her cheeks, pooling onto the pages.

"I can't… I can't believe this," she whispered through sobs, her voice catching. "Jessi… why would you do this?"

She wiped her eyes as she continued to read.

You are everything to me, Becca. Please forgive me, but if you don't, I understand. I've left the title to my car and the keys. I want you to have it because, frankly, your car sucks and you need a good ride. Please take care of it.

Please don't pass this opportunity, Becca. I love you with all my heart. Maybe, one day, you'll forgive me. I hope so. Right now, all I can do is dream of you.

Love,

Jessi

The apartment, empty and still, seemed to hold Jessi's presence in every corner, every shadow, every whisper of her devotion. Becca pressed the papers to her face, inhaling deeply, trying to commit the moment, and Jessi, wherever she was that morning, would always be part of it.

She sat on the floor as Bob trotted over and lay in her lap. She just cried as she petted him. Her world was gone, and she couldn't imagine her future without her. "Where are you, Jessi?" she whispered. "Please come back. I love you too."

* * *

Jessi sat quietly in the back of the SUV, the countryside sliding past in a blur of muted greens and browns. The driver said nothing, the hum of the engine filling the silence as her thoughts raced.

After several minutes, the vehicle slowed and came to a halt before a massive cast-iron gate, its ornate scrollwork gleaming faintly in the soft light. Beyond it, a sprawling three-story mansion rose into view, its stone façade pristine, exuding wealth and control.

The driver stepped out without a word, opening the door for her. Jessi hesitated for a moment, taking in the house's immensity, then stepped onto the pea-gravel driveway. She craned her neck upward, awed by the meticulous architecture and polished grandeur.

At the entrance, Marcus awaited her, his posture calm but commanding. He smiled, a slight curve of satisfaction in his eyes. "Are you ready for your new life?" he asked.

Jessi returned the smile, a mixture of nerves and apprehension tightening her chest. She nodded and followed him up the steps, through the massive double doors. She turned and caught a glimpse of the gray sky as the heavy door closed behind them with a soft thud, leaving the outside world and all her old life behind.

Maybe, just maybe, she would see the light again, the light of Rebecca's smile and grace. She could only hope.

The End

"Thank you from the bottom of my heart for reading Dangerous Obsessions. I pour everything I have into my characters, and knowing that you've journeyed with them is the ultimate reward. If you had fun reading, please consider leaving an honest review on Amazon. Your feedback helps me keep writing!"

Visit me at www.jmreines.com

www.ingramcontent.com/pod-product-compliance
Lightning Source LLC
LaVergne TN
LVHW100506110826
845146LV00002B/537

* 9 7 9 8 9 9 6 3 8 1 4 1 8 *